Metabyte

Cat Connor

9mm Press
New Zealand, 5018

ISBN Print: 978-0-4734974-2-2
ISBN Draft2Digital: 978-1-0670072-5-6
ISBN ePub: 978-1-3703040-3-5
ISBN: 978-1-9440772-4-2

Book design by *9mm Press*
Editor: Jayne Southern
First published in the USA by Rebel ePublishers

Published in New Zealand 2024

For Patricia

All truths are easy to understand once they are discovered; the point is to discover them.

- Galileo Galilei Italian astronomer & physicist (1564 - 1642)

Chapter One

Surfin' Safari

"Your phone!" Harley, my husband's niece, hollered. The opening bars of 'Wanted dead or alive' rang out.

"Coming," I called back.

Something flew at me when I stepped into the living room. My fingers snatched the object from mid-air. SSA Kurt Henderson. "Problem?"

"Potentially," he replied.

"And that problem is?"

"Two dead bodies."

Awesome. Nothing like the odd fatality to add to the ambiance of the normal evening at home that stretched in front of me. My eyes rolled.

"I'll pick you up in thirty."

"You at home?"

"Yes. I'll finish reading a bedtime story to Olivia then I'll pick you up."

"See you soon."

I hung up, noted the time on my phone screen. My night at home, struggling with the story idea from my brother's wife, Holly, was almost over. A little voice inside my head rejoiced, 'Woo hoo!'

"You going out?" Harley said from the couch.

"Yeah, work. You be okay? We can drop you at Gran's if you like?"

"I'll be all right," she said, turning her head to see me. "Besides Uncle Mitch will be here later, won't he?"

"He sure will." The time on my watch told me my husband would be home in about three-quarters of an hour. I'd miss him and that sucked. I sent a text saying I'd been called out. Criminals have no regard for our lives but on the plus side, job security.

Harley uncurled her legs and stood up. "I'm going to get a glass of water. Did you want anything?"

"No, thanks." I looked at the laptop on the coffee table. Write a story, she said. It'll be fun, she said. I'd sooner cut off my fingers with a butter knife.

A scream broke the silence.

My heart bashed against my ribcage. "Harley!" My hand reached for my Glock and came up empty. Dammit. "Harley!"

Another scream.

I grabbed my spare weapon from the drawer under the coffee table and crept into the hallway. "Harley!"

Sobbing. From the kitchen.

A voice broke through the sobs, "Ellie!"

In the kitchen I found Harley, pale and backed into a corner. "What's wrong?"

She pointed to a black shape on the tiled floor. Relief washed over me. My heart rate returned to normal.

"I can't shoot that," I said, placing the gun on the countertop and holding my hand out. "Come here."

She shook her head. "I can't. It'll get me."

Potentially. "Watch it and I'll get the bug spray."

Chemical warfare in a can.

"No! It'll run at me if you spray it."

Eyeing the black furry horror on the floor, I stepped closer. Yuck. Reaching for a glass on the counter I quelled my desire to squash the ugly fat horror.

"What. Are. You. Doing?"

"Helping it." I dropped the glass over the spider and looked up at Harley. "Placemat?"

She shook her head and backed away. Biting my lip, I walked around the kitchen island and took a thin plastic placemat from a drawer. Sliding it under the glass, I encouraged the hairy beastie to climb up so I could carry him outside. Holding the glass firmly over the placemat, I moved toward Harley. Horrified, the teenager leaped out of the way.

"Laundry door."

She shook her head.

"Then hold this," I said, pretending to pass her the trapped beast.

"No!" She raced ahead of me and opened the laundry door.

With mustered calm I let the spider go in the grass then went back inside. Harley squawked and flew at me. I hugged her.

"I hate spiders."

"Don't usually see any inside. You going to be okay?"

She nodded, her smile returning. "Sorry."

"Better put this away." I picked up the gun from the kitchen counter. "Can we reserve screams for life-threatening situations?"

Harley accompanied me to the living room. She settled in one of the armchairs. I dragged the laptop back to my knees and checked email, happy to give up on the story writing. Harley found the TV remote. Channels changed. Adverts mingled with snippets of TV programs. Peace returned.

"What's it about?"

"What's what about?" I squinted at the screen as clouds parted, and a ray of sun crossed my line of vision. "No sun for days and now it wants to shine."

"The story you're writing—"

"What about it?"

"You're not listening ..."

I lifted my fingers off the keyboard and looked at her. "I'm listening. Ask me again."

"What's the story about?"

"No story here, just email."

"Doesn't sound very exciting," she said, her interest diverted by the bright colors and chirpy music of a new television advert.

No, it doesn't.

All the noise stopped. I looked up to find Mitch's niece standing in front of me. One hand on her hip, and the other twirling the remote control around her fingers.

"Can I help you?"

"Holly said you were writing a story."

Did she now? "Yeah, nah. Not really."

"Show me?"

The file was still open under the email program. I closed my email and spun the laptop to face her. She picked it up and sat on the couch. I mooched off for a snack. I didn't have time to finish my peanut butter sandwich before Harley appeared in the doorway.

"Ellie, it's so funny."

"Good funny?"

"Yeah. But something needs to happen."

"It's a trip to the beach ..." Lots happened, I'm just not sure any of it is for general consumption. Okay, I know it isn't.

"You should just write about work, your work stories are the best."

"Thanks for the input, Harley. Unfortunately, writing about a case is frowned upon."

She shrugged. "Come on, Ellie. Please. What about the time you and Lee were in New Zealand. Didn't you go to a beach?"

Images filled my head. Special Agent Lee Davenport and I at a golf course by a beach. A flash from an automatic weapon caught my eye. Not that story.

"I'll think about it," I said. It's not happening.

Harley spun around and sat in her chosen chair, pulling her legs up underneath her. "It'd be a best seller."

"You sound like Holly," I said.

Her laughter bounced off the walls and collapsed in a heap of giggles on the rug. My phone buzzed. A text from Mitch saying he and Harley would cook dinner and they'd save me some. Winning.

For a moment, a memory of a different teenager curled in a large armchair overlaid the present. Her smile radiated, her laughter jingled in the air like a dozen fairy bells. The memory of my teenage daughter, Carla, glittered around the edges as it faded. I missed her laugh so very much. I finished the last of my sandwich.

Harley's perky voice plunged through the remnants of my memory. "What'd Uncle Mitch say?"

"He said you can help him cook dinner." A niggly-squirmy-unsure feeling grew in my gut. "I don't like the idea of you being on your own," I said.

"I won't be for long," she replied with a smile. "Anyway, Mom and Dad are going to FaceTime me soon. I won't really be alone."

FaceTiming from Germany, yeah, that's almost like they're here. With her parents on a business trip, we were Harley's guardians for a month. A week in and it was going well. She was a great kid. Yet the responsibility threatened to buckle my shoulders.

"Ellie, I'll be fine. Uncle Mitch will be home soon. I have Gran's number in my phone." Her blue eyes glittered with amusement. "I have *all* the numbers."

"Okay," I said, looking around the room for my bag. "I'd better get organized." I appreciated her not huffing and puffing and reminding me she was seventeen, not a baby.

"It's behind the couch," Harley said.

"Thanks." I attached my weapon in its holster, handcuffs, and spare magazines to my belt.

"Isn't that uncomfortable?"

6

Until she spoke, I was unaware she'd been watching. "Nah. Got used to it years ago."

"Is that why you always wear a heavy belt?"

I nodded and shoved my ID wallet into my left front jeans pocket. My phone lived in my right pocket. Harley handed me my FBI jacket. I pulled it on, not bothering to zip it up. Car tires crunched on the gravel driveway. A horn blasted.

"That's me, Harley. Be good." I gave her a quick hug. "Bug spray is in the cabinet under the sink."

She grimaced and her eyes darted furtively around the carpeted floor. "I don't like spiders."

No kidding. "Pretty sure there aren't any more inside." I crossed my fingers. "Uncle Mitch will be back soon."

Security lighting flooded the top of the driveway when I stepped out and illuminated Kurt's car with crisp white light. I gave the front door a sharp pull.

"Hey," I said, sliding into the seat and closing the car door.

"Sorry to drag you away from the family," Kurt replied. The engine rumbled to life.

"Where are we going?"

"Chesapeake Bay."

"The bodies?"

"Two bodies washed up on the shore."

"Boating accident?" I fastened my seat belt and got comfortable.

"I doubt it. State Police called us. One of the deceased is on our Most Wanted list."

"One down ..." I whispered. Scenery blurred beyond the windscreen. I leaned on the headrest and waited for more information.

"He was a bank robber, his partner is still at large," Kurt said, passing several cars.

"And the other person?"

"No ID yet."

"Lee and Sam?" I swiveled and peered into the back, just in case I'd missed their presence when I climbed into the car. No SA Lee Davenport or SA Sam Jackson.

"I didn't stash them in the back."

"Just checking."

"At this point, it's two dead bodies. No need to mess up the entire team's night."

Two dead bodies and a nighttime trip to the beach. I had a feeling this wouldn't be any better than any of my other beach stories: I don't want to be a writer. The night came back into focus, it was welcome but brief.

Visions of the last author I met danced before my eyes, backlit by oncoming headlights. It took a bit of convincing before my brain accepted that not all writers were psychopaths. And not all writers based their characters on real people. And not all writers went about putting those real people into horrendous situations just to watch how they reacted.

"I don't want to be a writer."

"Conway? Say again ..."

"Say what again?"

"You said something about writers?"

Ah, crap. That wasn't in my head after all. "I never wanted to be a writer," I said.

"You're a couple of years too late, Conway. You are, like it or not."

"A few poems do not a writer make," I said. "And I'm an Iverson now, remember?"

"I'm sorry, it's not easy remembering your new name after all these years."

I didn't have to look at Kurt to know he was smiling.

A tune I knew flowed from the radio. "Kansas," I said with a smile and turned the volume up until "Carry on Wayward Son" filled the car.

Chapter Two

Demons

I crouched near the body of the dead man. With a gloved hand, I brushed sand and seaweed from his face, revealing his features. Something about his face caused pangs of remembrance.

"All right, Conway?" Kurt said, from near the other body. I gave him a look. He shrugged. "Habit ... Iverson."

"Yeah, hard for me too," I said, staring at the death mask in front of me. "And I'm fine, by the way."

"Gunshot wound in this guy. Definitely not a boating accident."

I refocused on the body before me. Closing my eyes, I visualized the face animated.

"What are you thinking?"

I looked up at Kurt. "What makes you say that?"

"Either you're in pain, or you're thinking." He grinned.

"Smartass. He looks kinda familiar and he hasn't been in the water long enough to bloat and peel which is a bonus for us." I stood up and looked down at the dead eyes and contorted expression. "No obvious wounds here. Wasn't a peaceful death, that's for sure."

"Familiar how?" Kurt joined me.

"Pretty sure I've come across him before, just don't know the context." I snapped a picture with my phone.

"Give me a hand to roll him," Kurt said.

We rolled the deceased onto his side. The back of his shirt was torn. Kurt poked around then said, "There's a wound here." He leaned over and checked the front of the body. "Not a through and through."

"Stab wound maybe?" I offered.

He nodded.

"Stabbed in the back. Keeping it cowardly."

Cops milled about the area beyond the police tape. Floodlighting bathed everything in fake daylight. I stood up and looked around. No boat. No wreckage. Nothing to suggest they were on a boat. Where else could they have been to end up in the sea and finally on the beach? Washed down the river? On a bridge? On a jetty? On a dock? Thoughts caught on the dock. I saw the USS *Barry*, a ghostly gray ship on a gray day.

"Chesapeake is vast – where do you suppose these two hailed from?" Kurt said as we both stood up.

I looked at the photo I'd taken on my phone. I did know him. The USS *Barry* faded from my mind and cannons took its place. The Navy Yard. That's where I knew him from. I waited. A cross popped out of the sidewalk in front of NCIS headquarters.

"I think they came down the Anacostia."

"And you're basing this on ...?"

"This guy." I pointed to the man we'd just finished inspecting. "I think he's Derek Cross."

"Derek Cross." A frown creased Kurt's forehead. "Should I know that name?"

"I don't know."

"Where do you know him from?"

"I met him at an NCIS function. He is dating, or was, dating Jenn."

Kurt groaned. "Is he NCIS?"

If I said yes, our job here was done. We could hand over to NCIS and go home. "It's possible."

Kurt had his phone in his hand and made a call before I could even process his actions. He walked away talking into his phone and came back with a smile on his face. "We're out of here. Police can hand it over. Let's go home."

Guess that was my answer. We walked across the sand toward the car. A uniformed police officer held up the crime scene tape. I ducked under first and thanked the officer. He smiled.

"Getting cold," I said, zipping my jacket against the cool night air.

"Fresh out here, that's for sure," Kurt replied.

In the darkness ahead was our car; behind us police lights flashed at the floodlit crime scene. I preferred the dark.

My phone rang, the screen illuminated in my hand. "Crap," I said, showing him the screen.

He grimaced. "Bad news travels fast."

"Jenn."

"Are you sure it's Derek Cross?" she said. Her tone gave nothing away.

"No."

We kept walking into the dark. I wasn't a hundred

percent. It's not like I had anything apart from a twinge in my gut and something slightly familiar about his contorted dead face.

"El?" Jenn said.

"My gut, Jenn, that's all I got until there's been a formal identification. NCIS is sending a team. I take it you're not on it?"

"Too close."

"When did you last see him?"

Kurt opened the car door for me. I climbed in and buckled my belt with Jenn talking in my ear.

"Two weeks ago. He went undercover. I don't know what he was working on. I do know he was using a backstopped alias."

"Putting you on speaker, Jenn," I said, as Kurt slid behind the wheel.

"Hi, Jenn," Kurt said.

"That you, Henderson?"

"Yes."

"Jenn, were you and Cross a couple?" he said. Kurt pointed the car homeward.

"We dated a while ago and remained close."

This really sucked. "So, you have no idea why Derek Cross was in the Chesapeake Bay with one of America's Most Wanted?"

Silence.

"Jenn?"

"None."

"I'll let you go. I'm around if you want to talk."

"Thanks, El."

I hung up and dropped my phone into my lap. Gazing out the window into the night I caught sight of my reflection. The tiredness looking back at me made me yawn. I'm getting too old for this middle-of-the-night crap. Another yawn loomed. I fought it but it escaped anyway. The Cross situation wriggled and jiggled inside me. A children's song erupted within the confines of my overstretched brain. I was pretty sure I didn't swallow the spider to catch a fly. But maybe I did. What if Cross was the spider and the bank robber the fly? We needed to put an end to it before I swallowed a horse. I reached into my bag by my feet and extracted my tablet and typed Cross's name into our search engine.

"What are you doing?" Kurt said with a sideways glance.

"Looking up Derek Cross. It bugs me that he was with one of America's Most Wanted and they're both dead." It's not supposed to work that way.

"Find anything?"

I scrolled through several mentions until I found his employment records. Classified. Damn. Not what I wanted to see.

"Came up classified. Employee photo looks like him though."

"Jenn said deep cover?"

"She said undercover with a backstop, that implies deep cover," I said. My tablet chimed several times. I'd woken Satan's tool, and now it was downloading emails at a rapid rate.

Email banners rolled across the screen. Nothing caught my attention for long. I ignored them, trying another database to see if Cross had his alias registered. Nothing showed up there either. More email chimes sounded. They were current. Subject lines scrolled across the screen in my hand.

"Lot of email for two in the a.m.," Kurt said.

"Yeah. They can wait." Emails in the small hours were rarely good news.

"Anything useful regarding Cross?"

"Nada."

My phone rang. I knew the song. Mitch. "Babe, you should be long asleep," I said.

"Yes, I should."

"What?"

I felt Kurt glance at me. He knew the sound of trouble when he heard it.

"Harley went to a friend's and hasn't come home."

"Did you call her and the friend's parents?" Asking the obvious is what I do best because not everyone thinks clearly when stress hits.

"Yep. The friend's parents haven't seen her since they dropped her back here, outside the house, at ten."

I looked at my watch. The number glowed faintly in the dim light from my phone. Four hours. "Did you hear her come in?"

"No. I started making phone calls when she missed her curfew at eleven."

Jesus! "We're an hour away." There was another possibility. "Your mom?"

"I called just after eleven – didn't want to worry them, but asked if they'd heard from her."

"And?"

"Mom said Harley called her yesterday."

"Okay. I want you to go into her room and tell me what's missing. You might have to open drawers. You okay with snooping?"

"Not really, but I will."

Kurt touched the hands-free button on the steering wheel and spoke. "Call work."

The phone rang five times before someone in the bullpen answered.

"It's Henderson, we have a missing teenager, Harley Iverson. She's been gone four hours. I want an Amber Alert."

"Runaway?" I recognized Claude's voice: SSA of Delta B was on deck and involved.

"Doubtful. Conway's niece – Iverson's niece."

"Description?"

"Hey, Claude. Harley is a seventeen-year-old white female. Five-feet-six-inches tall. Weighs approximately ninety pounds. Long brown hair, no bangs, center parting. Blue eyes. Straight, even teeth, she had her braces off recently. One moment." I spoke into my phone, "Mitch, what was she wearing when you dropped her off?"

"Light blue Levi skinny jeans, a checked blue shirt,

16

olive green short jacket, and a pair of white Reeboks."

I relayed the information to Claude and told him there was a photo of her on my desk in a pile with other photos from our wedding.

Mitch spoke again, "She had her backpack with her. It's purple with a peacock design."

Kurt took over talking to Claude and I concentrated on Mitch.

"Mitch, anything obvious missing?"

"Nope, not even her charger."

She had an iPhone. She didn't take her charger, so she wasn't planning on staying long or going anywhere else.

"I know this is super obvious, but you did call her cell?"

"Of course, and sent a text. Her phone is off, Ellie. iMessage came up green instead of blue and sent as a text."

"Check current network status with her provider. Could be that the network is having issues and the phone's not off."

"Babe, the three of us use the same provider."

Guess the phone's off. "I'll be home soon." I hung up, leaned forward and flipped on the grill lights, muttering under my breath, "Under lights."

Dark thoughts stacked like building storm clouds. Lightning shot from the center of the blackest cloud. A missing teen. We'd been here before. A feeling of dread settled in the pit of my stomach.

"Breathe, Iverson," Kurt said, his voice low and quiet.

"We don't know anything yet."

Theories twisted and turned, words backflipped, sending shock waves through my system, but never made it out of my mouth. Missing kid cases rarely end well.

Chapter Three

Stay With Me

Kurt parked behind a police cruiser in my driveway. I climbed out of the car. Light from the open front door spilled over the porch and onto the gravel. The security lighting flickered on as I passed, bathing some of the stones on the driveway in an iridescent glow, reminding me of dragonfly wings. Eerie but pretty. Conscious of Kurt behind me but not waiting for him, I walked in my front door. "Mitch?"

"Living room," he called back.

I entered the room to find two police officers talking to my husband. One looked up from writing in her notebook and smiled at me. I recognized her face but couldn't remember her name.

"Agent Conway," she said. Her eyes paused on mine then her line of sight hovered over my shoulder. "Agent Henderson."

"Officer Hamilton," Kurt replied.

Ah, good, he remembered her name.

"Conway married. She's an Iverson now."

Hamilton. Officer Irene Hamilton.

"Congrats, Agent."

Mitch kissed me hello as I moved and sat next to him. "You all right?" I whispered.

"Yes."

The package on the table drew my eyes. New Zealand

candy. "Pre-dinner snacks?"

"It was after dinner. She's been asking questions about New Zealand."

Ah, Q and A over candy. Nice.

"There is nothing out of place anywhere?" Officer Hamilton asked, turning a page in her notebook.

Mitch looked up at her. "No. She's a tidy kid, her room looks like it always does."

"Laptop?" I said.

"On her bed."

"Ma'am, would you like us to take a look and see if there is anything in her social media that might help locate her?"

I looked at the cop. Did I? Or did I want to snoop on Mitch's niece myself? Did I think she was a runaway or something bad had happened? Mentally stumbling around the white noise created by thoughts I didn't want to face, I glanced at Mitch and then Kurt.

Kurt's head moved a fraction. "We'll take it from here, thank you."

"Yes, sir."

Both cops pocketed their notebooks and left the room.

"Harley's room?" Kurt said from the doorway.

"Up the front stairs," Mitch said, "Second on the left."

Then it was just us. "What do you think?" I said, leaning against Mitch. He wrapped his arm around my shoulders and pulled me closer.

"A boy ... I think she's with a boy."

"She hasn't mentioned a boy to me. You?"

"No."

"So you pulled 'boy' from thin air?"

"Not really. She hasn't mentioned a boy as such. She's talked about school friends and friends she plays online games with, chances are they're not all girls."

That's true. My mind spun over the online aspect of her life. Scary shit lurked in plain view on the internet disguised as teenage girls and boys. What game did she play? I cast my mind back to previous conversations held while she watched something intently on the screen. She'd said her character was a wolf. Feral Heart. "That Feral Heart game?"

"Uh-huh."

"What do we know about that?"

"Not as much as we should, I'll bet."

Kurt walked into the room carrying Harley's laptop, open, and resting on one arm. "She Skyped before she went to her friend's tonight."

A cone of silence fell over me. I did not want to be here again. How could that happen twice? It couldn't. Different situation. Different kids. This is not the same. This doesn't have to be sinister.

Kurt perched on the coffee table in front of us. His mouth moved. No sound. I shoved a finger in my right ear and wiggled it around. Expecting to hear again when I pulled it out. Nothing.

Kurt's mouth moved some more. I watched his lips. "Iverson."

"Henderson," I replied, watching closely for his next voiceless announcement.

"You all right?"

A loud bang jolted me from the cone of silence.

"Iverson, you all right?"

"What do you think?"

He sort of smiled then changed his mind. "I think we need to talk about Skype in relation to Harley and not let the past cloud our judgments."

Good call. "Yeah. Okay. Who did she Skype?"

He turned the laptop to face me. Mitch and I leaned closer to see the Skype window with more clarity while he spoke. "She was in a group chat with four other people. Emma in Perth, Australia. Tui in Wellington, New Zealand. Sarah in the US, and Katie in the US."

"No specific location on Sarah and Katie?" Mitch asked.

"Not in their profiles," Kurt said. "Email addresses are there. We can run those through a few different databases and see if they registered a location or two and see if anything else comes to light."

I waved an index finger at the chat window. "Did they audio or video chat?"

"Audio. This time."

"This time?"

"They have video-chatted in the past but not all the girls took part." Kurt pulled up previous group chats. "Emma has never video-chatted with the group. Harley has never video-chatted with Emma privately." He scrolled through her call history. "From what I can tell, Harley has had private video calls with Sarah and Tui. Group video calls with Sarah, Tui, and Katie."

"What's that?" Mitch pointed to something on the list in

red.

"Unanswered voicecall originating from this computer to Emma." He turned the laptop so he could see the screen with ease. "A few minutes after the time stamp on the call there is a message from Emma saying she's sorry but she has a sore throat and can't talk."

"Why do I get the feeling Emma does a lot of bunking on calls and has a ton of excuses at the ready about why she can't video chat?" I said. "There's a chance that Emma might be a forty-year-old man."

Kurt raised an eyebrow and looked at me over the laptop screen. "I'm getting the same feeling. I'll send the conversations between these five girls to the office. I think Cyber should have a run at it."

"Anything look like grooming?"

"No. Nothing."

"Catfishing?"

"Could be."

"Babe, catfishing?" Mitch queried.

"The phenomenon of internet predators who fabricate online identities and entire social circles to trick people into emotional/romantic relationships, usually over a long period of time." Sometimes years. "From what I've seen the possible motivations can be damn near anything." I was in danger of turning into a Wiki page. "The four big motivators seem to be revenge, loneliness, curiosity, and boredom." I heard my voice and even I thought, blah, blah, blah.

"Jeez. Why is it called catfishing?"

"After a documentary titled *Catfish*. I think it came out in

23

2010?" I looked at Kurt. He nodded. I felt Mitch's mind ticking over and waited because I knew it was something to do with what I'd just dumped on him.

"Wasn't there a scandal of sorts a few years ago involving sock puppets, is that the same thing?"

Kurt took over. I was done with the sound of my own voice and my walking encyclopedia status. And anytime anyone said sock puppet, Lamb Chop and that freaking song that never ends hijacked me. Thanks for that, Shari Lewis.

"They start out the same. They're both assumed identities. A sockpuppet is an online identity used for purposes of deception. The term originally referred to a false identity assumed by a member of an Internet community who spoke to, or about, themselves, while pretending to be another person. What you remember, I think, is that Amazon scandal where some authors created sock puppets and went around writing bad reviews of their counterparts and glowing reviews of their own work. Badly behaved authors."

In my experience, when authors go bad they start killing, not verbally tearing one another down. Mitch's voice interrupted my not-so-pleasant thoughts.

"I recall hearing something about that," Mitch said. "If I wanted to say great things about my own design for example, but didn't want to look like I was blowing my own trumpet, I'd create a sock puppet? But if I wanted a romantic relationship or a friendship and created an identity that'd be catfishing?"

"Yes," I said, attempting to banish Lamb Chop from my head. Painful, oh, so, painful.

"All right, I have it now. So it's possible that one or more of the people Harley talked to, and played her game with, aren't who they say they are for whatever reason?"

"Yes."

"Is it always bad?"

"No, not always. There are legitimate reasons to protect your real identity online, but I'm struggling to think of a reason why teenage girls would need to do that."

"WITSEC," Kurt said as if a light bulb had just gone on.

The flash was so bright it almost blinded me. "Witness Security? You're kidding?"

He shook his head. "There're lots of reasons for someone to hide their true identity, Iverson, but when you're a teenager, it's a bit different." Kurt spun the laptop to face me. On the screen was a photo of Emma. "Have you got your laptop here?"

I nodded, broke away from Mitch's hold and hurried to my home office. I came back with the laptop. Kurt emailed the photo straight from Harley's machine.

It took several minutes to arrive in my inbox. Funny how slow email can be when you're in the same room and waiting. "Got it. I'm running that photo now."

"These kids have been talking to each other for two years via Skype. Emma was the last to join the group. By the look of the conversations, they talk while they're playing Feral Heart. They all met through the game."

"Once upon a time it would've been pencils, paper, envelopes and stamps and now it's online games and Skype," Mitch said. "Did catfishing go on back in the days of pen pals?"

"Probably," Kurt replied. "Pen pals used to advertise in the personal column of newspapers. No reason to assume that catfishing is modern. People are people, technology just helps them find each other easier."

The program flashed an alert on my screen.

"Shit," I muttered, opening the alert. Inside I found a photo of Emma with a deceased stamp across it and a note saying all information regarding the person and their death was classified. It didn't even show her name. "Houston we have a problem."

"WITSEC?" Kurt said.

"She's in the database marked as deceased but information is blocked by the US Marshals Service. So yeah, Witness Security would be my guess. We've got nothing and the chances of getting anything are slim to none."

"Australia?" Mitch said.

"It's possible but unlikely," Kurt said. "The family would use an anonymous browser like we do."

"They could be anywhere and they're using proxies, so they can't be traced?" Mitch said.

"Yes," I said.

"This might not be sinister at all then." Mitch leaned back on the couch.

"Might not be." Think positive. She's a teenage girl who hasn't mentioned a boy and whose parents are in Europe. She went to visit a friend and went on to another friend. Nothing I wouldn't have done at her age given the opportunity. Lucky for me, my crazy mother used to do the disappearing acts, which as I grew older was a relief.

"You called all her friends?"

"Yes. All the ones I have numbers for."

"The Amber Alert is live."

As much as I hated it, there wasn't a lot more we could physically do. What Mitch had said about the iMessage being sent as a text and her phone being off bothered me. But depending on when she charged it last and what she was doing in the meantime, the battery could be flat rather than her having turned off the phone.

Instinctively I reached for my phone and iMessaged her. It came up green straight away. Still off. I wrote a message in the hope that she'd be able to charge her phone or turn it on at some stage. Or whoever had control of her phone would turn it on and see my message telling whoever had Harley exactly what I would do to them when I caught them and left no doubt that I would catch them. With luck, they'd read it to her. If she saw or heard it she'd laugh, if someone else saw it, they might think twice about whatever the hell they were planning.

Mitch caught the smile on my face. "What'd you do?"

"Liam Neeson in text."

He laughed. "I will look for you, I will find you, and I will kill you?"

"Yeah."

"You say who you were?" Kurt asked.

"No. My name will come up on the message. If pressed, I'm sure Harley will tell whoever is with her that her aunt is FBI."

"Now what?" Mitch rubbed his right eye and yawned.

"We wait," Kurt said. "Try to get some sleep."

"You going to the office?" I said, stifling a yawn.

"No." He frowned, and changed his mind. "Yes. I'll go check on the investigation and finish our paperwork for the scene we handed over to NCIS. You stay here with Mitch and get some sleep."

A protest rose within me but was quelled by a swift look from Kurt. He was right. I needed to sleep and so did Mitch. We were no good to anyone exhausted. Least of all Harley.

Kurt let himself out. Mitch followed me upstairs. I stopped in Harley's doorway.

"What?" Mitch came up behind me and wrapped his arms around my waist. "You need sleep."

His warm breath ruffled the hair by my right ear. "Her iPad."

He took my hand and pointed it to the nightstand by her bed. iPad. Might be something on it that wasn't on her laptop. Maybe I could use the Find iPhone app to locate Harley's phone. If it'd been turned on. If iMessage was off but the phone was still going. If it wasn't broken or dead. So many ifs. I sighed. Mitch kissed my neck.

"Let's have a look at that iPad, then maybe bed?"

"Yeah, iPad then bed." Sounded good to me.

We sat side by side on the bed. I opened the cover on the iPad and watched it spring to life. No passcode. That made it easier. I tapped the app I wanted. Moments later it told me the only device of Harley's online was the iPad.

Dammit.

"Nothing," I mumbled closing the app.

"What's that?" Mitch pointed at another icon on the screen. It looked like a picture of a SIM card and was called Locate_CI.

"I have no idea." I tapped it and the icon opened to reveal an app. It was a lot like the Find iPhone screen. There were options. One of them was turn iPhone on. Holy crap. This was one awesome application.

I tapped to turn on Harley's phone and waited. We sat on her bed staring at the screen. A map flashed up and a little picture of a phone blinked on the map. The blinking icon moved. I zoomed in enough to see the names of the major roads and highways.

The movement stopped. An alert flashed on the screen. iPhone off. Last known location popped up as 2227-2397 Reston Parkway, Reston VA heading toward Herndon.

"Someone else has control of her phone," I said, "If they continue on that road they'll end up on Ox Road, Fairfax. From there they could potentially get onto Lee Jackson Memorial Highway or even go to Fair Oaks Mall." I opened the settings panel inside the application. There was an interesting heading: Find HI.

"What are you looking for?" Mitch asked.

"Dunno, but it might be this ..." I tapped the heading and a menu emerged. "Yep, I think it's this."

Mitch leaned closer. "It's a tracker."

"Yeah, I think it is."

We watched the screen come to life and a map pick up where the last one left off.

"CI?" I queried, watching the screen. If it was tracking Harley, then she was moving as I expected.

"I'd say it was Chris and that he'd designed an app specifically for tracking his daughter."

"That's not weird." Mitch nudged my arm. I knew he was smiling.

"Think he'd let us use that technology?" Mitch said. "It might be handy with two of them to keep tabs on."

"Think we have a while before our twins are an issue," I replied, picking up my phone and making a call. The phone rang four times before I heard Kurt's voice.

"Iverson, you should be resting."

"Uh-huh. I know where she is, right now, we can track her. Meet us." I gave him the coordinates.

"On my way, bringing SWAT. We have no idea what we're dealing with here."

"Good call."

I hung up, pocketed my phone, thrust the iPad at Mitch and hurried to the bathroom trying to stem the tide of rising vomit. Resting would've been a good idea.

I returned with a question. "Mitch, how is the program tracking her? The phone was turned off again. So, where's the tracker?"

He stopped putting his jacket on for a moment; lines creased his forehead. "Good question."

I took a warm FBI jacket from the closet in our room and pulled it on. "Come on, we'll think about it on the way. Where is she now?"

Mitch handed me the iPad while he put his jacket on. The

screen said she was almost at Fair Oaks Mall. Bit early for shopping. It was even too early for Mall walkers.

"Chris had a pendant made for her last birthday. She always wears it. A silver locket." Mitch and I walked down the hallway. "The tracker could be part of the locket."

"Yeah, it could. Let's go to the mall, seems to be where they're heading," I said. I texted Kurt to let him know. "Why the hell would anyone go to the mall?"

The front door opened and closed behind me. The car door opened in front of me then closed as I settled into the passenger seat. I watched the screen in my hands.

Why go to the mall? Because there are several large parking lots? Because it's an open place to meet someone else? Because they want an ice cream? "Mitch, I want ice cream."

"There's a 7-Eleven up the road, they're always open."

"I want Cherry Garcia."

"Of course you do."

I saw his smile. Stupid o'clock in the morning was the perfect time for eating Cherry Garcia straight from the tub with a plastic spoon. Classy.

At the mall, two black Suburbans sat near the entrance to the parking lot closest to JC Penney's. Didn't look like any other cars were around. My phone rang. Kurt's image flashed on the screen. I jammed the spoon into the ice cream and placed the tub in Mitch's lap then answered.

"Anything?"

"Not yet."

I glanced at the iPad. The signal had stopped moving. A stationary flashing icon pointed to the Marriott. A wave of panic coursed freely through me.

"Iverson? What?"

"The Marriott. The tracker stopped moving."

"We're on it," Kurt replied.

Mitch grabbed my arm as I swung the car door open. "Not by yourself."

"Just let me walk."

"Babe."

One word, so much resignation. I smiled and climbed out of the car. "Stay here, please," I said over my shoulder. "Don't eat my ice cream."

With a flick of my boot, I shut the car door. Surveying the darkness that engulfed the parking lot and led to the hotel, I took a deep cleansing breath. My hand sat on the butt of the Glock, just inside my right hip. One fluid movement released the weapon from my holster. My shoulders squared, my pistol gripped in my right hand but by my side, I walked into the darkness. A chirp from my pocket broke the silence wide open. I checked the display on my phone. Kurt, wanting to know where I was.

I tapped a reply with my left thumb: Walking across the parking lot toward the Marriott.

Modern West and Kevin Costner's "Long Hot Night" erupted from the phone. I hit answer. Music dropped like frozen stars and melted into puddles of liquid silver on the night-shrouded blacktop.

"Conway ... Iverson."

"Henderson."

"Stand down and let us handle this situation."

A small laugh escaped. "You see that happening?"

"Probably not, but I had to try."

"Well, you tried, now can we get on with this?" The darkness swallowed my footsteps, increasing the temptation to run.

"We'll wait for you."

Chapter Four

I'll Be Waiting

Kurt leaned on the driver's side of his car. His head swiveled toward me. "Anything?"

"Considering we don't know what kind of car she's in or anything more than an app on her iPad puts her in the vicinity of the Marriott ... no. She's here somewhere. Or her necklace is." I pointed toward the well-lit hotel. An oasis in the night. "Let's go."

With a twirl of my arm in the air, car doors opened and closed, a hive of activity filled the space in front of us. We were far enough from the hotel to still be in semi-darkness.

"Listen up," I said, lifting my voice to be heard. Silence fell. "We're running on information sent from a tracking device inside a necklace. If we can't get a positive ID from the reception staff, then we'll conduct a floor by floor, room by room search. No one leaves the hotel until we determine whether or not Harley Iverson is here."

A low murmur of understanding flowed from the group of ten men and women in front of me.

Kurt motioned to the group, "You five are Echo, the rest of you are Foxtrot. We ..." He waggled a finger between him and me. "We are Golf."

A female agent stepped forward. Karen Christos. "We're heading to the back," she said. "See you inside."

"Be safe," I said, as the five agents moved out.

A man from the second group smiled and said, "In the front door for us."

"Thanks, Tommy, we'll go in first," I replied. "Be safe."

Kurt and I followed the second group, moving in front of them at the entrance. Inside the lobby, I scanned for the concierge.

A tightly wound woman with a strained smile stood near the front desk. Guess she figured out we weren't there to check in. For a moment I almost felt sorry for her, especially knowing what was about to happen.

"I'm SSA Iverson," I said to the woman as I showed her my badge.

"What can I do for you, Agent?" Her cold tone gave away more than the unwelcoming smile on her face.

"Have you seen this girl?" I handed her my phone with a photo of Harley on the screen.

She took a moment before handing it back. "Yes. That young lady's father checked in and she accompanied him." She moved sideways until she stood in front of a screen. Keyboard tapping followed. We waited.

"Suite 470."

"And the name of the guest?"

"Christopher Iverson."

Hooves pounded down a tilt line in my mind. The lance splintered as it hit me in the chest. Chris? "Do you have photo ID on file?"

"Yes, we do. Mr. Iverson's passport."

"I need a copy of that." Hoping my voice wasn't as

shaky as my insides felt.

Out of sight, a printer whirred. The woman passed me a copy of the image she had on file. It looked like Chris Iverson's passport and it was his image on the page.

"Thanks. Did you make a note of his car tags?"

She read the screen, scrolled, nodded, and wrote a number on a piece of memo paper for me.

I passed the paper to the nearest agent. "Alan, take Charlotte and secure the car."

"On it, ma'am," Alan replied, spinning on his heels and exiting the foyer with Charlotte close behind. Kurt called the second team and gave them the room number. I heard him talking; they'd secured the back of the hotel.

I pointed to two agents. "You two stay here. No one in or out until we're done here." They smiled. Neither said a word.

They took up positions near the door. That left us with one agent. Scott.

"You're with us, Scott," Kurt said, catching up with the play and pocketing his phone. "SWAT has arrived. They're outside if we need them."

"Good," I said heading for the stairs. "Let's resolve this without SWAT if possible."

I made a call to comms. "SSA Iverson, requesting QV." I gave them the tag number for the car Harley was in.

"Agent, that car is registered to a rental company, Hertz Rentals, Fair Oaks."

"Thanks." I hung up and spoke to my phone while holding the home button. "Siri, phone number for Hertz

Rental Cars in Fair Oaks, please."

Siri replied, "Hmm, I believe someone asked for that just the other day ... here's what I found."

Kurt chuckled. "Siri is more lifelike with every update."

"Yep," I said, calling the number on my screen.

A voice answered and I identified myself and asked who hired the car with license tag number EQR 5555.

"That car was rented by Christopher Iverson."

Again with the Chris Iverson thing. "Really?" From Germany to Fairfax without telling his family? I don't think so. Despite his passport being bandied about, I didn't think it was Chris.

"Yes, ma'am. He paid by credit card."

"Tell me you have his driver's license on record?"

"Yes, ma'am. We have a photo of it in our files."

"Email me the image and the credit card details, please, at the following email address, G dot Iverson at FBI dot Gov."

I hung up and pocketed my phone. We were on the fourth floor and I hadn't even noticed walking up the stairs. Kurt swung open the heavy door; I stepped through and moved aside to wait for him and Scott.

"The concierge said Harley is here with her father," I passed the piece of paper from the concierge to Kurt.

"Chris's passport," he said, looking at me while he folded the paper and pocketed it. "And the rental car company said Chris hired the car." Interest mingled with disbelief in Kurt's voice. He didn't believe it any more than I did.

"Yep, let's go see who opens the door." I doubted it would be Mitch's brother.

The hallway in front of me shimmered; through the haze and silvery ripples stepped Christopher Chance. Sometimes I wished I'd never read *The Human Target* comic books or watched the TV series. Chance walked toward me, grinning; as he drew level with my ear he whispered, "Ever heard of Devil's Breath?"

"No."

"Bet Kurt has." He disappeared into the wall by the stairwell door.

"What was that?" Kurt asked touching my arm.

"Chance."

We stopped one door back from our target doorway. Scott passed us and waited on the other side of the door.

"Do I need to know?"

"He said you'd know what Devil's Breath is."

Kurt lifted his phone and called paramedics. A brief conversation ensued where he mentioned the name of something that sounded nasty, scopolamine. I figured that was the real name for Devil's Breath.

Scott murmured something. I looked up. He flashed a quick hand signal telling me he'd heard noise from in the room. I pulled my weapon from the holster on my hip. Settling the grip firmly in my hand, I steeled myself and moved the ten remaining feet between us and the doorway to room 470.

I knocked twice and called out, "Room service." Then leaned back on the wall by the hinge side of the door, away from the security peephole.

A voice rang out from the inside, "We didn't order anything."

Thinking on my feet, "Complimentary champagne."

The security lock snapped back. The door opened a few inches. I stepped into the doorway and shoved the door hard. Sending the person behind staggering backward.

"Who are you?" he said, fumbling behind his back while trying to regain his footing.

"FBI. Hands in front of you." I glanced at him and confirmed my suspicions. "You're not Chris Iverson." My eyes searched beyond him. "Harley!"

The imposter in front of us moved, I saw black in his hand. His arm swung out straight. A pistol.

"Drop it," I growled, sliding my index finger onto the trigger of my Glock.

His finger twitched. I fired. The pistol fell. Kurt leaped forward, kicking the gun out of the way. He grabbed the man by his dripping bloodied hand and twisted it up behind his back. Too surprised to react, he complied. I moved further into the room. Two doors led off the living space.

"Harley?" I called opening one door.

I felt a presence behind me. My heart thumped harder as I glanced backward. Scott. He gave a quick smile and placed a hand on my shoulder. He squeezed my shoulder and we moved as one through the doorway. Inside, he broke left, I went right. We made eye contact across the perfectly made king-size bed once we were sure the room was clear. Scott motioned to the closet door. I nodded. He reached over and pulled one door open.

Air escaped through my teeth. Nothing but spare pillows.

We went back into the main room where the wounded male complained loudly about his shot hand, bleeding on the carpet. Kurt wrapped a towel around his hand, which was still handcuffed behind his back.

Next room, same procedure.

She lay covered by blankets in the middle of the big bed. Holstering my weapon, I strode to the curled-up girl. Scott remained vigilant.

"Harley," I said, touching her shoulder. She didn't move. "Kurt!" I yelled, pressing two fingers under her jaw trying to find a pulse. "Doc!" I shook Harley by the shoulder. "Wake up, Harley!"

Rising panic mingled with not too distant memories. Teenagers scare the living shit out of me. Why the hell did I think having Harley stay for a month was a good idea?

Kurt's hand came into view. "Right here, Iverson." He could've said anything. His voice always filled me with calm. "Paramedics are on their way," he said as he gave Harley a visual once-over.

I moved out of his way and took up position at the end of the bed. I glanced at Kurt, about to ask if he'd asked for two buses. He nodded before I voiced the question. I left it at that.

"These were in the bleeder's pockets." He threw me a

wallet and passport.

I snatched them from the air. Opening the wallet, I found Chris's driver's license and a credit card with Chris Iverson's name on it. The passport looked real.

"Questioned Documents lab needs to check these," I said. "I'm expecting at least the passport to be a forgery."

Scott took them from me.

"Come on, Harley. Wakey, wakey." Kurt rubbed her collar bone trying to get a response.

She didn't move.

"Doc?"

"I'm picking she was drugged. I don't know any other way to get a seventeen-year-old girl to be quiet or compliant."

That was a pretty fair comment. "Devil's Breath?"

"Worth looking into," Kurt said. "Chance is getting more random with every appearance. How often would anyone think 'zombie drug' in Northern Virginia?"

"What now?"

"Devil's Breath. It comes from the Nightshade family. In the right doses, it causes compliance and a zombie-like state."

Zombies. And they said my head shots were overkill. I knew one day zombies would be real. Chance appeared and high-fived me. I reined in my mind, resuming some control. "Explain."

"There've been cases in recent years where the drug has been blown into people's faces rendering the victims unable to think for themselves. They're then made to empty their bank accounts and so forth. I've heard of tourists in Europe targeted that way but nothing here."

Scott's phone rang. He listened then hung up. "Paramedics are on their way up from the lobby."

"Thanks." I left Kurt with Harley and went to get a better look at the bleeder before they took him. "Look at me," I ordered.

The bleeding man's head turned until I could see most of his face. Definitely not Chris but close enough to get away with it late at night. The later it gets, the less people could give a shit. And who looks like their driver's license or passport photo anyway?

"You shot me," he said.

Shit happens. Chris had an accent similar to Mitch's, one that hinted at a life lived somewhere exotic or at least not entirely spent within the Americas; this low-life sounded like he left a gator farm in Alabama last week. "You'll live," I said just as the first crew of paramedics entered the room.

"He's all yours. One of my people will accompany you to the hospital." An agent moved closer to the wounded man. Alan from Delta B.

"I'll be accompanying you," he said introducing himself to the medics.

They got on with their jobs and the second crew arrived.

"You're with me," I said, motioning to them to follow. I stopped just inside the bedroom doorway, then stepped aside. "Paramedics for Harley, Kurt."

He called them through and explained what he suspected was the reason why Harley wasn't waking. He said he would travel to the hospital with them then looked at me. "You okay with that?"

"Yes. I'll call Mitch and we'll meet you there."

The paramedics swung into action and before long Harley was on a gurney and wheeled from the room, with Kurt in tow.

I beckoned Scott. "Search the suite. You're looking for a drug of some kind, it may be a fine powder. Also, anything that tells us what that moron wanted with my niece and who he is."

"We've got half of Team Echo out there." He nodded toward the main room.

"Good, they can help. A thousand thoughts crashed into me at once. I swam through them picking one or two that wouldn't sink me. "I need to talk to my husband. Gimme a minute."

Scott nodded and left the room. I heard his voice but not what he said as he spoke to other agents.

Seconds later Mitch's worried face appeared on the screen of my phone. The worry turned to relief. He smiled. "I knew you were okay but confirmation is good."

"Of course." I smiled back. He would've heard sirens and seen the ambulances. "We got her. She's on her way to hospital with Kurt."

Lines creased his forehead. "Hospital?"

"We think she was drugged."

Worry blasted from his eyes, panic etched into the fine

lines. "Drugged? Is she going to be okay?"

I nodded. "Pretty sure she will be. Kurt is with her."

Panic faded. "How long will you be, El?"

"Not long. Doing a search. Hopefully get an ID on the guy who says he's Christopher Iverson."

"Jesus!"

"Yeah. We'll need to contact Chris and Susan."

"Together, okay?"

I nodded. Didn't want to tell them we let their daughter get drugged and kidnapped by myself.

"Drive over to the hotel. I'll travel to the hospital with you. One of the agents here can take Kurt's car back to work."

"See you soon."

"Yeah, you will."

I tapped the red icon and plunged the screen into darkness.

"Scott?" I spun on the spot, my eyes darting around the room looking for Scott's tall, black-haired self.

He straightened up, making himself obvious where he sat on a large leather couch. "Over here," he said. "Found something interesting."

I joined him on the couch. "What?"

"The coffee table."

"Nice. Wooden. Solid looking. Any of these things close to what interested you?"

"Nope. Watch." He moved his gloved hand under the coffee table and pressed something. A hidden compartment opened underneath the table. Inside it were several plastic document wallets and two small baggies of a white crystalline powder.

"He booked this room knowing about the table? Or all the suites in this hotel contain secret compartments in the coffee tables."

Not a bad idea. Like a safe but more Mission Impossible. I motioned to an agent standing by the door. "Get the concierge up here, please."

Scott opened a document wallet and pulled papers out, spreading them on the table. A dossier on Harley. There was a lot of information and a lot missing. Whoever compiled this did not know about the necklace or me. They had me down as the sister-in-law and as Mrs. Mitchell Iverson. No mention of my job. But they knew Harley was staying with her uncle and aunt and had our address. Deep in my brain, Robby waved his arms, 'Warning, Will Robinson.'

"Some of this stuff had to come from Chris and Susan," I said. The more I read the papers, the more I was certain the information was not gathered by surveillance. "I have a bad feeling."

"Then you'll love this." He handed me three passports. One Australian. One American. One Chinese.

I opened each one and looked at the photograph and name. Stephen Wall, Australian; Stephen Wies, American; Stephen Wong, Chinese. "At least he's consistent. Good chance he's actually Stephen something."

"Any ideas?"

I shook my head. Nada. Not a one. The kid was drugged. I was happy to believe Chance when it came to the drug of choice. Under the influence of the drug, she would've done as she was told. And I suspected some of that was to unlock her phone. She wouldn't get into a stranger's car and accompany the person into a hotel without any fuss. Drugging made sense. Luckily, her father was a clever guy. Why was Harley snatched? What was a man with three passports doing with the kid? What was he doing with a dossier on the kid?

I turned the American passport over in my hand. A small piece of paper fell out. I retrieved it from the floor. A phone number. A D.C. phone number.

"Let's see what happens when someone answers," I said, pressing the sequence of numbers on my phone. I counted rings as I waited. Scott busied himself with an app on his phone and paired his phone with mine, ready to track the call the instant it was answered.

On eight, a gruff male voice said, "Hello."

"Is that you, Stephen?"

"There's no one here by that name."

"Oh, he told me to ring this number when I had the parcel." I infused a little confusion and worry into my voice. "Sorry. I must've written it wrong."

Voices behind me grew louder. I held my hand up to silence them.

"I can send someone to pick up the parcel." The owner of the voice perked up, I imagined cogs turning as the hamster in his head picked up speed.

"I'm only supposed to give her," I paused for effect, "I mean ... the parcel, to Stephen."

"Trust me, he won't mind. Where are you?"

"I'm not sure about this—"

"Look, lady, Stephen works for me. He's an idiot. I'm coming to you. Where are you?"

Scott grinned.

"Room 470, Marriott at Fair Oaks."

"Stay put. I'll be there in twenty."

I hung up and turned to Scott. "Anything?"

"Location, location, location," he said with a laugh, looking at the map on his screen. "The call landed at an address in Vienna." He pulled a pen from his pocket along with a notebook and wrote down the address.

I pointed to two agents in the doorway. "Get me Andrews from SWAT and let everyone else know they need to stand down. I don't want anyone visible when our guest arrives."

Another agent appeared with the concierge.

"Come on in, ma'am," I said, beckoning the woman over. "Sorry, I didn't get your name earlier ..." Her name tag hadn't registered and now it was absent from her blouse.

"Blake, Sonya Blake," she said through tight lips.

"Sonya. The gentleman who checked into this room—"

"Yes, Mr. Iverson."

"Yes, Mr. Iverson. Has he stayed with you before?"

She shook her head. "I don't believe so."

"The furniture in this suite, is it the same in all your

rooms?"

Again her head shook. "There are fifteen rooms with that particular coffee table."

I'd seen something similar before at a home show. The one I saw was fitted to conceal weapons.

Tiredness washed over me. I hid a yawn behind my hand. "Did Mr. Iverson ask for a room with a coffee table like this?" I tapped the table with my index finger.

"Yes. He asked for a room on the fourth floor in particular."

"Thank you."

I looked up at the agent who'd escorted her in. "I need you to accompany Ms. Blake back to her post and stay with her, please. There is someone coming in who will be looking for this room."

"Yes, ma'am."

"Make sure he gets up here without any problem."

With a nod of his head, he escorted Sonya Blake back to her desk. Andrews passed them in the doorway.

"Hey, Iverson," he called, coming over and sitting in an armchair opposite me.

"We've got someone coming in who has something to do with the kidnapping of my niece. Stay close?"

"Absolutely."

For the next ten minutes, we all nailed down our parts for the next scene.

48

Chapter Five
Sweet Virginia

My heart raced when I heard a quiet knock on the hotel room door. I ducked into the first bedroom and checked on Andrews. "Okay in here?"

"Yeah," he replied from the bed.

"Try to look smaller." I tugged the blankets higher, so only the top of his brown hair was visible. "And don't move ... most seventeen-year-old girls don't have a five o'clock shadow."

The knock grew louder.

"Coming," I called. Scott and another agent were stationed in the next bedroom.

Walking into the main room in time to hear another knock at the door, I steadied my nerves with a deep breath. Pulled off my jacket, turned it inside out – seemed better not to confront the guy with bright yellow lettering that said FBI – and put it on again making sure my gun was hidden.

Time for the confused blonde act. With a steadying breath, I swung open the door. "Hello," I chirped. "Are you Stephen's friend?"

He pushed past me and into the room. "Where is the package?"

"In the bedroom." I pointed to the room and whispered, "You know it's not a real package, don't you?"

He stopped moving and stared at me. "Are you for real, lady?"

I blinked several times. "It's a girl."

He shook his head. "You're not real bright, are you?"

"What's your name?" I managed to pull in a ragged breath and inject some fear into my voice. "Stephen will be mad if I don't tell him." I cast my eyes to the floor and shuffled from foot to foot.

"Jake," he said and walked into the bedroom.

A smile flashed across my lips, I flipped my open jacket out of the way and pulled my gun from my hip and followed him. From just inside the doorway, I said, "Hey, Jake …"

He looked up just as he lifted the edge of the blanket off Andrews' shoulders. Surprise, then amusement, crossed his face as he focused on the Glock in my hands.

"Really? You think that's going to do … what?"

"FBI. Put your hands on your head."

Confusion mingled with sudden realization. Guess he didn't like the new game plan. His right hand strayed to his hip. Andrews sprang up from the bed, knocked Jake on his ass and grabbed the pistol that fell from his hand.

"You might wanna stay down," Andrews muttered, reaching for the disposable cuffs he carried on his belt. "Iverson's already shot someone tonight, don't give her a reason to double her paperwork."

A few swift movements followed; when Andrews straightened up, Jake was hog-tied. I stifled a laugh. A shadow caused me to glance over my shoulder. Scott smiled at me from the doorway and spoke into his phone.

"Eeny, meeny, miny, moe, one of us has got to go," I said with a grin. "Best be me. I'm too close to this to interview the suspect effectively." I holstered my weapon and shook Andrews's hand.

"Give my best to Mitch. Hope the kid is all right," Andrews said, smiling. "Good outcome, Iverson."

"You made a fine teenage girl, Andrews."

"I'll add it to my résumé."

"You should."

I said goodbye to the other two agents and left. Opening the door from the stairwell, I found Mitch pacing the lobby. He stopped when he saw me.

"You all right?"

"Yep," I said, slipping my hand into his. "Heard anything from Kurt?"

"Yeah, Harley's waking up and he thinks she'll be fine."

"Good. Let's get over there?"

"You're done here?"

"I am."

We exited the hotel as the gray early morning sky fractured, letting slivers of light turn the clouds pink and gold. Morning had broken. My mind filled with Cat Stevens singing. That couldn't be bad. I squeezed Mitch's hand and felt light pressure as he did the same.

"I ate your ice-cream," he whispered in my ear.

Chapter Six
Labor Of Love

There was a definite attempt on my part not to pay any attention to my surroundings as we walked through the main entrance of Fairfax hospital. If I refused to let the hospital walls close in, I might get out of the building without any more trauma to my psyche. I recognized my reluctance to be in a hospital with a teenager and, considering how it went last time, I was okay with being reluctant and okay with protecting myself. You do what you have to do. Halfway to the elevators, my name echoed against the walls.

"Agent Iverson!"

I kept walking.

"Iverson, wait up!"

Mitch turned to see who wanted me, tugging my hand as he did so and halting my progress toward the elevators. "Who's that?" he whispered in my ear.

"Alan, he's with Delta B," I whispered back before planting a smile on my face and greeting Alan. "Hey, you want me?"

"Yes." Alan puffed as he stopped in front of us. "Stephen, the man with multiple surnames and passports, is semi-patched up and in custody. We're taking him to the office in a few minutes." He took a breath and then another. "Heard you were heading in here and hoped I could catch you."

"And you did. Has Stephen said anything?" Multiple surnames but there was a good chance his real Christian name was Stephen.

"Asked for his lawyer and clammed up."

"You want me to have a run at him before the lawyer arrives?"

His eyebrows waggled. "Wouldn't hurt."

Right then I knew who Alan reminded me of – another Alan. Alan Alda. More precisely, Hawkeye from *MASH*. The struggle to rid my brain of the ensuing *MASH* theme was real. I was in a hospital with Hawkeye; the saving grace for me was the lack of khaki-colored canvas and mud.

"How about I send my husband to pediatrics to see his niece and I come with you to check on the welfare of Stephen Whatshisface?"

Mitch gave me a fast hug and a kiss that promised there'd be more later. I watched him step into the elevator and with a small wave, I walked away with Alan. A couple of nurses walked past us. Neither of them looked like Loretta Swit.

"I can't be on my own with him," I said, keeping my voice low.

"I'll stay in the room."

"Good. Thanks."

Alan nodded toward a door that said Emergency Room. "This way," he said, pushing the door open and holding it for me. "Four rooms down is a guard. He's in there. Ready?"

I let my eyes drift to the ceiling as I released a silent plea to God, please don't let that guard look like Klinger. Please, no wedding dress.

"Sure. I'm ready." Let's say I'm ready. While we're at it, let's say I'm calm enough to talk to the lunatic who grabbed Mitch's niece. I really could not be left alone with the loser. No telling how I'd keep my gun holstered if provoked by Stephen breathing in my presence. Breathe. Don't shoot the moron. Breathe. Just breathe.

A darkness crept over my soul. I felt it clawing at the light. All of a sudden it stopped and muttered about a hospital not being a good place to put a chunk of lead in a child abductor. The chance of survival was too high.

Wait. Just wait. The darkness shrank away leaving long shadows and remnants of murderous intent.

Stephen sat on a hospital bed, handcuffed by his good arm to the side railing. Anger flashed as he saw me walk in. "You! You did this!" The handcuffs rattled against the metal bed as he tugged his arm. "Don't come near me."

I don't need to be close to kill. That's what bullets are for. Cramming my voice with sincerity, I said, "Hello, Stephen. Feeling okay?"

"Lucky I still have a hand," he grumbled. His eyebrows knitted together, forming a scowl.

"That's what happens when you don't listen," I replied, sitting in the visitor's chair by the door. I decided to stay by the door. Too risky to be within arm's reach. My right hand alternated between fist closed and semi-relaxed. I kept my hand near my knee and well away from the weapon on my right hip.

"My lawyer's coming. I have nothing to say to you."

"That's okay, Stephen. Do you mind if I talk?"

His frown deepened. More ridges grew in his forehead. If the wind changed, he'd look like a Klingon for life. His head shook. "Do what you want. I don't have to listen." His eyes roamed the room and stopped on Alan for a moment before moving to me.

"Let me tell you a story about a man named Stephen who decided kidnapping my niece was a good idea." I watched him as I spoke, noting the smug expression on his face. "He had a fancy dossier on the kid but he didn't have all the information."

"You better hurry up with your stupid story."

So smug. So lacking in remorse. Nothing a lump of lead in his brain wouldn't fix. Ignoring his comment I carried on, "Ya see, Stephen didn't know that the kid he took was the niece of an FBI Special Agent or that she would summon angels to rain down the fury of heaven on him from a great fucking height."

"Angels? Wow. That sounds scary," he said. Furrows faded from his forehead as he relaxed.

Oh, if he thinks angels are all sweetness and light he needs to watch more *Supernatural*. "You ever seen a pissed-off angel?" He shook his head. "Then if I were you I'd shut up and listen to the story."

He rattled his cuffed hand against the bed. "You can't touch me."

"I'm sure you touch yourself enough for the both of us." I didn't give him time to speak again. "As I was saying, poor Stephen didn't know what he was doing. They found him with passports, drugs, a gun, and a dossier on the kid."

In case he didn't get where I was going, I spelled it out. "They found him in a hotel room with a minor who was not his daughter. They also found him with her father's passport, driver's license, and one of his credit cards." And I'm beginning to think something bad happened to my brother- and sister-in-law in Germany.

He stared at me for a moment. His shoulders shrugged. "So?"

"Stephen is in big trouble." I let that sit for a second. "And his friend Jake is very helpful." My left middle finger crossed over my index finger; I stuffed my hand in my pocket. Good chance he'll be helpful. Little lies for a good cause.

"What are you getting at?"

"Stephen's friend, Jake, told the FBI that Stephen was trafficking kids to be used as sex slaves."

His jaw dropped. As hard as it was not to smirk, I didn't. He shut his mouth.

"Now poor stupid Stephen will be charged as a human trafficker and it seems the foreign passports have irked various countries. China is talking extradition ... they seem sure they can pin some missing kid cases on poor stupid Stephen."

His mouth fell open again.

"I've heard stories about their prisons. Sounds like an interesting place to visit but I don't think I'd want to stay."

He closed his mouth again.

"You're okay in the cold, right?"

"My lawyer won't let that happen—"

"Of course not. And you've probably made zillions of dollars trafficking so you can afford the best legal representation." I pretended to think for a moment. "Oh, that's right, your bank accounts and assets will be frozen." I smiled at him. "I hope you have off-shore accounts."

"What assets? I don't have any money. I'm not a trafficker."

I pictured his mind scrambling to refute everything I said. He pulled against the bed rail. "Oh, dear. That's not what we heard and seems to contradict your behavior, doesn't it?"

"It's not true. He lied."

"Of course he did. Everyone we speak to lies. Ya see, Stephen, you want to make sure you're the first person to lie to us in any given situation. That way, everyone else has to work that much harder to have their lies believed."

A processing light came on behind his eyes. "I can prove that Jake is behind this and that I was only doing this one job."

I leaned forward a little and frowned as if I was thinking. "It will take a lot for us to believe you now."

Alan rocked from foot to foot beside me. I'd almost

forgotten he was in the room.

Stephen looked up at him. "Is my lawyer here?"

"Not yet," Alan replied. He checked his wristwatch then tipped his arm so I could see the time. We needed to hurry this along.

"Back to you, Stephen," I said with a small tight smile. "We have evidence that you kidnapped and drugged a minor, kept her against her will, used false documents, were in possession of false documents, attempted to use a weapon against a federal agent ..." I paused. "Shall I continue?"

His shoulders slumped. "I didn't hurt her."

"You administered a drug – that act constitutes harm."

His eyes watered. "I was just supposed to grab her, keep moving her around until Jake told me where to take her and then he would pick her up. After that, I don't know."

"Where did you get the drugs?"

"Jake."

"And the dossier?"

His voice dropped. "Jake."

"You need to make better friends." I watched him for a moment. "Where did you meet Jake?"

"I answered an advert on a website I belong to."

"For a kidnapper?" Because that's the kind of advert you see every day?

He didn't nod but his body language didn't disagree with my question. "It was good money."

"What's the name of the website?"

"You can't just Google it." He almost smiled.

"Darknet?"

He nodded. "Where do you live?" Be easier to get into the website via his computer. Something told me he wasn't super security conscious. Perhaps that thought was started by the discovery of the passports. Which begged the question of why he had aliases if it was a one-time thing?

"Thought you knew everything."

"Careful Stephen, this isn't over and it's your word against Jake's." I leaned back. "He got in first, remember?"

Stephen pulled back. He whispered an address. Alan stepped forward and asked him to repeat it then wrote the address in his notebook.

I contemplated how to obtain a warrant and was pretty sure we had enough information to satisfy the pickiest judge. Not really my problem anyway. "Good news, Stephen, if you harmed the kid's parents then we'll fight to keep you in the US until your trial here." I stood and left the room.

The guard stepped forward. "Everything all right, Agent?"

"Yes. Just waiting for Alan."

A suited male walked toward us with a briefcase in his hand just as Alan emerged from Stephen's room. I turned my face to him and said, "Get a warrant for his house. I want his computer. Make sure it goes to Sandra Sinclair in our office."

Sandra was the Delta A support person and a computer magician.

"Will do." He glanced at the male bearing down on us. "Must be the lawyer. Go see your niece."

I didn't look at the approaching male. Instead, I walked in the other direction.

Chapter Seven

The Ledge

Morning sun sent glaring rays into my tired eyes. The temptation to close the curtains grew as sunlight ricocheted off the shiny table surface. I squinted at my phone searching for the phone number I needed. Mitch handed me a glass of water. I took a few sips and set it on the table. I called Chris Iverson's cell phone. Mitch and I waited.

The call went straight to voicemail.

Mitch searched through texts on his phone and found the address of their hotel and their room number. I made a call to the hotel and asked to be connected to their room.

No answer.

I found myself talking to the reception desk again. "Please leave a message for Mr. and Mrs. Iverson. Tell them Ellie and Mitch called and will call back later." I hung up.

"I'm not super happy about them not answering," Mitch said.

"Me neither. Let me see if I can find someone who can swing by and check on them." I could notify the embassy and have someone look for them, and I would, but I wanted someone I knew involved. Scrolling through my contacts two names stood out. Seamus Kennedy and

Misha Praskovya. Both in Europe. Maybe. Hard to tell where Kennedy would be on any given day. My finger hovered over the phone icon next to Kennedy's name but moved on and touched the phone image next to Misha's name. I had no idea where he was or what time it was for him but I did know he'd pick up my call if he could. I listened for the dialing to stop and the ringing to begin.

Four rings and then silence right before he spoke. "Ellie!"

Misha's enthusiasm for my name always made me smile. "*Zdravstvuyte! Mne nuzhno odolzheniye.*" Hello! I need a favor.

"*Chem ya mogu vam pomoch'?*" How can I help?

"*U menya vozntkli problemy Vashe moy brat-v-zakone . Posledneye my uslyshali oni byli v Gamburge, Germaniya.*" I am having trouble contacting my brother-in-law. Last we heard they were in Hamburg, Germany.

"*Ya v Prage. Ya mogu puteshestvovat' v Gamburg noch'yu padat.*" I am in Prague visiting family. I can travel to Hamburg by nightfall. "*Eto srochno?*" It's an emergency?

"There is emergency potential. Their daughter was kidnapped. We have her. She is safe. But I am not convinced her parents are safe."

"Embassy?"

"Not yet. I'll call the State Department now and let them know there might be a problem."

"Send me all the details you have, including passport information and current photographs. I will book a flight

62

immediately."

"*Spasibo*, Misha. I shall send everything now."

"You are my friend. I am helping. No need to thank me," Misha said, hanging up.

Mitch was watching me when I placed the phone on the table. "Russian?"

"Picked up a bit, here and there."

He laughed. "That wasn't a bit."

"Maybe I picked up more than I realized over the years. He's going to Hamburg. Boots on the ground by this evening and his only mission is to locate Chris and Susan."

I turned my attention to my laptop. All the information I needed to send Misha sat in a file on my desktop. Before Chris left, I'd had him scan their documents and send the scans to me. It wasn't because something would happen, but because it's smart to have copies of important documents stored somewhere safe when you're traveling. I had photos of their passports, itinerary, travel insurance, and medical information. I added current photos to the folder, zipped it and sent it to Misha's email address.

My next call was to Iain Campbell in Homelands. "There could be a situation in Hamburg. This is your heads up."

"That doesn't sound good," Iain replied. "Could be a situation or already is?"

"It's not good, and I don't know for sure. My brother and sister-in-law are potentially missing. Their daughter was abducted here last night. The kidnapper had information that could've only come from her parents. Also, he had what appear to be Chris's passport, driver's license, and one of his credit cards."

"It is a situation. I'll contact the relevant people at the embassy. You going?"

"Nope." I forwarded to Iain the same info I'd sent Misha. "I have FSB officer Misha Praskovya heading to Hamburg as my representative."

"I'll get on it now, you'll hear from me as soon as I know something. Tell Mitch we'll find his brother." I heard the email tone. "Thanks for the info, Ellie. This will help. Is the kid okay?"

"Yeah, shaken but unhurt."

"Thank God."

Yeah, maybe God hasn't abandoned us after all. "Talk soon." I hung up and let a modicum of relief saunter through my being. Things were moving. People were looking. We'd have information coming back within a few hours. Until then it was business as usual.

Mitch wrapped an arm around my shoulders and pulled me close. "You need to get some sleep," he whispered.

"Let's head to bed. Harley will be in hospital until this evening and there's nothing more we can do for Chris and Susan."

"Let's not mention this to my parents yet." Mitch stood and pulled me up by the hand.

"Good call."

Hand in hand we walked up the stairs.

Chapter Eight

When The Rainbow Comes

I rolled over. My hand flapped at the nightstand hoping to connect with my ringing cell phone. Through sheer luck, my fingers grasped the noisy device and pulled it close to my sleepy eyes.

"Iverson, we have something," Kurt said. "You awake?"

"No. But tell me anyway." I rubbed my eyes in an attempt to force them to focus.

Mitch moved next to me. I tapped the speaker icon and dropped the phone onto the comforter.

"The credit card is a fake. The passport is a high-end forgery. The driver's license is real."

"They're sure?"

"Uh-huh. Although this is just a preliminary report. They're swamped at the lab as usual."

"Where are you?"

"Parked in your driveway."

Mitch threw off the comforter and climbed out of bed. He stretched then opened the curtains and peered out. "I'll put the coffee on."

I sent a grateful smile in his direction.

"Hey, thanks, Mitch." The comforter muffled Kurt's voice.

I flipped the blanket back. "See you in a bit," I said to the phone and hit the red call end icon.

Mitch called out from the bathroom, "This is bad, isn't it?"

"It's not great," I replied, extracting myself from our warm bed and following the sound of his voice. He'd washed his face and was running a brush through his hair when our eyes met in the mirror. I wrapped my arms around him from behind. I wanted to tell him it'd be okay but I couldn't because it probably wouldn't be okay. Ever. "We'll find out what's going on."

That I could say. With relative certainty. He turned and hugged me. It felt good to be in his arms.

"You shower. I'll let Kurt in and make coffee." Mitch stooped his head and kissed me. Warmth and happiness flowed through me. We were okay. We'd be okay, no matter what. Mitch reached behind me and turned the shower on for me. Long arms are handy things.

With one last kiss, he left the room and I stepped under the hot running water. Shampooing my hair sent foaming apple-scented bubbles cascading over me and down the drain. It was my new favorite shampoo and conditioner scent because the ones I used to like were sullied on a previous case by a serial-killing artist and his entourage. Breathing in the tangy green apple smell made me happy. Apple is a happy association and a happy smell. Smelled like early autumn and pie. My stomach rumbled. Pie. Pie for breakfast would be ideal.

I turned off the shower, reached for a towel and wrapped myself in it. Choosing clothes was the easiest part of my day. Long-sleeved button-down shirts, blue jeans, brown cowboy boots were standard in my life.

Warm dark coffee smells wafted up the stairs.

I blasted my hair with the hair dryer, filling the room with fallen apples. A light dusting of mineral powder and a couple of passes with black mascara and I was ready to take on the world.

My cup waited on the kitchen counter, full. A plate with a slice of apple pie sat next to it with a fork. Mitch must've read my mind. I scooped a forkful of pie into my mouth. Perfect.

"We're in the dining room," Mitch said.

I swallowed and replied, "Be right there." Pie first.

I scoffed the pie in record time, swigged some coffee, topped it up from the pot and took my mug to the dining room.

Sitting next to Mitch and opposite Kurt, I sipped more coffee. "Pie was delicious," I said, smiling at my husband.

"You're welcome."

"Pie, Iverson?"

"Yeah, well technically it's not morning, so it's not breakfast." I grinned. "Tell me what you have and what you think is happening."

"First up, you can pick Harley up this evening. I'll have her discharged. She's well. Have a psychiatrist talking with her this afternoon, just a precaution."

"That's a relief," Mitch said with a sigh. "We're not telling my parents yet."

"Good to know." Kurt sipped his coffee for a moment. "We know that Stephen Whatshisname had Chris's actual driver's license. He's still saying he got everything from Jake. Haven't found anything that disputes that yet."

"Sandra get the computer?"

Kurt nodded. "She's been all over the darknet website that Stephen used to meet people."

It smacked of the last horrendous case. Anything to do with the darknet sent my brain to a very scary place. Nice shit doesn't start with the word dark. I pulled my mind back to the present and Kurt's voice. "And?"

"No other contact regarding anything to do with the kidnapping. Only Jake. She got into their private messages. Traced the money. Stephen's role began and ended with Jake."

That information writhed like a basket of snakes. "Terror cell behavior," I whispered to my coffee cup then looked up at Kurt. "Okay, what about Jake?"

"This is a road trip that you'll enjoy. Finish that coffee then we'll saddle up." Kurt's eyes rested on Mitch for a second. "You come too."

Mitch nodded. "You sure?"

"Yes."

Fifteen minutes later we followed Kurt to an address on the other side of Fairfax County. Overgrown lawns, a driveway marked by cracks and weeds and grimy windows painted a picture of a house that'd seen better days. Curtains hanging precariously on their tracks by a few hooks, leaving the rest of the curtain to gape and fall, spoke of the lack of care. Crime scene tape sealing the front door spoke of something else entirely.

Kurt swung his car door open. Mitch and I followed suit and met him on the sidewalk in front of the bedraggled house.

"Who lives here?" I said.

"Jake Templeton. He lives alone."

Kurt led the way. He handed us disposable bootees and gloves at the front door. With a pocket knife he cut the seal to the door; he folded the blade back into the handle and pushed it into his pants pocket. He swung the door wide, sunlight illuminated dust motes in the air. For a moment it twinkled like fairy dust and then the smell hit me. Urine, feces, sweat.

My arm wrapped around my mouth and nose, burying them in the elbow of my jacket. "You couldn't have done this by yourself?" I said to Kurt, knowing he'd struggle to hear my muffled words.

Kurt pulled masks from his jacket pocket. "I think we should wear these." I gratefully accepted. "You need to see what I've already seen. Leave the door open and let in some air."

I doubted that would help. Mitch had dropped about five shades of tan. We walked into the dank hallway. Heat didn't help the smell. Figured the windows were never opened.

"There are five rooms opening off this hallway, the bathroom and kitchen are at the back of the house along with a small laundry room." Kurt stopped by the first door.

It was shut. I looked down the hall. They were all shut.

I prepared myself for an onslaught of grossness the minute the doors were opened. Kurt pulled another pair of gloves over his already gloved hands. Oh, that meant it was bad.

He looked at me with his hand on the door knob. "Touch nothing."

Yeah, double gloving, I'm not touching anything. He swung open the door. Even with the mask, I gagged at the smell. The only light came from small gaps in the badly hung curtains. Even so, I could see a cage. No. Bars, not a cage.

The bars ran floor to ceiling like an old holding cell in a police station. The bars created a cell in the middle of the room. Inside were two metal-framed beds with ratty mattresses. No sheets or blankets. A bucket of overflowing excrement sat near the cell door.

"Wireless cameras," I said, pointing at the top of the bars. One on each side pointed inward. "Who was kept here?"

"Teenage girls mostly, from what we can gather."

I swallowed and regretted it. I seemed to swallow the stench. "He was picking up Harley." I spun around to check on Mitch and saw him heading for the door.

"I'll be outside," he said without looking back.

I didn't say anything, I was too busy preventing my pie from escaping.

Kurt moved past me and out of the room. He opened another door. Same setup, but a bigger cell. Three beds. Chains attached to the frames of the beds. Another bucket of shit. More cameras. Three more doors. Three more cells with either two or three beds.

"He couldn't have held that many teenagers at once. All it would take is for one to yell out when someone came to the door or when he came and went." I looked around the kitchen. Surprisingly, not filthy like the other rooms. I opened the refrigerator. "No food apart from eggs and milk." The expiry date told me both were still good.

The pantry held more. Mostly packets and cans.

In the laundry room was a large tub and a stack of buckets. They needed disinfecting with more Clorox than I could see in the cabinet under the tub. I noted there were several boxes of latex gloves and a few packets of industrial rubber gloves. The bathroom wasn't super clean but nor was it filthy.

I opened the back door and walked out into a yard littered with mounds of fresh dirt. "What the hell?"

"He was digging holes and emptying buckets ... guess he didn't want to clog the sewage system by tipping buckets down the toilet."

"Anything else out there?"

"Crime scene techs are coming back here tomorrow. They're digging up the entire yard. If there is anything, we'll find it."

I soaked up the semi-fresh backyard air and the warmth of the sun before going back into the stuffy, stench-ridden house.

"Computer?"

"Being decontaminated so Sandra can work her magic."

"How many kids do you guesstimate he held at one time?"

"Judging by the filth in each room, I'd say the cells were full and probably more kids than beds."

"Where are they now?"

"No idea."

"The cameras might know. If the video was stored, we might get something usable."

"Sandra will find the information."

Yeah, she will. If there is anything at all to find, She. Will. Find. It.

"On the plus side, we have interrupted the trafficking of young humans by arresting Jake." At least temporarily. The thoughts that edged into the light were awful. We'd dealt with trafficking before and every single time it hurt my heart.

I headed for the front door not removing my mask, gloves, or bootees until I was at our car. Feeling a little unwell and light headed, I used the car for support. The heat radiating from the dark paint warmed my back and seeped into my cold bones. I was pretty impressed I hadn't puked up my pie.

Kurt locked the door and put fresh tape across it. Mitch and I waited in silence for him to join us. I could feel his thoughts and he could feel mine. No sense voicing our disgust and horror at what had nearly happened to Harley. No sense in giving that any airtime at all.

Chapter Nine

Dancing With Myself

A light knock on my office door preluded the entry of Executive Assistant Director Owen. I stayed seated behind my desk. Cold flowed from the Evil Queen, spreading across the floor like dry ice. It bit into my feet under the desk coating my veins in frost.

A cloud of thick perfume billowed in my direction. The scent reached my nose. Jasmine, rose, carnation and something else. Cinnamon? Underneath the flowery mid notes the true horror lay: sandalwood, cedarwood, myrrh, musk and the kicker, patchouli. Memories rushed at me from all angles, none of them were good. Self-preservation kicked in, I breathed through my mouth.

"Good morning, Agent Con—" She gave a small smile. "Agent Iverson."

"Assistant Director Owen," I replied, trying to loosen my lips into a smile and failing. "How can I help you?"

I have ideas. A shovel, a gun, and somewhere no one will ever find the body. Owen folded her perfectly put-together self in the chair in front of my desk. She looked way too pleased to be in my office and took her time before speaking.

"The resolution of your niece's abduction has uncovered a child trafficking enterprise."

No kidding, Einstein. "Yes. I saw Jake Templeton's

house and the cages or cells. Why does this interest you?" A few lines struggled against the Botox in her forehead but lost the fight before a wrinkle appeared.

"I don't want Delta A involved in this. It's now a Delta B case. Turn over all the information regarding Harley Iverson and her abduction immediately."

"Of course, ma'am." Fuck you and the horse you rode in on. May your nail varnish chip and your hair frizz.

"It's for the best, Agent. You're too close to this." She tapped her nails together in her lap. "I take it Delta B interviewed Miss Iverson in hospital?"

She knew damn well they did. Harley knew nothing and remembered nothing. "Yes, ma'am. I'll brief Claude this morning."

"Good." The Evil Queen stood to leave. "How is your niece?"

"Well and at home."

"Have you contacted her parents?"

My fingers crossed in my lap. "We've left messages for them to call." It wasn't a lie. I tried to gauge if she'd heard from The State Department. I doubted she had.

"See that all the information is given to Delta B and step away from this case, Agent Iverson." Owen's skirt swished as she sashayed from the room leaving a thick spicy perfume residue dripping from the air.

Struggling against rising bile, I dragged my bottom drawer open and took out a can of air freshener. I sprayed the room with enthusiasm. The fine mist fell cloaking the droplets of residual stench and ridding my office Owen's presence.

I dropped the can into my open drawer, gave it a shove shut and muttered to myself while massaging my temples. "Go back to 1977 and take your Yves Saint Laurent *Opium* habit with you."

The beginnings of trouble tweaked inside my skull. My top drawer held my aromatherapy Synergy that I have sent from New Zealand. I took it out and read the label. Didn't say I couldn't use it. Didn't say I could. Not helpful. Better not to. I dropped the vial back in the drawer. Slowly the warmth returned, and my bones thawed. A good indication that Owen was indeed gone. Just to be sure, I waited a few minutes before venturing from my office to find Claude.

His office was on a corridor that ran parallel with ours. Between the corridors were meeting rooms, interview rooms, bathrooms, and the bullpen. Access to the Delta B corridor was via the bullpen, or a hallway in the middle of the corridor, or from the foyer at the far end. I knew from the direction of the lingering smell Owen went toward the elevators. So I opted for the bullpen. Sam and Lee were at their desks. Alan and a few other Delta B agents were in a huddle in the common seating area.

Lee saw me and waved me over. "Hey, Chicky, everything all right?"

"Yep, everything's just peachy."

Lee's left eyebrow rose, he rocked back in his chair and gave an understated shake of his head. "Nope, not buying it."

76

Sam joined in. "That's an interesting shade of green you have happening there, Chicky Babe." He circled his finger in the air toward my face.

"Owen," I said.

A throaty chuckle came from Lee. "Still bathing in *Opium?*"

"Yep."

"Smells worse on her than on anyone else I've come across," Sam said.

He wasn't wrong. "It mixes with the evil in her soul and becomes a weapon of mass destruction." I rested against Lee's desk. A sigh escaped before I could stop it alerting Sam and Lee to another issue.

"You didn't come in here to see us, did you?" Lee said.

"Not entirely. I'm on my way to talk to Claude. The Evil Queen wants us to hand over Harley's case to Delta B."

"And we are?"

My left hand dropped as my fingers crossed. "Yep. I can't take a trafficking case that involves a family member."

Lee grinned at me. "This is a whole new side of you, Chicky. Kurt will love it."

"Let's not get too giggly too quick," Sam said, throwing a look of incredulity at me. "This is completely out of character."

"It's sensible," I countered.

Sam snorted. "I rest my case."

Shards of glass rammed into my right eye, rendering it

almost blind. I grimaced. My eye shut and refused to open.

"Okay, that's it," Lee said. He stood up, his chair rolled backward. He grabbed it and motioned for me to sit. "I know that look. I haven't seen it in a long time. But I know it."

I sat. Pain pushed through my eye deep into my skull. Nausea sloshed about in the empty space in my stomach. Voices softened, disappearing into the ethereal mist surrounding me. Moisture in the air felt cool as it settled on my clammy skin. If I let go, I knew I could drift forever on the clouds.

"Iverson?"

Words in my head scattered like lost sheep. I waited for one of them to show leadership potential and find my mouth. It wasn't looking good.

"Come on, Iverson."

Conversation felt like seven steps too far. I slipped back onto a small cloud. Maybe it was cotton wool.

"Open your eyes."

I understood the words. I recognized the instructional tone. Nothing happened.

My eyelids said no. Outside was light. Light was bad. No light for Ellie.

Chapter Ten
Shine A Light

I lay still, taking stock of the situation. I saw gray with patches of light. The gray moved, blocking the light. A cool hand brushed hair off my forehead. What was missing? The clinical smell of a hospital. That seemed like a win.

What did I know? Owen poisoned me with her stench.

I partially opened one eye and saw Kurt sitting on the coffee table next to me. Forcing my other eye open, I recognized my office. A light warm fuzz hung on the edges of my vision and in my brain. It wasn't unpleasant or unfamiliar. Best of all was the lack of pain.

Words fell from my mouth before I could censor them. "The Evil Queen poisoned me."

"Now you're Snow White?"

"Doc—"

"I'm a little tall to be a dwarf," Kurt said, following his words with a small laugh. "You feeling better?"

"I'm okay." I think. Yeah. I'm good. "Demerol?"

"Yes." His eyes roamed within mine. "I administered the lowest dose I could give you that would kill the pain."

"Okay. That's good. I have to hand over Harley's case to Claude."

I pushed myself up onto my elbows and waited for a moment to make sure there were no unwanted dizzy-making effects from the pain medication or the migraine. It took a little more effort to sit up properly.

"Take it easy, Iverson."

I swung my legs over the side of the sofa and felt my feet hit the floor. "Claude—"

"He knows. Lee and Sam had a word with him. Is there anything you need to hand over yourself or was everything in Sentinel?"

"Can't think of anything."

"Iverson? Are you sure?"

"Let's just let them work with what they have. They can chase the trafficking trail before it gets cold and find those kids. Harley is safe."

No need to mention Misha or Iain's involvement or Germany. They need to concentrate on finding the kids.

"Sandra is working her special brand of magic on the laptop that was at the house and doing her best to find where the feed from those cameras was stored. She'll pass any information to Delta B," Kurt said, standing.

"Great."

He looked down at me, offered me his hand, and helped me to my feet. "For the record, Sandra will keep you in the loop."

I smoothed my shirt. "I like Claude. He's a good investigator ..."

"But?"

"A lot of the time he doesn't know whether to check his ass or scratch his watch."

Kurt laughed and handed me a bottle of water. "Keep

your fluids up. Rest a bit. Try to avoid Owen."

"I better call Mitch."

"He'll be here in about five minutes to take you home." Of course. Kurt would've called Mitch. My phone buzzed on the coffee table. Kurt handed it to me.

"Owen," I said, showing him the text on the screen. "She wants me to go home and think about stepping away from fieldwork."

"She must have spies in the bullpen," Kurt said. "Her people are everywhere."

"Someone should cancel her birth certificate." I stabbed a pointy finger at the text and typed a reply: Thank you for your concern. It was a reaction to perfume. Please stay out of my airspace if you are wearing Opium. Thank you.

"What'd you say?" Kurt took my phone from my hand as I hit send. "She won't like that."

"Probably not, and I don't like her poison." Or her inability to lead, or her personality, or her willingness to use other people's work as her personal stepping stones.

I halted all thoughts regarding Owen, which prevented her hijacking my brain and a return of the migraine from hell.

Mitch leaned around the doorframe. "Hey, coming home?" His eyes sparkled.

Chapter Eleven

Garden Party

I lurked by the kitchen door absorbing the hum of the room as Delta A spoke with the occupants of the house. We'd heard nothing from Hamburg and Delta A was out on a new case. Jake the trafficker and Stephen the moron were being handled by Claude and Delta B with help from Sandra. Technically, Delta B should investigate Harley's abduction but I'd convinced Claude that their part of the investigation needed to center on Jake and Stephen, not Harley. Really, prioritizing trafficking was the smart move.

If Jake was trafficking and there were kids out there, they needed to be brought to safety. The kids Jake Templeton had taken were reachable if Claude followed that path.

I let it all go and settled into my morning role. A supervisory role; float and listen. Not actively involved in the discussions going on but active enough to jump in if required, or suited me.

So far I'd heard very little that rang any major alarm bells. The crime scene in the garage wasn't spectacular but it was messy. Brains on the wall type of messy. It looked like a homeless man shot himself in the garage but I'm fully aware that things are rarely how they look. So far three parts of the equation held some interest for me – why he was in the garage to start with, who locked the door, and why his name triggered a call to Delta A.

A mystery. The door locked from the outside with several padlocks. John and Martha Devereux used the garage for storage and had done so for several years. No car anymore. They had no need to go into the garage much, if at all, over the last few years. They'd heard a gunshot and called police saying it came from their garage but that John couldn't open the padlocks. His key didn't work. Not surprising as police said the locks appeared to be new.

Police cut the locks open and found brains all over the back wall. A search of the body revealed a driver's license and a name, Eric Simonsson. The minute his name entered the system a flag went up, a big red warning to notify FBI. This wasn't a regular flag though, this one specifically asked that Delta A be notified. So there we were listening, but none the wiser. The flag linked to a classified file and until we could get access, all we had was the homeowners' story.

The old couple didn't know him, had no idea where he came from or how he got there. They'd been staying with their daughter for a week and were home a matter of hours before the gunshot. Their story checked out. The taxi company confirmed picking up the couple from Union Station and the time they were dropped at their door. I'd viewed their train tickets. Washington D.C to New York City return. I'd even viewed CCTV footage as they boarded the train at Union Station in Washington and alighted at Penn Station New York City, and vice versa. Amtrak was in helpful mood: it took only one phone call to have access via my phone to the footage I required.

A voice rang out filling the space behind me with my name, "Agent Iverson?"

"Right here," I answered and stepped out of the kitchen into the hallway. "How can I help?"

"Two of your colleagues have arrived," the police officer said.

I glanced back into the kitchen where Kurt talked with the elderly female occupant. Sam and Lee chatted with her husband about his vegetable garden. Apparently, they had become experts on soil, but when I had no idea. Yeah, we were all present and accounted for. I hadn't made a call for backup and couldn't think why anyone from any other Delta team would stop by.

"I'll come out, where are they?"

"At the front door, ma'am, with Detective Konstram."

A smile flitted across my lips. Detective Josh Konstram. Our buddy. He and Delta went way back.

"On my way, officer." I darted into the kitchen and told my team I'd be out front for a few minutes. No one liked it when one of us disappeared. We might have a case of shared paranoia. I walked down the hallway as a suspicion cemented. It's not paranoia if they really are out to get you. Once upon a time that would've made me smile. Not so much now. It felt like every man and his dog'd had a crack at wiping Delta A off the map over the last several years.

Josh waved to me from the open front door. He was talking with two men in suits. The tall blond one needed a shave and the slightly shorter dark-haired one looked like he'd be more at home in jeans and cowboy boots. Not a judgment, just an observation. The awkward look of the dark-haired male made me smile and look down at my own jeans and cowboy boots. Some people aren't cut out for suits.

"Agent Iverson," Josh said as I approached. "Join us. I'm sure you know these two agents?"

Josh flashed a good-natured smile at me.

"I don't believe I've had the pleasure," I said and extended my hand to the shorter of the two agents and looked him square in the eye. He was about six feet tall.

He grasped my hand and shook it. "Special Agent Dane Wesson."

The taller man extended his hand to me. "Special Agent Stewart Smith."

Without missing a beat, I replied, "I'm Special Agent Heckler and my buddy Special Agent Koch will be along presently."

A smirk darted across Wesson's lips. "Thought you were Iverson," he murmured. "But I see you're actually Special Agent Wiseass."

I'm fairly good at placing faces and reasonable at remembering names. I'd remember if I'd ever met Smith and Wesson before. They weren't from the Washington Field Office. I didn't remember seeing either man at the

Hoover Building, nor had I run into them during my frequent lectures to recruits at Quantico.

My gut twinged and niggled. Something hinky was going on. I'm sure there are agents out there I've never come across before – it's a big country, we have a lot of offices – but something about Smith and Wesson kicked my gut into high gear.

Could be the names. Could be that they weren't agents at all? Whoa, back up the truck. I had no idea where that came from but it felt smart to keep it under wraps for now.

"ID?" I said to Smith. "Routine, ya know, crime scene an' all."

He tugged a black wallet from the inner pocket of his suit jacket and showed me. Wesson did the same. Their names really were Smith and Wesson, according to the Bureau. I nodded, they pocketed their ID wallets.

"Follow me," I said to the interlopers then turned to Josh. "Thanks for keeping these boys company. We'll chat soon."

"You're welcome, Ellie." Josh turned and headed for his car. "Take care."

"Hey, Josh," I called after him. "Are you leaving?"

"Nah. I'll be in my car," he called and waved over his shoulder.

Working no doubt. Catching up on paperwork. These days we could almost all work from our cars with laptops, tablets, smartphones and stable mobile Internet connections. Some days there wasn't a lot of need to set foot in a station house or office. I should work more from my car: prevent the risk of Owen polluting my atmosphere.

I stepped through the open door and beckoned to Smith and Wesson. "Stay close, gentlemen." They followed me into the house.

Wesson spoke, "Where was the body found?"

He had a notebook and pen in his hand.

"Garage," I replied.

"We'd like to talk to the homeowners," Wesson said.

I imagined they would. "Let my team finish up first."

"If you could point us to the crime scene, Agent Iverson," Wesson said straightening his tie. "We can make a start and interview the homeowners once we know what we're dealing with."

Wesson was close to me. I grabbed him by the arm and dragged him into the nearest room, pleased it was the living room and not someone's bedroom. Didn't need to add awkward to whatever this was. Smith followed.

"Talk," I growled. "You're pretty and look more like Dean Winchester than Dane Wesson, so I choose you to start this conversation. What are you doing here?"

Wesson bristled and shrugged my hand off his arm. "I'm all good with the television reference ... even if it doesn't make a lot of sense."

Really? Just me? "Nice try, sunshine. You're at my crime scene, why?"

"We're here doing our jobs, just like you," Wesson said. "You wanna make this hard?"

Their jobs? Oh, he was cute. Like they were all grown-up agents. Maybe it was just me that found that part hard to swallow. They weren't unlikeable by any means. Smith, the taller of the two, was quiet and less in my face. Felt like I should keep a close eye on him. Definitely brooding in a Sam Winchester kinda way.

Settle brain, I don't need your crap right now!

"I'm not making this hard. I'd like to know how you came to be here."

"We're your backup."

"How about you stop dispensing bullshit and start talking?" I said to Wesson.

"I don't know what you're talking about," he said.

"Why'd you use a reference to *Supernatural*?" Smith asked with a tentative half-smile on his lips.

Oh, he speaks.

"Because it seemed to fit. Now I have questions." I rocked on my heels. "What's going on? And why are you here?"

Wesson fumbled a black wallet from his pocket and flipped it open. I took it and looked at it again. Special Agent Dane Wesson. If it was fake, it was high end. "You know it's an offense, right?"

"They're real," Wesson said. "We're invited into this case."

"Yeah? Well, ya see boys, I do the invitations and you weren't on my list." I pushed his ID back into his hand. "Start talking."

"We're interested in the case," Wesson replied.

"And you know about it how?"

"Got a call from a buddy who heard it over the police scanner," Smith said. "It seemed like our kind of gig."

"That's not an invitation, dude."

The call would've gone out over the airways and the minute the name sent up a Delta flag, all communication would've ceased. Maybe they did have a buddy who heard it over a scanner.

"We heard about it and it seemed like something we'd be into."

"And you do what exactly?"

Wesson smirked. "You were pretty close with *Supernatural*."

"*Supernatural* is a TV show, boys." I could tell they were going to be all kinds of fun. "And last I looked, even reality television wasn't real."

"Whatever helps you sleep at night, Agent Iverson," Wesson replied. "Whatever helps."

"What helps me sleep at night is knowing lunatics aren't running around half-cocked, flashing fake badges, hearing shit on a police scanner, and inviting themselves into an FBI investigation. Never mind potentially scaring good folk half out of their wits."

I eyed Wesson. He looked uncomfortable but I suspected that was the suit's doing, not the situation. Smith was more at ease with himself. Definitely more the suit type.

"We're not running around half-cocked. We're not scaring people," Smith said quietly. "We're not flashing fake badges. We're doing our jobs just like you."

"And you went through Quantico just like me ..."

I witnessed a fast exchange of looks between Smith and Wesson. For a split second, I doubted my gut reaction to their names and wondered if their badges were authentic.

"We did twelve weeks at Quantico, like every agent," Smith said. "Then we took a specialist role as well general case work."

"Specialist?"

"Yeah."

"Waiting for an elaboration on your specialist field ..."

There was another exchange of looks.

"We have a unique set of skills. Not the sort that can be taught."

Really? Because they do a pretty damn good job teaching all manner of exciting skills at the academy. What was he trying to say? That they specialized in things that go bump in the night or little green men?

Then again, I have a unique set of skills and I don't think they're teachable. "Gimme a few minutes, fellas, because this conversation is just getting started and I'm fascinated to see where it ends ... but right now I need to let my team know we are leaving. It's interesting but I don't know that it's an FBI job." I lied, I wanted to see if they knew more than they'd let on.

Another silent exchange between them. They must've known each other a while.

"Can we at least have a look?"

I smiled. "You're kidding me, right? You think I'm going to let you two near my crime scene?" They had balls, had to give them marks for trying.

"We know how to handle ourselves in a crime scene, Agent," Wesson said with a hint of irritation in his words. "This case is smack within our directive."

"That won't be happening. I'd like to discuss your game plan with you, just give me a minute." I looked from one to the other, making sure they were tuned into me and listening. "Stay put."

I hurried to the kitchen and pulled Lee aside. "Finish up here. Unless you see something I don't?"

"No, Chicky. Not even sure why we were flagged, even with the red sticky shit on the garage walls, this doesn't seem to require our presence."

"That flag means something hinky is going on." I thought about Smith and Wesson. Hinky it most definitely was. "Could also be a good measure of paranoia. It's how we all roll now."

Lee chuckled. "Ain't that the truth."

An alert sounded on my phone. A message from Sandra. I motioned to Lee that I needed to read it. We were still locked out of the classified file pertaining to Eric Simonsson, and Director O'Hare requested my presence in her office. Interesting and potentially something to do with the flag. I sent a message saying I'd be there as soon as I could.

"All right?" Lee said, watching me put my phone in my pocket.

"Yeah, O'Hare wants to see me ... what do ya bet it's about this classified file?"

"Good chance," he replied with a crooked smile.

Lee's smile reminded me of his brother's. Every now and then they seem very alike. Something warm shuffled sideways inside me. Did I miss Mike Davenport and his flirtatious ways? Sometimes, yes.

"Josh Konstram is out front ready for a briefing," I said. "He's probably in his car."

"You want me to handle that?"

"Yeah. I've got a couple of characters to talk to."

His expression changed to curiosity. "You want company?"

"Nope, I got this."

I strolled down the hallway and into the living room where Smith and Wesson waited on the sofa. The air heavy with impatience.

"Can we see the crime scene?" Smith asked.

"Let's stick a pin in that idea for now," I said, sitting in an armchair. "You're here why?"

"Because we investigate unusual things," Smith said.

"This could be in our ballpark," Wesson added.

"So, you investigate unusual things ... you do realize that the FBI doesn't actually have an X-files division, right?"

"You sure about that?" Wesson leaned forward, elbows on his knees, hands hanging.

"Pretty sure. I've been with the FBI for a long time. X-files is more CIA than us and even then, it was more your

Cold-War-ESP crap." I smiled.

Wesson smiled back.

"How'd the dead guy get into a locked garage?" Smith said.

Pretty obvious it was locked after he got in, guess they didn't know that. "How'd you know about the job?" I countered.

Smith smiled. "Really?"

"Yeah. Hey, I can play all day." I remembered O'Hare wanted to see me. I could still play all day. O'Hare would understand.

"How'd Simonsson get locked in the garage?" Wesson asked.

I noted he'd switched from 'get into a locked garage' to 'get locked in a garage.' "How'd you know his name?" I shot back. "As I said, I can play all day."

Smith and Wesson exchanged looks.

"How'd the dead guy ... Simonsson, get locked in the garage?" Smith said again.

My phone chimed. I pulled it from my pocket and saw another request to meet O'Hare in her office. Must be important. Time to wrap it up here.

"I don't know, but I'm sure there is a reasonable explanation."

My money was on someone else being on the premises and locking him in there. Wouldn't have hurt me to mention the locks were brand new and that the owner told us the locks they'd had on there were rusted. Someone replacing the locks spoke of another person at the scene.

"Really?" Wesson said.

"Uh-huh."

"And when you can't find a reasonable answer?" Smith said.

"I'll be sure to give you boys a call."

Wesson's right eyebrow arched. "Awesome. You'll be making that call. I guarantee it."

"Meanwhile, you don't want to tell me how you heard about the job and I have somewhere to be and you don't need to be here." I lowered my voice. "There is no way on God's little green earth that I'm letting either of you into the crime scene."

They stood up. I gave them credit for the lack of petulance. That was refreshing.

"Just one thing ..." Wesson said. "You didn't smell sulfur in the garage did you?"

"Nope."

"Anyone see any black smoke?"

"Black smoke? This isn't *Supernatural*. You know how I mentioned television isn't real? Yeah, that."

"Just asking," Smith said with a tight-lipped smile. "If you do come across black smoke or smell sulfur, call us." He pressed a business card into my hand.

I glanced at it, noting the FBI logo. If they weren't real agents, they'd certainly gone all out to make it look like they were. Why did I even think they weren't real agents? Because I've watched too much television. Laughter rippled but thankfully stayed confined; instead, I poked the agents a bit with a pointy stick.

"You don't happen to have something with your real names on it, do you?" I said, passing them one of my cards and ignoring the confusion on their faces. "Smith and Wesson? Seriously? Couldn't have been more inventive?"

Nothing. Not a thing. Stony-faced.

"Anytime, day or night. We always answer that phone," Smith said.

"And you can reach me during business hours should you feel the need tell the truth." I ushered them to the door. "It's been a blast, now my team has a job to do."

"Awesome," Wesson muttered and followed Smith out the door.

I smiled as they walked away, no idea why, but I liked them.

Definitely going soft.

Chapter Twelve

Walking In Memphis

The sun warmed my back as I leaned on the hood of the car and scrawled notes with a scratchy pen in my notebook. Four lines into a quick case summary, the pen gave up. Footsteps behind caused me to straighten up and turn.

"Hey, gotta pen?" I tossed the dead pen through the open car window then held my hand out in hope.

"Yeah," Kurt replied sliding his pen into my outstretched hand.

"Thank you."

"You're welcome. We finished here?" Kurt inclined his head toward the house behind him.

"I think so. O'Hare wants to see me. Have a feeling it's about this job."

He nodded. "I called the crime scene techs and scene guards."

"Thanks."

"Metro will stay behind and turn the scene over to our guards once crime scene people are finished." Kurt leaned on the hood of the car. "You about done?"

"Yep. Just let me finish my notes."

"You know, if you just wrote them on your tablet ... you'd be done by now."

I shot him a warning look. He knew damn well why I wasn't using it. Every single time I touched the freaking tablet we ended up working the worst cases imaginable. We've worked a lot of worst cases over the years. This week, I'm not keen on being buried under an avalanche of hellish murders. So, no, tablet.

"If I touch that device bad shit will happen." And it hadn't been a great week.

"Never knew how superstitious you really are, Iverson," Kurt replied and grinned.

"I'm not superstitious, I'm just not prepared to tempt fate. But you carry on giving me crap and I'll try to handwrite these notes so we can get out of here." Handwrite them, and pass the notebook to Sandra back at the office, meet with O'Hare and then get home to my husband. I glanced at my wristwatch. I never expected it would be so hard to go back to work after a month away with Mitch.

"Can you hear that?" Kurt leaned into the open car window and picked something up from the passenger seat. He straightened up with my tablet in his hand. "Ah, forty unread emails ... hang on ... forty-one ... forty-two ..."

A groan escaped. I wrote the last word in my notebook. "I'm finished, let's get out of here," I said and closed the notebook.

Kurt stood next to me with the tablet in his hand. It chimed with increasing regularity as more and more emails arrived.

"You want to check any of these?"

"No, I do not."

"Isn't it curious that this tablet is going crazy with email alerts and yet your phone is silent?"

It was only a matter of time before he noticed. "I disabled my work email on my phone." My private account pinging at me was enough. It made it hard to relax at home with the work account's constant harassment.

"Iverson ..."

For a split second, I thought I detected disapproval in his voice. It vanished before I could comment. Wise move on his part.

I slid into the passenger seat. Kurt's turn to drive. He moved the seat back a little and tweaked the rearview mirror and wing-mirrors. I'd finished my notes and avoided mentioning Smith and Wesson. Props for the *Supernatural* reference they'd made. Black smoke and sulfur. Excellent. Laughter tried to bubble up. I forced it back down. Now was not the time to giggle like a maniac. I pushed the pair into a banged-up old drawer in my mind to clear space for a better perspective on the garage body.

Smith and Wesson kept popping out of a drawer and it took some effort to shove them back in. I worried I'd catch my fingers. I hadn't found out exactly what they wanted, or their specialty. Apart from wanting to look at the crime scene, their presence was a mystery.

My scene, not theirs. Request denied. Reaching forward I turned on the radio. There was a chance that music would distract me enough to let Smith and Wesson settle and stay in the closed drawer. Seems I still have some Pollyanna in me.

Three songs later, Kurt interrupted my listening. "Did

you bring your car in this morning?"

Did I?

I scrolled through the day until I reached my arrival at work. Confused, I glanced into the backseat and saw my jacket and a bag from Bed, Bath & Beyond peeking out from underneath it.

This is my car. "Yeah, I did. We're in it."

Kurt chuckled and adjusted the rearview mirror again. "So it is."

A smile settled on my face. "And I'm the one with a mushy brain."

"I was going to say I'd drop you home, but my car is at work, so work it is."

"I have a meeting anyway, remember?"

Kurt nodded. He seemed more distracted than me.

Six more email alerts sounded in quick succession. We had at least another twenty minutes before we'd be at work. I lifted the tablet from the footwell and looked at the growing list of unanswered emails. With a sigh, I opened and read them.

Oldest to newest. Hoping to find an email from Misha or the embassy in Germany saying they'd found Chris and Susan safe and sound. Despite Delta B having point on this case, I was still first contact for the parts I'd set in motion. No need to trouble everyone with family business.

Skimming over the email subject lines, I discovered they were pretty much all things I could forward to other agents. As I read the last one, two more arrived. One was from Misha. One had no subject but the sender intrigued me. It was an FBI email address and the name said Wesson D.

Pretty clever. Part of me didn't fully believe they were real agents. Maybe I was wrong. A laugh rumbled in my head; it sounded almost familiar but was gone before I could place it.

Misha's email included photographs of the Iversons' hotel room. It looked like they'd gone out for the day. Nothing unusual in the room. A suitcase sat open on a chair with another suitcase open on the floor. A pair of jeans lay on the bed. Susan's purse was on the desk with Chris's wallet. If I needed proof they didn't just go out for the day, it was the purse and wallet. No one goes out sightseeing without their purse. The room was tidy. He'd photographed the bathroom. A hairbrush and makeup bag were on the counter. Misha noted both passports were in Susan's purse along with cash and credit cards. He also added Chris's driver's license was missing from the wallet. No surprise there. I fired off a thank you.

Next, I opened the email with no subject. Dane wanted to meet me for a coffee and discuss the supposedly homeless man who died. He suggested I might be interested in two similar deaths in different towns in Virginia.

My heart sank to my stomach and bounced a couple of times. Dammit. Two others. Three deaths. If they were related, then this was a messy FBI problem. My gut twinged then back-flipped.

"What's up?" Kurt asked.

"The dead guy, Simonsson, isn't an isolated anomaly."

"Crap."

"Yeah. One of the agents from earlier wants to meet and discuss what he's found."

As soon as I said it, I knew I should've kept my mouth shut. A can fell over, worms tumbled out, and a little yellow duck waddled in and chomped greedily on the fat juicy wrigglers.

"I don't recall seeing any other agents. Who were they with?"

"FBI. Two agents turned up when we were almost finished at the crime scene. I wasn't entirely convinced of their authenticity but they were likable enough."

Kurt's fingers gripped the steering wheel a little tighter. He kept his focus on the road. "Their names?"

"Stewart Smith and Dane Wesson."

"Are you kidding me right now?"

"Nope."

"There is a conversation that needs to happen, Iverson. Are they even legitimate agents?" He paused and took a breath. "Why you didn't let us know that two more agents were on scene?" Kurt clenched and unclenched his jaw. "Smith and Wesson? Who are we, Heckler and Koch?"

I choked back laughter. Well, yeah.

Could I be losing my killer edge? Or maybe, losing my marbles completely? Being all loved up and gone soft now I'm a married woman? All seemed likely.

Moving into damage-control mode struck me as wise. Instead, my mouth opened and I spilled some more of the conversation with Smith and Wesson. The idiot in me told

Kurt about the black smoke and sulfur and how *Supernatural* they were.

Kurt changed tack before I could backpedal. "How confident are you, that they are legit?"

"My gut is confident," I replied. Semi-confident. Okay, it's flip-flopping like a fish on a hook.

Kurt smiled. "How do you want to proceed?"

"With caution."

He glanced at me. Not an unexpected look of surprise on his face. Kurt nodded slowly. "I'm liking the caution – it's refreshing, Iverson."

"Wiseass," I mumbled, looking beyond my reflection to the ever-changing scenery. Caution was the new approach. There was a balancing act or maybe a juggling act in play, aware that I needed my edge and also understood that my husband needed me home in one piece. The whole experience was new, challenging, and not without pitfalls. Making the best of a tricky situation was within my wheelhouse. I couldn't think of a time when I wasn't up for a challenge.

"Let's say Smith and Wesson are agents and ignore the fake feel to their names. You think they're on to something with their reasoning?" Kurt concentrated for a moment on the road before clarifying his question. "Regarding the other deaths being linked, not about the possibility of demons or some kind of external force at play here."

"Pretty much every violent death involves an external force."

The corner of his mouth curled upward. "That wasn't the

question," he said, negotiating traffic and crossing two lanes to the off-ramp.

"Sure it was."

"Then I should make myself clearer. Do you think the deaths are linked?"

"I have no idea. They think so, so maybe."

I sensed something else, something Kurt wanted to ask but wasn't sure. "Just ask, Henderson. Whatever it is, just ask."

Without taking his eyes off the road, he said, "Do you think it's possible that there are things out there that we don't know about?"

I arched an eyebrow in his direction. Really? He wants to talk about spooky shit? Okay. "I think we've all seen too many seasons of *Supernatural* and watched too many old sci-fi movies." The scenery changed. We were almost at work. "But that doesn't change what I've experienced in the past and nor does it prevent me from keeping an open mind."

"Ghosts, monsters, or aliens?" Kurt's voice seemed to drop a full octave.

"If you're asking if I believe in supernatural forces – I used to hold conversations with my dead husband in a Messenger window. Then he moved from being the ghost in the machine to a ghost in mirrors."

I wanted to stop talking but the crazy kept on coming.

"Don't forget that I also shot his incorporeal self in the head. Those things point to one of two things ... insanity or supernatural energies of some sort." I paused and looked at him. "As for monsters, I've arrested a lot of the human kind." A sigh escaped. "I don't know what to tell you."

"You've told me plenty."

I've lived long enough to know there's more shit out there than we know about and that real evil exists. Maybe they're not kidding about the black smoke and sulfur. Maybe we do have demons on the loose. I reined in my crazy before I convinced myself they were hunters of the supernatural and paranormal. "It used to make me feel nuts to think about Mac and how he appeared all those times."

"And now?"

"I think anything is possible."

"What does your ever-astute gut say about Smith and Wesson and this current situation?"

Nothing, it's just how I digest food? Untrue. It twinged with every perception of Smith or Wesson and their manifestation in my life. "My gut thinks we should keep an open mind," I whispered, checking phone messages.

It also thinks something horrible has happened to Harley's parents and it's starting to panic about the possibility that we just became guardians to a teenager.

Chapter Thirteen
What's My Scene?

Kurt held open the door; I walked through and settled behind the desk. My mind sought a plausible reason for not mentioning Smith and Wesson at the crime scene. Not having a reason really didn't make the task any easier. I felt Kurt's impatience growing. I opened my laptop and logged into the system.

Kurt sat in the chair in front of my desk and leaned toward me. I opened a search page within Sentinel and typed Wesson, D into it. "Anytime, Iverson. I've got all afternoon."

I hit enter. "I don't have an answer." As the honesty fell off my tongue and tumbled into the air between us, I cringed. "I kinda liked them and I could handle it."

"You kinda liked them?"

"I'm not entirely convinced they're who they say they are but my gut didn't react negatively," I said, hoping that sounded better. "There's something there, but I dunno what."

"Let's look them up," Kurt suggested.

"Way ahead of you."

The page on the screen in front of me held an answer. Dane Wesson existed. The photo in front of me was the man I'd met.

I beckoned to Kurt. "Check it out. I was wrong-ish."

Disbelief clouded his face. "Really?"

"I know, right?" We all knew the day would come but it felt

weird regardless. "Not entirely wrong because I never really committed to the idea they weren't legit agents, but I teetered on the brink."

He appeared next to me. Taking the mouse, he opened the employment record attached to the photo and Wesson's badge number. He was attached to Criminal Investigations, just like us, but unlike us worked with one partner and didn't appear to be part of a division or particular unit. Kurt clicked on the additional information button. The screen changed to black with a white box in the center. Classified.

"You have got to be kidding," I muttered, reaching for the phone on my desk and pressing three numbers. Cutting out the middleman and going to the top was usual for me. No one really minded too much except Assistant Director Owen, and she wasn't about to find out. I heard the phone ring twice.

"Director O'Hare's office."

"Kirstie, it's Agent Iverson, is the Director in?"

"Yes, Agent, she's waiting for you. Just a warning, the Director has wall-to-wall meetings this afternoon."

"I'm on my way."

Kurt waited while I straightened my shirt, ran a brush through my hair and tied it into a ponytail.

"I'll let you know if she tells me anything," I said, hurrying out the door. Before I got far, Sandra stopped me.

"Josh dropped off the homeless guy's phone," she said, holding out an evidence bag.

"Is that an iPhone?"

"Yes, O Goddess of technology."

I took the bag. "Thanks. It'll need charging."

"Josh charged it for you. Said you'd want to get into it."

He's good. "I'll have a quick look then go see O'Hare."

I scurried back into my office to Kurt. I showed him the bag as I passed him and sat back at my desk.

"How many homeless have iPhones?" Kurt said.

"I wouldn't imagine too many. Wonder if it's locked." Pressing the home button showed it was locked as expected.

"Not good."

I arched an eyebrow at Kurt. "There's more than one way to look for information on an iPhone."

"Dazzle me, Iverson."

"Prepare yourself," I said and touched the word 'Emergency' on the lock screen. The screen changed to a white keypad. At the bottom left I saw the red Medical ID icon and tapped it.

"Medical ID is partly filled. No name though." I scrolled down and back up. "There's something here under medical notes." Either one long number, broken into three sets of four, or three numbers.

I showed Kurt. "Credit card?"

"Not enough numbers."

"Phone number?"

Maybe. "I wonder if it's something else."

I wrote the number on the pad on my desk and carried on looking down the list on the screen. Allergic to penicillin. That was it by way of medical information. The numbers and an allergy. I canceled the Medical ID and went back to the lock screen.

Looking at the number on the pad, I started to see the

groupings differently. Nine-zero-one-two, three-four-five-six, seven-eight-nine-zero. The next number in the pattern was one-two-three-four. Not exactly rocket science but it'd probably throw a few people off. The fourth number of each set gave me two-six-zero-four. I entered the four digits into the lock screen. And the magic happened.

"I'm in. Now to find out where our mystery man has been." I flipped the phone around and showed Kurt.

"Your mind, Iverson, is a complicated nest of the unexplained and unfathomable."

"Nah, it just likes patterns and coded crap."

I opened settings then privacy and then location services and scrolled to system services and scrolled again to frequent locations. Location was on. Not surprising a lot of people don't realize how much information their phones retain.

A small smile flittered over my lips. Could be he left it on because he had nothing to hide or he's not a terrorist? I tapped the screen and read his history. Everywhere he'd been for the last two months.

"What'd you find?" Kurt asked.

"Before he ended up dead at the old couple's home, he visited the address five times over several weeks." I opened the map. "Kurt, we have the time of day he visited and how long he was there. According to his phone, those five visits lasted no more than three minutes each. He was there at various times, never the same time twice."

"Now that's interesting."

"Yeah, and he's been a few other places – most notably an address that appears as home."

"Not homeless then."

"Not according to his iPhone."

"How'd you know how to do that?"

I shrugged. "Read an article in the Post about iPhones and location services and figured it might be handy one day."

"Like next time one of us goes off the reservation?"

"Yeah, just like that."

I scrutinized his recently visited places. "Kurt – why do you suppose Mr. Not-so-homeless was at Langley?"

"How often was he there?"

"Often enough to say he was working out of Langley. Twenty times in three weeks ... for nine hours at a time." I looked at Kurt. "His last visit to the old couple's home was twenty-seven hours before he was found dead. He never left. Prior to that, he was at Dulles International Airport." I thought for a minute. "He went from Dulles to the property in Falls Church. This stinks. I think we're going to find answers at Langley."

"Where was he before Dulles?"

"St. John, New Brunswick. Canada."

"Before that?"

"Montreal, and before that Hong Kong." He didn't leave the USA for Hong Kong directly. I tracked his travel through three European countries before he arrived in Hong Kong.

"Strange travel."

"Yep." I looked at the frequency, times, and lengths of the visits to Langley. He kept regular hours, like he was going to a place of work. I didn't doubt he was working for the CIA. It stank like CIA. If he was CIA, why was it so easy to get into his phone? Scrolling back, I checked the old couple's address again. Smelled like tradecraft. A dead drop.

So if Mr. Not-so-homeless had a name, a job, a home ... why hasn't someone missed him? Because he was a spook and they don't announce when spooks go off the reservation?

If he had a phone, why not make a nine-one-one call? Why not call home or call Langley? Maybe he couldn't get to his phone? The phone was found in a built-in concealment pouch inside the back of his pants. Did that point to his inability to reach the phone and call for help?

A mystery.

As I pondered the possibilities, my phone rang. O'Hare. Shit. "I'm on my way," I said. "Something came up."

Chapter Fourteen

Help Is On Its Way

I smiled through the glass door at Kirstie as I swung it wide.

"Go straight in, Ellie, she's waiting."

I tapped lightly on the door bearing the words Director O'Hare, opened it and walked in without waiting for her response.

"Ellie, have a seat," O'Hare said with a smile.

I closed the door and settled into a deep, red leather armchair in front of her huge mahogany desk.

"Ma'am," I said, smiling back at her.

"I understand Delta was called to a job this morning."

"Yes, ma'am."

"Do you know who Eric Simonsson is?"

"No, ma'am, but I'm pretty sure he wasn't homeless as police mentioned. We hit a classified file and not much else." I wanted to say I had his iPhone and he'd been hanging out in Langley. And I didn't know why I didn't. I kept my views on Simonsson and his spooky behavior to myself.

"Eric Simonsson is a dead man," O'Hare said, her mouth set in a grim line. "He was dead long before his brains were blown across that garage."

"Ma'am?"

"Simonsson was killed in a car crash in nineteen

ninety-nine."

My brain spun off its axis thinking maybe Smith and Wesson might be more *Supernatural* than I thought.

"Ma'am, how is that possible and why was he flagged Delta A?"

"It's not possible, Ellie. He was flagged Delta A because he was Delta A."

"Excuse me?"

"The flag was an old flag attached to his employee file."

I tried to wrap my head around her words. "An old flag attached to a dead employee's records alerted us to his death today?"

"Yes." Cait O'Hare leaned on her elbows on her desk. "Back then Delta A was different. We ran a lot of undercover operations ... Eric Simonsson was an agent who spent most of his time with the FBI, undercover."

"Okay, so he was killed in a car crash eighteen years ago." I looked at O'Hare. She nodded. "And now he's dead again but this time in a garage?" That's not weird at all.

X-Files theme song played full blast in my head. Getting home to my family within the hour wasn't going to happen. "Simonsson was his real name or an alias?"

"His real name. I worked with him. Nice guy, good agent. Tragic the way he died, had a young family."

Questions fought for space but I waited to see what else O'Hare could tell me.

She tapped at her computer keyboard, moments later a printer by the far wall whirred to life. "I can't unlock the file for you, but I can print some of the information from my files, details from the crash that killed him."

Paper spewed from the printer. I retrieved it and thumbed through the pages. "This is his last case?" I looked at O'Hare.

"Yes. He died two days after the arrests were made."

He was undercover as an accountant by the name of Jeb Warner, investigating money laundering. I turned the page and read the next one. Organized crime. I took a breath. "Did he die or was he put into WITSEC?"

O'Hare looked up me as I stood by the printer reading. "He died."

"How was he identified after the crash?"

"I saw his body. I made the identification," she said.

Through her quiet tone, I heard her voice cracking, and saw deliberation on her face as she revisited that day. A slow dawning surfaced.

"The crash was significant, there was a fuel tanker involved. His body was severely burned."

It's very hard to positively identify a crispy critter even if you know them well, without using DNA or dental records. Fire does horrendous things to human flesh.

"Walk me through it ..." I said.

"His car was identified by the tags and engine number. I got the call because the car was linked to Simonsson and I was on record as his last partner." She paused for a second. "Local police came across the crash site, identified the car, and called Delta and me. I attended the scene. The body was still behind the wheel." She swallowed hard. "The smell was unforgettable. Police recovered personal effects from inside a briefcase in the trunk. His body was mostly unrecognizable."

"Personal effects in the trunk?"

"I know ... for almost anyone else that would be unusual. But Simonsson put his gun, badge and ID into a locked briefcase before going home. Always."

"Why?"

"He had young children and the real reason – no one in his life knew he was FBI."

"No one?"

She shook her head. "He got married while on the job, his wife knew him as Jeb Warner, a CPA. She had no idea."

"That's hard."

She nodded. "Very. His wife was someone we were trying to keep safe. As the investigation into the money laundering continued, we uncovered a plot to kill the daughter of our target by rivals. Simonsson married her to keep her close and safe."

"That's dedication."

"She was attractive, intelligent, and she made it easy for him to play the dutiful suitor and eventually the devoted husband."

There was more to it. Getting married while in a deep-cover operation and having kids – that's serious. An agent could get lost permanently doing something like that. Lines blur and the job becomes secondary. Hard question time.

"Was there any reason to think the body in the car was not Simonsson?"

"No."

"And now?"

"Every reason."

"What happened to the wife?"

"Six months after the crash she took the kids and moved to Canada."

"Did that seem strange?"

"No, not at all. She had family and friends in New Brunswick."

That was the second link between New Brunswick and our dead guy. Wonder if he dropped in to visit his estranged family? Wonder if they were estranged? "Either way Simonsson is dead now, I'll have the lab confirm the identity with DNA. If it's Simonsson, then—"

"Then it could get messy."

Yeah, messy; good description. If he'd been put into a protection program and just surfaced, there had to be a reason. Even if he staged his own death and disappeared of his own volition, that he turned up again, in Virginia, dead, meant something. Because I knew he'd been at Langley, I doubted any of it was his doing. I doubted seriously that any sort of protective program was involved. My money was on Simonsson being a spook from the beginning. And that brought me back to Smith and Wesson.

"Would anyone else be notified of Simonsson's death?"

"You mean the flag that notified Delta A?"

"Yes."

"Not that I know of." O'Hare scrolled with the mouse then paused and looked at me. "There's an addendum on the file." She typed something then waited. "Okay, the addendum leads to something called the Wayward Son Protocol."

Seriously? *Supernatural* sprang into my head and all I could hear was Kansas singing 'Carry on Wayward Son.' "And weird gets weirder."

"Yes," O'Hare agreed. "The names of deceased agents are flagged with a tag that's invisible to most people within the agency. So, the answer is yes, another flag went up when Eric Simonsson's name hit the system."

"We're tracking the dead now?" Just like that, I went from *Supernatural* to *The Walking Dead*. Seemed a good idea to track the dead, if they were up and walking.

"This protocol was put in place before I became Director. I just bet there's a fascinating reason why it's there."

"And back to the mostly invisible tag that alerted Delta A. Do we know who else can see it?"

Her eyes tracked across the screen in front of her. "There is a task force within criminal investigations that can see those flags." O'Hare typed a few more words. "Sometimes the FBI has a warped sense of humor."

"Sorry?" I said, dragging my attention off the file. "Did you say the FBI has a sense of humor?"

O'Hare laughed. "I did. As evidenced by the Wayward Son Protocol. The two agents who make up the task force are always called Smith and Wesson. No matter what their names actually are."

Well, hello! "So they give up their real identities?" I didn't want to tell O'Hare that I'd come across Smith and Wesson until I knew a bit more.

"Yes and no. They retain their own Christian names and adopt the task force surnames for the duration of their secondment. To date, there are six teams registered as having been on the task force. The system records their badge numbers."

The movement of her eyes indicated that she was still reading.

"The agents are approached at the end of their training at Quantico, from there they are given additional special training to enhance certain abilities that became apparent during psychological testing."

"Holy crap, they're talking about mental abilities like *X-files*?"

She looked up, the corners of her mouth curved upward but it wasn't really a smile, and I had a feeling I wouldn't like what she said next.

"There are a few people who can see things other people can't, or can come by information via methods that aren't understood by the general population and defy regular investigative techniques."

The bottom dropped out of my stomach.

I shook my head. "What are you saying?"

"They're like you."

My head carried on shaking; I didn't seem to be able to

stop it. "I don't have amazing mental prowess or powers. I just read situations well." And people. And dead people. I see dead people. I talk to dead people. Oh, man. I'm a freak.

"Ellie. I've known you since you graduated. I know what you are capable of. I am aware of how your mind has developed."

"Mostly it's just migraine meds and lack of sleep," I mumbled, wiping my palms down the thighs of my jeans. "Or overactive imagination and a bit of an irritable gut."

"Okay, fine. Smith and Wesson can read situations and have the ability to perceive things most people can't or won't acknowledge." She smiled. "I doubt they're on your level." She continued reading her screen.

"Stewart Smith and Dane Wesson turned up at the crime scene today," I said. "I kinda suspected they weren't real agents. Figured their names were fake and then I searched for them in our system and they were real agents and their names weren't fake."

Her blue eyes smiled at me. "And now you know their names are fake."

"It's not helping." I stood up.

"This might," O'Hare said. She motioned for me to sit down again. "They're the last names on the list."

A few seconds later, O'Hare turned her screen to face me. On it were two FBI ID cards. Stewart Worcester. Dane Worcester. The faces matched the men I'd met. They were brothers. And weird just spun out of control. Really, Worcester? Not that far removed from

Winchester. "Are you serious?"

"Yes."

"This isn't more FBI sense of humor stuff?"

"No, I don't believe so. What's the matter?"

"Ever seen *Supernatural*? The TV show?"

I watched the dime drop and make change.

"Sam and Dean Winchester," O'Hare said on an exhale. "Stewart and Dane Worcester." Disbelief settled on her face. "And they're actual brothers." Our eyes met. "Add to that the Wayward Son Protocol."

Skepticism didn't really cover it. "Why do I feel like I've been punked?"

"You and me both, Ellie."

"Who set the protocol up and when?"

She found the date quickly but not the person responsible. "I suspect this is the former Director's handiwork. The protocol went live on October thirteen, two thousand and five."

A Google search to find out when the pilot of the series first aired, pulled up September thirteen, two thousand and five. The former Director seems to have had a sense of humor? He couldn't have known how popular the series would become and that it'd still be running thirteen years later.

Also, the protocol would've been in the development stage before he ever saw the pilot, guess he named it after the song from the series. Google told me the song wasn't featured until episode twenty-two. He must've thought it fitted before they did. I checked when the names Smith and Wesson were first used in the series. Years later. So that must've been a fluke or just the Director having some fun.

Fun? Crazy life we lead. "This is twisted," I muttered. "How am I supposed to take the Worcester brothers seriously?"

O'Hare nodded sympathetically. "Let's be thankful they aren't Winchesters. At least Worcester sounds different."

"Not different enough for my mind." I had to find a way of making this work for me and stopping my inventive mind from confusing their names. The only recourse open for the moment was to shove it all aside and concentrate on the homicide of Eric Simonsson.

I scrambled through what we knew. We knew Simonsson died twice. We knew he was Delta, back in the day. The pages in my hand twitched. I needed to talk to the wife. Maybe she could tell us why her husband was in that garage and still breathing until his brains decorated the garage walls. And why no one missed him. And why he was spending so much time at Langley. And why his phone was easy to get into. And why he didn't make a distress call. I was back to him being unable to retrieve the phone from its concealed pocket.

"Anything else you can tell me about Simonsson?" My eyes settled on Cait O'Hare as she read more on the screen in front of her.

She looked over. "You have everything I can tell you."

"Would Smith and Wesson know more than us?"

"Possibly."

"All right, I'll take this," I leafed through the pages then rolled them in my hand. "You want to be kept in the loop?"

"Please, Ellie. If you need my help, holler."

I stood up. We shook hands and I walked back through the corridors and took the stairs to my office.

Chapter Fifteen

Jump In My Car

Kurt was waiting when I swung through the office door. I dropped the rolled-up papers in his lap.

"Little bit of light reading," I said, moving to my desk and settling in my chair.

"Related to?"

"A classified file pertaining to Simonsson."

"From O'Hare?"

"Yep. She couldn't unlock it for us but printed some of it."

I looked at Kurt. "I need more information than O'Hare could give me. Especially about the Wayward Son Protocol."

"The what now?"

I had his full attention. "Simonsson was a Delta agent."

There was no denying he was a Delta agent, but my gut twinged up a storm and I felt he was CIA the whole time.

"Guess that explains our involvement. What's the story with the protocol?"

"The former Director's wacky sense of humor became apparent when I started asking about Simonsson. There is a protocol to deal with the reemergence of deceased agents, or maybe just their names ... it's possible they don't become zombies." I paused. More than a little mortified that I'd said zombie aloud.

"Zombies, Conway?"

"It's Iverson. Yeah, not so much." My fingers crossed.

Probably not zombies.

"Okay, moving on, Iverson."

"We weren't the only ones who got a flag from Simonsson's name. A flag went to a task force assigned to clean up things like this."

"Smith and Wesson?"

"Yep. And I need more information." About their wackadoodle way of doing things.

"Iain Campbell ..."

I smiled. "Good thinking on the Campbell idea."

Iain might have heard about the protocol. He was Homeland but that's not why he might've heard something. He was CIA for a lot of years before he was Homeland. It's been my experience that the CIA knows a lot more about what goes on within our agency than they like to let on. He may have even come across Simonsson.

I put the call through. If he didn't know, his and my former boss over at the CIA might. I saw Tierney's name flame, burn, and drop from the sky. It landed on my desk, a smoldering charcoaled mess. Crap, that wasn't a happy moment.

Iain answered just before I hung up, thinking he was out of the office. "Iverson?"

"Took your time," I replied with a smile in my voice. "Trying to avoid my call?"

Our direct dial numbers come up with a name within Federal agencies.

"Not at all," he replied. "To what do I owe the pleasure?"

"Wondering if you've ever come across FBI agents by the name of Dane Wesson or Stewart Smith—"

"You're kidding me, right?" Iain's voice filled with amusement. "Smith and Wesson?"

"Nope, not kidding, they're legit agents."

"You ever watched *Supernatural*?"

"Uh-huh." You learn something new every day. "Surprised you do though."

My mind shuffled all the things I knew about the show into order and overlaid it with the small amount I knew about the actors, Jensen Ackles and Jared Padalecki. Wesson and Smith looked a little like Ackles and Padalecki but not enough to make this an episode of *Punked*. The fact that Stewart and Dane were brothers set off another ripple of weirdness.

"Still with me, Iverson?" Iain said.

"Yeah, was just thinking."

"A couple of seasons back, Sam and Dean Winchester used the names Smith and Wesson and posed as FBI agents."

I knew that. The Winchester boys were always posing as FBI and often used distinctive names, quite often names from rock groups. Favorites of mine being the aliases Agents Collins and Gabriel.

"Have you heard the names previously? Or at any time over the last ten years?"

"I think I'd remember if I had, Iverson. What's this about?"

"I'm getting to that. I found Wesson in the system, he exists. Problem is it's a basic employment record and the bulk of it is classified. Turns out he's an agent but his real name is Dane Worcester."

"And you want in to that file?"

"Well, yeah. I had these two turn up at a crime scene and

want in. They came across like a couple of imposters and I believed that was a possibility."

"But you found Wesson in the system and ..." His voice petered off.

"And? I didn't catch the rest."

"And ... you were wrong?"

"Yeah," I replied. "It had to happen one day."

"Might take me some time to digest, Iverson."

I laughed. "Meanwhile?"

"I'll do some digging and see if I can find something useful."

"So you haven't come across them before?"

"No. I'd definitely remember if I had. What else, Iverson?"

He knew me well. "Wayward Son Protocol, ever heard of it?"

Iain laughed. "Have I been punked?"

"O'Hare and I had the same reaction. Seems there is such a thing as coincidence after all."

"I find that hard to believe. Never heard of that protocol but I'll look into it." He was silent for a beat. "What else?"

"Ever heard the name Simonsson associated with the CIA? Think back eighteen years or more."

"No, don't recall it but that doesn't mean much, El, it's a big ol' world and I was offshore a lot once upon a time."

"If you remember anything ..." Thoughts of Chris and Susan wriggled in. "Have you heard anything from Hamburg?"

"Not yet. We've opened an investigation. I've talked to Misha Praskovya. He's working with German police. I'll be in touch."

There was a long pause. I sensed cogs turning.

"Delta B ... what's happening there regarding your brother-in-law?"

"Nothing, they're investigating the trafficking of minors and should be leaving the Chris and Susan situation the hell alone."

"I heard from the Embassy in Germany that AD Owen had been in touch saying that Delta B is investigating the kidnapping of Harley Iverson and would like someone to locate the parents."

"And?"

"The embassy said they were working with Misha Praskovya."

"Make sure anything regarding Chris and Susan is passed to me first."

"Will do."

"Thanks, Iain."

I hung up the phone and leaned back in my chair. My right index finger twitched. I clamped my left hand over the spasming muscle in my trigger finger and attempted to think happy non-Owen thoughts. Kurt rose and crossed the floor to my desk. I glared at him.

"I'm okay. You don't need to go all Doc on me."

His eyebrows knitted as his facial muscles formed a frown. "What's with the eye?"

"Nothing." Just Owen. "I'm giving Wesson and Smith a call and telling them to come in."

Kurt nodded, rid his forehead of the frown and went back to his chair. I called Wesson.

He answered quickly. "Agent Iverson."

"My office. A-sap. Bring coffee. Kurt and I take ours black."

"From?"

"The Firehook."

"Awesome, see you soon."

I looked at Kurt's expectant expression. "You going to share the phone info?"

"We're on the same team, Henderson."

"I'm sure we are," he said but wasn't convincing.

I sighed. "Why did that sound a lot more like 'the fuck we are' instead of 'I'm sure we are'?"

Kurt laughed. "Not intentional."

I didn't come down in the last shower. Thrusting my hand toward him, I said, "I'm Ellie, and you are?"

"Funny, Iverson, real funny."

"I know, right?"

Chapter Sixteen

Carry On Wayward Son

"They're here," I said.

"I'll go," Kurt replied, disappearing out the door.

I snooped around the iPhone in my hand looking for a name, still hung up on why the phone was so easy for me to get in. If he hadn't secreted the passcode in the medical ID, we'd be unable to access anything except emergency information. If Simonsson died eighteen years ago, who has he been since?

Phosphorus flared as a match stuck. I held the home button until Siri popped up. "Who am I?"

"You're Wayne, well, that's what you told me anyway," Siri replied.

On the screen sat contact and personal information for Wayne McEwan. I jotted his address in my notebook and noted it was on his frequent location list but not marked as home. This was looking a little too easy. Now I had a name, address, and birthday.

Voices outside the door heralded the arrival of Stewart, Dane, and Kurt. I scrolled through the phone contacts looking for something that stood out. I found an emergency contact, Tracey Games. Just as I touched the call icon, in walked Stewart, Dane and Kurt. I held up a finger and put the call on speaker.

Five rings and a man answered. "Wayne! Where've you

been?"

"Sorry, not Wayne."

"Why are you using his phone?" was the suspicion-laden reply.

"I'm SSA Iverson, FBI. And you are Tracey Games?"

"Yes. Where's Wayne?"

"He can't talk right now." Not a lie. "When did you last see him?"

"Ten days ago at work."

"And that is?"

"I'm not happy continuing this conversation via phone."

"Then we'll meet. My office or yours?"

"Yours."

My office was popular. I glanced at the clocks on the wall. "Be in the foyer of the Hoover Building at seven tonight."

"I'll be there."

I hung up Wayne's phone and addressed the questions I felt simmering in the three men sitting in front of my desk.

My fingers tapped the iPhone in its life-proof case. "This is Eric Simonsson's phone, our so-called homeless guy." The case alone was nearly worth eighty dollars.

Stewart leaned forward. "Since when do homeless guys have iPhones?"

"Since when do homeless guys trigger flags within two FBI systems?"

"Fair call," Stewart replied.

"Our deceased male was having a fine time. He is both Eric Simonsson and Wayne McEwan. One of those men has been dead for eighteen years." I looked at Stewart and Dane. "Yeah, that means I know who you are."

Dane nodded but said nothing.

"His body was found with a driver's license saying he was Simonsson and no other identification. The phone was discovered under the body inside the back of his pants, not in a pocket, but in a purposely constructed pouch. I got the other identity from the phone."

"Whoever killed him didn't look for a phone," Kurt said.

"It was pretty well hidden," I countered.

Kurt nodded. "He was lying on it, so maybe they didn't look beyond checking his obvious pockets, and maybe he had a phone they did find."

That would make sense because there was no wallet on the body either. "Whatever the reason, we have one man with two identities. And a job and a home."

"And we have two more deaths where police are calling the victims homeless," Stewart replied. "Just as they did with Simonsson."

"Stick a pin in that, let's wrangle Wayne/Eric for a moment." I rocked in my chair. "I have a feeling his partner, Tracey, might have some answers. I also think we'll find more in Langley."

"Central Intelligence Agency?" Dane glanced at his brother.

"Let's just say he's made frequent visits to Langley and spent a minimum of nine hours there on each visit, feels like that could be where he works. Tracey confirmed seeing him at work ten days ago but as you heard, didn't want to continue the conversation via phone. But until I get out there and confirm, let's say it's a possibility he was CIA."

And FBI? Messy.

"And you knew who to call?" Kurt said.

"I discovered that our victim had an emergency contact listed on the phone, Tracey Games. He's coming to talk to us."

"He doesn't know about McEwan?" Stewart asked.

"No. I'll tell him in person and get him to identify the body."

"You taking him to the morgue?"

I shook my head gently. "I have photos of the deceased, best angles possible to maximize facial recognition and prevent trauma to whoever makes the ID." A good chunk of his skull and most of his brain was all over the garage, it didn't leave a very pretty picture but it was better than viewing his body in the morgue.

"Do you know anything about how he ended up locked in that garage?" Dane asked. "Any evidence that someone else was present?"

"He didn't lock himself in the garage, so ya know there's that." Forensically there was no evidence of another person. No fingerprints, no hair, no fibers, no footprints. So far we had jack shit and new locks. "Not yet. His phone puts him at that address for twenty-seven hours prior to his death."

The old couple swore they didn't know him and hadn't seen him. My gut churned. Dead drop still felt like the best answer. But then, why he didn't he leave? What kept him there the last time he visited?

"He was there that long ... so why didn't he use his phone and call for help?" Stewart said.

"Because he couldn't," I replied. "There is no other explanation."

"Restrained?"

Kurt spoke, "No evidence on his body of him being restrained. I'd expect to see chaffing from cuffs or tape residue or rope marks."

My mind ticked. "Someone kept Simonsson alive, unrestrained, but unable to escape or summon help. Drugged?"

Zombie flashed up on my internal screen. But why keep someone drugged in a garage for twenty-seven hours?

Stewart lifted his head and made eye contact with me. "Zombie?"

"Why'd you say that?" I leaned back in my chair and scrutinized his face for a few seconds.

"It popped into my head."

I turned to Kurt, he nodded. "Could be drugs. Could even be scopolamine."

"What are the odds of the zombie drug being used in two seemingly unrelated cases within days of each other? Is it that common now?"

"No, it isn't."

"And the purpose of this zombie drug?" Dane seemed okay with Stewart picking the word zombie from my mind.

"It renders a person compliant and unable to use free

will."

"They can talk? They can do as they're told?"

"Yes." Kurt played with his pen, tapping it on his knee. "Is anyone else curious why Eric Simonsson's driver's license was found with his body when his name has been Wayne McEwan for a very long time?"

Silence fell. What was it that the killer wanted us to know about Simonsson? Why did he leave the old driver's license? Why was he held for so long before his death? Did he kill himself or did someone else pull the trigger?

"Murder weapon?"

"Not at the scene," Kurt said, reading a report on his tablet. "GSR on the victim's right hand and stippling on the skin."

Stippling. The gun wasn't in contact with his skin. "He killed himself?" I questioned.

"Not necessarily," Dane replied. "Simonsson was a lefty."

"Okay, let's say someone else shot him. Someone could've told him to hold the gun and held his hand in position," Kurt said. "Someone wanted it to look like suicide?"

Anything was possible. I flicked my eyes to Stewart. All quiet in his direction. I swung back to the license. "That old license should've been destroyed with the rest of his previous identity," I said and motioned to the coffee on the desk. "Mine?"

"Yes," Dane replied.

"Thanks. Now what have you got?"

"I've got a black coffee and Stewie here has a low-fat soy latte with extra foam plus cinnamon and chocolate," Dane said. "He's almost a girl."

"And I bet you didn't order that." I couldn't help but smile.

Dane grinned.

"Can we get back to work?" Stewart muttered.

"Sure. What have you got?" I shot a warning look at Dane. "Case related."

"Another two locked garages covered in brains and containing dead bodies."

"Hold up. Extra? Like more than the two previously?"

"Uh-huh," Stewart said. "They're piling up."

"And you still think this is some kind of ooky spooky supernatural whatever?"

Kurt chimed in, "Spooky it may be but I got a feeling it's more alphabet soupy than anything."

I stifled a laugh. He wasn't wrong. Who do we know that likes to make homicides look like something they're not? "Crime scene photos and reports of the new scenes would be super handy," I said, sipping my coffee.

"Already in Sentinel. Case number Three zero six-HQ-six-seven-one-eight," Dane said with a cocky grin.

"Three zero six?"

"Five murders with the same MO attached to the same initial case generated a Three-zero-six prefix."

Five. Whatever was going on was escalating faster than I liked. Three-zero-six is the serial crime/murder prefix. The good thing about a Three-zero-six is it gets us priority in the lab. I almost laughed aloud. Priority in the lab. Everything that hit the lab was a priority for someone. It'd been my experience that jumping the queue with a Three-zero-six just pissed people off. Making friends and influencing people again, I rock. Luckily I also rock at buying bottles of scotch to say thank you.

"Do we actually think this is the work of a serial killer?" Dane said. "Regardless of the system wanting to tidy this away under a classification, is this in your opinion a serial killer at work?"

I let that sit for a moment. Yes and no. "I don't think this is a serial killer in terms of how the media view a serial killer." I let my mind wander over the serial killer myths perpetuated by the media and hoped it didn't get stuck in the quagmire.

All serial killers were raised in dysfunctional or abusive families. They are loners who are incapable of maintaining long-term relationships. The violence they inflict on the victims escalates as the series progresses. They attempt to engage the police in dialogue and learn about the progress of the investigation by frequenting police "hangouts." Once a killer starts murdering, he can never stop. If there is a time break in a series, the offender was either in prison, joined the military, went away to college, or was admitted to a mental health facility.

"Can we steer clear of a label at this point?" I said. My response elicited nods of compliance.

"Are we investigating this together?" Kurt said.

"Same case," Wesson replied. "Our trajectory might be

slightly different."

Oh, I don't think so. I leaned back and watched them for a moment before speaking. "If you know about the other deaths, then this is more than your run-of-the-mill potential serial killer or spree killer at work." Wesson tilted his head. Reminded me of a parrot. "I know," I said with quiet deliberation. "I know about the Wayward Son Protocol. I know who you are."

"All of it?"

My turn to tilt my head. "All?"

"The protocol doesn't just flag deceased agents, there's more to it than that," Stewart said. "It flags their names, sure, and we investigate why the names popped up – because dead people shouldn't be roaming around."

Glad he said that because they really shouldn't be.

"But it also flags deaths that defy usual explanation. We lucked out. This case has both, well at least with one of the bodies and I'm picking some of the other scenes will exhibit the same interesting attributes."

He paused; cogs turned, I saw the sparks the cogs created on his face. "Or the same deliberate placement of evidence, like that old driver's license."

Yeah, that was reasonable. My mind took his words and ran with them. Deaths that defy usual explanation led to thoughts of creatures that lurked in the night. "And when the answer isn't monsters from another realm?"

"We'll leave you to it." A slight smile tweaked at his eyes.

"You. Are. Hilarious. Hope you enjoy working with

Delta A."

"Are you saying you want to work with us?"

"I'm saying this is starting to look like an interesting case." It's also a tad freaking weird. "We might need all hands on deck."

"Good point," Kurt said, wiping the surprise off his face.

Guess he never expected me to invite Smith and Wesson into a Delta case. Well, I didn't, The Wayward Son Protocol did. I just made them feel welcome. Something about keeping friends close and enemies closer lurked at the edges of my mind.

Stewart looked at me. "We're not enemies."

Freak. I needed to build a wall and keep the friends out of my mind. A disembodied voice said, "Good luck." Stewart grinned. Damn. Blocking them wasn't going to be as easy as shutting out Mitch.

I picked up my phone and texted Sam and Lee: My office now.

Twenty seconds later my office seethed with wall-to-wall testosterone.

"Case number Three-zero-six-HQ-six-seven-one-eight," I said. Everyone typed the number into whatever device they used, my chosen device my laptop, just like Lee's. I left the tablet on my desk, taunting me with its insistent email chimes, reminding me to silence notifications, as I had on my laptop but probably shouldn't disable it like the phone account.

"Crap," I muttered, looking at the geographic spread. So far, five deaths on the Eastern seaboard, all apparently homeless according to the reports. I found it very hard to believe and skimmed, looking for personal effects, in particular, phones.

"We've got two more iPhones, homeless my ass." I picked up my phone and called the agent down at the evidence locker. "It's Ellie Con— sorry, Ellie Iverson, I need any evidence logged against case three-zero-six dash HQ dash six-seven-one-eight brought to my office."

"Yes, ma'am. I'll send someone up with the boxes. We've only just received some and there are more coming in."

"Thanks." Leaning on my elbow, I looked sideways at Kurt.

"What?"

"Thinking about the iPhone."

"I can tell you're thinking, Iverson, now spill the content," Kurt said.

"Without a passcode, we can't get into iPhones. We all know that. It's part of Apple's security. There's no way in at all unless someone allows you in. All we can see is what someone leaves unlocked for us in their emergency information."

"And?"

"It's interesting."

"Yes, it is,' Kurt said. "There's a lack of names associated with most of these bodies. What's that about?"

"Lazy policing?" Lee offered.

My eyebrows rose. "From five different districts? I think not." With no identity, there'd be no flags. Did that mean whoever killed them knew not to leave ID on the bodies? Or was there something special about Simonsson? I looked at the new guys. "You received a flag for each one?"

Smith nodded.

"So, there are names?"

His head shook. "The MO alerted us with all of them but Simonsson. No names for anyone else."

"Let's get some names attached, shall we?" My mind somersaulted over the lack of identity. DNA. "I want the lab to run DNA on all the bodies."

There was a collective nod from the room.

"You know we probably won't get anything back for weeks from the lab," Lee said. "And there is no guarantee there will be DNA samples on file to match any results too."

Yep. The way the case was shaping up I fully expected DNA to be disappointing rather than the magical key that unlocks identities. "Meanwhile let's use some real live investigative techniques, gentlemen."

Chapter Seventeen

Escape

Night fell. Lights flickered, brightening as the dark deepened. So much for getting home early enough to have dinner with Mitch and Harley. My phone rang: Mitch requesting FaceTime. "Hey," I said as soon as I could see his smiling face.

"Don't work too late, babe," Mitch replied, walking through the house. "I'm cooking." He turned the phone around, Harley waved at me from the kitchen table.

"Hi, Ellie."

"Homework?" I said by way of reply.

"Yes, ma'am." She saluted.

The image on my screen was Mitch again. "What are we having for dinner?"

"Roast beef. I started late. You have an hour to get home."

My stomach growled and mouth watered. "Is there roasted garlic too?"

"Of course."

"Oh, yum. Love your roast beef."

He grinned. "I know. Is it a new case?"

"Yes. It's getting out of hand fast."

With each body adding to the confusion. An alert sounded. I saw the banner flick across the top of my phone screen. Another body. A sigh escaped.

Mouthwatering visions of roasted beef and garlic slid out of view.

"Babe, we got another body. Can you save me some dinner, please?"

"Of course. Don't be too late."

"I'll try not to be." He smiled and I wanted to go home, not just for roast beef.

Mitch disappeared from my screen. I checked the message containing the alert just as Kurt walked into my office, followed closely by Lee and Sam.

"Another one," Sam crooned. "Field trip?"

I nodded. My phone chirped and the screen lit up. "Tracey Games is downstairs waiting for me."

"You want company?" Sam asked.

I shook my head. "I'll chat with him downstairs. Back in a few." I hurried out the door and down the corridor to the stairwell. Games waited patiently by the front desk.

I strode across the expanse between us and thrust out my hand. "Ellie Iverson, Tracey Games?" His handshake felt firm.

"Yes."

I turned to the agent manning the desk. "Anyone in A-1?"

"No, ma'am."

"I'll be talking to our guest in there."

"Yes, ma'am."

I asked Games to join me. I flipped the lights on and closed the door. The neutral color scheme extended to a functional beige couch, two matching armchairs and a pine coffee table. I opted for the couch and suggested Games make himself comfortable. He didn't seem upset to be here. I gave him a few seconds to settle.

"You and Wayne have been together how long?"

"Five years. We were married two years ago."

My stomach sank. Delivering bad news isn't my favorite part of the job. Telling a spouse that their other half is never coming home is something I hate doing. "Where did you marry?"

"In the District."

D.C. stopped discriminating in early 2010, giving same-sex couples the right to marry. Until death do us part just like everyone else. I scrawled 'married in D.C. two years ago' in my notebook. "You're happily married?"

He nodded. "Where is my husband, agent?"

Don't say in the morgue. I ignored his question and forged ahead. "I'll get to that. Bear with me. How long has Wayne been with the CIA?"

"A long time."

"How long has he worked at Langley?"

"Five and a half years."

"You met at work?" He nodded. His fingers clasped so tight, his knuckles whitened. I'd have to tell him soon.

"Agent, what's this about?"

"Do you know what Wayne's role was prior to being at Langley?"

"He was an officer with the Directorate of Operations. Wayne spent quite a bit of time overseas."

The DO served the clandestine arm of the CIA. Tierney

was with the DO. Flames shot across my line of vision. I blinked and they were gone. "Where overseas?"

"I believe he spent most of his time in China." He looked at me. His brown eyes filled with questions and frustration at my lack of answers. "Where is Wayne?" Exhibiting just enough control to keep his voice even.

"We found a body and believe it may be Wayne." I held his gaze for a moment then opened photos on my phone and passed it to him. "Is this your husband, Wayne McEwan?"

He swallowed. His breathing changed to shallow and fast. Tears welled. "That's Wayne." He dropped the phone, I caught it.

Standing, I fetched a cup of water from the water cooler by the door. "I'm very sorry for your loss," I said, pressing the cup into his hand.

"How? Where?"

"Ongoing investigation I'm afraid. We don't have a lot to tell you yet. Although it appears Wayne was shot. His body was discovered yesterday."

"Where?"

"At a residential property outside the Beltway. Do you have any idea why he would visit the same residential address several times before being found dead there?"

A deep frown furrowed his brow. He shook his head. "He was away working."

"Inside the USA?"

He shook his head. "No. Wayne was supposed to be overseas. A situation developed in China. I don't know the details except that's where he said he was going." He paused and wiped his eyes with the back of his hands. "I dropped him at Dulles International Airport myself."

So he didn't know he was here. And we knew he'd been out of the country and came back in via a strange series of flights. The man in front of me was wrecked; he needed to go home and attempt to process his changed world. Yet, I carried on, hoping to get some answers before I released him. "How much do you know about Wayne's life before you met him?"

"He was CIA for a long time. An experienced clandestine operative who spent most of his career overseas. He was in the Middle East before moving to Asia."

"What about his personal life before he met you?"

Games looked confused for a moment. I waited.

"He was married to a woman ... before he accepted who he really was."

"Do you know much about his wife?"

He shook his head. "He talked about what a mistake that was once. After that admission, he refused to enter into conversation about that time in his life."

Mistake is right. I bet Tracey had no idea about the children. "Was Wayne in the habit of keeping his phone in a concealment pouch?"

Tracey looked at me for a moment before answering. "We both do when we're working. That was a decision we made when we married."

"Why?"

"Because we wanted to know if something happened and we wanted law enforcement to be able to use our data." He wiped his eyes. "We're CIA, our work phones are removed and destroyed in the event of an ... accident." Tracey took a big breath. "No data from those phones would ever be turned over to law enforcement, no matter how we'd died."

That explained why the passcode was in the Medical ID. "So you keep personal phones in concealment pouches and life-proof cases."

"Yes. Bodies aren't always left in a dry location."

My thoughts skimmed the two bodies recently pulled from the Chesapeake Bay. Nope, bodies aren't always dry. And phones don't generally like water too much. "Was it Wayne who came up with that plan?"

He nodded. "He made sure we both had location on as well. If you have his phone, Agent, then you have access to the data regarding his last movements." He looked at me. "Use it wisely."

"I intend to." I scrolled back to the mention of a work phone. "Would Wayne have had two phones on his person?"

"Yes. He always carried his work phone in his front left jean pocket and his wallet in the back right jean pocket."

"Thank you for your time."

"You will keep me posted?"

"Yes." I gave him my card. "If you think of anything that might help, call me. And again, Mr. Games, I'm very sorry for your loss."

We stood at the same time. I shook his hand and sent him on his way. Nothing like a grieving family member to put shit into perspective. An unsettling feeling grew; I knew I was looking at the tip of the iceberg. The best I could hope for was state of the art radar to prevent us doing a Titanic.

I had a horrible feeling I'd have to talk to Jonathon Tierney at the CIA. Pretty sure I didn't want to and I sensed it would cost me. Last time we spoke was after I smashed my fist into the mouth of one of his officers. The knuckles on my right hand twinged. Tierney and I had disagreed on the reason the officer was in the Navy Yard. Relations had been strained ever since I killed Tierney's wife. We were working through that, but smacking Tierney's clean-up guy, John Miller, and threatening to keep on interfering with the job he was on didn't help. Some people are so touchy.

Chapter Eighteen

All Along The Watch Tower

My phone rang before I got back to my office – Josh Konstram letting me know about another body that fitted our investigation.

"Josh, we got an alert about a new body three-quarters of an hour ago. Same?"

"No. This is body number two tonight," he said. I was already losing count. "This one is not far from you."

"As the crow flies or using actual roads?"

Josh's guttural laugh reverberated down the airways. "Actual roads."

"I'll be there as soon as I can." I hung up and hurried to my office. My stomach grumbled in protest and demanded food. So much for roast beef. I really wanted roast beef.

"Call Squirrel and Moose," I said, walking through the door, seeing Delta waiting and noting the absence of Smith and Wesson. Shoving my phone back in my pocket, I kicked the door shut. The door closed with a bang. I grabbed a candy bar from the fridge in my office and peeled the silver wrapper back, revealing chocolate goodness; I took a bite and hoped it would assuage my hunger.

All eyes remained on me. No one moved. "Hello? Squirrel and Moose, get them in here," I said, irritation spilling forth as I bit into the chocolate again.

"Iverson, do you mean Dane and Stewart?" Kurt asked, taking his phone from his suit jacket pocket.

I swallowed my mouthful of chocolate. "That's what I said."

An eyebrow shot up. "No, Iverson, you said Squirrel and Moose."

I did? "Well, I meant Stewart and D ... Dane." Yeah, that was going to be too hard for me. My brain was too busy having fun with the *Supernatural* craziness. Just a matter of time before I slipped up and called them Sam and Dean.

Kurt made the call. Lee and Sam sat in silence for a few beats. I knew one of them would have to say something. I managed another few bites of the candy bar before anyone spoke to me.

"Chicky Babe – *Supernatural*?" Sam said as the dime dropped through a few layers in his brain.

Play it cool, Ellie.

"Squirrel and Moose," Sam said with a beaming grin. "I see where you got it, suits them."

And right there I knew the decision was made. They'd be Squirrel and Moose from now on. Sam knew it too. "Nickname achievement unlocked," I muttered, leaning back in my chair and closing my eyes for a second as I savored the last of the bar.

"Lemme guess ... Moose is the tall one?" Sam said.

I opened an eye and looked at him. "What do you think?" Both eyes sprang open. I balled up the wrapper and threw it at the trash can by the door. "Score," I said as it dropped into the can.

His deep throaty laugh was infectious: I had to rein in my laughter before the arrival of Moose and Squirrel. I needed to give up on ever having a normal brain or one that didn't associate life with TV or music. Maybe everyone did it?

Kurt attracted my attention. "Trust me, Iverson, not everyone does it. You're unique."

"I didn't say anything."

"You didn't have to."

It didn't bother me that Kurt often knew what I was thinking. We'd worked together for a long time. We were close. Didn't bother me that Mitch and I could communicate non-verbally. It did bother me that Squirrel and Moose might be able to tap into my thoughts.

Closing my eyes, I concentrated on putting up a protective wall. For appearances' sake, I left one or two of the more mundane thoughts on the outside of the wall. My eyes pinged open when I heard footsteps in the corridor, followed by a knock at my door. Kurt opened it. Moose followed Squirrel in.

All that testosterone. Zero air. Why didn't we have any female agents wanting to join Delta? Because they were smarter than me, and didn't want to devote their lives to the cause? Delta is life. Delta sometimes feels like a life sentence. "We've got a new scene," I said as the hum in the room settled.

No one spoke.

"Also, I spoke to Wayne McEwan's husband. He was aware McEwan was married to a woman a long time ago but didn't seem to know any details. Doesn't sound like McEwan wanted to talk about that or work. Mr. Games believed McEwan was in China, so he was a little surprised to find he was deceased in Virginia."

"CIA might demand the files and shut us out," Lee said.

"As far as we're concerned, McEwan is Simonsson and Simonsson was FBI." I smiled. "You're right though. They might. I'll consider talking to Tierney later. I want to make sure that the rest of the deaths are ours, no crossover, and then CIA can argue all they like ... they won't get anywhere," I replied. Could I really talk to Tierney after all that had happened? Yeah. Nah. Iain could.

The clocks on the wall above the door showed me I'd missed dinner.

"Are we going, Chicky Babe?" Sam asked.

"Yep. Kurt and I, you and Lee, Squirrel and Moose," I said. "Best if we stick to our usual teams."

To their credit, neither Wesson nor Smith reacted. I dipped my hand into my desk drawer and pulled out a salt shaker. "Heads up," I said, throwing it across the room to Moose.

He caught it, looked at it, and smiled. "So, you're not a low-sodium freak." Then threw it back.

Yep, we'd get along fine. They had a sense of humor.

Relief followed the discovery that Squirrel and Moose

drove a black Chevy Suburban just like ours and not a black '69 Impala. A sense of humor was one thing but '69 Impala would've pushed funny into crazy territory.

Kurt and I arrived at the scene first. I asked for a rundown on personal effects while I donned protective booties and gloved up.

"Found a cellphone hidden on the body, Ellie," Josh said. "No identification. No wallet."

"Thanks." I took a breath and walked through the door. I paused and let everything cement in my mind.

High velocity spatter told me the victim was facing the door when he was shot. His clothing didn't suggest homelessness. I walked over to the body. Clean, tidy, but casual. I crouched next to the deceased. Under the sharp metallic smell of blood, I detected soap and laundry detergent.

"What are you thinking?" Squirrel asked, crouching next to me.

"That he's not homeless and someone is killing to send a message." My eyes roved over the body. Usually, I could see or hear the deceased person's final moments. This body felt like Simonsson's. Too quiet.

"Really? You think there's a message?"

"Uh-huh." Maybe. "No clue what that message could be. And that's annoying."

I checked the phone. A number within the medical ID was similar to one I'd seen before on Simonsson's phone. Helpful. Made me wonder if they knew each other. I wrote the number in my notebook. Three sets of four.

One-zero-nine-eight, seven-six-five-four, three-two-one-zero. So the next number should be nine-eight-seven-six. That gave me eight-four-zero-six. I put the passcode into the phone.

Our dead guy visited this address multiple times over a two-week period. Two to three minutes each visit. Searching further within the phone's meager contents I found a name. "Our vic is Adrian Lee, or at least that's what his phone says."

"Hmm," Moose said. "Adrian Lee, FBI. Found him."

He showed me a photo. Yep. Same guy apart from the dead eyes.

I crouched next to the body. "Okay, Adrian, we're going to need some help here." He still wasn't chatty. About to stand up, I saw a piece of something underneath his arm "What have you got for us?" I said, moving the fabric of his jacket and revealing a business card. I picked it up, noting the FBI logo. "Thank you, Adrian." I stood up, straightened my back and worked out a kink.

"The dead ever talk back?" Squirrel motioned to Adrian with one finger.

"Usually," I said. No big deal. "There's a name here, see what you can find," I said to Squirrel and Moose, showing the card.

Moose stood ready to input the name into his iPad. "Go."

"Shaun, that's S-H, not S-E. Shaun Rowe."

Moments later both Moose and Squirrel's phones chimed.

"Is that from the name?" I asked.

"Yes. Shaun Rowe died six years ago," Moose replied. He handed me his phone for me to read the incoming information.

"Diving accident. Coroner ruling says the body was more than likely swept out to sea."

Lee spoke, "When was that again, Chicky?"

"Six years ago."

Kurt finished his inspection of the body and joined us. "Another dead agent?"

"Yep." I looked at the photo attached to the document. It was Shaun Rowe and Adrian Lee – the deceased lying on the floor. He'd been working out of the Manassas field office prior to his death. The only family listed was a sister in Australia. I handed Moose the phone and left the garage; stepping into the darkness helped me think. I heard Kurt's voice behind me tell Squirrel and Moose to leave me alone for a minute or two.

Walking down the driveway toward my car the night enveloped me. Streets lamps dropped pools of white at regular intervals up and down the suburban street. Sitting on the hood of the car in a patch of darkness I let the events of the past twelve hours replay in my mind. So, it wasn't someone using dead agents' names, it was dead agents returning. Perplexing. My hand opened.

The phone belonging to the victim begged me to investigate it further. I checked out his recent conversations. There were none. Who has a smartphone in their possession and doesn't text or use social media or make calls? Someone who wants their whereabouts recorded, just like Simonsson. I scrolled back through Adrian Lee's last recorded whereabouts. No mention of Langley.

That was comforting because our system said he was FBI.

Any comfort gleaned from that was short-lived when I saw Williamsburg, Virginia as a location. Closer inspection revealed a heart-dropping tidbit: Camp Peary. Among other things, Camp Peary hosted a covert CIA training facility known as The Farm. He'd come and gone from Camp Peary which indicated a job – maybe. So CIA wasn't off the table yet. It was possible there was another reason. Location entries for the three weeks prior to Camp Peary did nothing to alleviate my concern. He'd been at Harvey Point, North Carolina. At least the CIA wasn't the only alphabet involved there. ATF, Navy, CIA and FBI all occupied The Point. What did I know about The Point? It was the sister facility to Camp Peary.

Not exactly good news.

Why did the CIA have people inside the FBI and why did we not know about it? Why are they dead now? Why are they twice dead? Why did the killer want us to know Eric Simonsson's name? Why did someone leave an old business card of Shaun Rowe's near Adrian Lee's body?

So many questions.

Footsteps echoed down the quiet street pulling me out of my head. Focusing on the approaching figure, I waited, hand absently resting on the grip of my Glock. The person stepped into a pool of light ten feet from my car.

He grinned. Lopsided and cute. Running his right hand through his blond hair, he winked as he grew closer. "El ..."

"Chance. To what do I owe the pleasure?"

He laughed. "Glad you said pleasure."

"Don't make me change my mind."

His dimples deepened as the grin on his face widened. "What are you doing out here?" He looked around. "By yourself."

"Thinking."

"About?"

"Why do I think you know?"

He laughed again. "Because, El, your mind is one fucked-up place but I couldn't exist without it."

Well, that was true. "Whaddaya know, Chance?"

"It's not just about CIA officers. Dig deeper."

"Okay, but why are CIA officers posing as FBI?"

"You'll figure it out. Think in broader terms, El."

Broader terms? "What does that even mean, Chance?"

"You got this. You'll find the answer." His image shimmered. "Don't get caught up with perceived CIA involvement. It's not all about them."

"What is it about, Chance?"

He faded a little more and smiled. "What kind of person would keep a dress with DNA on it and not wash it?"

A bright burst of laughter came from Chance before I could reconcile the comment with the situation. He moved on to be more case-specific. "Who would keep a driver's license from a dead man and an old business card belonging to another dead man?"

Somewhere behind me a door slammed. I looked over my shoulder. Chance was gone when I turned back.

Not super helpful.

I doubted Monika Lewinsky's involvement. But that's not what he meant. I dredged my memory banks for what I knew about that unfortunate situation. Someone told her to keep the dirty dress and gifts, and also encouraged her to document her relationship with Clinton, and that person apparently acted on advice from a literary agent.

To me, that smacked of a book in the making. Some kind of tell-all exposé crap designed to make money and ruin lives. So the question becomes, how did that situation equate with the one in front of me? Someone told our killer to keep the driver's license of a dead man? Someone also told our killer to keep a business card from a different dead man?

Okay.

Or, someone was told to keep them and hand them over to the Unsub when it was needed. Layers of culpability. A twisty fucking web of deceit.

Why? What did they hope to achieve? Why kill the already dead? How would someone get that license?

The license bothered me more than a business card. Business cards are handed out by Delta to the tune of almost two-hundred and fifty per agent per three months. I supposed it was similar for other agents.

Before his death, Simonsson kept his ID in the trunk of his car in a locked case. O'Hare knew that. My brain screeched to a halt.

Surely other people he worked with knew that. Not just O'Hare. Not Caitlin O'Hare.

And just like that, the ground felt unstable. I cornered the thoughts about Cait O'Hare and jammed them into a box marked 'later.' It looked a lot like the 'too-hard basket.'

If it's not all about the CIA, then why two dead people with CIA connections? What is so important about Eric Simonsson that we had to know his name first? We had eight bodies last count, and only two came with names. Why?

I slid off the car and propelled myself back to the crime scene. We needed to get back to the office and go over the evidence from the other deaths. I needed my team around me.

At the door, I stopped. Two more questions vied for attention: How the hell were the victims willingly going into garages? Drugs had to be the answer. Toxicology would confirm that. I hoped. Why were they in garages of houses that appeared to be dead drops? Dead drops.

I didn't like that at all.

Tradecraft. CIA operational inside our borders ... wouldn't be the first time. The warning from Chance surfaced again. I growled internally. If it's not about the CIA, why are they featured so prominently?

A slightly raspy male voice on my right made me jump.

Wesson. Squirrel.

"Sorry, thought you heard me," he said, humor filled his words and matched the smile on his face.

"I didn't."

"I could tell."

"Did you want something?" I asked, stepping across the threshold.

"Yeah. Kurt wants you to see something else in the garage. You might want to see it."

"Okay. Gimme a clue?"

He grinned. "Come and see for yourself."

I followed him. He stopped, stepped aside and ushered me into the garage.

"Kurt?" I said. He stood with his back to me. "You find something?"

"Come here, Iverson. Tell me what you see," Kurt said, waving me over.

We faced the back wall of the garage. My nose wrinkled, irritated by the metallic smell of blood. Messy crime scenes aren't much fun. A symbol about a foot-high, halfway up at the wall, rough, painted using fingers not a brush and a reddish brown.

"Any paint anywhere?" Kurt scanned the garage before his eyes settled back on me.

"I found a pail of ceiling paint," Moose replied, using a screwdriver to lift the lid. "It's white."

"That definitely wasn't what created this," I said, looking closer at the wall. "It's crude. Not the best wall art I've ever seen." Thanks to a case where the artist used blood and created what he called 'Forensic Art,' I'm an expert on blood art. The more I looked at the painted wall, the more it looked like blood to me.

A glance at Kurt told me he thought it was blood too.

I extended my hand toward the image. I could've painted it without stooping or stretching. The strongest color and thickest coverage was at a comfortable height for me.

"How tall is our dead guy?"

"Just under six feet, by the look of him," Squirrel said.

"Any red on his fingers?"

"Yes."

"So he could have painted this before he died."

"He could've painted it before the fatal wound, even hours before." Kurt looked from me to the wall. "He didn't do it after the gunshot to his head."

"Is that a compass, a pyramid, and an eye?"

"Looks that way," Kurt agreed.

"And?"

"Ever seen anything like that before?"

Yeah. I had. My hand slipped into my pocket and before my brain caught up, I'd called Dad. Squirrel attempted to speak but gave up and let me talk.

"Hey, sorry, question ..."

"El ..." His voice fought sleep. "Must be important."

"The ring you wear sometimes—"

"Masonic, El. Remember?"

"I do now."

"Anything else?"

"Not yet."

"Can I go back to sleep?"

"Yes. Sorry, Dad."

I hung up. Kurt waited with as much patience as ever. "Iverson?"

"Secret society shite. That's the Masonic symbol." I waved my right hand at the wall and the rough-painted symbol. "Nothing good can come of this." Before we know it, we'll be knee-deep in Illuminati. That'd make things interesting, as if they weren't already.

I stopped short of trying to imagine things getting any more interesting, because tempting fate wasn't my thing. Not this week anyway. An internal laugh caught me by surprise.

Kurt sparked with questions. I watched him process his thoughts. The spark died down. "Masonic. Guess that's a new spin."

"Not a welcome one," I muttered.

"Not a fan of the Freemasons, Iverson?"

A smile lurked but never made it to my lips. "Secret societies ... I dunno." I shrugged. "Been doing this job too long to find anything good in secrets."

I'm not keen on my father belonging to a secret society but he's belonged to the Freemasons longer than he's been my father, so I ignore it as much as possible.

"That I understand," Kurt said. "Feels like we've got more secrets and hidden agendas with this case than we've had in any one case for a few years."

Yes, it did. It could be something else entirely. I pulled

a dollar bill from my pocket and unfurled it. I handed the note to Kurt.

"Tip?"

"Ha, funny man. Check out the back."

"The Eye of Providence."

"Could be the wall art is about money, not the Freemasons," I said.

"It's an avenue we should consider."

Dane Wesson coughed.

"Yes?" I turned toward him. He crouched next to the body.

"Our vic has a connection to the Freemasons. Look at his hand."

I moved closer and leaned down. On his left hand, he wore a ring bearing a similar design as the wall.

Maybe not about money. Damn. "Nice ring," I said.

"Points down ... he might belong to a Virginia Lodge."

"Specific information."

"Southern states tend to wear the points down, northerners wear them point up."

My dad wore his ring points down. He was most definitely southern and when I was a kid he'd belonged to a Lodge in Christchurch, New Zealand, and subsequently a lodge in Richmond, VA.

"You're not one, are you?" If he knew so much why didn't he tell us what the symbol was?

"No."

"How come you didn't say you knew what the symbol was?"

"I was about to then you made that call."

"Talk faster and louder next time." Squirrel smiled. "So why make something of the Freemasons connection?"

Squirrel opened his mouth to reply. I held up my hand to silence him. Figured he'd get used to the way I worked sooner or later. My habit of thinking aloud can be confusing for new folk.

Why draw attention to Freemasonry? Painting the symbol was hardly likely to be random. The ring would tell us he was a Freemason, so, the large symbol on the wall's purpose was what? To make sure we got it? Someone with a problem with Freemasonry? Someone liked finger painting in blood? Whose blood?

I checked the hands of the victim again. Red smudges on the underside of three fingers of his right hand. I turned his left hand over and saw a cut across his palm.

"Could that blood on the wall come from a cut palm?" Already knowing it wasn't likely.

Kurt checked the cut. "It's healing. Could be three or four days old. I don't think it's his blood."

"Do we have another victim or did the killer bring a bag of blood with him?"

"Just what we need, more questions and no answers," Moose said, his voice quiet and just audible from the far side of the garage.

He was right. I looked at the ring again. "Squirrel. The red stone – does it mean anything?"

"Scottish Rite."

"And that means?"

"He wears a red ring." Squirrel grinned.

"Helpful."

"There's a Scottish Rite Temple in Alexandria."

"That's more like it." He was shaping up to be the fount of all things Masonic.

I could do with a fount.

Kurt tapped my shoulder. "Iverson, how many others among our deceased—"

"Have Masonic links?" I finished for him.

"Yes."

"No clue. Might pay to find out though."

Squirrel cleared his throat. "A few past presidents have been Freemasons."

I briefly wondered if Clinton was, then silenced the crazy notions building in my head. "That's helpful, not. Don't suppose you have a membership list in your pocket?"

"Nope."

"Can we get one?"

"That I don't know, but we sure as hell can ask."

"You wanna do that?"

"Sure." Squirrel left, taking his partner with him.

I called after them before they disappeared, "Check in regularly." Moose's hand rose and he waved in an acknowledgment without looking back.

'Error 404: Species not found' popped into my head. That was weird, even for me. For a moment I tried to imagine what it meant. Species not found? Yeah, nah. Smacked of *X-Files* and *Supernatural* all mashed into one. Enough.

Behave brain. I can't deal with your shit right now.

Chapter Nineteen
The Devil's In The Temple

Early morning light filtered through the wet gray cityscape. Raindrops racing down the window held my attention. One, in particular, fascinated me, gathering drops of moisture as it rolled. Growing bigger all the time. With a splash, it hit the sill.

Kurt burst through the door. I jumped and spun around. Settling my insides, I glared at him as he strode to my desk waving several sheets of paper in his hand. "Ya had to make an entrance?"

"Didn't mean to startle you." The papers in his hand rustled. "I think this will make up for it."

"Problem?"

"More of an interesting development." Kurt dropped the papers on my desk then looked around the room. "Smith and Wesson? Sam and Lee?"

"Moose and Squirrel are trying to get information from the Masons regarding our growing list of dead. Sam and Sandra aren't coming in until nine today. Wedding planner or something. Lee is ..." I shrugged. "Bullpen, I think."

"Great. Read." He dragged a chair to my desk.

I picked up the papers and skimmed the header on the first page. It was from the Forensic Computer lab and addressed to Delta B. A report on the Skype conversations

Harley had with a group of online friends.

Damn, Owen must have intercepted the results and changed their designation so I wasn't notified.

I read the lab report regarding the identities and whereabouts of the girls. It started well. They were who they said they were and yet I felt growing disaster. Reaching Emma, the girl we thought was deceased, I sat up straighter in my chair. My heart plunged to my stomach then cartwheeled down my legs to stop at my feet. The call originated in Perth, Western Australia.

A ghost? An Australian ghost.

The prospect of another ghost in another machine caused a string of expletives to queue behind my teeth, ready for spitting across my desk. Keeping them in check, I kept reading.

I looked at Kurt over the top of the papers. "This would've been handy information a few days ago."

"Yes, it would've."

"Lucky we got Harley back without having to rely on the lab to give us a hand and before the Evil Queen turned the case over to Delta B."

He nodded. "Have you finished reading?"

I shook my head and turned the page. The person posing as Emma was suspected to be a forty-five to fifty-year-old male according to the experts. Emma couldn't have videoed or called via Skype with any of the girls; it would've given the game away. We had an address.

Excellent.

The forensic team had trolled through every word Emma

typed to Harley and checked everything Harley said with the dossier we found. It was a match. Good chance that the information came from this person and not an Iverson, although it wouldn't have been hard for their abductors or captors to fact check. None of the other conversations contained anything of interest. Emma didn't talk to anyone else one-on-one. There was no mention of how Emma died or who Emma really was or why this male targeted Harley.

"Why?" I said, more to myself than to Kurt.

Kurt leaned an elbow on my desk, thinking. "We need to open that classified file," he finally said, "and find out what happened to the real Emma. And who she is. We haven't got a name beyond Emma."

"Yep." One hand was on the phone receiver, the other punched Director O'Hare's extension into the keypad.

The phone rang five times before I heard Kirstie's voice. "She's not in, Ellie."

"Can I get hold of her?"

"Not right now. Family time."

Our fearless leader didn't take a lot of personal time but when she did, she was not to be interrupted with anything less than a world war. As much as I wanted to tell Kirstie the terror alert just hit red and it's an emergency, I controlled my impulses.

"Thanks, Kirstie." I hung up, chewed my lip, and tapped the phone receiver with my fingernails. I needed someone inside the US Marshals office. "Who do we know who is a Marshal?"

"Sarah ... ah, no, she's gone. How about Marcia Gomez?"

"Maternity leave. I went to her baby shower."

"Normal channels, send a request via Owen."

Laughter tripped off my tongue. "How about I walk on over to the Department of Justice and sweet talk someone?"

"Or Sandra ..." Kurt's voice dropped to a harsh whisper. "Can't believe I'm suggesting hacking the DoJ computers."

A light switched on in my head. "There could be another way."

"What?" Kurt said leaning closer.

"Caine."

The boss has been around since stone tablets were cutting-edge technology. He had to know someone. I picked up my phone and a put a call through.

"How can I help?" Eight in the morning and he already sounded like a pissed-off black bear. It was his go-to response for all situations.

"We need to get into a classified WITSEC file."

"The hell you do." I imagined steam coming from his ears. "They're classified for a reason."

"It's important to our investigation."

"Ellie, it's not going to happen."

"Just gimme a name. There has to be someone I can talk to in the Marshals Service. Please, Caine, I wouldn't ask if it wasn't important."

A drawer opened. Something was placed on the desk. Paper turned. A smile crept over my face, Kurt saw it. I touched the speaker button so he could hear pages turning. He smiled. Caine was the only person we knew who still used an actual physical address book; even my dad used his phone to keep contact information.

"Got a pen?" Caine grumbled into the phone.

"Yes." I waited, pen poised over my desk blotter.

"Call Audrey Adams and she'll tell you which marshal you should talk to. They won't give you access, Ellie, but talking to the marshal responsible is a better option."

"Thank you."

"Don't piss off anyone over there." He growled once more and hung up.

Kurt punched the number into my landline; we wanted Audrey to know this was a legitimate call. Four minutes later we had a coffee date with a marshal by the name of Joanna Brock at our usual cafe.

I checked my watch then looked at the row of clocks above my door. I stopped short at checking the time on my phone as well. That'd be overkill. "We'll walk?" I looked at Kurt staring past me and out the window.

"Rain's stopped. Walking sounds good."

He pushed his chair back, opened the closet and took out two waterproof FBI jackets. After a quick label check, he threw one to me and put the other one on.

We opted to leave via the bullpen so we could let Lee know we were leaving the building.

"Take those stairs," he said, motioning to the emergency stairwell door.

"Why?"

"Owen is in with Claude, she's been there about ten minutes."

"Good call. We'll bring you coffee."

"If anyone asks, you're on a coffee run," Lee said. "You better get out of here before the Wicked Queen steps out of that office."

Kurt and I wound our way past the desks to the emergency exit. He pulled the door open just far enough for us to slip through. Fluorescent lighting filled the stairwell. Concrete steps with reflector strips on the edges ran down as far as I could see. The air was clean. People leave behind trails of scent. Mostly it's pleasant, sometimes it's overpowering.

"You okay?" Kurt slowed his pace until we were side by side on the concrete steps.

"Yep."

"Nothing bothering you?"

"Nope." I kept my hand lightly on the handrail as I walked. "Not a fan of stairwells these days but this one seems remarkably fresh compared with the other stairs."

A quiet laugh sprang back off the plain white walls. "Bit more sensitive to smells than usual, Iverson?"

"Yeah, and I was pretty sensitive to start with but this bonus sensitivity is downright cruel."

"You'll be back to normal before you know it." Kurt held the final smoke-stop door open for me.

"You do realize you just implied I was previously *normal*."

I stepped into the main foyer. Kurt laughed. The agent manning the desk looked over then went back to whatever he was staring at on his screen.

Cameras probably.

The elevator dinged. I didn't turn around but strode to the

outer door. Just as I crossed the threshold, I heard Owen screech. "Agent Iverson!"

Feigning deafness, I hurried to the sidewalk dodging puddles. Kurt fell into step next to me. Neither of us looked back. I was thankful for the drizzle and generally unappealing weather. Water and Owen didn't mix. She'd probably dissolve.

At the cafe, we took off our jackets and hung them on the backs of our chairs and waited for Joanna Brock. A woman with short curly brown hair wearing a jacket not unlike ours approached the table.

"Agents Iverson and Henderson?"

I offered my hand. "Agent Iverson. You must be Joanna Brock?"

We shook, she smiled. "Yes." She dropped her jacket on the back of her chair and sat down. Kurt took coffee orders and disappeared for a moment, returning with a number.

"What's this about, Agents?"

"A kidnapping case. We uncovered something and think you might be able to help fill in the blanks." I passed her my phone with the photo of Emma from the system, with the deceased stamp on it. "She is apparently a friend of my niece. They've been talking for over a year."

Joanna frowned, handed me back my phone. She used her phone. Tapping the screen and reading. Joanna started to speak. I held up my finger to warn her our coffees had arrived. The server left and we resumed our conversation.

"She's dead. It's not possible for her to be talking to anyone."

"Really dead or WITSEC dead?" Considering how things were going lately, it was a fair question.

Joanna's green eyes lit with a splash of amusement. "Really dead. She died eighteen months ago."

"And she was in WITSEC?"

"Yes."

"What's her name?"

Joanna sipped her coffee. She placed the cup on the table, picked up a napkin and pressed it to her lips. Folding it, she placed the napkin back on the table. "Emma."

"What's her full name?"

"I can't tell you that."

"What about the name she was given by WITSEC?"

Her head shook. "I can't give you any identifying information."

"Why would someone pose as a dead teenager and target my niece?"

"I have no idea." She picked up her cup again, sipped her coffee, replaced the cup, picked up a napkin and pressed it to her lips. With the napkin neatly folded and back on the table, she looked at me. "She's dead. I can confirm her death."

I drank some coffee. "Did she die in the United States?"

"Yes."

"Did they have family in Australia?"

"Yes." Joanna picked up her cup.

I waited, watching her ritual with interest. OCD or self-soothing? Pressing the napkin to her mouth could be what she does to stop from talking. "Joanna, is there a relative in Australia who is a forty-five to fifty-year-old male?"

She nodded.

"Did Emma make contact with that male while they were in protection?"

She nodded again. Took another sip of coffee and repeated the whole napkin ritual.

"Did that lead to her death?" It was like pulling teeth. I just wanted her to talk. Just fucking tell me!

The coffee-napkin ritual happened again. Once it was over, she made eye contact.

"Yes."

My mind whirred, filling in the blanks and trying to ask the right questions. "She made contact with the uncle." Fishing. Big time. "Unbeknownst to the parents."

Joanna pressed the napkin to her mouth and held it there a few seconds longer than previously.

"She missed him. She was a kid. Understandable." I thought about Harley. I thought about Carla. Teenagers. "The kid made a decision to remain in contact with her uncle even though she knew she shouldn't. Someone tracked the family down through the uncle."

Coffee. Napkin. Silence.

Kurt placed his cup on the table. "Joanna, we've uncovered a human trafficking enterprise. The teenager Iverson is talking about was rescued just before she disappeared forever. We think she was targeted for a reason, it wasn't opportunistic, this kid was the target. Why would Emma's uncle be targeting a kid, similar age to Emma?"

She leaned forward and placed her elbows on the table. "I don't know. To my knowledge, there was zero criminal activity by the brother."

"But not so Emma's father or mother?"

"Mother."

"Related to the uncle?"

"Only by marriage."

Okay, so father's brother. Mom was a criminal probably turned State's Witness and would be in protection for life, or Mom had information on organized crime that she decided to impart for whatever reason.

"Did they have other children?"

"No."

That wasn't the right question. "Did the mom have other children?"

"Yes. Grown children. She left them behind. It was not her choice."

Finally a better response. Okay, so the uncle would've been in touch with the other kids. Emma was probably using her uncle to pass messages to her siblings. "And Emma was killed while in WITSEC?"

She nodded, checked her phone and stood up. "Sorry I can't be more help."

"Thanks, anyway … we know more than we did." I rose to my feet and shook her hand. "Okay if I stay in touch?"

"Of course. Nice to meet you, Agents."

Joanna pulled on her jacket and left, leaving me feeling mentally exhausted.

Chapter Twenty
Where Do You Go To My Lovely?

It was mid-morning when I arrived home. My plan was to spend time with my family before going back to the office. Simple. A day and dinner with the family. Just to let the new case settle in my head a bit and hang out with Harley and Mitch, then have dinner with Mitch's parents. It was time we told them about Chris and Susan before Delta B did, or worse, before Owen. It wouldn't go well for us if they heard it from anyone but us.

Harley walked into the room. "Dad didn't message me or anything yet." She flopped onto the sofa, phone in her hand.

"How are you feeling?"

"Good," she replied, checking her phone.

Truth time. "We haven't been able to get hold of your parents."

Harley sat up straighter and looked at me. "They don't know?"

That's not what I said. But I had a feeling they did know. "They're not answering their phones." Or the hotel room phone. And reception hasn't seen them to give them a message.

"Why?" A kaleidoscope of emotions crammed her face, crowding her bright blue eyes. She touched the screen on her phone. Two taps later the phone rang. It went to voicemail and I heard Susan's voice say she would call back. "Why aren't they answering?"

As I attempted to answer, Harley came up with her own scenarios. "Maybe the phones are off. They could be traveling. Coming home."

They could be. Without their passports and luggage. Sure, why not? Let's say they're traveling. Their phones weren't in the hotel room, so maybe they are. I nodded. "Harley, I have someone in Hamburg trying to find them."

"We should go." She paused. "No. We should be here because they're coming home."

Yeah. I felt her conflict. I'd fought the urge to jump the next flight to Hamburg since Harley's abduction. "We'll find them. They'll be coming home." Hopefully without need of body bags. Meanwhile, we had ourselves a teenager for a bit longer. So far we'd coped. I still hoped it wasn't permanent.

"What do I do now?" Harley asked, dropping her phone on the couch.

"You stay with us or Gran and Granddad if you'd prefer. And you carry on being the best version of yourself that you can be until they get home." Because what's the alternative?

"Why was I drugged? What did that man want?"

"We think he wanted ..." The truth was not going to help and anything else would screw her up more. "... he wanted you. It might have something to do with your parents but we're not sure what yet."

"Why do you think that?"

More truth. A censored version. "I found a document that contained some information. It's possible that information came from conversations you had on Skype with Emma and maybe from your parents too."

"Emma is my friend. How did you know about Emma?" Suspicion swaddled her words.

"Part of the investigation into your disappearance centered on online activity. It's routine." I did my best to downplay our snooping into her laptop. "I didn't think they could've gotten that information from anyone except your parents."

Harley sank into the sofa and pulled up her legs. Her long hair partially obscured her face.

"But I was wrong, the information matched what you'd said to Emma. We had the conversation analyzed."

Tears rolled as her anger took hold. "My private conversations with my friends."

"You were missing ... we wanted you back," I said by way of an explanation. "Safely."

Her head snapped around. "You violated my privacy!"

"Yes, I did."

"You read my conversations!"

"Where are you Harley, right now?"

She glared at me. Daggers of anger, fueled by a sense of betrayal, shot from her eyes.

"Where are you?" My voice remained calm but firm. I'd been here before with a different teenager.

"At your house."

"And?"

Her anger ebbed, spilling a single whispered word. "Safe."

"I did my job. You're welcome." I shuffled closer and wrapped an arm around her shoulders, pulling her into a hug. "I will not apologize for doing my job, Harley."

Her body twisted, I held firm. Efforts to escape were futile. Her shoulders shook as she struggled to contain tears. The shift from anger to acceptance was complete when she hugged me back. "The person in Germany. He's the best right?"

"Yep. He's Russian, FSB." I detected confusion in her. "What I do, but in Russia. He's charming, formidable, and hates to lose."

"He'll find them and bring them home." Her statement punctuated by sobs. My shoulder grew progressively wetter as Harley's eyes leaked onto my shirt.

"I have faith in Misha," I said, mindful that I couldn't guarantee Chris and Susan's safety and how dangerous it would be to go down that road with Harley. Bringing them home was one thing, bringing them home unharmed was another.

Harley pulled back until she was looking at me. "Promise you'll tell me things as you find out. No matter what it is." Fear spilled from her being and emerged from her mouth. "Promise!"

"I promise."

She extracted a hand, curled her fingers into her palm, leaving her pinky crooked. "Pinky swear."

We linked pinkies. "I promise, I will tell you what's

going on."

Her shoulders sagged as she relaxed. "What about Gran and Granddad? Do they know?"

"No, they don't." I attempted a smile. "We are going to tell them this afternoon. Everyone together."

"All right." She looked around the room like she was seeing it for the first time. "Where's Uncle Mitch?"

"He's down the hall in our office finishing up some work."

"Someone kidnapped me. My parents could've been kidnapped too?"

I nodded. "It's possible."

A tear rolled over her lashes and down her cheek. "What if Uncle Mitch is in danger too?" Harley brushed more tears from her face. "Him and Dad both own Iverson Tech."

Yeah.

I've mulled that over. Interesting that she considered it was something to do with the company. "What makes you think it has something to do with Iverson Tech?"

She shrugged. "I don't really know. Seems logical I guess."

Maybe. Or maybe she overheard something.

"Do you remember something?"

Harley shook her head. "Don't think so. It seems like it could be something to do with Dad's job. Because why else would this be happening?"

Good question. "I thought so too but couldn't figure it out." Also, another case got in the way and I'm not sure about that twisty web of bullshit either.

"You can't go to Germany, can you?"

"Not really. I'm a bit close to this. Better if it's Misha." Two more reasons: The chance I could shoot someone and it's better if I don't put myself in the position of becoming a bargaining chip.

"Uncle Mitch, he's safe?"

"I want to tell you that nothing will happen to any of us. But. We're not a hundred percent sure what's going on or what we're up against." So much truth. "I will do all I can to ensure we are all safe. Deal?"

"Deal."

"That might mean security at the house and a security detail with you and Mitch. All the time."

"Like the president?"

"Yep. You have to respect your security detail, do as they say, let them do their jobs."

"I can do that."

"Good." I gave her one last hug. "Go get ready. We're going to your grandparents. Can you give Uncle Mitch his five-minute warning?"

She took a breath, wiped her face on her sleeve, and stood up. "I can do that."

I smiled at the kid. She displayed resilience and a good deal of mental toughness. Handling it like a pro. For now.

With Harley gone from sight and her footfalls silent, I called Sean O'Hare. He's our Director's twin brother and owner of the best private security company I'd ever worked with.

"Hey, Ellie, got something for me?"

"I need three Close Protection Details, and I need them now."

"You got it. Do I know the clients?"

"One of them, Mitch Iverson. Also, his parents Alan and Joan Iverson. The other is Harley Iverson, she's seventeen and Mitch's niece."

"This can't be a good scenario. If they're under threat, then you are too."

"It's me," I said with a sigh. "I'm good. I'm tracked twenty-four seven. Delta is never far away."

"I can have three details with the clients in forty minutes." A smile crept into his voice. "Where do I send them?"

In forty minutes we'd be at my in-law's place. I rattled off an address and added a proviso. "They need to blend in. More Secret Service than black Gore-Tex."

Sean laughed. "Because the Secret Service really know how to blend in."

"You know what I mean. Suits are fine, jeans are better, but leave the tactical gear out."

"Gotcha. Assignment length?"

"Open-ended. Potentially the threat is abduction but they need to be ready for anything." I heard typing. "Sean, bill me not Delta A."

The typing stopped. "No problem." The typing resumed. "I've assigned two Close Protection Officers per client. The teenager gets a female officer and a male."

Good thinking. With two officers per detail that meant

one would drive and the other ride shotgun wherever Mitch and Harley went.

Keyboard sounds continued. "Are Joan and Alan retired?"

"Yes."

"Two officers assigned to them with a third and fourth on standby should either of the parents need to leave the property."

"Thanks. Verify identities and I'll meet them at the address. Have someone text me when they arrive."

"Done."

I hung up. Before long, a document arrived in my inbox containing photographs. I thought I knew one of the officers. Hang around D.C. long enough and you meet nearly everyone. I looked at the photo again. He was someone I knew. That was very good.

My phone buzzed. A text from Sean: J.C. 63.

I stood up and went to the kitchen. From the glass cabinet above the counter, I chose a Julia Child recipe book. Checking the number in the text, I turned to the appropriate page in the book. Filet Mignon. That was our identification phrase. All it did was make me hungry. I'd developed a real love of beef. I drank a glass of water and made another call, this time to Mitch's mom.

"Joan, it's Ellie. We're leaving in a few minutes."

"It'll be nice to see you all. Dinner is cooking."

The growling in my stomach resumed. I doubted our visit would be nice but at least the food would be good. "Anything you want me to pick up on the way?"

"I don't think so, Gabrielle." I heard her mind ticking in the pause. "If you pass the supermarket, a loaf of fresh bread would be welcome."

One day maybe Joan will stop calling me Gabrielle and embrace Ellie like everyone else. "I'll get some. See you soon." My stomach growled louder. I shoved a handful of raisins in my mouth and chewed fast.

Twenty minutes later I raced into the supermarket, grabbed two loaves of fresh bread from the bakery, paid, and hurried back to the car.

"That was quick," Mitch said.

I detected surprise in his voice as I dropped the bread on the seat next to Harley and clambered into the front.

"I know, right?" Buckling up, I said, "I picked the right checkout for the first time ever."

Things were looking up.

Time disappeared into a haze of traffic and the smell of fresh bread. My phone remained silent. Clinging to the feeling that things were looking up was easier when my phone did nothing to refute it.

Joan waited on the porch, apron on, large slotted spoon in hand. She smiled and waved. My brain automatically committed her smile to memory. I was about to crash her world.

The greetings were quick and affectionate. Harley took the bread to the kitchen, leading the way for the rest of us. Roast beef, garlic, and apple pie with a hint of cloves filled the air. My mouth watered. From the kitchen door, I spotted the origin of the delicious aromas. Beef cooked in the oven, surrounded by vegetables. Pie cooled on a wire rack on the counter.

Yum.

Growling activated in earnest. Loud. Cranky sounding. Black bear terrifying.

Mitch's eyebrows rose as he looked at me. "Hungry, El?"

"Apparently."

Joan invited us to sit at the kitchen table. She cut a slice of pie, slid it onto a plate then placed the plate in front of me. A fork appeared in my hand. "Eat," Joan insisted. "Hunger like that is not good."

No argument here. I demolished the warm pie with gusto. It was the best pie ever. Once fed, a cup of tea appeared in front of me. Even that tasted good.

Mitch and Joan chatted. Harley drank hot chocolate. Alan came in from the garden, kissed his wife, shook his son's hand and washed up. It was all so TV normal; *7th Heaven* sprang to mind. Knowing I was about to shatter the normal and drag them all into my world was hard to handle. A voice in my head told me it wasn't my doing. Something Chris was involved in did this.

It's not me.

It's you.

It's. Not. Me.

I touched Mitch's leg. Reminding him we had to tell them. He smiled at me and nodded. Harley moved her chair closer.

Time ticked.

The protection detail would be outside any minute. Just say it like it is.

Alan sat at the table. "I take it you haven't heard from them either?"

"No. We haven't." I stifled a sigh, swallowed all emotion, and put my work face on.

Joan looked from me to Mitch and back. "What's wrong?"

"They're missing." A gasp met my ears. Joan blanched. There was no other way to say it. Missing is better to hear than abducted or dead. The words in my head didn't help me feel any better. I forged on. "Their phones are also missing, so hopefully with them. Passports and luggage are still in their hotel room in Hamburg."

"How do you know they're missing?" Alan said. Quiet, calm, thinking, as always.

"Their bank accounts haven't been touched. No one has heard from them. They're not answering their phones."

"You've known a while then?"

"A few days." My imaginings swerved to the edge of the cliff and threatened to jump. Reeling them back in wasn't easy. "When they didn't answer calls, texts, or contact Harley, I sent someone to Hamburg to knock on their hotel room door."

"That's extreme."

"Nothing felt right, Alan."

"And?" Alan said, taking Joan's hand and giving it a squeeze.

"Just what I told you. They're missing without their

185

passports. No sign of any struggle or anything stolen from their room."

"An accident ..." Joan said. "They could've been in an accident."

"I've checked all the hospitals. They had a rental car and that's still parked at the hotel. Police are looking into their disappearance."

"What else is happening here?" Joan asked, her blue eyes teared up.

"There's a chance this has something to do with Iverson Technology."

"That's not all, is it?" Joan said, her attention now on Harley. "Where were you the other night when Mitchell called me?"

Snapped. I looked at Mitch. Harley squirmed.

"I got this," he said. "Mom, the other night Harley was abducted from outside our place. We traced her using the tracker Chris put in her necklace."

Made me wonder if Chris knew something like this was a possibility. I glanced at Harley. Puzzled, her fingers sought the locket around her neck.

I nodded at her and mouthed, "We'll explain that later."

She faltered for a second then mouthed back, "Okay."

Mitch's voice remained steady and calm as he explained the rest of that night to his uneasy parents. I waited. Not really listening, instead gauging their reactions so I knew where to install damage-controlling flood barriers.

Typically hard to read, Alan always appeared calm, his eyes the only betrayal of his real feelings. Today the sparkle was minimal. Joan was the opposite. Her face read like an open book. An annoyed open book. One with creased pages and small tears in the fragile paper.

Mitch stopped talking and Joan said, "I'm disappointed that you didn't tell us right away."

"I know, Mom. We're sorry. Until we realized Chris was missing, it seemed like a random happening."

Liar, liar, pants on fire.

He didn't tell them about the dossier on Harley or that the abductor posed as Chris. Or the frightening detail of his brother's driver's license found on the abductor.

"No excuse, Mitchell."

"Gran, I'm fine, really," Harley said with a small smile.

Joan sized up her granddaughter in one long, penetrating gaze. "Yes, I believe you are. But, we're a family. We don't keep secrets."

Point well made. Suddenly it was my turn.

"Gabrielle, does Simon know?"

"No. He doesn't." I didn't want to say I didn't discuss cases with my father but that wouldn't help and wasn't entirely correct. "I'm sorry. We're trying to find Chris and Susan. At this point, we have no idea why they're missing or why someone wanted Harley." I took a deep breath. "The only thing that makes any sense is that it may have something to do with work."

Another deep breath. "Which is why ..." My phone buzzed. I laid it on the table and replied to the message: I'll be right there. "... which is why there are three protection details outside the house now. One for Harley, one for Mitch, and one for you two."

That took a second to sink in. The horrified look on Joan's face said more than any words could.

Mitch turned to face me. "You didn't tell me about that."

I smiled. "I made the call before we left home. I'm not apologizing for worrying about the welfare of your family. In the light of recent events." I watched his face for a second. I readied myself to use phrases like 'It's my job' and 'You need to let me work this.'

"Fair enough."

Whew. "I'll be back in a minute." I stood up and went to the front door. On the porch stood four of Sean O'Hare's finest, two more stood on the path in front of the house.

"Casey O'Rouke, ma'am," said the petite young brunette female agent, as she reached for my hand. "I believe you like Filet Mignon."

"Yes, the way Julia Child cooked it," I replied shaking her hand. "Pleased to meet you, Casey."

Another person stepped forward. He was maybe five years older than Casey. Just over six feet tall. Broad shouldered. Dark haired. "Aaron Langford, ma'am." We shook. "Casey and I are assigned to Harley Iverson."

"Go on in and wait for me in the hallway."

A dark curly-haired male, standing approximately five feet eleven took a step sideways and held out his hand. "Paul O'Brien assigned to Joan and Alan Iverson with this reprobate." He inclined his head to the lighter-haired male standing on his left as we shook hands. Paul moved around me into the hallway. His buddy grinned and took my hand; instead of shaking it, he lifted my hand to his lips.

"It's a pleasure to meet you Agent, Jefferson Cullen at your service." He kissed my hand and let it go. "Don't believe everything O'Brien says."

"I prefer to make my own mind up about people I meet, Cullen."

And he smacked of charm and trouble; I had a feeling O'Brien wasn't far off the mark with his reprobate comment.

A six feet tall, blond, thirtysomething male stepped up. "Murray Fletcher. Assigned to Mitch Iverson."

He smiled, shook my hand, and joined the others inside. The last man grinned at me as he walked up the porch steps. His brown eyes twinkled; creases around his eyes told a story about his sense of humor and a ready smile.

"Ellie Conway," he said sticking his hand out. "I hear you married." I shook his hand. He pulled me in for a hug. It was brief but warm.

"Diego Juarez, I heard you were dead." His presence felt good, comforting. Diego was a hell of an agent and I expected he'd be just as good at close protection.

He laughed. "Common misperception. I've been assigned to Mitch Iverson."

"My husband."

"Ellie Iverson," he said. "That works."

"Let's go in."

I closed the door behind us, threaded my way past everyone and led them to the kitchen. Joan and Alan smiled at me as I entered. The smiles froze as the group behind me emerged. Introductions were brief. The room felt overstuffed and claustrophobic.

I gave Joan a reassuring smile. "You'll see a bit of these six. Everywhere Harley or Mitch go, they will be driven and escorted. Round-the-clock protection."

Joan's attention moved from one to the other. Her smile felt welcoming but I knew ripples of fear lay beneath the surface. "Cullen and O'Brien will stay with you and Alan. If you need to go somewhere separately, then two more officers will be assigned, so there is a team each."

"What about you?" Alan said. "Where's your detail?"

I almost said I didn't need one. Almost. Then self-preservation kicked in. "These guys are private Close Protection Officers. Not FBI."

"Who's paying for them?" he asked.

"The bill goes to me as the SSA responsible for Delta A expenditure." Me actually. This was a private arrangement until I was prepared to acknowledge professionally whatever the hell was happening; that way Owen wouldn't be notified.

His face gave little away. "Where's your security?" Alan reiterated.

I am my security. And the Glock on my hip. And the partner in my car. And, shut up, Ellie. Just shut up before those words fall out of your mouth. "I'm rarely alone. Delta watch me very carefully." I struggled to keep my fingers from crossing.

"All right."

No. It wasn't. That much I could tell.

Mitch interceded, "Dad. She's got me."

Harley laughed. First time I'd heard her laugh since the incident.

"Nice," Mitch said with a smile directed to his niece. "Real nice."

Alan smiled too but I sensed a comment coming. "When your Uncle Mitch was a youngster—"

Harley chuckled some more. "Makes him sound like an old man."

"He is, compared with you," Alan replied. "As I was saying ... your uncle was a champion target shooter back in his youth. His trophies are still on the shelf in his bedroom."

She pushed her chair back and leaped to her feet.

"Where are you going?" I asked.

"To see these trophies," she replied. As soon as she moved, Casey moved.

I sighed a quiet sigh of relief. Even in the house, Casey was on it. Some weren't. With a teenager, they needed to be. Diego and Cullen also left the room. I knew how CPD worked. They'd all take turns patrolling the interior of the house and the perimeter of the property. The space lightened. I could breathe again.

"Mitch the sharp shooter," I said with a grin as I bumped him with my elbow.

"Had to do something to keep me occupied when you

and your family left New Zealand."

Joan smiled at me. "He moped around without you."

"I came back."

A few times. Until one day I didn't.

"El, we'll get through this like we have everything else," Mitch said, "This time we're together. It's got to be easier as a team."

"Till death do us part," I replied. Because that's what it would take.

A little warning light came on in my head. Tempting fate wasn't the smartest move.

Mitch's dad looked at us. I saw cogs turning. "What happens now regarding Chris and Susan?"

"I've got someone on the ground. You met him at our wedding. The Russian, Misha Praskovya."

"Is this an FBI matter now?"

Kinda. It's complicated. "German police with assistance from FSB on my request."

"There have been no demands?"

I shook my head. "We've heard nothing. I don't think this is about money."

"What then?" Alan asked.

Joan stood and checked the oven.

I watched her pull the roasting pan out. "Maybe a design? Perhaps something Chris was working on?' Information.

"Mitch?" Alan turned to his son. "Could that be it?"

"I don't know, Dad. It's possible. We do a lot of work for big companies and we've won a few contracts with various governments."

Hang on a cotton-picking minute. "Governments. Plural. Not just ours?"

His head moved a little. "Plural. We've worked for several governments."

"Anyone dodgy or unfriendly?" What a question to ask. But it didn't feel like a time to be super politically correct. And to be honest, unfriendly described most of the world since our last election.

"New Zealand, Australia, Canada, South Korea."

"Allies." Or at least not enemies, although I wasn't sure about South Korea these days. Our political failings changed how the world saw us and not for the better. Scenarios plowed the fertile ground in my head. No work for Germany then. South Korea.

Guess anything that helped them, would also upset the jumped-up little dweeb in North Korea. I set that on the back burner for a bit, forcing the encroaching scenes from *Olympus Has Fallen* off my inner screen. Nothing pointed to Olympus falling or Gerard Butler saving the day.

Standing, I shoved everything aside and joined Joan by the kitchen counter. "We'll find them," I said.

Joan finished turning the vegetables and put the dinner back in the oven. "I don't think I have enough for six extras."

"It's okay. They don't expect to be fed."

She opened the fridge and mulled over the contents. "I can make sandwiches, will that do?"

No sense arguing. Feeding people is her go-to response.

"They'll be very grateful for sandwiches, Joan." I leaned on the counter. "I'll help."

"That would be nice. Thank you."

Alan and Mitch talked. The five men from the protection details looked on. Every now and then one of them left to patrol the house and the other the perimeter. Casey and Harley were still gone. I guessed Harley had a million questions for Casey about her job.

My phone remained silent. I checked my email notifications were on. The silence began to feel creepy. Joan and I made a plate of ham, cheese, and tomato sandwiches. She carried them to the living room. I followed with a tray laden with a pitcher of freshly made iced tea, glasses, side plates and napkins. We set out dinner for the CPDs and let them know.

The family would eat in the kitchen as usual, monitored closely by the CPD as they took turns to eat and continue surveillance. We were comfortable in the kitchen; it added a sense of normality to a strange new situation.

A nagging wiggle of a notion jiggled around in my mind. Dad, Aidan, Holly and baby Lucy should be included. This is a family situation. Attack one, attack us all.

Sam was imitating Mr. T in my head. 'Pity the fools who try to bring down this house.' His impression faded as Bon Jovi started up. So loud I thought it was a radio. 'This House Is Not For Sale.' The words wrapped around me and I knew there was a message there.

Background noises broke through the song intermittently. A clatter of plates. A knife dragged across the wooden cutting board as Alan sliced the beef thinly. Metal on metal as Mitch stirred gravy with a fork, scraping the bottom of the pan.

I weighed up everything, careful measurements. Whoever had Chris and Susan didn't know about me, well, no more than that I married Mitch. They only had me as Ellie Iverson in the dossier. If that's the case, then they don't know about the rest of us.

Mitch touched my arm. "All right?"

I nodded. "Yeah. Just thinking."

"Can you do your thinking sitting down with a fork in your hand?" He pulled a chair out for me. Plates were being distributed. Harley was at the table.

I slid into the chair. "This looks and smells wonderful," I said to Joan. She sat opposite me.

"Good. Now eat up."

I got halfway through my piled plate before I knew I had to get Dad here. They needed his support. His no-nonsense military background wouldn't hurt either. I placed my fork on the edge of my plate and stood up. "Excuse me a minute." I pushed my chair away. "I'll be right back."

Mitch caught my hand as I moved past him. "Okay?"

"Yes." He smiled and let me go.

I used Mitch's old bedroom and called Dad. He didn't pick up. Sitting on Mitch's bed, I saw the trophies. My husband the marksman. Looking around I doubted this ever was Mitch's room or if it was, it wasn't for long. They can't have been back in the States long before Mitch left for College. This room was a replica of his room in New Zealand with updated furnishings.

My phone rang. The noise reverberated off the bookshelves and hit me full force, breaking the memories of our childhood wide open.

Dad. "Hey. Can you and Aid come to the Iversons?"

"Guess so. I've just gotten back from the Foundation. I'll grab a snack and come over. Problem?"

"Yeah. Chris and Susan are in trouble."

"Time to circle the wagons?"

"Sure is. See you soon."

Hanging up, I realized I was standing in front of the trophy shelf. My fingers traced the name on the first trophy. Mitchell Iverson. Fourteen-year-old Mitch sprang into view. Long hair, sparkling blue eyes, lanky, and wearing a smile that lit my heart. The memory warmed me.

Back in the kitchen, I stooped and kissed my husband's head. His hair was shorter. Nothing else had changed.

"You call your dad?' he said as I planted my butt in my chair.

'I did. They'll be along soon."

Joan heard. She placed her fork on her plate. "Thank you, Gabrielle. We should all be together. Simon is Chris's godfather, after all.'

Harley nudged me. "Are they bringing the baby?"

"I expect so."

She grinned. "She's cute."

Joan rose from the table and began clearing. Harley

jumped up to help.

Alan smiled at me. "Don't look so worried, Ellie," he said, passing dishes to Harley. "I'm sure you'll find them and all will be well."

"That's a lot of faith you have there."

"I've known you all your life," he said as if that explained his unrealistic faith in me.

If I wasn't feeling pressure before I had it in spades now. And what I needed was extra stress in my life. Extra stress and a side helping of teenager. Do you want fries with that?

My phone rang, interrupting all conversation and sent silent exclamations of what-the-fuck through me when I saw AD Owen's name on my screen. I injected polite into my voice before I answered, "How can I help Assistant Director?"

"You can explain why you have requested Close Protection Details from a private company for four of your family members, in particular, the child who is part of a Delta B investigation."

How in God's name would she know that? I scratched around my brain trying to work out how the Evil Queen heard about a private arrangement. Nothing surfaced. "Because they are needed," I said, clenching and unclenching my right fist. "Why are you concerned about what I'm doing?"

"It involves a Delta B case."

Bullshit. "What exactly is the problem?"

"This is a case involving a family member and you need

to step aside. You are not capable of remaining objective. You must stand down."

I'm sorry, what now? An order? "I provided protection for my family out of my pocket. It is none of the FBI's business."

"Agent Iverson, you were asked to hand the case over. You will follow orders or face the consequences."

"Delta B is investigating a trafficking case. We are *not* investigating a trafficking case. I am protecting my family because I don't believe the FBI can." I crossed my fingers. "I'm *not* disobeying orders. Delta A is working a case under a directive by Cait O'Hare." Take your flying fucking monkeys and back off from my family.

There was a very good chance that the missing Iversons had something to do with our Wayward Son cases, I just couldn't prove it yet and wasn't sure what or where the overlap was. I just needed time to unravel the mess. Something told me I was right, I chose to believe that and worry about proving it later.

"If there is overlap you must stand down." Her voice grated like a squeaky wheel. "I heard about Praskovya. You should have run that by me first. Involving an agency from another country without your superior's knowledge and support."

Superior? Can you say delusional? "Is there anything else?"

There was a sharp intake of breath and I knew she was rallying. "Perhaps you should be thinking about your future and a part-time desk job. It would be safer."

I swallowed hard and resisted the urge to scream down the phone, 'Get the fuck out of my business!' Safer? Desk job? Part time? Death wish much? Mustering every ounce of pleasantness still within my reach I said, "Thanks for calling. I'll take your concerns on board." I hung up.

I'd be changing the access to Sentinel as soon as humanly possible to lock the bitch out of our case. Maybe we needed to install nets to protect ourselves from her flying monkeys or sweep our offices for bugs

General chitchat carried on around me, no one but Mitch seemed aware of the phone call. For a moment I wondered what it'd be like to do something else. McDonald's seemed like a possibility. Complete career change. Pretty sure AD Owen would be thrilled and fully supportive.

Reality snuck in and reminded me I wasn't cut out to deal with the public on a never-ending processional basis. There'd be death, horror, and cold fries.

A small laugh broke free and tumbled onto the table top. Black outlines in a variety of thicknesses appeared around my world. Color faded to the more muted tones of a comic book. At the top of the page, a cream narration box appeared and filled with black words 'Just at that moment.' My eyes scanned the page. A warm breeze lifted the corner, revealing Chance sitting at his desk.

He looked up. "You're here," he said, waving a hand at a chair by his desk. As I moved, I saw my boot. We were both comic book sketches. Fascinating. I sat on the chair and wriggled a bit. Black and red ink drawn leather felt comfortable.

"What's going on, Chance?"

"Your father-in-law's faith is not misplaced."

"I don't think you can say that." I'm talking to a drawing in a comic book office, and I don't think he can say that?

"El, you are that chick. Remember?"

"The stakes have never been higher. If I fail, I have to live with my family's disappointment. I don't think I can." Hard enough living with my own.

Echoes of my greatest failures to date haunted me: Mac and Carla were dead, haunting was all they had left. And I'd failed them both.

"You won't fail. Just don't drink Owen's Kool-Aid, Ellie. The FBI didn't spend a fortune training you to stand behind a counter and serve fries."

I laughed. "Early retirement isn't going to work for me, Chance. I think we both know how my career path will end and it won't be in sitting on my porch in a rocking chair watching a sunset."

"Don't say bloody, El. It's not going to end like that."

"Yeah, it is. I just don't know when."

Chance frowned. His countenance darkened. "And you're okay with that?"

"I don't think it's up to me." Truthfully, I'd resigned myself to a sticky, bloody end many years ago. It's not how I go that bothers me, it's when.

As Chance looked at me, the color began to run. The blond from his hair picked up the blue in his eyes and trickled down his face, leaving cream streaks as it dripped off the page.

An arm tightened around my shoulders. The musky scent of Mitch's deodorant brought me back to the present. "All right?"

"Yeah." I looked up at Mitch. "Decided I'm not going to drink Owen's Kool-Aid. We're not stepping aside and I'm not taking a desk job."

Mitch bowed his head slightly until his lips met mine. Warmth flowed in all the right places. I knew I had his full support no matter what. Any doubt I had about my ability to bring Chris and Susan home needed to take a hike in the deep dark woods and stay there.

Chapter Twenty One
This House Is Not For Sale

Mitch's phone rang. He tapped the Bluetooth on the steering wheel. "Kelsy?"

"Mr. Iverson, our computer system is under attack."

"Say again, Kelsy?"

"We are experiencing a cyber attack."

"How's the system coping?"

"So far so good." She paused. Line noise filled the car then suddenly Kelsy was back. "Sir, it's almost as if they know what to do but back off at the last minute."

"Clarify."

"If they kept doing what they were doing, they'd have a chance but the attacker pulls back before breaking through our defenses then tries again."

My mind whirred. Maybe they didn't have all the information, or maybe it was something else, not an actual attack. Why did I think that? Because I'm weird. No. Because strange things happen all the time and for whatever reason, my mind notices.

I called work. "Sandra?"

"O Genie of the Underdog, how can I help?"

"Iverson Tech is experiencing a cyber attack." Mitch glanced at me, I smiled back.

"I'll see what I can do," Sandra said.

Both our calls ended at once.

Mitch spoke, "Chris designed our system to meet government security standards."

Of course he did. And if anyone knew how to find a way in, it'd be him. Shadows wandered through a flowery field in my mind, leaving brown dying wild flowers in their wake. "If there is a backdoor, Sandra will find it. If she gets in and joins the fight, what will she find?"

He glanced at me again. "What does that mean?"

"Could Chris be doing this?"

"He can just use his password and sign in. No need to attack the system from the outside."

"Then everyone would know he was in there fiddling around."

"Yeah, I suppose." His grip tightened on the steering wheel. "But why create an attack like that and stop before breaking through?"

A sharp crack sent flashes of light across the field illuminating the trail of dying plants. My mind's eye showed me a bird's eye view. Not everything was tainted. Purple and blue wild flowers sprang from the edges of death, creating an outline. The blue and purple pattern continued beyond the crispy dead streak. "Someone could have a gun to his head."

Or Susan's. An idea lurched to the fore. I called Sandra again.

"O Genie of the Cyberattack—"

"Is there a pattern?"

"I'll let you know." We hung up.

"Explain," Mitch said, keeping his eyes on the now

heavy traffic.

"The gun to his head or the pattern?"

He sighed. "Pattern, babe."

"This could be a total left-field situation—"

"But you don't think so, or you wouldn't have asked Sandra about a pattern," Mitch said.

I could be way off, time would tell. "When we were kids we used to get those code cracking magazines, remember?"

"Vaguely, go on."

"Chris and I were good at them." I chuckled. "You and Aid, not so much."

Chris and I always won code-cracking competitions when we were all on vacation. Used to be fun making codes up and using them to communicate and not just because it drove our respective brothers nuts.

"There could be a message in the attacks."

"Would he know to do that?"

"If I were Chris, I would try to make contact anyway I could."

"And he'd know you'd be investigating if he was missing, even if police weren't involved yet ..." The corner of Mitch's mouth turned up. "If it is him, we might have something?"

"If, Mitch." Big IF. Let's not count those chickens.

And *bam!* A little yellow chick popped out from behind my phone in my lap and peered up at me. It peeped once and disappeared. A voice in my head said, "Don't count it." Too late. It was one.

I stared at my phone screen for a few seconds as if it were a crystal ball. My reflection jumped from the surface as thoughts aligned like colored squares on a Rubik's Cube. If I were Chris ... I'd use whatever I had to make contact with people who could help. If that meant hiding information within hack attempts, that's what I'd do.

Mitch pulled into our driveway. The gates swung open and he drove up the gravel drive followed closely by a black Ford Expedition. In the wing mirror, I watched the gates close.

Mitch's CPD parked behind our car in front of the house. Both men alighted. They went in different directions, checking the perimeter. I'd given Diego a door and gate code and instructions to make themselves comfortable in the house, which included helping themselves to coffee and food. By the time we were inside the house my phone was ringing again.

"Sandra, what've you got?"

"Sending you screen shots of the incoming activity on the Iverson Tech mainframe. I think you're right about a pattern."

"Great." I like being right.

"It's recurring. From what I can see it's been repeating for the last hour."

"Thanks. Send me screenshots from the last three weeks too, please."

I hung up, went into settings and reinstated my work email account on my phone and dropped my bag off my shoulder onto the kitchen counter. Through the window,

I saw a figure heading for the back door. I lifted my hand from my weapon. Don't shoot the help.

My brain placed the figure and gave him a name. Murray Fletcher. Having people around would take some getting used to. I joined Mitch in the living room. Doors opened and closed as the CPD checked the house. A shadow passed the living room door. I sank into the big leather cushions of my favorite sofa.

Mitch smiled at me. "Not easy for you, is it?" His hand waved toward my holster.

"Nope. I really don't want to shoot the help."

He laughed and I relaxed. Right then, on the echo of Mitch's laugh, everything was okay.

"Chris hasn't been missing three weeks," Mitch said as he lowered himself into the big leather armchair opposite me. We were separated by a coffee table and there wasn't any coffee on it. Oversight. I knew of a remedy.

"Comparison," I said. "I need to make sure it's a pattern that means something, not just a pattern."

He nodded. "Yeah, as soon as I said it I realized." Mitch moved his neck from side to side and gave the base of his neck a quick rub with one hand. "Do you really think he's trying to send a message?"

"I hope he is."

Because that would be super helpful and if I were him, I would.

"You think drugs are involved?"

"I think that's probably how someone took control of them initially."

"Like Harley." It wasn't a question.

They probably used Devil's Breath any time they needed compliance or to move Chris and Susan. I didn't know enough about the drug to know how it affected the victims' ability to use their brain for complex tasks, like hacking. Good chance it would hinder someone's ability to operate at that sort of intelligence-rich level.

"Hey, when Chris left the country, are you sure his password was active and could the status have changed while he's been gone?"

Mitch frowned. He scrolled through a series of screens on his phone. The frown melted. "Yes, it was active but within two days of him leaving, the system demanded new passwords. So his wouldn't work now. We can't change our passwords remotely, they have to be changed on the main computer in the office."

"That's a blessing." And another reason why he couldn't just log in. Stealing a log-in or forcing someone to log in would be a lot easier than getting someone to hack such a secure system. Wonder if that held true for the person who designed the software. My money was on Chris having free will and trying to make contact and give us information.

And the reason there were no unicorns on the Ark was because they were too busy playing. Leprechauns hide pots of gold at the end of rainbows and my brother-in-law is trying to tell us where he is or something. One of those things is probably true.

A sudden unwelcome rush of guilt replaced my earlier

feeling of warmth. I shouldn't be lounging around. I should be working this case. I started to move from my comfortable seat.

"El, just rest for a few minutes," Mitch said, his voice soft. "As much as I want Chris and Susan home safe, I want you well and safe."

"I'm good." I paused listening to noises in the house. Footsteps. Doors. More footsteps. A chair moving. Maybe we should have some music on to mask the intrusion. "Stereo. Listen. Bon Jovi." Moments later Bon Jovi's 'Real Love' filled the room. Maybe I won't shoot anyone today.

"You're better than good, baby. And I'd like you to stay that way." Mitch ran his right hand through his hair.

"What are you saying?" I arched an eyebrow at him.

"I'm saying you are better at looking after yourself but still not great at it."

Yeah. Okay. Can't really argue with that. "What time are we expecting Harley?"

He checked his watch. "About an hour."

Email alerts chimed on my phone, glancing at them told me they weren't the ones I wanted. Forcing myself to wait wasn't easy.

Don't hound. Just wait. All the images will arrive at the right time and if they don't, there's not much I can do about it. Hey, when did I become so ... trusting? No, more like Doris Day.

And without an invitation, Doris Day singing 'Que Sera Sera' came from nowhere overriding Bon Jovi on the stereo. A twinge of irony followed as an Alfred Hitchcock movie loomed, *The Man Who Knew Too Much*. Part of me wondered if Chris and Susan's disappearance and Harley's abduction could be anything like the plot of the movie. What were the chances of them stumbling onto an assassination plot and the conspirators using Harley to try to silence them? Enough.

I reined in my imaginings.

More email alerts rang out, sounding almost musical. "Okay, we're up," I said picking up the phone from next to me on the couch. "I need to use the PC and all the screens."

Mitch smiled. "I'll make the coffee. You do what you do."

He lurched to his feet and grabbed my hand, pulling me up into his arms. I tipped my head back, our lips met. I could think of better things to be doing with a free hour. Mitch held me against him.

"Let's do this." I kissed him again and extracted myself from his arms before I was incapable.

Firing up the PC was not a long process, unless you were waiting. Then it was like watching grass grow through two feet of snow.

The aroma of freshly brewed coffee drifted from the kitchen. Under the music coming from the speakers hidden in the walls of the office, I heard the soft *clunk* of mugs on the tiled counter. Saliva pooled at the prospect of sipping on the black nectar. I swallowed. Mitch's hand reached around me and placed a steaming mug of coffee on the desk. Life slowed down.

I clicked the email program and found the emails containing screen shots. I sipped my coffee and dragged images into the order I wanted them. Right away I could tell there was no pattern in the older ones and moved them to the third monitor and pulled up recent images. Mitch breathed quietly beside me.

"Do you see it?" I looked at him.

"I do."

One pattern repeated over and over, then another pattern, rinse and repeat. Two patterns.

"Yeah."

"What does it mean?"

"That I'm right. Someone is trying to make contact."

"Chris?"

"I hope so."

Leaning back and sipping the hot brew I let the pattern speak to me. As I watched the screen, color faded. A warm, muted color scheme outlined in black emerged. I turned in time to see a black pen draw a door. The door opened but I couldn't see anything. From somewhere beyond the door I heard a comfortable-sounding hybrid Upstate New York/Canadian accent; it sounded like he was singing. As I watched, the door swung open.

Chance stepped through with a dimpled grin on his face. "What are you looking at?"

"Screenshots showing the times and length of repeated hack attempts."

His hand appeared and pointed to the pattern I saw.

"Did you like codes when you were a kid?" Chance laughed. "Look who I'm asking."

I still do. I smiled. "Yep."

"What are we really looking at?" His tone changed.

"Something from my childhood I think. I just can't quite get it."

Chance perched on my desk. Close. So close I couldn't use the mouse. "Think back, El. You know this. You created it."

"Yes, I did." It's not time. It's words.

Chance pushed my thigh with his knee. "Coordinates?"

"Nope, it's an alphabet-based code." I needed a pen and paper.

Chance winked. "I'll leave you to it."

I reached through him and picked up a pen as he dissolved. By the time I'd pulled a notebook from my drawer everything was back to normal with Mitch in his desk chair next to me. He never said a word. Guess I didn't speak aloud to Chance.

The scratching of the pen nib on paper broke the silence and felt productive. Until that moment I hadn't realized the album we were listening to had finished.

I can't have been staring at the screen for over an hour. "Mitch, music?"

"I turned it off."

"Okay. Good. Back to the code."

Despite knowing I created the code, it seemed to take forever before I had two vowels and a starting point. A lot had filled my mind since I was that twelve-year-old kid playing with codes on wet days during family vacations at the beach.

"Frustrating," I muttered, looking at the paper in front of me, then the screens.

"You're making progress," Mitch said. "Reminds me of those summer vacations."

"Yeah."

Long summer days at the beach in the Marlborough Sounds with our mothers, while our fathers worked and joined us for weekends. If it hadn't been for Joan, Mitch, and Chris, our vacations would've been spent hiding from the crazy that was our mentally ill mother, with her ill-disguised love of booze, parties, and anyone or anything that wasn't us.

Words jumped off the page. There was a code within a code or rather a memory within a code.

"It's a game, Mitch. Remember how your mom gave us words and we had to make other words from them?" Anagrams. They were fun.

"Yeah, and she always had a candy bar for the best effort."

Yes, she did. Joan Iverson provided stability and unconditional love peppered with a lot of laughter and hugs. Not a gin bottle in sight. Such a contrast when set next to my mother's idea of mothering.

Okay. Anagram time, then. Mitch was just as good at them. "The first word is technology."

"The company?"

"Maybe." I passed him a pen and another notebook.

"Descending order, nine-letter word first."

"How do you know that?"

"It's in the code. He put numbers after the word and what might be the first letter of the word he means. Nine E, eight T, seven L, six T, five H, four L, three C."

Mitch reached for the iPad on his side of the desk. "Better idea than sitting here all night trying to figure out what he means ..." He searched online for anagrams of technology.

Together we looked at the list. I started writing and so did Mitch. We compared and had the same relevant words.

"Ethnology, theology, lengthy, techno, hotel, Lyon, CEO."

"That doesn't sound good," Mitch said. "What's the next main word?"

"Antipodes. Eight S, seven D, six P, five S, four D, three N."

He searched and a list popped up. "Nothing good here either. Sedation, detains, ponied, spite, Dane, NSA." Mitch hissed air through clenched teeth.

"It's definitely Chris."

"Yeah."

"Lyon is in France. So it could mean they've moved from Hamburg and we missed the move, or they're going to move."

"A hotel in Lyon," Mitch said.

"Hotel is good, there's a chance someone might've seen them. Better a hotel than a private residence. That could be what he's saying but we've skipped ahead and this is an ordered process. Let's go back to the beginning and start with technology and the derivatives of that word."

"Ethnology and theology," Mitch said. "What's that about?"

"Could be telling us there is a different belief system, or even a religion, behind this."

"Is this terrorism?"

Because that would be the only reason for the word theology and ethnology to be there together, telling us that whoever is behind this is not like us. As in Catholic? Or as in Western?

"If I make that call, then all bets are off and we go in guns blazing. And then it becomes a full-blown international incident and ugly gets uglier real quick." Catastrophe threatened: good chance we wouldn't get Chris and Susan out alive. Could I make that call based on a code, a few anagrams, and a family history?

Hell, yes, I could. Focus. "Lengthy." What could that mean? "That this is not going to be over anytime soon or it could refer to a process."

"That doesn't sound good either." Mitch took a big swig of his coffee. "Lukewarm. Ick."

"Techno – something else pointing to the company?" Or something more specific – as in something created by the company? I stuck that thought to the corkboard in my mind with a big shiny gold pin.

"Sounds like it," Mitch said. "That brings us to hotel and Lyon. Which we think we understand, but what about CEO?"

"He's not the CEO of Iverson Tech, is he?"

Mitch shook his head. "We co-own the company but I'm the CEO and he's the Director."

I looked at Mitch. "I'm very glad we have a CPD with you."

He nodded. "It could mean something else, could be about his abductors, not me."

"Highest ranking person ..." I just left the words sitting there all dark and ominous. And watched Mitch try to ignore them. He did well.

He moved on. "Could they be intending to travel to Australia or New Zealand?"

Antipodes suggests as much. "Looks that way."

He tapped the word 'sedation' on my page. "Drugs being used? Is that your confirmation?"

"I'd say so." We were moving closer and closer to the words I didn't want to try to explain, but first we had ponied. "Ponied."

"As in pony up ..."

"That's where I'm heading with this. To my knowledge, there has been no ransom demand. Pretty sure you would've told me if there had been and if they were after money you'd be the best starting point."

Mitch nodded. "I've heard nothing."

"Good. Then I don't think he's telling us his captors want money from him."

"What then?"

I visualized Chris and Susan in a hotel room with at

least two captors who were trying to get information, data, something, from him. Something only he could provide. Why? Because someone else wanted it. They were hired hands or maybe the hands-on part of a terror cell and someone was paying them for the information.

"Could be about the captors and whoever is paying them or whoever is willing to buy information they get from Chris."

I ran my fingers through my hair, lifting the weight of it off my neck. "Spite seems an odd word."

"Chris is probably in a position to overhear conversations. Why wouldn't he? He can't exactly repeat anything to anyone."

That in itself made me think that the end game wasn't to release Chris or Susan. Tension knotted my shoulders. That wasn't something I needed to share with Mitch. Yet. "Spite means to hurt, annoy or offend."

"Someone acting out of spite?"

"Someone who was hurt by Iverson Tech?"

Mitch recoiled. "I'd never have gone there. We're not in the business of hurting people."

Yeah, but shit happens and there are byproducts of designing tools for the military. "I don't think we can rule it out, babe. It's possible that someone was hurt by something designed by Iverson Tech." Iverson Tech is a soft target compared with going after the military.

The horror on his face spoke volumes. He didn't need to say anything. I felt the need to distract him regarding his company's potential involvement.

"Could be about the captors," I said, with a smile. "I don't think for one second that those bozos are kind, caring, and all about anything that's not in their own best interests. Maybe they're spiteful?"

The horror flittered away, came back, and then disappeared to be replaced by something I hadn't seen in a long time. Fear. I wasn't helping.

"El."

"I know. I'm sorry. I should be going over this with Delta, not with you. It's too close."

We looked at each other as Mitch's finger rested on the word Dane on the paper. "What are the chances of him talking about someone from Denmark?"

"Nil, I would've thought." But, hey, I could be wrong. I'd like to be wrong. Really like to be wrong. I don't want this to be about Squirrel.

Clenching and unclenching my jaw didn't change anything. I rubbed my temples and told myself it didn't have to be bad.

"El?"

"I know someone called Dane. He's seconded to Delta A for the time being." What did Chris have to do with the Wayward Son Protocol?

"Is his name being mentioned a bad, El?"

I didn't know how to answer that. "I hope not." The sinking feeling in my gut crushed my hope. "NSA. Chris must have a connection. I need to get to his office and his computer. Can we make that happen?"

Down the end of the hallway, a door opened and

closed. Two female voices floated down the hallway. Harley and Casey.

Harley called out, "Uncle Mitch? Ellie?"

Mitch stood up and went to the door. "In the office," he said, loud enough that she'd hear him from the living room.

I packed up everything and made sure nothing was visible to her or anyone else who came into the office. Screen savers blocked out the photos.

Chapter Twenty Two
Knockout

Mitch's dynamic duo trailed us to his office within the complex of buildings that was Iverson Technologies. We walked hand in hand through the foyer, greeted the receptionist, and made our way down the corridor to the executive offices.

I called Misha from Mitch's office. "*Privet!*" Hello.

"Ellie!"

"Anything to report?" I leaned my backside against Mitch's desk.

"I have someone from your embassy helping me. We are watching the hotel. So far, nothing."

"Nothing," I repeated. "CCTV?"

"The hotel has CCTV in the reception only. If anyone exited via one of the other doors, they would not be seen."

My heart sank. "Can you access the room again, check to see if their passports are still there?"

"Of course. Do you know something?"

"Whoever has them might be about to move them to Lyon, France."

"I notified the relevant agencies, border patrols were advised. It will make it harder for anyone to move the Iversons from Germany."

"How many countries in Europe now have no internal

borders? Is that still what's happening over there even with the upswing in terrorist activity over the last few years?"

"The Schengen Agreement? Twenty-six countries are involved. Checks are still made but passports aren't stamped."

So not entirely free movement then. "Are there other ways to cross borders without being detected?"

"Yes. Of course. People always find ways to discreetly cross borders."

"Check for me? Lyon might not be the final destination." Australia or New Zealand did require passports. If Chris was right, if it even was Chris, they'd have to get new passports or retrieve theirs from the Hamburg hotel.

"I will. I'll let you know what I find."

"*Spasibo*." Thank you.

"Wherever they are being held, they probably are kept away from public areas. Germany requires tourists be able to produce their passports when asked. That they are still in the hotel means someone took them from the hotel not from outside."

Yeah, that made sense. Phones on them but not passports. Phones. Why the phones? "Hang on a second, Misha."

I turned to Mitch. "Do Chris and Susan carry their phones on them at home? In pockets or whatever ... or do they keep them close but not on them?"

Mitch's expression hinted at a smile. "Close, not on

them usually. They might have their phones on their person when they travel because of Harley."

Good point. Maybe we don't need to worry about the missing phones. "Misha, I need you to photograph the room again and send me the images."

"I will do that, Ellie."

"*Spasibo*." The line went dead.

My phone rang as I held it. Default ring. Insistent and loud. Dane Wesson. "Agent Iverson speaking. How can I help?"

"We're at another crime scene only this time we're not alone. There's a drone buzzing around."

"How big?"

"Small. Like a small bird, sparrow, or something."

I put him on speaker and tapped Mitch's hand. "Where'd you see the drone?"

"It came inside the garage we're in."

"Can you see it now?"

"Yeah, it's out in the yard about twenty feet off the ground."

Mitch wrote on a piece of paper and handed it to me. Short range. "I'm coming, send me the address and keep an eye on it."

"You think it's got something to do with the bodies?" Squirrel said.

"Maybe." My voice dropped. "Or the media." Either way, it wasn't good news.

Squirrel texted the address and I hung up. "Could it be one of yours?" I said, pushing off the desk and propelling myself to the door.

"Yes. But other companies produce small drones. If I see it, I can tell you if it's one of ours."

I smiled. That wasn't an unexpected comment. "Come on then." I swung the door open and came face-to-face with Diego. "We're going to a crime scene. It's gonna be fun."

"Iverson, I recall your idea of fun." He shook his head and sighed. "Mitch is going too?"

I nodded. "And that means—"

"We're all going to a crime scene."

To his credit, he contained his excitement well. I might've been a little too keen to get my hands dirty and hunt the owner of the drone. There was a growing need for less cerebral investigating.

Chapter Twenty Three
Lies

Dusk edged over the sky. Police cars sat at the curb, lights rolling, red and blue flickering. Squirrel waited for me in the driveway of the latest crime scene. The cheap suit replaced with blue jeans, a green checked shirt, and a soft-looking brown leather jacket. A better fit for his personality. I glanced at his feet. Brown cowboy boots. Nice.

"Iverson," he said, looking past me to Mitch and his Close Protection Detail. "You brought friends. Awesome."

His awesome was unconvincing. "My husband is an expert in drones." I beckoned Mitch closer. "Mitch Iverson this is ..." Don't say Squirrel. My mouth formed a D eventually, " ... Dane. Dane Wesson."

They shook hands. I watched Mitch's face. He was trying to work out if Squirrel was the person Chris mentioned in the code.

One helluva coincidence that the name Dane would be mentioned right when I'd met a Dane, the only one I've ever met. Then again, it could be Dean that Chris was trying to say. I didn't know a Dean. Would be nice if whoever was involved or behind this mess, wasn't someone I knew.

"And the entourage?" Squirrel asked.

"CPD, Diego and Murray." I pointed to each in turn as I

said their names. They did a chin/eyebrow lift in response then resumed their surveillance of the area. My attention turned to the house.

Traditional style home. Mushroom-colored clapboard exterior with off-white painted trim. Manicured front lawn. Well-tended gardens. Not a weed in sight. Impressive. My own garden was more weed than plant. I decided they weren't weeds at all but self-seeded wild flowers. I'm a bee-friendly honey-hater. "Police?"

"Inside with the homeowners. They're shaken."

"Understandable. Did they call it in?"

"Yes. Lady of the house came home, zapped the garage door as she drove up, and saw the body. She called the police."

"Occupants are what age range?" Not sure it mattered but it seemed that the killer liked to use garages of the elderly, and the manicured front yard spoke of retired people to me, or maybe an employed gardener.

"Retired couple who travel a lot. Early seventies."

Squirrel and I walked up the asphalt driveway, around a car parked in front of the two-bay garage attached to the house. Mitch and Diego were just behind us with Murray bringing up the rear. Moose was inside the open garage. Squirrel paused at the doorway.

"Problem?" I said.

"It's okay to call me Squirrel," he said quietly and with a grin. "I get the reference and no one's given me a nickname before."

Oh, I bet they have but kept it to themselves.

Apparently, some people have social filters. Imagine that? "Don't get too excited, pretty much everyone ends up with a nickname from me."

Moose stood up from his crouched position by the body. "Hey. This guy comes with a drone," he said, inclining his head toward the sky outside. "It's been inside the garage twice ... by the time we saw it, we were too late to try to catch it."

"I'll get a bit closer," Mitch said, moving toward the hovering drone with Diego and Murray in tow. I noted the phone in Mitch's hand.

"Anything else?" I said, looking at the body. Head shot again. Blood and brains blown out the back of his head. Facedown. Crumpled. Awkward. Dead.

I looked at Moose, he nodded and pointed to the back of our victim's pants. "There's a concealment pouch."

"Phone?"

"Yeah, I could feel it. You wanna do the honors?"

I smiled, pulled nitrile gloves from my pocket and put them on. Reaching into the back of the victim's pants, I extracted the phone and held it up for Squirrel and Moose to see. "Another iPhone. Loving this part of the game."

"And this." Moose handed me a card in a plastic evidence bag. "Library card."

"Fascinating," I said, reading the name on the card aloud, "Jenkins Laking."

"He was FBI," Moose said. "Died in 2003."

"Lot of fresh blood for a zombie," I muttered. I checked his phone, found my way to the code, and wrote the numbers in my notebook, I figured out the next set and found the passcode. "We're in. Let's have a look and see where this zombie has been hanging out." I jumped when someone touched my arm.

Mitch chuckled. "Sorry. But you should see this." He held out the drone in his hand.

My eyebrows rose. "How?"

He showed me an app on his phone. "This little fellow is a prototype and it's ours."

"Jeez."

That was not good news.

"But, how'd you catch it and who is operating it?"

"I overrode the control. This drone still has an override. As for who ... someone with access to Iverson Tech and our drone program. They need the app. I have it on my phone. Chris has it on his phone. No one else had access."

"Range?"

"Within a mile of us."

"Chris's phone ..."

He nodded. Chris's phone was on. Mitch handed me his phone and I saw the Find Friends app running. Chris's phone was on the map and close. "Stay here," I said to Mitch. "Not in the garage. Stay with Murray and Diego." I looked at Squirrel. "With me."

He nodded.

"Babe, be safe," Mitch said.

"I will. I'm taking your phone."

Squirrel and I ran down the driveway. "My car," Squirrel said. "I'll drive, you navigate."

"Okay."

We jumped into his car. I reached for the switch and activated his grill lights.

Chapter Twenty Four

Jump In My Car

"We're close," I said, a block away from where Mitch interrupted the drone shenanigans. "Whoever has that phone is right here somewhere."

Squirrel slowed, easing the car along the street. A couple passed us, walking. We had no idea who we were looking for. I doubted whoever it was would stand out. There wouldn't be a neon flashing sign with the word Unsub on it above the house. Maybe one day GPS satellites would illuminate houses with some kind of bat signal and make our lives easier. Maybe that's something my husband's company should be developing.

Scanning the sidewalk and houses, I let the suburban vibe wash over me. The area was green, with many trees. That'd make flight tricky for a drone. The operator would need to be skilled. Probably played a lot of flight simulator games or used to operating drones and navigating via the drone camera.

"Stop," I said. "Let's try that one." I pointed to the house across the road. "Looks promising."

It was a slightly worse for wear colonial home with a two-bay garage attached. The light moss-green paint was chipped and peeling in places, revealing pink undercoat on the clapboard sidings. The garage door was tilted half open.

"Do you think the Unsub knows someone grabbed the drone and who?" Squirrel peered at the front of the house.

"Maybe."

"Then we approach with caution."

Squirrel and I approached the semi-open garage door. "Knock knock," I said, hoping my voice sounded friendly. "We're trying to find ..." I looked at Squirrel and shrugged then pulled a street name from thin air. "Brenton Point Drive? I think that's it."

A male voice echoed in the garage. "You're not even close."

"Be great if you could point us in the right direction."

The door groaned then moved. Lifting, it revealed a tidy garage space with a large workbench on one side. A man in his mid-twenties shoved a phone into his pocket before walking out of the garage. Squirrel greeted him before I could.

He stepped forward with his hand outstretched. "Hi, sorry, I'm Dane this is my wife, Ellie. She's hopeless at directions."

"Kiss my go-to-hell," I said with as much annoyance as I could muster.

Squirrel widened his eyes at me and smirked.

The young man laughed. "I get it, man." But he didn't introduce himself.

Mitch's phone hummed in my pocket. Odd. I pulled it out and looked at the screen. Find Friends flashed an alert on the screen. We were right on top of Chris's phone. I walked away a little bit so I could use my phone.

While Squirrel tried to get the young man to give directions, I called Chris's phone. Ringing came from the man's pocket.

"I better get this," he said, pulling the phone from his pocket. Confusion clouded his face as he saw the screen. I wondered what Chris had me under in his contacts list. He answered, "Hi."

"Chris?"

"Yeah."

"You don't sound like Chris," I said. "Right about now would be a good time to take stock of the situation you're in."

Squirrel's shoulders shook as he failed to contain his laughter. I walked over to the man. "Hey, whoever-you-are. You might want to say goodbye."

Shock registered as he looked from me to Squirrel as we both produced badges and held them up.

Curious to see what the call came up as on Chris's phone, I extracted the phone from the man's hand. My brother-in-law had a sense of humor. The call was from Lily Rush. I hung up. It was hard to suppress my delight at being the main character from *Cold Case*. Good choice. Too clever for the idiot in front of us, though, or maybe he was too young?

"And you are?" Squirrel asked, grabbing the man by the wrist and spinning him so he could snap cuffs on him.

"No one." He grunted as the second steel bracelet closed on his other wrist.

"Did you lose something this evening?" Squirrel gave him a small shove in the middle of his back, toward the house. "Where's the drone you were playing with?"

Nightfall fast overtook the dusk, throwing long shadows over the area. Security lighting flickered then flooded the area near the garage with yellow light.

He shrugged. "It didn't come back."

"Who lives here?" I stepped up beside Squirrel, who marched the man-with-no-name to the front door of the house.

"No one," he replied.

I phoned Mitch and told him I had Chris's phone in my possession. Then I called for backup.

Squirrel knocked three times on the front door. We waited. Nothing. He knocked again.

Nothing.

"I'll go around the back," I said and hurried away.

Darkness crept after me. Security lighting popped on as I moved with care on the wide plant-edged pathway that led from the front of the house to the back, where a soft glow of electric lighting emanated from the porch light on the back of the house. A shadow moved in a window. I knocked on the wooden back door and waited.

Sounds of movement filtered through the closed door.

I knocked again. This time the movement noise was purposeful. A shadow appeared behind the glass. I took a breath and stepped sideways. Just in case. My heart pounded in my throat.

The door handle dropped and the door swung inward.

An aged female voice said, "Hello?"

I moved into the brighter porch light and smiled. "Hello, sorry to disturb you. I'm FBI Special Agent Ellie Iverson, and you are?" I showed my badge to the elderly woman wearing a lilac leisure suit.

"Mrs. Daniel Shivers," she replied.

"Do you have a young man staying with you by the name of Chris?"

She peered at my ID and badge then at my face. "I have a young man visiting with me. His name isn't Chris."

"What is his name?"

"Nathan. Nathan Moffat. He's staying with me for a week while he attends a men's study program."

Studying in Reston. Studying? My brain buzzed. "What is he studying?"

"How to better serve God and mankind," she replied with a small smile.

Serving God and mankind would be admirable if he hadn't had Chris's cell phone on him and if I hadn't come across the terms ethnology and theology in connection with Chris and his disappearance. "Is anyone else in the house?"

"No. My husband passed five years ago." She crossed herself. "Come in, won't you, Ellie, is it?" I nodded. "I'm fixin' dinner and I hear boiling on the stove top."

She turned and walked back into the kitchen, I followed her inside, closing the door behind me. I gave Squirrel a quick call. "I'm inside, come around the back with Nathan."

"Be there in a few."

I hung up and watched Mrs. Shivers lift the lid off a pot of boiling water. Smelled starchy, like potatoes cooking. Steam curled toward the ceiling. She flipped a switch on the wall. The steam changed direction, sucked from the air. Another pot lid jiggled. She tilted that one and the noise stopped. Green swirled, breaking the surface of the boiling water. Beans.

"Mrs. Shivers, how well do you know Nathan?"

"Not very well. He's a nice enough boy."

"Why is he staying with you?"

"I belong to the church, we have the young men studying at the center stay with members of the congregation." Her smile revealed newish-looking false teeth.

Made sense. Hide the little fuckers in the community with elderly folk where no one will notice them. "It's very nice of you to open your home to a stranger. Do you do it often?"

"You have a lot of questions, young lady." Her smile slipped off her shiny teeth. "Is there something I should know about young Nathan?"

A rap on the back door alerted me to Squirrel's presence. Mrs. Shivers started to move.

"It's my partner and your house guest," I said. "I'll let them in?"

"Thank you," she said and sat heavily on a kitchen chair. "Such a lot of questions and fuss."

I opened the door. Nathan didn't look too happy. With

a smile on my face and in my voice, I said, "Nathan, how good of you to join us."

He said nothing. His expression hardened as Squirrel encouraged him through the door.

Mrs. Shivers looked at Nathan and then Squirrel. "Has Nathan done something wrong?"

Squirrel introduced himself, "I'm Special Agent Dane Wesson, ma'am. And yes, he has."

Disappointment flooded her face, setting her mouth in a grim line. "Nathan. What have you done?" She pushed herself up from the table and scuttled over to the counter. "We can't have this."

My gut tweaked.

Mrs. Shivers opened a kitchen drawer. Her hand closed around something.

In a blink I had my weapon in hand. "No!"

She angled her body toward me.

Silver. Gun.

"Mrs. Shivers. Put down the gun."

"He's a stupid boy," she said. Vitriol cascaded from her words. She held the gun in a two-handed grip pointed at Nathan. Her index finger locked on the trigger.

Dammit, God, don't make me shoot an old woman. "Lower the weapon!"

Her old washed-out eyes steeled. The grim line of her mouth set as if in stone.

Squirrel shoved Nathan out the kitchen door into the hallway. Unable to stop himself, he fell head first into the wall. The thud shook the floor.

Mrs. Shivers swung her gun to me.

"Lower the weapon!"

Her finger moved.

I squeezed the trigger. A crack from next to me told me Squirrel had fired, too.

Mrs. Shivers lived up to her name and froze. The gun tumbled from her hands, smashing into the tiled floor, followed by the slow-motion crumpling of the old woman. Vomit filled my mouth. I stepped over the woman's outstretched arm, grabbed the sink edge for support, turned on the faucet, and retched into the sink until spots danced before my eyes.

"You okay?" Squirrel crouched near the woman's body, checking for a pulse.

Booted feet sounded on the path outside the kitchen window. Seconds later a booming voice filled the house. "FBI!"

I looked at Squirrel and nodded. "That's Sam."

"Sam, it's clear! We're in the kitchen," Squirrel called.

Heavy footsteps thundered into the kitchen. "Chicky Babe?"

"We're okay," I replied, as Sam took stock of the scene in the room.

"What the hell happened?"

"Squirrel and Moose found a drone at another crime scene. We tracked it back to here." Sort of. "Found Nathan, the unconscious guy in the hallway with Chris Iverson's phone. The old lady, Mrs. Shivers, was apparently billeting Nathan while he studied ... she pulled a gun from the kitchen drawer and when prevented from shooting Nathan, decided shooting at us was smart." It really wasn't.

Vomit rose again. I spun back to the sink and puked until there was nothing but foam coming up.

I was right. Chris Iverson had something to do with the dead previously dead agents.

Chapter Twenty Five

Come on up to our house

"Where is Nathan?" I spun my chair until I faced Sam who sat on the sofa in my office.

"In an interview room," he said, reading something on his phone. It held his interest, so I waited.

Just as I started to wonder where this new-found patience originated, Sam looked up. "And?" I said, meeting his gaze.

"That old woman liked to lurk on Darknet." He waggled his phone. "Sandra sent me a report from the old woman's computer."

Before I could check it, I'd channeled my very much alive father. "Well butter my butt and call me a biscuit."

Sam's eyebrows danced with amusement. "One of your dad's?"

I followed a nod with a half-assed shrug. "Did we find anything out from her Darknet-loving ways?"

"Not much. She answered an advert on a Darknet religious page asking for God-fearing folk to billet young men, the so-called Foot Soldiers of God."

"I thought she was doing that through the local church … I didn't know about the Foot Soldiers. That is most definitely something, dude." And not for the first time I considered this was some kind of terror cell behavior.

"Mrs. Shivers used her own name on the site."

"Doesn't surprise me. Anything about the Foot Soldier of God movement?"

"Screeds."

"Reader's Digest version, go."

"Their mission statement is to bring back Christian values, through the practice and acceptance of a patriarchal society."

"Already they scare me."

Sam laughed. "Me too, Chicky Babe, me too."

"What else?"

Sam blew out a sigh. "The ad was placed by an anonymous user. We have nada on the origin. Nothing we can find connects Nathan to any other crime scenes."

That didn't surprise me.

"Also," Sam said. "Nathan didn't know the victim. They'd never met before."

"Why'd he put a drone up and how did he get his hands on an Iverson prototype?"

"Why he put the drone up ... because he's an idiot and he wanted to watch the body being found and the aftermath."

"Ah, he's a perv." A perv with my brother-in-law's phone. "How'd he get the drone and the phone?"

"Sounds like a question for Dr. Seuss," Sam said with a deep throaty chuckle. "I do not like the man with the drone. I do not like his stolen phone. I do not like his stinky cologne. I am Sam, I have a plan, to make the man atone."

I high-fived Sam. "All right Sam with a plan, where'd

Nathan get the phone and the drone?"

"Mrs. Shivers, according to him."

"How'd she get her hands on that stuff?"

"There is a message on the site she used, saying a courier would drop a package to her and that she was to give it to the young man when he arrived." Sam read down the page then looked at me. "He'll know why. She was instructed not to touch or open the package. Her place was to cook and take care of him."

"Charming."

"It gets better. Underneath her instructions was an addendum stating that if Nathan drew unwanted attention, then she must absolve him of his sins and send him to God."

My eyebrows rose. "Good grief."

"Not grandma material."

"Nope." Not even close to being grandma material. "Get someone to turn that house inside out, I want the courier bag the equipment came in or anything that points to which courier company it was."

"Consider it done, Chicky. I'll get back to you."

"This is a mess, Sam."

Sam didn't disagree. He walked over to the small fridge and took two bottles of water from it, twisted the top open on one and handed it to me before opening his. "We're good with messes, it's what we do."

Doesn't feel like we're making much progress with this particular mess, though. Every turn brings another dead end or more death. "I didn't know Chris had a drone with him. He omitted to mention to his brother he was leaving the country with a prototype. So I didn't know it was missing."

"Why is he in Europe?"

"Vacation perhaps. Maybe he's combining work with pleasure."

"I'm going back to talk to Nathan." Sam downed half his bottle of water in one long pull. "That drone probably had a purpose, I doubt it was to spy on the happenings at Nathan's first kill."

"Good thinking, Kemosabe." I took a few decent gulps of water. "I'll talk to Mitch about the drone."

Chapter Twenty Six

Born Again Tomorrow

I stood in the middle of my office and tried to envisage the walls another color. Anything but off-white. Time for a change. Something new, fresh, and not prone to shadows.

Turning on the spot, I searched the walls for any hint of the dragonfly I thought I'd seen minutes earlier. Five floors up. Windows shut. Night had long since blanketed the city. How the hell would a dragonfly get into my office?

Walking to the window, I looked past my reflection and into the night. Flickering Lights. Deep dark doorways. Traffic lights. People moving on the street below. What else that could account for the dual-winged shadow I saw on the wall? The air around me chilled as I considered it could've been a drone.

A light rapping caught my attention. Turning, Sandra poked her head around the door frame. "Gracey is at the front desk."

"Pardon?"

"Gracey. Front desk."

The muscles in my forehead tensed. Gracey? I only knew one Gracey. "From Grange?"

Sandra nodded. "She'll only talk to you and said it's important."

Of course. Everything is always important. A vice tightened around my head, squeezing. "A-1 free?"

"Yes. Shall I tell the desk to show her through?"

"Please."

Sandra smiled and left. It'd been a long time since I'd seen Gracey. Intrigue piled on a plate in my mind with a small portion of I-don't-wanna on the side. The last time I saw her ...

I couldn't even remember the last time. Well before Rowan Grange, my then boyfriend, and I very publicly parted company. Another shadow on the wall tweaked the corner of my eye. Gossamer wings. I blinked. The shadow vanished.

Footsteps came closer. I listened, I knew those footfalls. Two more strides and he'd be level with my open door. Kurt swung into the doorway. "Okay?" he said, leaning on the door jam.

"Yeah. Ever think maybe these walls could do with being another color?"

"Not a fan of off-white, Iverson?"

"Not so much."

"All right, I'll play. What's up? This isn't about wall color ... I know you."

I rested on the edge of my desk and chewed my bottom lip. Yes, he did know me. "Gracey from Grange wants to see me downstairs."

"Been a while since we've heard from anyone from Grange." His eyes darkened. "You want some company?"

My head nodded before the words came. "Yes. I. Do."

A rumble of discontent rattled within me. Gracey. What the hell? I couldn't imagine how her wanting to see me was good. Worst-case scenarios vied for my attention.

"We going?" Kurt asked, taking a step toward me.

I pushed off my desk and met him in the middle of the room. "Yeah, of course." I walked out the door ahead of him, smoothing away the frown I felt in my forehead with pure willpower.

"Penny for them, Iverson." he said and pulled the door shut behind us.

"Don't think they're worth it."

"How about we go find out what brought Gracey to our building before you start concocting horror scenes in your mind?"

He did know me. "Elevator," I said before Kurt opened the stairwell door.

"Mixing it up, Iverson."

The agent at the front desk looked up as we alighted from the elevator. "Agents," he said then paused. "Agent Iverson, your guest is in A-1," he said and went back to whatever he was looking at on the screen in front of him.

"Thanks." I don't know if he heard me; it didn't really matter. With a deep breath, I pressed the door handle and pushed the door open fighting a feeling of disquiet. "Gracey?"

She was staring at a painting of the Chesapeake Bay on the wall; she turned and met my greeting with a smile. "Thanks for seeing me."

"Of course. What's going on?" I motioned to the couch.

Grace sat and twisted a ring on her right ring finger then moved onto fiddling with her watch on her left wrist. As she let the watch strap alone, she moved back to the ring. "It's Rowan," she said. Trepidation filled her eyes and spilled over her lashes.

I handed her the tissue box on the table. "What about Rowan?"

She balled a tissue up in her hand. More ring twisting and watch tormenting followed. I waited.

"He's missing."

Missing? "There's been nothing in the media ..." I looked at Kurt for confirmation that I hadn't missed anything vital in that regard. He shook his head.

"His publicist and manager don't want the media involved."

Of course they didn't. Nothing's changed then. "Where's Jed?" I knew Rowan's head of security; if anyone needed to raise the alarm, it should've been him. I glanced around the room in case he was hidden in a corner.

"He's back at the house. He asked me to come here." She fumbled in her jacket pocket and pulled out a piece of paper. "It's from Jed." She handed an envelope to me but I didn't know Jed well enough to recognize his writing on the front.

Why couldn't he pick up a phone and call me? I slipped a finger into the corner of the envelope and slit the paper. I widened the gap but decided not to pull out the contents. Gloves.

Kurt opened a cupboard in the corner of the room and took out a box of latex gloves. "Here," he said and dropped a pair of the gloves into my outstretched hand.

"Thanks."

"Why?" Gracey said as the second glove snapped against my wrist.

"Why didn't he call me or why the gloves?"

Her eyebrows knitted together in a frown. "Why everything."

Opting to address my glove comment, because that was the easy question, I said, "This could be evidence, that's why the gloves."

My gloved fingers ventured into the envelope and extracted the white paper. I felt the thickness between my finger and thumb: copier paper. Nothing out of the ordinary. Every office had printer paper or copier paper. I recognized the handwriting as Rowan's. My vision blurred. I refocused. My eyes skimmed over the paper and stole a look at Gracey. She didn't know it was from Rowan. "Why did Jed ask you to come see me?"

She attempted a smile but it fell short of her eyes and vanished. "He said I'd attract less attention than the head of Grange's security team rocking into FBI HQ."

Of course. They can downplay Gracey's appearance as an old friend in town wanting to catch up. But Jed sauntering through the doors would spark media scrutiny. Guess no one wanted that.

"Give me a minute to read this." I shook the paper in my hand. "Then we'll talk some more."

Dear El, sorry in advance, I imagine I'm the last person you expect or want to hear from. The only reason you'd be reading this is because something has gone wrong and I need your help. I left this letter with Jed in May because of an escalating situation. If you deem this to be serious then you'll probably need access to my laptop. Remember the last song?

I stopped reading for a minute. The last song? The last song we wrote together or the last song he wrote for me? What is it with everyone and their cryptic clues?

Earlier this year I started getting email from a fan, not unusual as you probably remember, and of course, I didn't answer the woman. The emails increased in frequency and content. Not much unusual in that either. You know what fan fiction is, right? This woman was concocting fantastic scenarios and publishing the stories on Tumblr and sending links to my publicist. Fans can get a bit intense sometimes. She posted a bunch of photoshopped images of her and me. Jed deconstructed the images, originally they were photos of you and me, but not photos I'd seen before. Then she started telling people I was going to marry her. Jed was concerned enough that he tracked her down and the lawyers handled her. It was all quiet for a few months and then I started getting letters addressed to Mrs. Grange care of my New York apartment – my mail is forwarded to the country estate. Jed investigated and found the woman was living in my apartment as my wife. I'm not married. That's you caught up. And something has happened to me, otherwise you wouldn't have this letter. Find me, El. The name of the woman posing as my wife is Christina Goretti.

I skimmed the information included after her name. He seemed pretty certain that this Christina Goretti person had something to do with me getting the letter. The last thing he wrote in the letter was 'I'd like to buy you a quad espresso when I come home.' A smile filtered through my unease and grasped the meaning of the words. The last song we wrote together was called 'Coming Home' and it spoke of quad espressos.

I handed the letter to Kurt and stood up. Wearing a track in the industrial carpet somehow soothed me and helped me think. I felt Gracey watching me as I paced and sensed her worry and confusion.

"El. Photos?" Kurt said halting me in my tracks.

"Guess they're on his laptop."

He nodded. "His timing isn't spectacular."

His timing was shit. Not the first happenstance this week that sucked out loud and gave change. Not the first time this week someone I knew had gone missing. He was lucky number four in the missing persons' stakes. One home, three to find.

That I knew them all felt hinky on a grand scale. I looked at Kurt. He shook his head as if he knew what I was thinking. "Gracey, when did you last see Rowan?"

"Yesterday afternoon."

I watched Gracey twist her ring. "Tell me what happened before he disappeared."

Kurt poured her a glass of water and placed it on the coffee table in front of her.

"We'd been recording in the studio for the best part of a month. Long days, long nights. About lunchtime yesterday, we finished putting down the last track on the album."

"Which studio?" I had visions of some swanky studio in New York.

"Rowan's studio at the house."

Ah, the country estate.

I dragged up memories of the grounds and house; I'd never liked being there after Carla died. She had loved it and spent a lot of time with Rowan Grange in the country because I was chasing killers and doing other non-family orientated stuff.

Kurt caught my sadness and intervened before it took hold. "What happened after you finished the last track?"

"The housekeeper called and said lunch was ready. Rowan told her we'd be there in a few minutes and would eat on the patio. He said we needed fresh air." Gracey smiled. "He was right. We'd been holed up day and night and needed to see the sun."

"Did you all walk over together?"

"We left the studio together. Rowan said he'd catch up, he wanted to stretch his legs. I said I'd go with him but he said he wouldn't be long and we should go ahead and eat. So I walked with Tony, Derek, and Martin. We went through the front door and out to the patio. Lunch was set out. We all settled in and ate. He never turned up.

After lunch, we all went for a walk to the stables to see the horses. I thought maybe Rowan was there. He wasn't."

"Rowan went for a walk on his own property and never came back?" She nodded. Okay. It's a large property.

The main house alone could house half the State. Then there were the recording studio, stables, staff quarters, six-car garage, and indoor swimming pool. Tennis courts. Expansive. Set amidst fields with a tree-lined driveway. The whole place felt secluded and calm.

What else was there? Hazards? A small man-made lake? Lake or large pond? Body of water. The horses. Guess they could be termed a hazard. "You searched for him?"

"Yes. No sign of him. No cars missing, no motorbikes missing, all the horses accounted for."

"No one heard anything? Car in the driveway?"

"No. Have you heard from him?" She appeared hopeful.

"I haven't heard from him in a long time." Not since I told him to fuck off. Not since I found out he'd cheated on me. Who does that to an FBI agent? An idiot that's who. "His parents?"

"They've heard nothing as far as I know."

"Is he missing, Gracey, or is he with someone?" I wanted to know if she knew about the crazy stalker or maybe if he was seeing someone.

Anger flashed like lightning. "You too? That's been everyone's response."

Interesting. Not Jed's though. "Jed?"

"He's worried."

"Where was he when Rowan wandered off?"

"Don't know."

Kurt leaned forward rested his arms on his legs. "What do you think happened, Gracey?"

"I don't know. But I think it's bad."

I stood and moved towards the door. Time was fleeting and many things required my attention. "We'll make some inquiries. Is his manager still the same person?"

Gracey nodded.

Damn. We weren't exactly friends. "Who knows you're here?"

"The boys and Jed." She stood up and wiped her hands down the thighs of her jeans.

"I'll be in touch," I said, trying not to sound dismissive. "If you hear anything or think of anything, call me. If I don't answer fast enough, text or call Kurt. You have our numbers?"

She didn't seem entirely sure. I handed her one of my cards. Kurt passed her one of his.

"Thanks, Ellie. Kurt." She shoved the cards in her jeans pocket. "Congratulations," she said, pointing to my wedding bands. "Hope you're very happy."

I smiled and all the tension vanished. "We are. Thanks." Mitch's voice filled my head confirming my affirmation.

Kurt showed Gracey out then met me at the elevator. "Are they worth a penny now?"

I pressed the up arrow twice because that makes elevators hurry. Not. "Perhaps." The elevator dinged. We stepped in and the doors closed. Sealing us in the moving steel coffin. "Did Rowan vanish without a trace? Was he taken? Has he gone off with someone for some R&R?"

"You knew him quite well. Which is it?"

"I want to say he's off with a lady friend but I have a horrible feeling he's been abducted and not necessarily by the crazy pretend-wife."

We exited the elevator at our floor and walked in silence down the corridor to my office.

"Could your thoughts be clouded by recent events?" Kurt held the door open for me.

"Absolutely."

Kurt smiled. I brushed past him and settled behind my desk.

"Let's stick with the facts."

Agreed.

"What do we actually know?" I opened my laptop and placed my phone on my desk.

Kurt pulled his chair closer. "That Rowan thought the crazy woman could act on her fantasies more than she had already. That he's the fourth person to disappear without a ransom demand."

My head shook and eyes widened. "We can't put him in the mix when it comes to Chris, Susan, and Harley. It's not the same thing at all."

Kurt arched an eyebrow at me. "You're sure?"

"Aren't you?" Seeds of doubt I did not need

"At this point, we can't rule it out."

Why the hell not? "Chris Iverson, software engineer/ Iverson Tech co-owner, has nothing to do with Rowan Grange, rock star/philanthropist."

"Again, you are certain?"

"I knew Grange pretty well once. He's not the techiest guy ever. As far as Grange knows Java is coffee and C# is a musical note. He's a songwriter and a musician, I doubt they'd cross paths."

"Are you deliberately ignoring the link?"

"The what now?"

"The common denominator. What do Rowan Grange and the Iverson family have in common?"

"Nope. Not me. This is not about me. Harley's abductor didn't know about me, so I doubt Chris and Susan's did either." Although that may have changed now.

"Time frame?"

"Chris and Susan, then Harley, then Rowan twenty-four hours ago."

I watched Kurt's mind working. It was his job to play devil's advocate, however silly it seemed to me.

"Is it possible ... whoever grabbed C and S needed more leverage?"

"I guess it's not impossible." CPD teams rendered Harley and Mitch much more difficult targets. The parents? "Why not make a play for the parents? Rowan isn't that easy."

Kurt looked up from his iPad. "Yeah, he is. That crazy

chick is documented. Rowan posted photos from within the studio on several social media sites. I just grabbed them and the location information is intact."

Oh, man. "He must've got a new phone, I had location turned off on his previous phone."

"What's security like at the country place?"

"From memory, relaxed."

"I'm not saying someone's used this information to get to him or that it's connected. I'm saying let's keep that in mind."

"It's what we'd do. If you and I went to the dark side, we'd use location info, we'd use anyone we could get our hands on." I took a breath and looked at Kurt. "We'd use soft targets that people wouldn't immediately connect." And my brain kicked into high gear. "Taking people to apply pressure to me will only have a shot at working if I know about it and know what they want." But taking Rowan ... if all else fails, they could ransom him for millions.

"Yes."

"I don't – I have speculation and assumptions. There's been no contact or demands made of me."

"What was it you told me once? That family and friends are the Achilles' heel of life as an agent."

True. "In this instance, I have nothing anyone could want."

"We can debate this all day. I just want you to broaden your scope on this case and accept it could be something to do with you."

I'm not buying that today. It really doesn't seem like anything to do with me. My phone rang. The screen lit with Caine's grumpy face. "Caine?"

"Have you seen Owen around tonight?"

"No." Thank you, God.

"Thanks. Everything okay your end?"

"Sure."

With a grumble, he hung up.

My gut writhed and contorted. I didn't need Owen popping up to confuse things with her special brand of helpfulness. Pushing her aside, I reflected on my Achilles' heel.

"Iverson?" Kurt leaned over, his hands flat on my desk. "Problem?"

Conclusion jumping seemed akin to puddle jumping in sneakers: a quick way to spend a day miserable with cold, wet feet. Not on my favorite things list. "Let's see if we can track down the crazy woman and then we can move on."

"Sounds like a good plan."

At that moment Squirrel barreled through my door clutching a manila folder.

"Can I help you?" I asked. His uncharacteristic haste amused me more than it should.

"Two more dead formerly dead agents. A flag alerted us."

"Current names or former names?"

"Former."

"How is someone finding these agents? And how is it

that some of them are popping up with their previous names attached?"

Squirrel dropped the folder on the desk in front of me. "Whoever it is must have a list of names or a database."

"And something like that would exist on our servers, wouldn't it?"

He nodded. "We don't have access to a list like that. Wayward Son Protocol has no list attached. It's reactive. Requiring a flag to alert us to a potential problem."

Guess the unasked question was obvious. I smiled. "Okay, but someone does."

"You can bet on that."

We stared at each other for a beat. Every ounce of me wanted this to be external not something on the inside.

Chapter Twenty Seven

Free Fallin'

Footsteps resounded in the corridor outside my office. They passed. I went back to my task. They returned. I waited. They paused. The pacing continued. A loud sigh escaped. My jaw clenched and released.

Jeez!

The pacing continued. Distracting.

Two minutes later, I shoved my chair back and jumped to my feet bellowing, "Come in!" at the closed door. The handle turned. The door inched open. "Get in here!" Excruciating. Planting my palms on my desk, I leaned forward trying to see who was behind the door.

An unsure looking Lee came into view. "Chicky ..."

"Are you kidding me? What the hell was that pacing out there?" I slumped back into my chair with a sigh.

"Sorry. It's ... um ..."

Lost for words? Really? "Spit it out Lee, this ..." I flapped a hand at him, " ... is not like you at all." A wave of worry crashed over my desk, foaming white caps covered my laptop then disappeared.

He shut the door and walked toward my desk. I saw a courier pack in his right hand. His brow creased, shoulders sagged. Everything in front of me pointed to something bad. A voice in my head said 'No sense getting too giggly too quick.' Yeah. It might be nothing. Another voice laughed like a hyena.

He dropped the courier pack on my desk with a light clunk. I stared at it without touching it. Addressed to me. It was no bigger than a regular envelope. Reaching into my drawer, I took out a pair of scissors. "Who sent it?"

"Don't know for sure. Doesn't say."

"X-rayed?" He nodded. Good, that meant the chance of it going bang was slim.

"Chicky, I think ... that's Noel Gerrard's handwriting."

That explained the behavior. Last time any of us heard from Retired NCIS Special Agent Noel Gerrard, he was in big trouble and had gone to ground.

I looked at the scissors in my hand and the package. My mind reeled with the last conversation I had with Noel Gerrard. He said if anything happened to him, I'd get a package and to sanitize it before telling his mom. None of me wanted to think about why I'd received the package. Denial seemed the best option. Life as an ostrich looked like a viable way to live my life from here on out. "What's in it?"

"Mailroom said a key."

I slit the end of the bag with the scissors and tipped the contents onto my desk. A note and a door key. Well, they were right. I read the note to Lee, "Wish I could send you a bouquet of a dozen roses. Stay frosty." Since when would Gerrard ever send me flowers? Let alone a dozen roses? Twelve. Bouquet.

The words collided and pulled together pictures of Gerrard and things I knew about him until I settled on one image. The two of us, drinking Scotch, and watching a movie. I Googled the twelfth Bond film. *For Your Eyes Only*. IMDb was next to check the cast list. Carole Bouquet.

So it was that movie. Would be nice if people would just say what they mean outright. This cryptic stuff is tiring.

"Do you think ...?"

"Looks that way," I replied, reading the note again. "He doesn't say what the key unlocks."

Lee started to speak then stopped. I looked at him. He pulled up a chair and sat down, head in hands.

For your eyes only. Well, that's something right there. Did he mean the movie or a song? I read the logline. Agent 007 is assigned to hunt for a lost British encryption device and prevent it from falling into enemy hands. Didn't feel like that was what he was trying to tell me, but, I'd keep it in mind. The song then.

I found the lyrics to Sheena Easton's 'For your eyes only' and a YouTube clip of the song, I played the song and read the lyrics. By the time I was done, I had a place to start.

"How did you get from, 'Wish I could send you a bouquet of a dozen roses' to Sheena Easton?" Lee asked.

"A code of sorts. A dozen is twelve. Last time we watched a movie together, it was *For Your Eyes Only*, that's the twelfth Bond movie."

"Okay."

I continued my explanation. "He confirmed that he

meant that title by the bouquet reference. Carole Bouquet played Melina Havelock. The log line for the movie didn't dredge anything up, so I figured he meant the song."

Lee's eyes met mine. "You're sure?"

"Oh, yeah."

"Can we hear it again?" Lee dropped his hands to his knees and leaned forward. "It's something, isn't it?"

I nodded and wrote all the lyrics on a yellow legal pad before hitting play again. We knew each other well. My dad trained Gerrard. My mind mulled over the lyrics. What better way to tell me something, than with a song? No one else would get it. It's not a code just anyone could crack, you'd have to think like me. And as Gerrard told me often, no one thinks like me.

And here he was telling me in a song that I could see what no one else could and how well I knew him. He was right, I didn't need to read between the lines. I knew what the key unlocked and exactly where it was. Where his passions collided. I saw the river and the cabin he told me about. Fishing and hunting.

"Road trip," I said, shoving the key in my pocket, and sliding my holster onto my belt.

Maybe getting out of the city would help clear my head. It needed clearing. Dead agents. Missing family members. Owen. Squirrel and Moose. A missing rock star. The elephant in the room. My mind definitely needed clearing. And somehow I knew Gerrard was mixed up in something and that something had spilled into our laps.

"Where?"

"You'll see."

"Mysterious."

"Nothing wrong with a bit of mystery."

It was an hour and a half away, two hours on a bad day or in traffic. I checked my watch. Ten-thirty. Traffic was less of an issue mid-morning.

"Kurt and Sam?"

"Where are they?"

I checked the charge on my phone. Sixty per cent; I could charge it in the car. Then skirted around Lee to get my go-bag from the cupboard in the corner. I didn't think we'd be gone overnight but being prepared never hurt anyone. I would've been an excellent scout.

"Kurt is in the bullpen and Sam was last seen talking to Sandra."

That figures, they have a wedding to plan. "Get your gear, Lee. And let them know we are out of the office for the rest of the day, they can come if they'd like."

"You know they will."

Yep. Retired or not, Noel Gerrard was family and Delta A always makes time for family.

Lee put the chair back and left.

I called Mitch at work. "Hey, I'm heading outta State for a few hours. Should be home for dinner, but let's eat late, okay?"

"New case?"

"More curiosity, I'll let you know if it develops into a full-blown case." Something in the song, and the way

Gerrard made contact, triggered twinges in my gut that said it was a case but it wasn't new.

"Intriguing."

"I'm all about the intrigue. Remind the teenager that her CPD must stay with her." I said with a small laugh. "Three things." Love. Want. Need.

"Three things, baby. Be extra careful out there."

I hung up smiling. There was a good chance Gerrard was dead. I was smiling and carrying on as normal. That wasn't right. Why wasn't I upset?

I stared at the dragonfly painting on my wall. Iridescent wings against a blue backdrop. Gerrard gave it to me. No, he didn't give it to me. He sent it to me.

It was the last communication we'd had and it was one-sided. I never thanked him because I never got a chance. I hung it on the wall and looked at it every day. The colors exuded life as they danced from the wings. I always thought I'd know if he was dead, that maybe the painting would change. Now that's something that shouldn't be allowed breathing space.

The last words he said to me were: "Sanitize my life before telling my mom what happened."

I flexed my right hand. It still ached some days. Every time it ached I wondered if Gerrard really was Tierney's target. Every time my gut roiled I knew he was, and I was glad I'd smashed my knuckles on the guy Tierney chose to do his wet work. That day was the final straw and the end of a long mutually beneficial relationship with the CIA.

So why wasn't I upset about the potential death of Retired NCIS Special Agent Noel Gerrard?

Because my whole being said Gerrard wasn't dead. I wasn't just going to find out what the key opened. I was going to bring him home. I swallowed hard. My inner Pollyanna wouldn't let negativity take over but reality was insidious. I adjusted my thinking. One way or another, he was coming home.

Kurt walked through my open door. "You all right?"

"Yep."

"You think it's really from Gerrard?"

"Yes."

"You're staring at the dragonfly painting like it holds answers." Kurt took a step closer to me and faced the picture.

"Maybe it does. Gerrard sent it to me."

"Butterflies are supposedly the souls of the dead, right?"

"Yeah."

"When you said you saw butterflies in strange places I figured it was something to do with Mac or Carla." Kurt shoved his hands in his pockets. "What does the dragonfly mean to you?"

"Change, transformation, adaptability." I felt more questions, but before he could ask I offered an explanation. "I always saw butterflies, I associated them with Mac. A little while after Carla died, I was in a scary situation with Mike Davenport, Lee's brother. I watched a dragonfly chase a butterfly away. It happened a few times after that, until one day the butterfly was gone, and the dragonflies stayed. Always felt like a lesson. You adapt, or you stagnate."

"You're full of surprises, Iverson."

"So you like to tell me, Henderson."

"And you're okay?"

"Apparently."

His head tipped toward the go-bag on the front of my desk. "Good thinking. No telling what we'll find."

Gerrard, that's what we'll find. "You ready?"

"Sam and Lee are briefing Sandra on our impending absence. Just need to get my bag on the way out."

"Let's do this thing."

"What about the gruesome twosome?" Kurt asked, closing my office door behind us.

A laugh caught me by surprise. I was rubbing off on him. Usually me that comes up with nicknames for people. "I'll call Squirrel and Moose when we're on our way. They can carry on here." They had two more deaths to investigate, that'd keep them busy while we ducked out for a bit.

"Is whatever Gerrard is involved in related to the rest of this murk?"

"I think so."

Kurt stopped walking and turned toward me. "Are you kidding? You think Gerrard could have something to do with the deaths of agents?"

"Yeah, but not in a hands-on kinda way." My fingers crossed. I hoped not. Felt to me like he was caught up in something, not behind it, or causing deaths. *X-Files* theme music filled my head: we're not so different from Scully and Mulder, we all hunt monsters. Monsters are real. The music switched to the theme for *Supernatural*. Maybe we're not so different from Sam and Dean either.

Chapter Twenty Eight

Hello

The occasional green running man signage, pointing to stairwells or elevators, broke the monotony of the battleship-grey parking garage walls. Kurt and I strode across the polished concrete floor to the Delta A parking area. Four black Suburbans in a row. I pressed a button on the fob in my hand. Brake lights and indicators flashed on the car closest to me. Kurt and I put our bags in the back. Lights flashed next to my car. Sam and Lee were stowing gear. We'd chosen to take two. In case ... I stopped.

Preconceived notions have a way of backfiring. Open mind.

"Chuck the keys, Iverson," Kurt said, standing by the driver's door.

He snatched them from mid-air and climbed into the car. He didn't know where we were going. I opened the front passenger door and stood on the running board and grinned at Lee over the roof. "Follow close."

"You got it, Chicky," he said with a grin. "In case we get separated?"

"Harpers Ferry."

"Be right behind you. Radio or cell?"

"Neither, unless it's unavoidable and then cell."

I didn't want anything regarding Gerrard or our destination to hit the airways. If he were alive, then he was still a target and I had no intention of leading anyone to him.

We'd left Washington before Kurt said anything. "The Potomac starts up there."

"Yep."

I knew he was thinking about the bodies fished out of the Chesapeake Bay and how one was an NCIS agent. I was pretty sure they'd come down the Anacostia but all rivers lead to Chesapeake, so maybe not.

"We've got time for you to tell me why we are going to Harpers Ferry and what is it you think we'll find."

I felt the key in my pocket. "Answers."

"And the questions?"

Oh, come on, really? I glanced at him. He appeared relaxed. No white-knuckle grip on the steering wheel or jaw clenching. "First, I'd like to know what led to the delivery of a key to me."

"His death, Iverson. That could be it."

"Perhaps. I'd also like to know where Gerrard's been, and what put him on Tierney's radar, and why he disappeared without reaching out. Even for him, this is unusual."

He might have known ahead of time something bad was going to happen because he sold his house before disappearing. That spoke to me of forward planning and having a fair bit of time up his sleeve before whatever it was that sent him underground happened.

Plenty of time to reach out to me, or Dad, or his old team. Yet, he didn't. Or maybe it was a coincidence. I had a hard time believing that Gerrard was a bad guy. It was way up there with thinking O'Hare had something to do with the driver's license found on Simonsson's body.

"A key? Nothing else?"

"A note saying he wished he could buy me flowers."

"Iverson ..."

"Henderson?" I didn't feel like explaining.

Kurt let out a long slow sigh. "Code?"

"Yeah." Always with the codes. I tugged my phone from my pocket and called Squirrel.

"Agent Iverson."

"I'm heading out of State with Delta. You two can carry on here, yeah?"

"Sure. We're on scene at one of the new homicides. Once we're clear here, we'll follow up the Masons."

Excellent. But I didn't think that was actually going to help. More like a red-herring but as long as they were busy and not sniffing around me while I tried to work out what was happening with Gerrard, it was all good. "Keep us posted. Sandra is on deck if you need anything." I smiled. "I can't believe I let you two get away with the black smoke and sulfur reference the first time we met."

He chuckled. "If I'd said sigils written in angel's blood, you might've freaked out."

"Nah, but if you'd said Windigo you might've got a faster reaction." I shuddered. Something else tugged at me. The Masonic symbol. "The Masonic symbol, have forensics confirmed what's it written in?" I wanted him to say red paint. Just say red paint.

"Preliminary field tests confirmed blood. We'll know if it's human or animal when all the tests are in."

"Dammit, you were supposed to say red paint."

"Sorry."

"Me, too." I hung up.

The conversation for the rest of the journey was minimal but not uncomfortable.

We stopped at a diner in Harper's Ferry for coffee and something to eat. Kurt swung open the door onto a decor of bright red upholstered booths and scratched red Formica tables with chrome edging. Comfortable echoes of a bygone era.

It'd been a while since we'd visited Harpers Ferry. Some way, seeing the diner look just like I remembered it, was good. I headed to a booth on the left toward the back and swiped a menu from the counter on the way. Pushing my sunglasses up onto my head, I slid into the seat and shuffled over to the wall. I wanted grilled cheese and tomato soup.

"Agent Conway?"

I looked up to see a friendly face peering at me. "Carmel." I grinned. "Didn't think you'd still be here. How are you?"

She flashed her left hand at me, a diamond ring on her finger sparkled in the light. "Engaged!"

"Congratulations." Last time I saw Carmel, she was bleeding from gunshot wounds in the middle of a road in a storm.

Her smile faded. "Has something bad happened?"

I shook my head. "No, just visiting a friend, that's all." Kurt, Sam, and Lee arrived at the table. "Do you remember these guys?"

She nodded. "I'm sorry, I don't remember your names but thank you for saving my life." A tear slid from her dark-lashed eyes. She wiped it away. "I always hoped to be able to thank you all."

Lee wrapped an arm around her shoulders and gave her a squeeze. "Just doing our jobs, but, I think I can speak for everyone here when I say, we're mighty glad you're well and back at work."

"What can I get you?" Carmel pulled a pad and pencil from her apron pocket.

Everyone sat down and gave their orders.

She assured us it wouldn't be long and carried on to the next table. Splashes of memories from the last time we were in Harpers Ferry dropped on the table like a biscuit dropped in gravy, and mingled with today's visit. Last time I was looking for someone and the deception uncovered involved NCIS. This time I'm looking for a retired NCIS agent and I'm pretty sure it's not a deception-free scenario. In fact, Gerrard retired because of what we uncovered about his Director and that all began up here.

The food arrived. Halfway through the first of my two grilled cheese sandwiches the memories surrounding Gerrard's retirement surfaced again. I placed the sandwich on the plate and wiped my hands on a red napkin.

"Good?" Sam asked, looking up at me from across the table.

"Yeah."

"Something wrong?"

I lifted my coffee cup and took a sip. Strong, black, nectar of the Gods. Life without coffee took me too far down the rabbit hole for my liking. It felt good to be able to drink it again. With care, I placed the cup back on the table.

"Something Carmel said." I looked at each of my team, in turn. "I don't know when I last thanked you for walking into hell beside me, time and time again."

Sam raised his coffee cup. "All for one." We followed suit. With a clink, our raised cups touched. "One for all."

Eating resumed.

Sam's words rang in my head. Something niggled at me.

Guilt. I'd pulled us away in the middle of a case to chase Gerrard. It felt there was a connection to whatever the hell Gerrard was mixed up in and our weird case. I refused to let the missing Iversons and Rowan Grange into the mix.

Enough with the guilt already. "The cabin we're going to is not far from one we've been to before."

Sam's fork paused in mid-air. "Iain Campbell's hunting cabin?"

"Yep."

A clatter of forks resounded. I had everyone's full attention.

Lee spoke first, "I didn't want to ask."

A smile let loose. Don't ask don't tell. I didn't want to say. I looked at the men in the booth with me. There was a good chance we were stepping right into a new version of hell. United we stand, divided we fall. "Anyone else have a hinky feeling about this trip?"

Sam's index finger rose. Lee nodded. Kurt wiped his mouth on a napkin and regarded me with curiosity.

"This is great soup," I said, dipping more of the sandwich into the delicious liquid in the bowl in front of me. "No way this is from a can. You can almost taste the tomatoes ripening on the vine. I bet they used fresh basil too."

"Glad you're enjoying it," Kurt said. "You have any other observations?"

Wiping soup from the corner of my mouth, I smiled. "Maybe they added fresh basil pesto. It's really good. Try some."

"Iverson ..."

From the corner of my eye, I saw Sam smirk. He reached over and dipped a piece of his grilled cheese and ham sandwich into my bowl. "Feels like it's been a long time since we've sat down together for a meal." He bit off the dripping chunk. His head nodded as he chewed. "Damn, that's good soup."

"You're not helping," Kurt said. He turned toward me and dipped his spoon into the bowl. "You're right though Sam, it's been too long since we shared a meal."

"Slurp, and you die."

He tipped the contents of the spoon into his mouth and swallowed. I waited. "That really is good."

Winning. "Lee?"

He didn't need to be asked twice. He too dipped a spoon into the diminishing puddle of red. "Excellent."

"Are we going to talk about what you're thinking?" Kurt

forked some of his salad into his mouth.

"Nah."

His eyes met mine. The look on his face changed, little furrows in his brow and a harder look to his eyes settled. "You're thinking something and I want to know what it is."

You might be sorry. "If we know about the cabin who else knows?"

"We didn't, you did. Without you, we wouldn't have a clue about the cabin."

"Doesn't mean no one else knows." I still thought there was a connection to our current case and felt like we running headlong into smoke and broken mirrors. Never mind the coded message from Chris Iverson that said NSA and mentioned Dane. The shards of mirror reflected bullshit in all directions.

A collective intake of breath followed. Kurt's expression stayed the same. No surprise. He was there when I smashed my knuckles on John Miller's face. He heard me telling Tierney to call him off, not long after that Gerrard called and said everything would be explained eventually. CIA involvement wasn't a big stretch.

"You think Miller is still after Gerrard," Kurt said.

Gerrard was one of the good guys and yet I deemed no one and nothing off limits. Judgments regarding innocence or guilt were not helpful as an investigative tool.

"Chicky, have you heard from Tierney since the sniper in the Navy Yard incident?" Lee said.

"Nope."

"Iain still with the State Department?" Sam said. He

helped himself to more of my soup.

"Yes," I replied and dipped the last of my grilled cheese, letting the saturated toast slide down my throat.

"He might know something," Kurt said.

We finished eating, paid the check, and said goodbye to Carmel. No doubt we'd be back one day. There was something about Harpers Ferry that drew us in. I could see why Iain and Noel both chose this area for their getaway cabins.

Did they know each other? Gerrard retired not long after I met Iain Campbell. I scoured my memory but couldn't determine if they'd met.

Silence enveloped our car as we drove out of town and up the same road we'd been once before. This time I didn't expect to call in USERT to look for a body. There was still a good chance we'd be shot at. Depending on who was at the cabin.

Chapter Twenty Nine
When We Were Young

I stood on the shoulder of the road and fastened the Velcro on my bulletproof vest. Quiet clicks and metallic sounds of weapons checked and rounds chambered surrounded me. Serious best described the collective mood.

Kurt wore a medical backpack. Sam, Lee, and I carried backpacks too. Spare ammunition, water, granola bars, duct tape, plasticuffs, wipes, Ziplock plastic bags, a lighter, emergency charger packs for our phones, field first-aid kits, and at least one knife, were the standard things we carried in our light packs. We each had our preferences when it came to extras. I liked to have chocolate with me. Because you just never know when you'll need an energy boost. Practical. I also carried a tactical pen.

"Okay, let's get this over with," I said. "Phones on silent."

Kurt pressed a button on the key fob. The car locked and alarmed. If anyone in a five-mile radius missed that sound, I'd be very surprised. Sam and Lee played paper, scissors, rock, real quick. It ended with Sam taking point and Lee coming up the rear. We walked up the gravel-covered cutting in the woods that passed as a driveway. About two-hundred yards in, the wide driveway became a narrower dirt path that veered to the right. The path grew darker as trees met overhead. We walked on. Dappled light eventually gave way to a clearing. Across the clearing I saw the cabin; it was a lot bigger than I imagined. I heard nothing but cicadas and birds. Surveying the place from the edge of the clearing partially hidden in shadow, nothing seemed out of place, and there was no outward sign of life.

My stomach sank. What did I expect? Windows open, coffee brewing, a smiling Gerrard waiting on the porch? Yeah. Nah. It wouldn't have hurt.

"This is one helluva fishing cabin," Kurt said, his voice never rising above a whisper.

He wasn't wrong. At the front of the house were two sets of French doors and one large window. A wide porch ran the entire width of the house. No vehicles anywhere that I could see. No obvious garage.

"How many external doors, do you think?" Lee said.

"At least three," I replied.

"Sam and I will take a looksee round the back."

We watched them leave. Lee went left, Sam right, sticking to the tree line and moving with slow care. Kurt and I waited.

My phone vibrated a few minutes after they left. Lee: We're in position. One back door. A lot of windows on your right, fewer on the left.

I replied: We'll knock on the front door. I figured the main door was directly in front of me. I pulled the key out of my pocket and looked at it. "Let's do this," I said to Kurt.

I rotated my shoulders, adjusted the Velcro on my vest, and left my weapon holstered. Kurt had his Glock in hand. My boots clunked across the wooden decking on the porch.

I knocked three times on the frame of the double doors

with stained-glass inserts. Fish leaping out of water. The panels were beautiful, resplendent in greens, blues, and golds. Above one of the fish, I saw a dragonfly. This was Gerrard's house.

Kurt moved to the window and peered inside. "No sign of anyone."

As I expected. I slipped the key into the lock and turned it. The lock tumbled, I pressed the handle down and pushed. "Well, that was easy," I said, entering the warm room.

From where I stood, on a large Turkish rug in the living room, there were closed internal French doors to the left and matching closed doors in front of me and to the right. He liked double doors and stained glass.

"Gerrard built this place?" Kurt said, with admiration.

"He did. It was just after he retired. When he said fishing cabin, I expected a cabin. You know, one room and maybe a bathroom." I swept my arm around the huge living room, taking in the massive stone fireplace in one corner and the two big, brown, distressed leather sofas and four matching chairs with ottomans. "A bunk bed and maybe a ratty old sofa."

Kurt chuckled. "Me, too."

"What do you suppose the floor is?"

"Maple," Kurt replied, tapping his shoe on the wood. "Natural maple."

I pointed to the doors on the left. "Bedroom?"

"Let's go see."

Lee and Sam were still out back. I called Lee's cell. "Keep

an eye out. We're inside."

Kurt opened the double doors. "Wow," he said, walking into the room.

Another leather armchair, two armoires, a large wooden chest of drawers, a queen-size bed, nightstands on each side. Another large Turkish rug, same colors as the living room rug, deep reds, blues, and gold. A room opened off the far side of the bedroom. No door. On closer inspection, it was a bathroom with porthole windows.

"Show home much," I muttered, opening one of the armoires. Five suits and three jackets. I closed the door.

Kurt opened a drawer on one of the nightstands. He picked up a book and flipped through it.

"What was he reading?"

"*Eraserbyte*," Kurt replied, showing me the cover. A bluish cover with a dragonfly.

Stands to reason. No papers. Nothing hidden.

Back in the living room, I opened a drawer in the coffee table by the fire. A box of drink coasters. Dragonflies again. I put the box back.

"Shall we?" Kurt asked, waiting by the as yet unexplored French doors.

I joined him and nodded. "Let's."

The door led to an office which flowed through to a big kitchen.

On the left of the door was a large wall cabinet, on the right, facing a window was a spacious mahogany desk. Apart from the lamp, there was nothing on the desk. The drawers were locked. I used my key. Several notebooks, pens, a few business cards. Rifling through the contents, I found a phone.

"This could be useful," I said, showing Kurt.

He agreed. We moved on to the kitchen. Kurt checked the fridge. I checked the coffee maker. Priorities. A fresh filter and full reservoir. Next to it was a silver canister full of coffee, a scoop, and four mugs. Felt like an invitation. I scooped coffee into the filter and flipped the switch before moving into a laundry room where I saw Lee outside the back door.

Unlocking the door, I said, "Coffee's on."

"This is a nice place," Sam said, heading into the kitchen followed by Lee.

A door led off the laundry; I opened it, figuring it led to another bathroom. Yep, shower, tub, toilet, basin and vanity. Porthole windows and another large Turkish rug. The cabin would not be out of place in *Home Beautiful*.

The smell of coffee lured me back to the kitchen. Lee leaned on the counter and looked out the window. Sam opened and closed cabinets. Kurt rested near the built-in refrigerator. "There's fresh food in the fridge."

No surprise there. "Any juice?"

Kurt moved out of the way so I could check out the contents of the refrigerator. No juice. "There's a small open carton of half and half." I gave the container a shake. "Hardly anything left."

"Doesn't look as though anyone is living here," Sam said. "It's too tidy."

"It's tidy all right, but someone was here, probably with

Gerrard." I closed the fridge door. "Someone who takes cream in their coffee."

"Gerrard doesn't," Kurt said.

"Most people wouldn't consider an almost empty carton of milk anything out of the ordinary," Lee said. "Glad you wanted juice, Chicky."

Yep. "I found a phone," I said. "It was in a locked desk drawer." I pulled it from my pocket.

"iPhone?" Sam asked.

"Yeah and guess what? It's not locked."

I searched in the settings for the phone number. It didn't match the one I had on my phone for Gerrard. While the coffee maker gurgled I scrolled through everything on the phone. The email app wasn't associated with an account, no texts or iMessages to read. Facebook wasn't connected. I opened photos.

"We have a photo," I said. "The photo is date- and time-stamped. Today, four and a half hours ago." I showed everyone the image on the screen. It was a photo of the book cover we'd already seen.

"What's with the dragonflies?" Kurt poured dark steaming liquid into the four mugs.

"I'm not sure, but, I think Gerrard's trying to tell us something." Like he's not dead.

"You're kidding me ... and that was taken today?" Kurt said.

"Uh huh."

No one contradicted my thinking. One by one we all took a mug of coffee and walked through to the living room. I opted for a chair in the corner nearest the office door. Sam and Kurt sat on the sofa. Kurt planted himself on the farthest chair.

The coffee smelled fantastic. Whatever it was Gerrard needed us to know was still mostly a mystery, but at least it was a mystery wrapped in tasteful surroundings, comfy leather, and delicious coffee. I placed my cup on the coffee table, then picked it up. Didn't want to leave a ring on his table. Sam leaned forward and pulled open a drawer.

"Coasters." He placed four on the table.

Dragonflies again. Different from those I'd seen in the other drawer. Sam fiddled with his coaster then turned it over. "We have a small piece of paper." He peeled a small folded yellow piece paper off the back of the coaster and handed it to me.

I opened the pale yellow sticky note. Noel's handwriting. "It says, the mercury is rising and it's signed Art Jeffries." Ha! I hauled in the movie reference. Clever. I turned the paper over. Nothing. I dropped it on the coffee table.

"Bruce Willis and Alec Baldwin movie, *Mercury Rising*," Lee said.

"Yeah."

"Seen any puzzle magazines in the house?" Kurt asked.

I shook my head and smiled. "He's telling us he had to leave, that it got too hot here and he's protecting somebody."

"A kid?" Lee turned his phone to show us the movie poster. Bruce Willis and a boy.

"No, not a kid but whoever it is, it's important." And

takes cream in their coffee.

"In the movie, the kid cracked an NSA code, that code was supposed to protect covert operatives all over the world," Lee said. "IMDb is awesome."

"He's not coming back." Sam picked up the note. "And he sure likes the cryptic shit."

I was pretty sure Sam was right and Noel had gone with whoever he was protecting. "What if there's something in that book ..." The song from earlier mentioned an open book.

"Worth checking," Kurt said.

I set my mug on a coaster and went to get the book from the bedroom. As I walked through the bedroom door, something outside caught my eye.

One long stride took me out of view via the bedroom window. I opened the drawer next to the bed and retrieved the book. Straightening up, I took a breath and listened for any noises outside. Nothing but a light breeze among the fir trees. The gentle rustle of branches. I stayed still for a moment. Just in case it wasn't my imagination.

A shadow passed the window. Silently, I drew my weapon, and hurried back to the living room, keeping as far from the windows as I could. Lee looked up. I pointed to the window behind him and covered my left wrist with my right hand. He nodded and rose from the couch. He and Sam moved, weapons in hand, toward the kitchen. A shadow passed the windows behind the sofa.

Reminding myself to breathe, I placed the book on the nearest coffee table and proceeded to the French doors. If someone was out there, they hadn't walked on the decking in the porch but stuck to the grass around the house. I hoped it was Gerrard but I doubted it. I opened the door and looked out. Nothing untoward. I knew Sam and Lee were going out the back door.

Kurt's hand landed on my shoulder. "Left or right?" he whispered in my ear.

"Left."

We separated. I crept around the side of the living room and saw Sam coming my way. He shook his head. I nodded. Nothing. Imagination? Trees? Wind? Clouds?

We walked back to the front door. With one last look, we went back inside. Kurt and Lee joined us in the living room.

"Anything?" I asked, holstering my weapon.

"No," Lee said. "What'd you see?"

"A shadow."

"Jumpy, Chicky?" he replied.

"Cautious." I picked up the book and thumbed through it.

"You think there's something in there?" Sam asked, settling back on the couch. Lee prowled through the bedroom and back. Guess he was jumpy too.

I held the book by the spine and shook it. "Yeah, but nothing obvious." I sat in the chair and flipped pages until I came to the first page of chapter one. My eyes skimmed the rows of words. A sentence jumped off the page made from the first word of rows one, ten, thirteen, nineteen and twenty-three. 'You believe justice report committee.'

I turned the page. The pattern jumped out again this

time one row down and carried on longer. Two, eleven, fourteen, twenty, twenty-four, twenty-nine, thirty-two. 'Should screen email we forty-five abandoned structure.' Turning the page, I saw more. Three, twelve, fifteen, twenty-one. 'Down followed clear information.'

Writing in my notebook adding commas where I felt they worked netted tentative results. 'You believe justice report, committee should screen email, we forty-five abandoned, structure down, followed clear information.' No matter how many times I read the words, I couldn't make anything good out of it.

And there was something missing. More than something. What justice report, what committee, who was abandoned and why? The 'structure down' comment made sense if forty-five were abandoned. Followed clear information? Okay, but where did that information come from?

I read the passage aloud, several times. "Ideas?" The faces before me looked painful.

"Question," Kurt said, leaning forward. "Forty-five?"

"We, forty-five. You think that means Gerrard is among them?" Lee said.

And that's a clue. I looked at Kurt. "John Miller." Kurt nodded and that enlisted questioning looks from Lee and Sam. "He was after Gerrard, or it looked like he was, months ago. We need to know what Gerrard was doing prior to landing himself in hot water."

"You think it's possible that a committee has sanctioned whatever action this is?" Sam asked.

That didn't feel right.

I shook my head. "Maybe the committee has an email problem? Why screen email?"

Kurt looked up from his phone. "Screen – verb. Conceal, protect, or shelter someone or something with a screen or something forming a screen. Synonyms are conceal, hide, mask, shield, shade, protect, guard, safeguard, veil, cloak, camouflage, disguise."

"So the committee should protect their emails?" That made better sense but didn't feel like the whole story.

Lee looked at me. "Gerrard is working within the confines of the text. He's hoping we can fill in the blanks and work out exactly what he's saying. This is an imperfect code."

"Yeah." Chances are it's not email at all but that was the closest word. "Could be data, could be files, could be emails," I said. Could be everything or nothing. Would've been easier if he'd just left a post-it note inside the book spelling it out. Or put a note on the damn phone instead of making this so much harder for us to figure out.

"Working on the premise that this is bigger than email, worst case scenario?" Sam said.

"Compromised data that leads to forty-five people being abandoned."

"Maybe not abandoned, might be something similar. Stranded for example," Kurt offered.

"Black ops," Sam said in a half-whisper.

That fitted with Tierney being involved and John Miller. "Disavowed," I said. Damn, that was it, I just knew it. Deny any responsibility for forty-five people. That's a lot of people to turn loose.

"Coming back to John Miller," Lee said. "Explanation please."

"John Miller cropped up in the Navy Yard while I was putting out some feelers regarding Gerrard's whereabouts."

"You smashed your hand up in the Navy Yard," Lee said.

"Miller has a hard face."

"His role in this?" Sam asked.

"I believe he was after Gerrard." And maybe he still is.

"Who is he?"

"A dickhead working for Tierney."

"A CIA cleaner?" Sam said.

"Potentially."

Everyone stopped. Silence dropped like a fire blanket.

"Why are the CIA after Gerrard?" Sam eventually said with slow precision.

"That's the million-dollar question." I had a feeling it was something to do with the email or data or whatever needed protecting.

"What was he involved in after retirement that drew such a negative reaction?"

"Who says it's after retirement?" I thought about our recently deceased agents. One was NCIS. "Deep cover."

Kurt picked up the thread. "Compromised deep cover and or aliases. There is a CIA database of aliases."

"Kept in Langley on internal servers. There is supposed to be no way of accessing that from outside." Supposed to be. Famous last words? There was another database. "We have access to a database of registered LEO aliases. The dead NCIS agent from Chesapeake didn't have his alias registered with the LEO database."

"We have no way of knowing if he was using a CIA manufactured alias," Kurt said. "Unless we can get into that server."

"Maybe he didn't retire," Lee said.

"Gerrard?" Paid to check where we were and which conversation.

He nodded.

That was possible. Perhaps when his mom thought he'd disappeared, he was working.

The sticking point for me was the sale of his house. Who handled it and where did the money go? I filed those questions for later.

"The forty-five, could they all be aliases, or undercover agents or operatives?" Lee said.

"We can't rule that out." The more the words swam around in my head, the more it sounded plausible. That made the locked garage deaths and lack of evidence seem less ooky-spooky supernatural and definitely more ooky-spooky-alphabet-soupy, just like Kurt said. Felt like he was right. Didn't stop me associating Wesson and Smith with Squirrel and Moose.

I needed to know about the Wayward Son Protocol. Time to call the Director. "Director. Quick question. Is the Wayward Son Protocol ours or a joint venture?"

"I was about to call you. Let me check." I heard Cait typing.

"Definitely ours, Ellie."

"Thank you."

"How's it going?"

"It's muddy but we might be onto something."

"Be aware, I've had a recent conversation with Jonathon Tierney."

So that's why she was about to call me. "I'll keep in touch." I hung up and put my phone on the coffee table.

Kurt flipped through the book. "Everything okay?"

"Tierney's talked to the Director."

"About?"

"She didn't say but wanted us to know there was a conversation."

"My money's on his call being fact finding because he doesn't want us pissing in his pool," Sam said. "More coffee?" He hauled his muscular frame from the sofa.

"Do you suppose there is hot chocolate powder in that amazing kitchen?"

"Depends how well Gerrard knows you," Sam replied with a grin. "I'll check the pantry."

He knows my coffee preferences but not sure if he knows I've developed a love of hot chocolate.

Lee helped Sam take the mugs out. Kurt and I looked at each other.

"This is going to get ugly," Kurt said.

"Going to?" Because this mess was so pretty now?

"Yeah, this is just starting, Iverson."

"Tierney must've heard about the death of Simonsson or McEwen or whoever he is when he's CIA."

"Batten down the hatches."

Some timely advice. I called Sandra.

"How can I help, O Esteemed Leader?"

"Get a new flash drive and download everything to do with case number three-zero-six-HQ-six-seven-one-eight from my laptop. Then remove all trace of the files from the laptop. Lock the Sentinel file pertaining to this case. It needs to be TS. Delta A only."

"What about Wesson and Smith?"

"Only Delta A."

"Yes, O Instigator of the shutdown. Anything else?"

"Yes. I need to know whose name is on the property tax records for this place." I doubted it was Gerrard's name. "Do you need the address?"

"Nope, I got your location on my screen."

"I'll be in touch."

Kurt waited until my phone was back on the table. "What about Smith and Wesson?"

"They popped up out of nowhere, on the whim of a previous Director. It bothers me."

"We can't shut them out, Iverson."

"I know."

I didn't want to shut them out. I just wanted to make sure they were who they appeared to be, and ours. It irked me that Chris had put the name Dane into his message. His NSA reference didn't thrill me either especially after Noel's note about the movie.

Lee came back from the kitchen and sat on the couch.

"What?" I recognized a question in his eyes.

"Committee," he said. "Do you think that's what we think when we think committee? Political? Or more imperfection with the code?"

What does committee mean? I Googled it on my phone. "A group of people appointed for a specific function, typically consisting of members of a larger group."

My gaze drifted to locate a faint quacking sound somewhere on the floor. Four little ducklings broke away from the main group. The little breakaway group quacked and lined up.

"Technically Delta A is a committee. We are members of a larger group, namely the FBI. We were appointed for a specific function." Tracking and apprehending serial killers and other assholes is a specific function. The ducklings dispersed amidst a flurry of yellow down.

Kurt agreed with a nod. "So the committee he's speaking of may not be a committee as such. It could be an agency. It could even be us."

"Or the CIA," I said. We needed some insight into possibilities. Sean O'Hare. I touched Sean's name in my recents list. The phone rang and rang. Voicemail. "Sean, it's Ellie. There's a seven-fifty game tonight." I hung up.

Kurt grinned. "Refresh my memory."

"Columbus Fountain outside Union Station at eight-thirty tonight."

Sean and I had developed a way of communicating meeting places over the years. Six-fifty tip off meant we'd meet at the Navy Memorial at seven-thirty. Five-fifty kick off was code for a meeting at six-thirty at the Dupont Circle

Fountain. I like fountains.

Sean wasn't the only one I used this particular code with. The other person was Iain Campbell. My next call was to him. He didn't pick up, so I left the same message. May as well get everyone on board and get moving toward a resolution. Be nice to tell Gerrard's mother something good or bring her some closure. Not knowing is worse than having a body to bury. I looked at my watch. "Wonder what's keeping Sam and the coffee?"

"He's probably still looking for some hot chocolate," Lee replied.

"He's been in there almost ten minutes," Kurt said.

The three of us looked at each other for a beat.

"Sam!" Lee called, "Wanna hurry on up?"

No response. No doors opening or closing. No sounds of mugs being filled. No scuffling. Nothing that suggested distress. I breathed in through my nose. The coffee was ready.

Lee stood and moved through the doorway and I followed. Still nothing from Sam. At movement outside the window, Kurt's hand flashed fast signals as he hurried. Back door. We moved on and found ourselves in an empty kitchen. The only sign that he was there earlier was the full coffee pot.

"Bathroom?" I suggested.

Lee nodded. Kurt was outside the back door. I let him in. "Anything?"

"A deer. Probably what you saw before."

Woods and deer. That made sense. I heard Lee knock on

the bathroom door. He joined us in the empty kitchen moments later. "Bathroom door is locked. He didn't reply. Might pay to give him a minute."

"Or not," Kurt replied, he left the room. I heard him knock. A few seconds later he said, "I'm coming in."

Chapter Thirty
Jigsaw Puzzle

Lee and I looked at each other. Kurt hurried back into the kitchen.

"The door was locked. He is not in the bathroom."

"Was locked?"

He shrugged. "You're not the only one who knows how to pick a lock."

"Window?" I recalled porthole windows in the bathrooms. "Are they big enough?"

Kurt shook his head.

"He didn't just vanish in a puff of green smoke," I said, opening cabinets.

"I don't think Sam would fit in any of those," Kurt added.

"Where is he?" Lee asked, scanning the room. He looked at the screen on his phone then made a call. It rang several times before it went to voicemail. I heard Sam's voice. Lee left a message, "Call us, bro."

I moved closer to the counter where the coffee maker sat. Coffee was ready. Sam had located hot chocolate powder for me and the kettle was still hot. No evidence of foul play. Nothing spilled or dropped on the floor. No signs of a struggle in the kitchen. I was fairly certain Sam hadn't fallen into the toilet or disappeared in a puff of smoke.

Pulling my phone from my pocket, I tapped the Find Friends icon on my home screen and tapped Sam's name. "He's not answering calls but his phone is active," I said, watching the screen on mine as a map emerged. "He's here. With us." Confused, I added, "Maybe he left his phone in the house?" We hadn't heard it ring when Lee called but maybe the volume was down or on silent.

Splitting up, we searched high and low. No phone. My phone still said he was right with us. We needed to get closer.

I called Sandra. "Can you get a fix on the tracker in Sam's phone?"

"One moment, O Genie of the Tech-O-Sphere." Her fingers moved at speed over keys. "He is northeast of your location."

"Thanks, Sandra."

"Everything okay?"

"Yep, just playing a little hide and go seek." I hung up. No sense worrying her yet.

"Under?" Kurt said.

We all looked at the large rug on the floor of the kitchen. Lee lifted one corner and peeled the rug back.

Nothing. No secret trap door. Looking disappointed, he dropped the rug back down.

My phone still said he was here. Sandra said he was northeast. I opened a compass application. "He's over that way."

An alert popped up on my screen. Sandra had activated an app on my phone that could access the Delta

A GPS trackers. Seconds later it confirmed what she'd told me. He was here. And now he was there.

But how? And where is there? The app showed he wasn't moving. I stared at the ceiling for a second. "Up?"

A rapid walk through the home office, kitchen, and laundry room showed no access to the ceiling space.

"Maybe not up," Kurt replied.

"I still think he's down or sideways." But I hadn't found any evidence of secret rooms or trap doors. "Lee, is there a rug like this one in the bathroom?" I pointed to the floor rug.

"Yeah. Won't hurt to look," he replied.

The three of us traipsed into the bathroom. The rug was just inside the door. Moving aside so Lee could lift it, air rushed over my lips as I saw the edges of a trapdoor.

"The rug doesn't come off the trap door fully," Lee said, giving it a tug. "It's designed to fall flat on the floor again once the door is dropped."

Movement from Kurt caught the corner of my eye. Gun.

We had a potential tunnel and the trap door. So Sam somehow discovered the trapdoor after using the bathroom? Possible. He could've kicked up the edge of the rug by accident and noticed there was something under it. Or someone could've come up through it and found Sam. We were talking in the living room – maybe we wouldn't hear voices way over here behind a closed door.

"Don't anyone move." I ran back through the house

and grabbed my backpack from the living room, swinging it on and hooking my arms through the straps, I ran back to the bathroom.

Kurt glanced at me. "I don't want you down there," he said, but I could already hear the resignation in his voice. He'd voiced his opinion and knew damn well I'd do it my way.

"I hear you, coming or not?" I lowered myself into the hole, finding a ladder with my feet.

Lee squatted by the opening. "I'm coming with you. Kurt can stay topside. He might not be down here."

"Can I?" Kurt replied with zero enthusiasm.

"Yeah. Don't go missing," I said, descending.

Voices circled the opening of the tunnel as I climbed down into the dim passageway and waited. Anyone in the tunnel would've heard something. Lee dropped down beside me less than a minute later. We stood in the pool of light from above. I held my finger to my lips then cupped one ear with my hand. No sound anywhere. We made eye contact. Simultaneous thumbs-up followed.

"Not bad," he whispered. "Not made for midgets at least."

Lee stepped forward to the edge of the light puddle. The ceiling was about a foot above his head. I stretched both arms across the width. My elbows bent a little as I held my palms flat on the walls. About five feet across.

"Bonus," I said, keeping my voice low. I shone my flashlight up the walls. Cinder blocks. The ceiling looked like poured concrete, as did the floor. This was a tunnel meant to last and built with purpose. Behind us, the concrete corridor extended out of my flashlight range. Ahead of us, more of the same. It wasn't as dark as I expected.

"There's a light source somewhere," I said, moving forward. "It must be filtering from somewhere, not just the trap door we came from. It's not dark enough down here for zero light."

"Yeah. Let me take bearings." Lee opened the compass app on his phone. "We're heading northeast."

I let my pack slide quietly to the ground and handed the torch to Lee. "Hold this." I pulled out the duct tape and ripped three lengths of tape with my teeth, and stuck the tape on the wall in an arrow to mark the trapdoor and the direction we were walking.

With everything back in my pack and my flashlight in hand again, we moved on. About a hundred yards later, I spotted a dim pool of light. It faded slowly to a deep shadowy gray like the rest of the tunnel. "See that?"

"Briefly. Maybe someone closed another trap door or a door at the end of the tunnel."

There was nothing to indicate Sam was anywhere near, except the constant vibration of the app on my phone. I had no idea what I expected. Chalk marks on the wall, a big sign that said 'This Way.' Something. Anything.

Another dim pool of light faded into shadow as we walked. "I don't think the light we see is another trapdoor," I said, shining my flashlight up and down the walls. Beams reflected from a glass dome high on the wall. "There are dim lights down here. Maybe they're slowly switching off?"

"Wonder what switched them on ..." Lee commented.

"Motion sensors?" I looked back. No light. If there were motion sensors, surely we'd trigger the lights?

"Maybe a sensor that's triggered by a fob, like a keyless car."

"Or maybe someone turned off the lights when they left but they dim before going out?"

His arm brushed mine and knowing he was close was comforting. Shadows played tricks on me tugging thoughts of demons and ghouls from my subconscious. "Sam's a big guy ... how is this happening?" It was rhetoric meant for my brain to work on, not for Lee to answer. "Why would he go willingly without hollering out to us? Without picking up his phone and calling or sending a text or coordinates?"

I knew Lee was mulling over the events as we knew them. Only his mind worked quietly and mine liked to vocalize.

A buzz in my pocket alerted me to an incoming call. Sandra.

"O Chief all things Hinky, I have something for you."

"I'm listening."

"There's a paper trail for the property. It was sold by Noel Gerrard two years ago, to a corporation. Grange Corp. Five months later the property was leased to Arthur Jeffries."

"Grange Corp?"

"Yes. Grange Corp owns three other properties in the area. They own more residential properties in Colorado, Pennsylvania, New York and California."

"Grange Corp, one of Rowan's holdings?"

"Yes. The corporation was set up by lawyers working for Rowan Grange. Those lawyers have limited power of attorney. Meaning they can buy and sell property on his behalf. Apart from the original company documents and filed power of attorney papers, there is nothing to suggest Rowan Grange is actively involved."

"Thanks."

Chapter Thirty One

Country High

"Up ahead," I said, shining my flashlight beam on a ladder fixed to the wall. "Just like the one we climbed down."

"Whoever built this place figured they'd need a tunnel. That's probably not good. How many people think they're going to need an escape tunnel?"

We both laughed. "Paranoid people or maybe people who know that one day they're going to end up on a hit list? It's an escape tunnel, not a panic room. They needed to save themselves," I said. If you can't rely on the cavalry coming, you need to be your own cavalry.

"That'd account for the rug being attached to the bathroom trapdoor. No need to worry about putting it back once the door's used."

"Yeah, makes sense." Anyone with a fancy tunnel like this would've planned details like that. They didn't want to be followed.

"And to hide a property, sell it and then lease it back under an assumed name?"

"That's one way of slowing down a hunter." I slowed my steps and scanned the ground. No scuff marks. No footprints. No drag marks. Nothing to suggest Sam was incapacitated. Nothing to indicate anyone came through the tunnel before us.

"How far have we walked?" Lee didn't require an answer;

he was looking at a map on his phone, the image reflected in his iris. "Almost a kilometer. I'm starting to feel a bit like a rat in a tube."

The walking continued until we saw another ladder attached to the wall. "Ya think there's cheese up there?" Hungry was my new normal.

"Here's hoping."

Whatever was up the ladder didn't feel right. Adrenaline tweaked without pumping yet. I was sure Sam went willingly. I just didn't know where or why. I switched off my flashlight and jammed it into my waistband.

Leaving my weapon holstered, I grabbed the sides of the ladder and clambered up. The door at the top was easy to open and fell back as I pushed. The ladder moved under my feet as I climbed out into the light. Lee caught up with me. We stood in a small empty room. Windows on two sides let in plenty of light.

"This is weird," he mumbled, turning on the spot.

"Yeah." I dropped my pack, unzipped it and stowed the flashlight. Leaving my pack on the floor, I moved toward the only door. No lock on the inside. I twisted the handle and pulled.

Our eyes grazed each other as the door opened. He stepped past me into the doorway. His involuntary exclamation caught me off guard.

"Step aside," I said. "You make a better door than a window."

Lee moved, two steps to the right but no further, allowing me viewing space. Sam sat in a large armchair. His feet planted on the floor. Hands on his knees. Elbows on the armrests. His half-closed eyes stared straight ahead. I'd never seen his face blank before.

Before I realized it, I'd taken a photo of him. I blinked, looked at the phone in my hand and the image on it. Terror erupted within me. "Sam!"

He didn't reply. No acknowledgment. His expression frozen.

Lee propelled himself forward, breaking whatever spell held him. He leaned over Sam, his fingers searching for a pulse in his neck. He looked at me and shook his head.

"No. No! No!"

"Chicky ... Kurt."

Lee grabbed Sam by the shoulders and dragged him to the floor. He ran his hands all over Sam. Checking as he went. No blood. Lee started chest compressions. I called Kurt. He answered on the second ring. "Sam. No pulse."

"I'm coming. I'll use the tunnel."

"There's an arrow on the wall – go that direction until you see another ladder. We're a kilometer away."

I heard him thump to the ground and figured he was already in the tunnel. I hung up. Lee was working on Sam.

Where were we? An open-plan living area. Weapon in hand, I checked the rest of what appeared to be a fishing cabin. Four rooms. The bedroom contained two sets of bunk beds. A bathroom and the main living area with a tiny kitchenette. No rugs. No trapdoors apart from the one we used. The front door locked from the inside with a dead bolt. No backdoor. A rustic log cabin. Devoid of life.

Lee worked. Sam stared from under half-closed eyelids. People like Sam don't just die.

How did anyone kill Sam? Why did he leave? Why didn't he call for back up? I knelt next to Sam's head. "Fuck it, Sam, don't do this!"

Nothing. "You don't get to die on us!"

A noise in the room next door alerted me. I scrambled to my feet and hurried to the door and saw Kurt straightening up after climbing the ladder.

"Where?"

"In here." I stepped aside to let him through.

Lee moved and Kurt took over. Lee's eyes locked onto mine as he walked toward me. "How?" he said, his voice low.

"I don't know."

Anger flashed in his brown eyes. Streaks of gold flew like daggers. "Gerrard?"

"Really?"

He shrugged. "Who else?"

"We can put Gerrard at the other house over five hours ago. But not here. Not without evidence."

"Chicky."

"We can't, Lee. But Sam had to be with someone." I watched as Kurt worked. He made a call, his phone on speaker. "Someone was with him. He's not a fucking cat looking to die under a house."

Lee unlatched the front door. A breeze floated in carrying an accent I didn't expect to hear.

Rowan Grange? "What the hell is going on? Why is

Rowan here?" I yelled at nothing and even knowing that, couldn't stop myself. Waves of anger crashed over me. "Why couldn't you just tell us what the fuck you want us to know and not leave cryptic goddamn clues? Where the hell are you, Gerrard!"

Rowan stepped in front of me and grabbed my shoulders. "What happened to Sam?"

"I don't know. I don't even know why he's here." I looked into the same eyes I'd looked into so many times in the past. "How did you get here?"

He shook his head but maintained eye contact. "I don't know. All I know is I was sitting in that chair," he pointed to the chair Sam had been in, "when the world came back into focus."

"Focus?"

"Everything was hazy. I sat there for a bit before going outside. Thought fresh air would help."

"You could just get up and walk out?"

He nodded. "I wasn't restrained in any way. The deadbolt on the door needs a key from the outside not inside, I could leave." I watched the thoughts flickering across his face and waited. "I don't even know where I am."

"Really? Because you are a kilometer away from a property owned by Grange Corp."

"I'm fucking what?"

"You heard."

"The corporation owns investment properties. I'm not involved in the buying and selling."

Resisting the desire to punch him, I let Grange Corp go,

for now. "Do you think you were hit in the head? You feeling okay now?"

"My head feels fine. I don't know if I was hit."

My breathing quickened. "You got up out of the chair and went outside. Then what, Sam sat in it and died?" Controlling my rising anger was difficult. "People don't just sit in a fucking chair and die!"

"I didn't even know Sam was here."

"The exterior door was shut when we arrived. Where were you?"

"It locked behind me when I went out. I didn't want to wait around for whoever deposited me here to come back."

"What were you doing outside? You obviously didn't leave."

"I don't really know. I must've walked into the woods a little way before ending up back here."

I looked around the cabin. "We found Sam alone and suddenly you popped up."

His voice dropped, pain and memories etched lines into his face. "Are you accusing me?"

Was I? No. Just looking for answers. I looked at Sam lying on the ground with Kurt working on him. "Was anyone else here?" I said to Rowan.

"No. I was alone. I didn't see anyone." His gaze fixed on Sam. "That doesn't make it look good for me, does it?"

Lee spoke, "Call it, Kurt. He's not coming back."

Kurt growled a response that none of us could decipher. Moments later he made a second phone call; while on the phone, he addressed me. "Where exactly are we?"

304

"Hang on." I went out of the door and stood on the porch looking at the cabin. I'd been here before. We all had. I'd shot through one of the windows and taken out a killer holed up in the cabin. I walked back inside and closed the door.

It's different than it used to be. There was no indoor plumbing before. "This is Iain Campbell's hunting cabin." I gave him the address and grabbed my phone and called Iain Campbell. "Why the hell am I standing in your cabin in the woods when I was out here trying to locate Noel Gerrard?"

"Nice to hear your voice too, El."

Maybe I was a tad brisk. "Sorry. Is this still your cabin?"

"No. Gerrard bought it from me a while back."

Everyone knows everyone. Don't know why it surprised me – them not knowing each other should be the surprise. "Washington is becoming more incestuous by the day," I said and hung up. I'd call when I could and explain.

"I can't believe he's not coming back," Kurt said, placing his hand over Sam's eyes while whispering something unintelligible into his ear.

Lee's foot kicked back into the wall he was leaning against. At least it wasn't his fist into Rowan's face.

Helpless, I waited.

Kurt glanced up. "I called for a medevac. They know it's a Delta body recovery."

I clamped a lid on the opening bars of the *Ghostbusters* theme song. Now was not the time for inappropriate interference.

"Who's coming?" Lee said.

"THU."

Tactical Helicopter Unit. Our people. Tears prickled. Sam would be in safe hands. They'd escort him like the fallen hero he was. I'd been on one of those missions before and seen firsthand how much respect is shown to fallen colleagues.

"Now what?" Lee said.

"Autopsy. I don't know what took him. His heart was in good shape according to his last physical."

"Then what?" I leaned on the wall. "A poison of some kind?" Without intending to, I found myself staring at Rowan.

"I didn't," he mumbled.

I knew that. Why would he? It's Rowan, he doesn't kill people, he sings to them.

"Maybe poison. Possibly a drug." Kurt paused. "This could also be a sudden Intracranial Catastrophe."

Worry reared its head when I realized that I knew what Intracranial Catastrophe meant. Sudden massive brain bleed. Intracranial hemorrhage. It's as bad as it sounds. "No trauma, correct?"

"Correct. There doesn't need to be."

"Sam's brain could've just gone bang? No warning, nothing?" Rowan said. "I didn't know that was possible. If I'd been here, could I have helped him?"

Kurt shook his head. "Time Is Brain."

"I thought time was money," I said, causing Kurt's eyes to flash in my direction.

"It means intervention has to be fast. It's not always possible. If that's what happened, then I don't believe anyone could've saved Sam."

That didn't answer the biggest question. "Kurt, if this is a brain event of any kind … it doesn't explain why Sam left us and why he didn't call for backup. How did someone get a big guy like Sam to climb down a ladder, trundle along a tunnel, up another ladder, and not cause a fuss? There were no signs of struggle, no blood, no scuff marks, or directional indicators." It's Sam. I've seen him in action. There is carnage. There is always carnage.

Lee watched me. "Chicky is right. Nothing indicated Sam went unwillingly. I think a fatal intracranial event is not the answer here. Sam's death may be the result of something else. Like whatever made my partner compliant." He rocked from foot to foot. "Overdose of something?"

Kurt looked up at Rowan. "And you were just sitting in a chair but have no clue how you got here or where you are?"

"Yes."

"Then we could be looking at two drugged people but only one fatally," Kurt muttered. "Why?"

"Kurt … the zombie drug?"

"I've been thinking that's one of the few scenarios that would get compliance from a guy like Sam."

Rowan spoke, "Zombie drug? What are we – in a B-grade horror?"

Wouldn't really surprise me. "They blow a fine powder in the victim's face." I said, "Kurt?"

"Possible."

"But could it kill him?"

"Maybe. He could've had a reaction. Or he could've been given more and this is the result of an overdose."

Silence sank from the ceiling like a frigid fog as the four of us watched Sam grow colder by the second. I expected him to jump up grinning. There was no jumping. There was no grinning.

Dead is dead. The finality of the situation opened a chasm and threatened to swallow me whole.

The need to protect myself and be able to function took over. Everything from the last hour was crammed into a filing cabinet drawer in my mind. Slammed shut and marked 'Do not open.' A pencil drew heavy black lines as it sketched the outline of the room containing the filing cabinets. Lines curved as wind blew through the scene. Muted paint filled in the gaps, bringing the drawing to life.

Christopher Chance strode across the floor from an open door. His hand ran down the first set of filing cabinets, stopping at the drawer where I'd stored the last hour. His hand slid along the edge of the cabinet. Turning, his cool blue eyes watched me. The drawer popped open, dark leaked from the broken seal. Chance jammed it shut and leaned on it. "I got this, you carry on."

A sharp crack jolted me into the present. "Gunshot!" I spun around looking for Rowan. I looked over my shoulder, everyone was armed. "Rowan!" I called, as loudly as I dared. He was right with me moments ago.

Chapter Thirty Two
Water Under The Bridge

I flung open the bathroom door. Not in there. Not again with missing people.

Another crack rang out. Glass blew through the air, covering half the room in shards. I ducked and crept to the open door. Another shot. This time it hit the wall. Lee appeared next to me.

"Civilians are a liability," he whispered. "Think he stepped outside."

"Go, we'll cover you," Kurt said, firing a few rounds through the broken window.

"Chicky, get the rock star," Lee said, exasperation evident in his voice.

Breathe. I nodded at Lee and Kurt. The shooter was in front of us. I needed to go out the back. "I'm going through the bathroom window. Gimme a minute to get out." I stayed low and hurried into the bathroom saying a silent prayer that there was only one shooter. Holstering my weapon, I pushed the window wide, climbed onto the toilet seat and over the windowsill and dropped with care to the ground below.

Rustling in the undergrowth. I pulled my weapon from my holster. Gunfire from the front of the cabin broke the silence. Eyes on a long face peered at me from the trees. Deer. Breathe.

Avoiding anything on the ground that would make noise under my feet, I moved to the corner; using the cabin as cover I peered into the woods. No sign of Rowan. I couldn't call out. I rounded the side sticking close to the wall. About ten feet away from me, before I got to the front corner, I heard a twig snap. Following the noise, I saw a figure crouching behind a smallish tree. A hand waved.

Rowan. He was closer to the shooter and would have to cross open ground to get to me. Or I'd have to cross open ground. I sighed. Civilians. I tugged my phone from my pocket and sent a text to Lee: Now's good.

Seconds later, gunfire erupted from the cabin. The shooter in the woods fired back. I ran for Rowan, my plan simple: Grab him and get out of there. Silence enveloped the area again.

"We are going to the back of the cabin," I whispered to Rowan. "When I move, you move. Don't mess this up."

He nodded. I texted Lee again: One for the road.

Gunfire followed. I grabbed Rowan's arm and we ran for the cover of the structure and kept moving to the back. The bathroom window would be tricky to get in without a toilet to stand on.

"In," I said. Rowan was just over six feet tall and not built like Arnie. Well put together but more sinew than muscle mass.

I watched the woods and listened for signs of trouble as Rowan jumped for the window sill and pulled himself up, head first, into the bathroom. I pulled myself up onto the window sill and slid legs first until I felt the toilet seat under my feet.

Safely inside I turned my attention to Rowan. "You okay?" I asked. "Not hit, hurt, bleeding?" He shook his head. "What were you doing out there? One minute you're with us, then you're gone."

"I didn't think you wanted me around."

"Don't make this about you." Anger simmered. "Not the time, Rowan."

"What's going on, Ellie?"

"I have no idea."

Kurt called out, "All right in there?"

"Yep." I opened the door. Sam still lay on the floor. I couldn't see Kurt or Lee from the bathroom doorway. Just Sam.

"Iverson, keep him low," Kurt said, moving into sight.

"Do you think the shooter knows about the big house?" I motioned to Rowan to sit on the floor near the bathroom door.

"No idea," he replied. "We've got a helicopter inbound and need to get the situation here under control."

"I'm going back out. Let's stop this shit so we can get Sam out of here." The words burst into flames as soon as they hit the air.

"No," Lee and Kurt said.

"Really, no?" A smile ventured across my face. "Got a better idea?" Silence. "Thought not."

"Be safe, Chicky," Lee said.

"I got this." More gunfire.

"Keep your head down."

"I'll be back. Don't shoot me," I said, as Lee crouched next to me.

I stayed low and hurried to the bathroom and climbed on the toilet seat.

"Be careful, El." Rowan's voice brimmed with concern.

"It's what I do. Just stay put."

He didn't reply and I didn't turn round.

Chapter Thirty Three
She Came In Through The Bathroom Window

With a deep breath, I jumped out of the window, landing softly on the ground below. Weapon in hand, I made my way across the small grassed area and into the woods, avoiding anything that would alert my target, taking as wide an arc as I could. It would make sense if the shooter were near the rocks Lee and I once used as both a vantage point and cover. I paused, used the compass on my phone to make sure I still on track. Gunfire from the direction of the rocks was a great indicator.

More gunfire. Return gunfire. Time ticked. Above my thumping heart, I could just hear the low *thwok* of a helicopter's rotors. Another deep breath and I moved on until the rocks ahead of me were in view. A shadowy figure lay prone on my side of the rocks.

I moved. One tree at a time. Within ten feet of the shooter, I had to remind myself again to breathe.

Eight feet out. Definitely male.

Seven feet. If he turned now, I'd be in trouble.

Six feet.

"Drop the weapon!" His body jerked. He squeezed the trigger. Another shot smashed into the cabin below. His fright would've been funnier if he weren't holding a rifle. "Drop it!"

Slowly, he released his grip on the weapon and rolled

over. He was still in shadow and I struggled to make out his features. "Hands where I can see them. No sudden moves."

He planted his hands on top of his head and said nothing.

"Are you alone?"

A small laugh caught me by surprise. "I always work alone, Conway."

He knew me. "Sit up."

He sat with his hands still on his head. The dappled light sent shadows over his face.

"Miller. John Miller. How's your jaw?" The knuckles on my right hand twinged.

"It's fine, How's your hand?"

"It's fine. And you're shooting at us why?" He smirked. I wanted to smash the smirk off his face. Memories of doing just that reminded my hand and it protested. I kept my weapon on Miller and spoke to the phone in my pocket. "Hey, Siri. Call Kurt."

"Calling Kurt," said a disembodied female voice from my pocket.

The phone rang once Kurt said, "You okay?"

"Yes, I am. Come get this prick."

"Coming. Leave the line open."

Miller glanced over his shoulder as noise from the cabin filtered up to us.

"Miller, what the hell is this about?"

"It's about ... how about you mind your own business and let me get on with my job?"

"I don't think that's going to work for me."

His voice dropped and developed a menacing edge. "You're the bane of my existence, Conway."

"Then I'm already winning."

"Don't you ever quit?" His eyes narrowed as he looked at me.

"Gave quitting up for Lent."

About twenty years ago.

I fought the smile that encroached. "It's taken you a while to track Gerrard down."

"He's wily."

Wily. Good description. Wily old salt. Better description. Except he's only ten years older than me. That doesn't seem so old these days.

Kurt spoke from my pocket. "The bird is almost here."

"Wait for them and send me Lee," I said, never taking my eyes off Miller. A small smile lurked on my lips. "And you failed again. Tierney won't be thrilled." I'd seen what happens to people who fail Jonathon Tierney. At best, it's unpleasant.

He shrugged. The darkness in his eyes belied the shrug. He cared. Tierney would lose it and Miller would be on the receiving end.

The helicopter overhead filled the air with thumping rotors and generated a massive disruption in the plant life around us. As trees swayed and branches moved, ropes tumbled into the sky and four dark figures slid down. Fast roping.

They have all the fun.

I figured we could hold Miller for maybe two hours before Tierney had a meltdown and stormed into our Director's office demanding Miller's release. I knew we wouldn't get anything out of Miller in that time, but we could annoy him and slow him down.

"I'll take him from here," Lee said stepping up beside me.

"Thanks. I'll go back to the cabin and check on our guest."

"We'll follow," Lee replied, dragging Miller to his feet and cuffing his hands behind his back.

"Frisk him." Lee nodded. I moved away, disconnected the phone call in my pocket, and took the shortest path to the cabin. The helicopter hovered overhead, filling the air with noise and tormenting the tree tops. I looked up in time to see it move away and disappear from view. A radio crackled.

Two agents dressed in combat gear stood close to the cabin door. I heard voices inside. Two other agents would be in there with Kurt and Sam. The one on the left of the front door nodded at me. He was kinda familiar. "Sorry for your loss. Jackson was a fine agent."

"Yes. He was." Gradually the agent's face and deep velvety voice triggered a memory. "Tyler Nicholas."

Tyler and Sam trained together at Quantico. We'd met at parties at Sam's a few times. I remembered him and Sam arm wrestling. He nodded.

"I'm sorry, Tyler." I felt the prickle of tears behind my eyes and in my throat.

We'd all lost someone today and it hurt. Chance's voice filled my head 'I told you I got this, so carry on.' I swallowed hard, took a deep breath, and tried to bury the shit.

"We'll take him on his last ride," Tyler said. "The bird is landing on the road. We'll carry Sam out."

I swallowed again and tried to speak but the words got tangled around my uvula and trapped behind my teeth. So I nodded.

"He won't be alone, Ellie. We'll be with him all the way … to the … all the way."

Morgue. That was the word he didn't say. I nodded again.

"There'll be a sentry posted with him."

The ramifications of Sam's death filtered through, evading Chance's attempts to corral them and shove them in the drawer. Kurt and I would speak to Sam's family. The three of us would talk to Sandra. I couldn't even begin to imagine how that conversation would go. I knew how it would end though. The way they always end – with disbelief followed by anger and then tears.

"Sam would appreciate everything you're doing for him." How could one person make so much saliva? I swallowed again. "Lee's coming down from the woods with a prisoner."

Tyler stiffened. "He responsible for Sam?"

"I don't know."

"How did he die?"

"Not bloody, Tyler, but other than that, we don't know

for sure. Drugged, maybe."

John Miller is CIA. If any agency were to use something like a zombie drug, it'd be them. My opinion of Miller was low, but I wasn't persuaded he'd seen Sam, let alone knew about the tunnel. Whoever facilitated Sam's death knew about the tunnel and the other house.

Footsteps, dull, headed our way from the woods. Movement in the cabin made me peer in the open door. They had Sam strapped to a stretcher that looked more like a long basket. Kurt beckoned to me.

Kurt asked the two men with him to step outside for a minute and for Rowan to join them outside. "Thought maybe Sam would want to talk to you before he goes," Kurt said.

"He didn't before."

"There's less chaos now."

I knelt down next to Sam. The black body bag wasn't zipped all the way, leaving Sam's head exposed. The feeling of waking sealed in a body bag rushed at me. Sweaty, stuffy, full of condensation. Guess if you're not breathing, they're not like that.

Bringing my lips close to his left ear, I whispered, "Sam, it's me. We've got a few minutes. I really need you to tell me how this happened."

A warm scent lingered on Sam's clothes. Washing powder. Slightly musky and floral. I breathed in and exhaled slowly. Waiting.

As I sat with Sam, letting my hand rest on his shoulder, memories of his laughter filled me. My eyes closed. Movement under my hand startled me. Pinging open my eyes, I expected to see his chest rise and fall. It didn't. "Sam ... I need you this one last time." A tear trickled down my face, I brushed it away. "Don't be the only dead person with nothing to say."

His head turned to face me. Cloudy eyes stared past me into the nothing. "Come with me, Chicky Babe. I'll show you," he said, extracting an arm from the body bag and grabbing my hand. Cold clogged my veins as Sam pulled me closer to him. "Use my mind, see what I saw."

"Just don't show me your junk," I said as Sam's mind opened. "I know you were in the bathroom."

A throaty laugh burst through the veil of fog surrounding us. "Chicky Babe, you know what they say about black men. It's all true."

"Shut up!" And then I was watching Sam washing his hands in the bathroom sink. We both heard a scraping noise and turned. The rug moved. Sam watched the rug lift up and fall backward. I felt what Sam felt. He wasn't worried or anxious.

He mumbled in my head, "Glad that didn't happen when I was draining the dragon." He stepped toward the hole in the floor and beckoned to me. "You need to see this, Chicky Babe." I moved closer. A face looked up at us as a person climbed up a ladder from the dark below. The light shining through the windows illuminated his features. A rush of relief flowed over me. It wasn't anyone I knew. It wasn't Gerrard. He didn't kill Sam.

The unidentified male climbed up and spoke. "You're

not Gerrard."

I looked at Sam and knew right away he didn't recognize the person. And whoever he was, he'd expected to see Gerrard if he saw anyone.

Someone else after Gerrard? Miller has a buddy or something else entirely. If Miller had a buddy, his buddy would've told him about the tunnel and that Gerrard wasn't there.

Sam touched my arm. Cold wriggled through my veins. "Watch," he said.

Just when it looked like the men were going to have a conversation The Unsub pulled an envelope from his pocket and blew a fine white powder into Sam's face. He faded. His mind closed down. Cold tendrils dragged themselves from my body and slithered back into Sam.

"Thank you, Sam," I whispered to his lifeless corpse. "Say hey to Mac and Carla."

I sat for a moment and analyzed what I'd seen. The unknown subject. Our Unsub. A white male. Brown hair. Short but not military short. Light brown eyes. Not as tall as Sam, but close. Potentially six feet three inches or so. Thirty-five to forty years old. American?

He didn't say much. It was hard to determine much from his brief sentence, except I didn't think he was European. He wasn't built like a powerhouse, he was no Arnold Schwarzenegger, but he wasn't scrawny. Worst body type of all, average build. My eyes closed as I conjured the Unsub's image and paused it on my internal screen. The hand he used to hold the envelope was missing part of his index finger. I squinted: Half his index finger. And he opened the trap door without gloves.

"Iverson?" Kurt crouched beside me. "Anything?"

"Sam was helpful. I can put together an Identikit image. He's missing half the index finger on his right hand. He opened the trap door without gloves. He said Gerrard's name."

Kurt stood and helped me up. He signaled to the men waiting by the door. All four came.

"We'll take him now," Tyler said. He bent down and zipped the bag over Sam's face whispering, "Godspeed, my friend."

My body moved, hand outstretched, ready to rip open the bag and let in air. A voice that sounded very like mine said, "He can't breathe like that. Don't shut him in."

Kurt's hand grabbed my forearm and slid down my arm until I felt the warmth of his fingers close around mine. Our eyes met. "Iverson." Kurt's eyes flooded with unshed tears. "Let them take Sam."

Tears fell from my eyes. I wiped my sleeve across my face and took a sharp breath. Not now. We have work to do. One day there will be time to deal with what happened.

In silence, the men lifted the stretcher, two on each side, and carried Sam from the cabin. We followed. Sunshine bathed the area in warmth yet my bones were chilled. A butterfly flew into their path; it seemed to hang in the air above the stretcher. Before they were gone from view, a dragonfly with its iridescent wings chased the butterfly away.

I gave Kurt a half smile, extracted my hand from his and looked around. Miller sat on the edge of the porch with his head bowed. His left foot kicked at a clump of grass. Lee stood on the other side of Kurt, at parade rest. Rowan sat on the opposite side of the porch to Miller. He rubbed his eyes, ran his hands through his hair, and tried to smile at me.

Despite a cloudless blue sky, I felt a storm brewing. No one moved or spoke until the helicopter lifted off.

Chapter Thirty Four
Your Song

Training and my sense of what was right overrode the part of me that didn't want to take Miller back to D.C. Sometimes I amaze myself. As much as I hated John Miller for what he was doing, Tierney was the problem. Miller followed orders.

Whatever Gerrard was involved in, and whoever he was protecting, painted a big-assed target on his back. The way Tierney pursued him made me think that it did indeed have something to do with the increasing list of recently deceased former and current agents.

Someone was trying to silence Gerrard. Could more than one faction be after Gerrard? Or did Miller have something to do with Rowan Grange being at the cabin? Maybe, but Rowan didn't recognize him and it wasn't Miller who drugged Sam. We found nothing on Miller that indicated he had drugs of any sort in his possession.

I didn't think Miller had any clue what was going on in the cabin. He didn't seem to know anything about Sam being there. He believed he'd find Gerrard. So, who took Grange to the cabin and why there? What the fuck was the point of taking Grange at all? And who was it who blew that shit into Sam's face?

I opened the identikit program we used to create images of felons and other miscreants. Using the memory

Sam shared, I put together an image that I hoped was close enough to get us somewhere.

White male of average build wasn't the best start to a description, and really the rest of it wasn't great either. He was forgettable right up until the partially missing finger. I knew that would help. Especially with the prints we lifted from the trapdoor. Mine, Kurt's, Gerrard's, Lee's, and two other people we had yet to identify. I felt fairly certain that one of those prints would be our guy with the missing finger.

My phone rang. Mitch. "You okay?"

"No, but I will be, eventually. Everything okay with you and Harley?"

"She went to school with her CPD in tow this morning. No doubt everyone will enjoy that."

"Did you call the school and let them know she's got armed protection with her and why?"

"I sure did."

"How'd they take it?"

"The principal wondered if Harley should remain at home and access her lessons via the internet. I gently informed Mrs. Vincent that unless Harley is stood down, she will be in school with her CPD."

I laughed. Go, Uncle Mitch! "Her response?"

"She reluctantly agreed to have the CPD in class with Harley." Mitch chuckled. "She didn't understand that my phone call this morning was simply a courtesy call as I'd already spoken to the chairman of the school board."

Guess having the FBI override school policy regarding

weapons on campus is not easy nor would it go down well. "They have my numbers?"

"Yes, and mine. I've already heard from Harley. She's having a good day."

I heard a door close. "Where are you?"

"At the office. And before you ask, I have Diego in my office with me, and Murray outside."

"Good. Going okay?"

"It is. Missing my wife. Any chance I'll get to see her soon?"

A smile filled my heart. "I'm missing my husband."

"It's worse for me."

Laughter broke free. "Of course it is."

"Will you be home for dinner?"

Maybe. If I were to be perfectly honest, there wasn't much chance of me being home for dinner. But I wanted to be. I badly wanted to be.

"I'll try, babe. I'd really like to spend the evening with you."

"Good enough. Three things."

"Three things, babe."

I hung up. With my elbows on my desk, I rested my forehead in my hands and closed my eyes. Disjointed thoughts became Lego bricks and none of them wanted to fit together. A little yellow duck quacked and roamed aimlessly around my office floor. I stood up and walked to the large white board on the far wall. Choosing a blue marker, I wrote a timeline.

Chris and Susan left the country a week before

Harley's abduction. Financials told me the last time they touched their bank accounts or credit cards was four days after they left. They called Harley that day and no one heard from them again. The same night Harley disappeared, we were called to two dead bodies in the Chesapeake Bay. One was an NCIS agent working undercover. We turned the case over to NCIS.

I stood back and gave that more breathing room. Related or not? I circled NCIS with a red pen and moved on.

We found Harley. Found scopolamine. Arrested the kidnapper. Who interviewed him? I circled that with red as well.

I asked Misha to look into Chris and Susan's disappearance.

Delta A was called to a crime scene. A dead formerly deceased agent.

Squirrel and Moose showed up. I circled their names in red.

An alarm on my phone chirped like a thousand birds on a sunny morning. But it wasn't morning, it was evening, and I had to be somewhere.

I left the building without fanfare or issue. Parking near Union Station I made my way to the fountain. Sean and Iain were waiting.

"A security specialist, an ex-CIA officer, and an FBI agent met at a fountain in D.C. ..."

"Sounds like a bad joke to me," Sean said, giving me a small smile and pulling me to him for a hug. "Losing Sam is utter shit."

No arguing with that. Sean released me from his bear-like grip.

"How you holding up, El?" Iain asked, wrapping an arm around my shoulders and giving me a friendly squeeze.

"Getting by." Trying not to think.

"What'd you want to see us about?" Sean perched on the back of a bench seat.

"Either of you know what Gerrard is mixed up in?"

Iain leaned next to Sean.

"Haven't heard from him in months," Sean said. "Why?"

"The cryptic bastard had a key and a message delivered to me. It led me to a cabin." I looked at Iain. "You would not believe how incredible the cabin he built is."

"He rebuilt my old place because I heard he sold it."

I shook my head. "Nope. He built another. He sold your place?"

"That's what I heard." Iain tapped on his phone screen then passed it to me. "Yes, he sold it."

I looked at the property tax information on the screen. "He sold it to Nicholas Kudrow. Well, that's just perfect."

"El?"

"The place he built, he sold to Grange Corp and leased it back under the name Arthur Jeffries. He left a message for me signed Art Jeffries. Both Art Jeffries and Nicholas Kudrow are characters in *Mercury Rising*."

"He's gone to some effort to conceal his interest in both properties," Iain said.

"Yes, he has." I sighed. "Anyway, I found the place, I know he was there at some point. I also found more cryptic crap. Talk of a list with forty-five names on it. Compromised data. It felt like he set up everything at the cabin to try and tell me what was going on."

"Forty-five names?"

"Yeah."

"Big list," Iain added.

"I think Gerrard was at the cabin with someone and that person doesn't want him telling anyone anything, or maybe it was too dangerous to leave anything obvious like a note of explanation. He managed to let me know he had to leave. Sam was taken and then died. Rowan Grange turned up. A CIA sniper was in the woods ... and by the way, he was after Gerrard, not us. I hope Gerrard can stay in front of the CIA. Far as I could figure he maybe had a five-hour head start before Miller showed up guns blazing."

"Grange?"

I shrugged. "Yeah, he was clueless about how he came to be there. I knew he was missing, but to be honest, I kinda expected he was off with a girl."

"Rockstar life," Sean muttered. "They do have an image."

Iain was thinking; his lips moved. "Someone took Grange and left him at the cabin." Sean and I looked at Iain, waiting for more. "What could be gained by taking

Grange?"

"Money," we said.

"Then why leave him there? Any demands?" Iain pushed off the back of the bench and straightened up.

"Not that I know of," I said, sitting down. "I don't think anyone meant to leave him there. I think it all turned ugly when someone stumbled upon Sam thinking he was going to find Gerrard."

"Gerrard knew about a list. The person who took Sam was looking for Gerrard," Sean said.

Iain sat next to me. "Is there a link between Gerrard and Grange?"

"Yeah, me."

"Aside from you?"

"Grange Corp."

The sound of the fountain both soothed and made me want to pee.

"And that is?"

"A company owned by Grange's lawyers to buy and sell property. They own the cabin Noel built, he then leased it back under an assumed name."

"Does Grange have anything to do with that company?" Sean asked.

"It doesn't look like he does. He didn't know where he was or that the company owned the cabin."

"What else could connect Rowan Grange to your case?"

Torrents. "The connection might not be Gerrard ... it might be with Iverson Tech or Chris Iverson."

"And that is what?" Sean asked.

"Torrents. Grange, like all musicians, artists, writers, and so forth, wage war on a daily basis against sites that offer their work for free. Downloads. Torrents. Pirates." A rain storm gathered in my mind and unleashed a deluge. "Chris is a software engineer, he could be helping in that fight." And if site owners and pirates are being prosecuted because of his software, I guess that would piss off a few people. Kim Dot Com sprang to mind.

"Abducting Rowan Grange could be because they knew Chris did some work for him and they can get a decent chunk of cash by ransoming him?" Iain said. "Might not be anything about the properties or Grange Corp."

Sean stood up. "He could just be an accessible prominent person, or this is an attempt to discredit Iverson by going after people he designed for?"

Discredit didn't feel right. Destroy did. "Systematic destruction of Iverson Tech by attacking clients."

"Someone really has it in for the company."

"But why only attack through Chris, why leave Mitch alone?" Sean said, raising an eyebrow at me. "You?"

I shook my head. "The dossier we found had my name as Mrs. Mitch Iverson. They didn't seem to know I'm FBI." Bit of a blessing.

"That doesn't mean they don't, it means they didn't tell whoever had the dossier," Iain said watching something.

I followed his gaze to a couple walking arm-in-arm on the sidewalk deep in conversation. They kept walking, neither looked in our direction. We were three people talking by a fountain.

"Was Gerrard there?" Iain said.

"No. He had been there. With someone."

"Did he find Grange and take him to the cabin?" Sean said.

"I have no idea." I doubt it.

"So neither of you know what Gerrard is involved in, or why the CIA wants him dead, or what list he was talking about?"

They shook their heads.

"The only way we are going to find out is to find Gerrard. Or Tierney," I whispered. "He's pulling John Miller's strings."

Iain jammed his hands in his pockets. "Tierney isn't taking my calls right now."

That couldn't be good. I dragged my phone from my jacket pocket and called Rowan. It rang. Guess he hadn't changed his number. It rang and rang. Finally, a female voice picked up. "Is Rowan there?" I asked, not introducing myself.

"He's not taking calls," the voice snapped.

"He'll take mine," I said. "Tell him it's the FBI."

Half a beat later Rowan spoke. "Ellie?"

"Do you know Chris Iverson?"

He paused. "No."

"You're sure?" Really, I was questioning his memory?

"You haven't used any software created by Iverson Tech?"

"Don't think so, El. I'm not a gamer."

A smile edged into my voice. "They don't make games. They're known for their drones."

"I don't think I've come across them."

"Thanks, Rowan. Hope you're okay."

"I am. Sorry about Sam."

"Me, too."

I hung up and stuck my phone back in my pocket. Darkness descended, dropping an obsidian blanket over the city. The fountain glowed, lit by underwater lighting.

Chapter Thirty Five

There'll Be Sad Songs

"What's the matter?" I said as he walked toward me. Seemed like a stupid question. His usually ridiculously good-looking face bore the strains of the last day and this case. He'd aged overnight. I suspected we all had.

"I've got a list of names for our deceased men," Lee replied. "We probably should sit down."

I sighed. "Couch?"

He nodded and we moved to the couch along the side wall of my office. Lee placed a pile of manila folders on the coffee table. He picked up the first one and opened it.

"Jared Gellman, died March 18, 2002." Lee passed me a photo. "And then there's this ..." He handed me another photograph. "But this one was taken yesterday by crime scene photographers. Initially identified as Lyndon Walmsley, until his fingerprints came back as Jared Gellman."

I bet that sent a flag. No wonder there is a protocol in place to investigate the previously deceased newly dead. "So Jared didn't die in 2002."

"Nope. Not unless he came back as a zombie. He looked more homeless than zombie."

"Homeless or someone wants us to think homeless?"

"Good point."

"Where was Lyndon Walmsley between March 2002

and two days ago?" I set the photos side by side on the table. He'd aged but it was the same person. Less hair. More lines. "Because he was somewhere." And I doubted it was under a bridge.

Lee looked up at me. "Jared Gellman was FBI."

"Any CIA lurking in his deep past?"

"Haven't found any yet."

Good. "Next?"

Lee opened another folder. He placed a photo in front of me and over the first of the other two. "Marconi Ausiello. Deceased June 7, 2001."

"Let me guess ... he's also a zombie?"

"Something like that." Lee added the next photo to the pile. "Victor Atwood, died in a locked garage in Reston last night."

He looked very like Marconi Ausiello. "And before he died again, he was where?"

"Don't know yet but Marconi Ausiello was FBI. Texas mostly."

"We got Social Security Numbers for these zombies?"

He passed me a piece of paper with Social Security Numbers for both Marconi and Victor. Different. "Any chance they changed their names by deed poll – filed for new Social Security Numbers and just walked away?" Did it have to be sinister? Faking deaths was sinister.

"Whoever changed their SSNs has blocked access to the records." Lee opened another file. "I doubt information attributed to the original Social Security Numbers was attached to the new ones."

"That's serious disappearing." I leaned back on the couch and gave mind power to the manufacture of new lives. They weren't temporary creations to hide them before they testified. They were whole new lives. Complete. Manufactured death. The whole nine. "Why?" I said, leaning forward again and moving photos around on the table surface.

"Why?" Lee repeated.

"Why do we have dead agents turning up dead?"

"I have no freaking idea."

I looked at the photographs again. "We need to get ahead of this – if there are potentially forty-five compromised agents, that's a big death list." If Gerrard was right, forty-five people were in deep shit.

"How many do we have now?"

"Seven. That we know of." Part of me counted Sam as one of the case casualties. I wasn't sure if I should add him to the list of the dead or add him to a collateral damage list. As far as we knew, Sam Jackson was Sam Jackson. No aliases lurking. No reason to suspect otherwise. Did I have to have a reason? Not usually. A smile flickered across my inner screen and disappeared.

"How can we determine who is next?"

"Find the list and start tracking them down," I said.

"Easy," Lee said running his hands through his hair. "I'll just pull the full list outta my ass and start contacting them now."

Hard not to smile. "Gerrard told us about a list, so if he's right, it does exist and we can get to it. Otherwise, why tell us?"

"Where'd he get his information?"

"I don't know. You know all I know, Lee." I stood up and walked over to my desk.

Lee's voice followed me. "Did he find something or did someone come to him with information?"

"I don't know, Lee. I wish I did. I don't know if he was at the cabin but it looked like he had been. Maybe he wanted to talk to us but when Sam ... and Rowan, and then Miller. And then the helicopter." It was a big fucking mess.

"Can we reach out? Bring him in and protect him?"

"I'd like to think we could but I don't know that we can. He knows how to get to us. He has to want to." We needed help. "I'll talk to Caine. About time he was useful." I lifted the handset off the cradle on my desk. I pressed zero-zero-one.

Moments later a customary growl that sounded almost like 'Ellie' greeted me. "I need to talk to someone about backstopped aliases."

"Thought you might. I saw the case summary."

"Who should I approach?"

"There are two people who run a department and provide that type of support for us. I'm not sure who is working this week but it's either Debbie Barnes or Michael Addison."

"Where do I find them?"

"Call extension four-zero-two-seven."

"Okay, thanks."

I hung up wondering why I'd never heard those names before. Probably because I hadn't needed their services. My long-term alias, Laura Graham, was a Delta A creation, not even Caine knew about her until the very end. I'd spent years keeping her identity current and making sure she came across as a real person. There was no official record of Laura Graham as anything but a Private Investigator prior to her marriage to Mike Davenport and her subsequent tragic death on her wedding day.

The only person outside my immediate team who knew anything about Laura was a now retired US Marshal who helped me set up Laura's life. He provided the social security number, birth certificate, driver's license, PI license, education records, credit and medical records just as they do for relocated witnesses. Dark clouds gathered. Perhaps keeping Laura out of the system was a smart move.

Lee watched me as I made a call.

"This is Debbie Barnes, how may I help?"

"Agent Ellie Iverson here, I need to see you."

"Come on down to my office, Agent. You'll find us in sub-basement four, room seventy-three."

"Thanks. I'm on my way."

"Want company?" Lee asked, pulling himself to his feet.

"Nah, you carry on and see what else you can dig up. I'll go meet Ms. Barnes." I hoisted my bag onto my shoulder and left the office.

The basement levels under our building were legendary. The elevator stopped at the first basement level below the parking garages. Beyond that, stairwells descended into the bowels of the building. Gray concrete, steel pipes, ducting, and cooler air marked the deeper levels like signposting in a B-grade horror movie. All that was missing was the customary steam. My mind skimmed *X-files*. Didn't Mulder have a basement office? Not comforting.

I stopped thinking and kept walking. The next door opened into a white corridor. Light reflected off the walls and the ceiling. My footsteps rang out in the empty space announcing my intention to anyone in the vicinity. I doubted there was anyone nearby with the exception of the woman I was looking for.

The hollow hallway mirrored the hole left in Delta by Sam. I whispered, "The drawer must be open a crack, Chance. You need to shut it again."

His voice echoed within me, "I got it." A key turned and a lock clunked. "It's locked, El. You'll be okay."

Sanity is a fine line and it felt like I was dancing on the very edge. I found a white door in the white wall that had a small plaque that read, 'Sub 4. 73.' Damn, I was deep underground. Four levels below the lower car-parking garage. Good chance monsters lurked this deep. Good chance I am that monster.

Chance's laughter flowed through his words. "You're not a monster ... Yet."

I took a breath, sent Chance packing, and knocked

twice on the white door.

A voice called, "Come."

Swinging open the door I entered a hive of activity. I took my time closing the door behind me. I'd expected a lone desk and a disheveled basement dweller sitting at a computer. My mind cartwheeled over the large room filled with desks and people. Massive screens hung on three walls showed news footage along with graphs and static images.

Orchestrating the activity was a tall woman with shoulder-length blonde curls. She stood in the center of the room, pen in one hand and a clipboard in the other, calling out to people, directing their attention to various screens or avenues. She paused mid-direction and looked at me. "Agent Iverson?"

"Yes, ma'am."

"I'll be right with you."

No one else took any notice of me. After several more directives to various people she walked toward me, pen and clipboard in one hand and right hand extended. After a brief but firm handshake and introduction, Debbie ushered me through a door in a glass wall. The office beyond the glass was quieter. She sat behind a large desk facing the glass wall. I took a chair from the far wall and placed it in front of her desk. "What is it you need, Agent?"

"Can you look up these names and see if they're in your system?" I passed her the folder in my hand. It contained aliases of four of the dead. I wanted to know how much she could tell me without my needing to divulge too much of my intelligence. I watched her skim the list of names. Wayne McEwan, Bryan Messing, Stephen York and Victor Atwood.

"Bear with me, Agent. There's a lot going on here this morning," she said, reading something on her screen.

"Bad?"

"Let's hope not," Debbie replied. "I'll run these names and see what I can find out for you." She pulled the file closer and began typing.

A knock on the glass caught her attention. The typing stopped. She motioned to the short, rotund interrupter. He opened the door flooding the quiet office with sound. Leaving the door open he approached the desk. "Sorry to interrupt, ma'am. We have a second ..." he paused as if unsure how to continue. "... problem."

"The same as last night's or a separate issue?"

"The same."

"Shut down that system."

"Ma'am." He scurried away, closing the door and dropping a blanket of silence over the room.

The message from Gerrard popped into my brain. The imperfect code. I looked at Debbie Barnes as she continued typing. "What system did you shut down?"

Her fingers paused over the keys as she looked at me. "What's your security clearance?"

I handed her my ID. She nodded and passed it back.

"We have three systems that talk to each other. Only one of them talks to external systems. That's the one we've taken offline. We now have no access from here to Sentinel or the web."

"Why?" Part of me knew.

"Because something is going on and I don't know what it is. It could be someone trying to gain access to our part of the FBI system." She beckoned me to join her on the other side of the desk. "Those names of yours, they're on a list. That list resides on one of our protected servers."

"Are there forty-five names on that list by any chance?"

"Yes."

Fuckadoodledo. Gerrard was right about the list. So who else knew about it? "Can that list be accessed externally?" Cold pitted in my stomach.

"Not in theory. As I said, it's on a protected server. It's not an external system ..."

"In theory?"

"There have been some anomalies of late."

No fucking kidding. Dead already-dead agents aren't exactly a normal everyday occurrence, even in my warped life. "What sort of anomalies are you talking about?" My money is on them being different from my anomalies.

She sighed. "Unusual hits on the system, they last seconds in duration and we have been unable to find an explanation. At this stage, we do not think any data has been compromised, but the activity is making me anxious."

Hence taking the system offline. "And?"

"The only way to access our system is from this suite.

The activity did not come from here."

"You're certain?"

She nodded. "Everything in this area is under surveillance. Our movement in the offices, our accessing of computers, it's all monitored with both video and audio. Anyone using a computer down here has to sign in, nothing works without a personalized authorization code."

"When did you first notice unexplained activity?"

Debbie turned her monitor a little so I could see what she was looking at.

She typed and pulled up a log. Scrolling through data, Debbie stopped at a log sheet from six months earlier.

"Six months and nothing was done about it?" Unfreakingbelievable.

She highlighted an entry. "This is the first instance. A six-second burst of activity from an unknown source. It wasn't trackable. It didn't happen again for some days."

"What did you think it was?"

"A glitch. Power surge maybe. A ghost in the machine." She almost smiled. "Everything seemed in order. The system with the activity isn't externally accessible. In theory, it could only be accessed by being in these rooms and using our computers. No one was here when that peculiarity occurred. It was after hours. The video surveillance picked up nothing. The computers themselves showed no access." She scrolled on. "In short, it wasn't worth worrying about."

I nodded. "Glitch would've been my go-to." Or

gremlin. I would've probably gone with gremlin. Nasty evil little cave-dwelling gremlin.

Debbie scrolled through more logs and pointed out several more 'glitches' over the next few months. They varied in length from four to eight seconds.

"What exactly was accessed?"

"Nothing that we can see." She typed some more. "The system is designed to record all activity and it hasn't shown anything bar these glitches."

"What could this be?"

"Hacker. Someone testing the system, maybe."

"No downloads?"

"Given the situation, I can't be sure. Our specialized system is supposed to prevent downloading of all stored information."

"Yeah, well, it's also not supposed to be accessible apart from in here, right?"

"Good point."

I have a lot of good points but I don't know what they're adding up to, yet. "Could information be downloaded using short bursts such as you've recorded?"

"It's not impossible. It'd be an irritating way of doing it, but that doesn't mean no one would try, but again, the system should send alerts and block any attempt as well as record everything."

"For a minute, let's pretend someone circumvented your fancy system."

"Devil's advocate, I like it."

"How is the information stored?" I didn't want to think

it was just sitting there in folders and readable by anyone.

"Encrypted files. Even if they are downloaded, our encryption is from NSA, it's not simply a matter of opening the file and reading it."

Their encryption is from NSA. The code Chris left in the Iverson Tech attempted hacks sprang to mind. My gut told me it was all connected even if the evidence didn't yet. "Okay, so, the software required is on the computers in here and nowhere else?"

"Exactly. It was created for us. Only we use it. It creates small file sizes and secure encryption."

"Small enough that several could be downloaded in seconds?" She looked at me. Her eyes betrayed her thoughts. Yes. It was a yes. Files with the information I suspected they contained wouldn't be big to start with.

Debbie sighed and turned her screen back to its proper position. "We need to find out what is behind these glitches," she said, her words punctuated by fingernails clicking on her keyboard. "If you're right, this could be a disaster."

"You can work on that. I need the list."

She stopped typing and stared at me. "The list?"

I didn't come here to fuck frogs. "The four names, they're in a list within your database. I need you to give me the list."

A frown burrowed into her forehead. "I can't simply hand over our data to you."

"I have dead agents. I don't want to have another thirty-something dead agents."

Her stare remained but behind her light blue eyes, I detected active brain cells. The little voice in my head told me to be still and let her come to a better decision.

Seconds ticked by.

The staring continued.

My impatience hid behind a calm exterior. The energy it took to keep my expression neutral was unbelievable. At the two-minute mark, I was ready to jump over the desk and throttle her.

"It's not just a list of names, Age—"

"Names, aliases, location details. In short, everything needed to track these people down?"

Her eyes widened. "Has that happened?"

"Debbie, seven former agents are dead. Do you think it's a coincidence that the four names I gave you are on your list? If I'd given you all seven, I think you'd find them all. Is it a coincidence that I know there are forty-five people on the list?"

"Obviously not."

"Have you got the list on screen? Because if so, I want to know how many are still government employees."

"How does that help you?"

"I want to know. Will you answer the question, please?" I watched her eyes move up and down the screen in front of her and her right hand move the mouse as she read.

"Most of the people on this list still have a connection to a federal agency."

"And they're all male?"

She nodded.

Dead male agents, who remained Federal after their deaths. "Do you know why their new lives were instigated?"

She nodded.

"Are you going to give me the file?"

She shook her head. "It's not possible."

"You've seen my clearance."

"The Director of the FBI, the Director of NSA, and the Secretary of Homeland Security are required to authorize movement of the file."

"Director O'Hare knows about the list?"

"Not necessarily. Unless I put in a meeting request with notes, most of the hierarchy has no idea we even exist down here."

"That could take days."

The mouse clicked a few times. A printer behind her whirred and chirped. "I can print everything I can see for you. Will that do?"

"I guess it'll have to."

"Please retain ownership of this list, Agent. I like this job and would hate to leave in disgrace."

"I will."

Paper spewed from the printer. Barnes spun her chair around and gathered up the pages, fastening them together with a stapler. She handed the wad of white paper to me. "Don't copy it. Don't let it out of your possession."

"Understood." I rose to my feet and shook her hand.

Stuffing the pages into my bag, I left her office and her secret lair in sub-basement four.

Chapter Thirty Six
Before They Make Me Run

Keith Richard's voice surrounded me but came from nowhere obvious. The radio was off, iPod was off. I let his words flow over me; not like it'd never happened before. I listened as he sang. The lyrics settled uncomfortably on a blade's edge in my mind. Images of Sam lined the spongy surface of my brain. Keith sang on. Was Sam finding his way to heaven? There was no doubt about him having served his time in hell.

Sadness swamped me. Unprepared to say goodbye to another good friend, I let the images and music dissolve into silver puddles on the surface of my desk. The voice in my head yelled for Chance to make sure the drawer in my mind was locked and the key somewhere safe.

My door opened. "Everything all right?" Kurt said, walking toward me.

"Of course."

"And the sad face, this about Sam?"

"Why couldn't we save him?"

"Don't, Conway."

I nodded and couldn't even correct my name. Looking at the names on the list I noticed some of them jiggled as I read them. The dead jiggled like an app waiting for deletion. Gerrard's name joined in. Music rose from the silver puddles on my desk and grew louder. Maybe it wasn't just about Sam. I drew a green question mark next to Gerrard's name on the list. All the jiggling and music stopped.

"Why?" Kurt stared at the green question mark "Everything pointed to him being alive when we left Harpers Ferry."

"Yeah, well, that's not a guarantee that he is now."

"Confirmation?"

I shrugged. "Just a song ..."

"What song?"

"'Before they make me run.'"

He nodded. No argument. "Did Barnes have anything that sheds light on what's happening?"

"Not that I've found. The attacks on the system started six months ago. I'm thinking they got everything they need."

"Any idea who they are?"

"Someone who doesn't like our way of making agents disappear?"

"That's pretty much all I came up with too."

"Squirrel and Moose?"

Kurt's turn to shrug. "I haven't heard from them since you sent them off chasing the Masonic link."

More a Masonic let's-get-them-out-of-the-way trip than a link. Go me. I picked up my phone and called Squirrel. He answered on the fifth ring.

"Iverson?"

"Where are you?"

"Heading back in." I heard trepidation in his voice.

"Where'd you disappear to for so long?"

"Chasing a ghost." Ended up creating a ghost. Stop thinking, Ellie. It'll turn to shit if you let that out now. "I'm in my office. We have information I'd like to share." I can share. I'm all about teamwork. All. About. It.

"We heard about Sam—"

"Shit happens."

"Iverson—"

"Don't."

"Okay. We're twenty minutes away. I'll bring coffee?"

"Please … make mine a mochaccino."

"Done."

I hung up.

Kurt grinned. "Mochaccino?"

"In this story, the heroine needs a drink." And I can't exactly pour a tequila. Working here and it'd be super-frowned on considering the current situation with me.

"What makes you think you're the heroine?"

We laughed and just like that the world was back how I liked it, despite the large missing piece of Delta A.

Stepping into my first impression about Gerrard now the world felt right, he was alive when we last saw him. That had to be my focus from now on. Losing Sam was bad enough, no need to create reasons to turn the world black. Until Gerrard's body turned up to refute his status as a living breathing human, he was alive.

Schrodinger's cat sprang to mind. Gerrard was both alive and dead until we opened the box. Laughter spiraled up from the depths. I quashed it. Chance's voice rose above the remnants of a giggle. "Don't lose it now, El. You've got this."

I lifted the handset of my desk phone and touched three buttons.

"SWAT."

"Iverson. Andrews, there's a sticky situation."

"I'm your man. What do you need?"

"Manpower. Our meeting room in half an hour."

"I'll be there."

I hung up and made two more calls. I called Delta B and C, requesting their help. Both SSAs agreed to be in our meeting room in half an hour. My next call was habit. My thoughts stumbled when Sandra answered. Why did she answer? She shouldn't be here. "What are you doing here?"

"Manning my desk. Delta needs me. And it's what I do, O Leader of the Elite."

"You should be home."

"I need to work. This is home."

Fair enough. Better to work than make friends with the worms in a tequila bottle. Or that might just be my coping mechanism. "Okay. Find Lee. Set up the meeting room and invite Caine to a meeting in half an hour. I'll invite the Director."

"Yes, O Genie of the War Council."

"Andrews will be down for the meeting, both Delta SSAs are coming."

"Do you want the division chief or Owen?"

"No, I do not."

"Understood." Sandra hung up.

The temptation to ask Sandra to gather as much salt as she could find and use it to seal the room once we were all safely inside, was huge. Just to make sure Owen couldn't get in. No, that wouldn't work. She's not a ghost, she's a demon. We'd need to ward the room.

I called Director O'Hare. "Meeting in thirty minutes in the Delta A meeting room. I have the list and we're going to find the live agents."

"Can we push that out another fifteen minutes?"

"Of course."

"If I'm not back, start without me. The President doesn't always run to time."

Squirrel and Moose vied for position as they both tried to squeeze through my doorway at once. Moose conceded. Squirrel smirked and sauntered in.

"Children ..."

"Iverson," Squirrel said. "We've got something."

"Seriously? From the Masonic Lodge?" Amazing.

They grabbed chairs and sat.

"The Masonic link wasn't what we thought but we got something from surveillance cameras outside the temple." Squirrel produced his cell phone. A few seconds later he handed it to me. "Press play when you're ready."

Watching, I saw Simonsson sitting in front of the temple with a cardboard handwritten sign. I couldn't read it. A man walked around the corner and dropped something, possibly money, into Simonsson's lap. A few minutes later another man appeared; this time, he sat down next to Simonsson. I zoomed in on their faces. Two dead men talking: Eric Simonsson and Shaun Rowe. I continued watching. Then clicked on the next video and then the next. There were eight in total over a period of seven months. Each time, Simonsson or Rowe sat outside the temple looking homeless, the other came along and joined him for company.

I passed the phone to Kurt. "Watch it all." Squirrel looked pretty pleased with himself. Rightly.

"Okay, so, Simonsson and Rowe definitely knew each other. Did we hear back on the blood?" Moose opened his notebook with a flourish. Excitable. My eyebrows rose.

"The blood was a match for Rowe."

"Now that's interesting ... so, he left the symbol in case we didn't think the ring was important ..." It was almost a question.

"That wound on his hand was healing ..." Kurt said as he handed the phone back to Squirrel. "Good work."

"Could he have been in the garage longer than we suspect?" Moose said.

We all considered that. And the answer was yes. He couldn't have been drugged the whole time. So why didn't he make a call for help? If he could paint the wall, he could make a call.

Good grief, I am a poet.

"Something you want to share with the class?" Squirrel said.

"No."

"Share …"

As much as I wanted to tell him to shut up, I didn't. I shared. It's like I don't even know me anymore. "If he could paint the wall he could make a call."

"Poetic," Kurt said, grinning. "But potentially you are correct. Unless someone told him to draw the symbol."

"Okay." I'll bite. "Why would someone do that?"

"Because people are sick. So sick," Moose replied.

"Squirrel?"

"My money is on him having a little bit of clarity. He probably wasn't all there but enough of him clawed back to want to leave a message of sorts."

I nodded. "He couldn't exactly write 'Hey, I know Simonsson and that's the clue that will blow this wide open.' Whoever held him would notice something like that."

Kurt stood up and walked to the white board. He drew a line under my timeline. "What do we know now?"

"That Simonsson and Rowe are linked. And they were the two who had things on them that identified who they used to be," Moose said. "And now we've seen them together."

I opened an internal browser on my laptop and plugged Rowe's name in. I wanted to see what cases he had worked that had the potential to overlap with Simonsson's. There wasn't a lot to choose from; Simonsson's cases were all classified, even after his death. The only one I really knew anything about was his last one. Nothing seemed to show any overlap.

Simonsson 'died' eighteen years ago. Rowe 'died' eight years ago.

I looked at Rowe alone. He was undercover. He worked an organized crime case. There was a case name and number for his last job. Operation Cannoli. He was investigating Angelo Moretti, supposedly a baker.

"Hey, did anything the Director give us have the name of Simonsson's wife on it?" I looked at Kurt who was still at the whiteboard.

"No. No names. He wasn't Simonsson when he married. He was Jeb Warner. We don't know who her family was either."

I rocked my chair as possibilities scrambled around gathering more probabilities and dust bunnies from the corners of my mind. "I want his marriage certificate," I said to no one in a room full of men.

"Way ahead of you," Moose said. He had a tablet in his hand, concentrating on something. "Jeb Warner married Josephine Moretti."

A flurry of activity followed as we all searched for information on Josephine Moretti and her family.

"I'll put money on Josephine being related to Angelo Moretti, the subject of the last operation Rowe worked," I said. It felt like progress. Finally.

"Good upstanding crime family," Squirrel said.

I had to agree. "Vito Moretti was jailed for money laundering, murder, attempted murder, intimidation, blackmail, assault, tax evasion, drug trafficking, and pandering," I said, reading from my screen. "He got thirty years without parole. He's still serving time in a federal prison and will be for another thirteen years."

"Doesn't exclude him as a suspect," Kurt said.

"No, it doesn't," I replied, looking at information popping up about the family. "Mom, Marina Moretti died two years ago of stomach cancer. Oldest son, Angelo Moretti, the baker, is in prison for pandering, intimidation, double murder, and assault. He's serving two consecutive life sentences. He's been inside for ten years."

Squirrel spoke, "Jenoah Moretti, second son, is a math teacher at Oakton High school."

Oh boy. Harley went to Oakton. "How long has he been at Oakton?"

"This is his third year."

"How long has he been a teacher?"

"Four years, prior to taking the position at Oakton High school, he was at South Lakes High School in Reston."

"Reston ..."

Squirrel and I looked at each other, then at Kurt. "Add it to the board," we said in unison.

Kurt wrote Jenoah Moretti on the whiteboard with Reston and Oakton written in big red letters next to his name.

"Lastly we have Nazario Moretti," I said. "Nasty Nazario is a real charmer by the look of his rap sheet but he hasn't done any long stretches, yet." I read more and it cemented my opinion of Nazario. "He's got a court appearance pending, looks like he'll get prison time."

Kurt stepped back from the board. "What else do we know about Josephine Moretti and her life since Simonsson or Warner as she knew him?"

"Sending a link," Squirrel said, looking at me.

My laptop pinged. "Josephine Warner took her two children to Canada after her husband, Jeb Warner, died. A few months later she gave birth to a baby girl. She met an American in New Brunswick. Josephine Warner became Josephine Willows. Her husband, Callum Willows is an electrician. They returned to the USA." I scanned more information breaking it down quickly into the important points. "The family disappeared off the radar two years ago."

Moose read aloud, "Two years ago more charges were laid against Vito and Angelo Moretti. The trial is still pending but the evidence was provided by an unnamed witness. Caught up in this round of charges is Nazario Moretti."

Kurt leaned on my desk. "Okay, so, Josephine and her family disappear at the same time as new charges come to light and a secret witness."

"Did the whole family disappear?" I thought aloud as I read more about the Moretti's and the Willows. "What were the kids' names?"

Moose went to speak. Kurt stopped him with a glance.

And there they were on my screen in glorious Technicolor. "Dane Moretti-Willows, Michelle Moretti-Willows, Emma Moretti-Willows."

Dane. So, Chris may not have meant Dane Wesson. He might have meant Dane Moretti-Willows. That changed things. Maybe Dane is more like his granddad and his uncles than his real dad or his stepdad. "Kurt ... Emma?"

"The brother, the one who was posing as a kid and talking to Harley."

Dammit. "Find Callum Willows's brother. Do it fast. He's in Perth, Western Australia." I stood up and stretched.

Kurt threw me a bottle of water. I caught it and twisted off the cap. The cold water felt amazing on my hot raw throat.

"Help yourselves to whatever you want from the fridge," I said to Squirrel and Moose. "Sandra keeps it well stocked." I glanced at my watch and the wall clocks. We were running out of time.

Squirrel jumped up, threw his hands in the air and yelled, "Got him!"

I leaned over my desk and high-fived him. "Who is he?"

"Brayden Willows, forty years old, works in IT." He laughed. "Doesn't everyone these days?"

"Can we get an address?"

"Yeah, baby, we got an address. He's still an American citizen but has been living in Perth for four years working in the insurance industry."

"I think—" I changed my mind. "My gut thinks that Dane Moretti-Willows and Brayden Willows have something to do with the ugly situation we have growing before us."

"Elaborate," Moose said.

"See if you can keep up ... two years ago a family went into witness protection because the mom, Josephine, turned state's evidence on her own family. That can get ugly enough without what happened next." I typed then stopped and looked at the screen. I loved the LEO system. Entering a few details netted some fascinating results. Nazario Moretti received several mentions.

"We've got something here. An FBI agent working another case noted unusual activity around the Moretti family a month after Josephine and her immediate family were placed in WITSEC. Chatter and movement that caused him to note an opinion that they were building up to something. There was another flurry of activity centering around Nazario nineteen months ago, then there was an impromptu gathering of the family and extended family three weeks later."

"What happened to make the family come together?" Kurt straightened up.

"I'd say this next piece of information has some bearing," I said. "A military drone was stolen nineteen months ago. It was found crashed two weeks later. The report was marked classified. Nothing was said publicly." I scrolled down the page. "Marked classified by the US Marshals."

Cogs turned. Possibilities germinated. "This is speculation, perhaps, Nasty Nazario used his niece, his innocent sixteen-year-old niece Emma, to find his sister.

Emma couldn't handle the WITSEC life, she missed her Uncle Brayden, she missed her big sister and big brother. I don't know why Josephine's other children, Michelle and Dane were not included in the WITSEC move. It's possible that Dane was already in with the family. If that's the case, he was too big a risk."

I swigged water. "Emma talked to Brayden, he passed messages to Michelle and Dane. Nasty Nazario found out where the family was and stole a military drone."

I called Joanna at the US Marshals office. "It's me. Was it a drone strike that killed Emma?" My finger tapped the speaker button as I set the phone on the desk. "You're on speaker."

"Tell me this is a secure office."

"It is. Now, was it a drone strike?"

"Yes."

"Thank you."

"I will deny ever saying that."

"I know." I hung up.

Kurt nodded. "It makes sense now. Nazario killed Emma by mistake. The drone crashed. His sister and her husband were moved again. The uncle, who up until now has been a good man is angry and wants someone to pay."

He threw it back to me. "Brayden can't lash out at Nazario for fear of getting his other niece and nephew killed. Because even though they're not blood, they're his brother's stepkids. They're his family. Brayden lashes out at the company who made the drone, Iverson Tech. He poses as a teenage girl after his homework tells him Chris Iverson has a teenage girl who was about Emma's age when she died."

"He didn't do it alone, did he?"

"Nope. Dane Moretti-Willows was the other person involved. His agenda is slightly different. He wanted the FBI to pay for what they, we, did to his family. I'm not talking about his uncles and grandfather, I'm talking about what Warner did to his mom. He lied. He faked his own death. He ran. Dane was a little kid who only had vague memories of his real father. Who knows how he found out that Jeb Warner was Eric Simonsson, but I think he did. Could be what pushed him over the edge when his sister was killed."

"So we have a two-pronged attack ..." Squirrel said. "Dane, great name, shame he's not living up to it, going after the former undercover agents, picking them off one by one, because he can. And Brayden going after the Iverson family, wanting to extract revenge for his niece's death?"

"They work together. There's more overlap," I said. "Chris Iverson is more than a software designer for drones. Chris designed NSA-grade encrypted software used by governments and government agencies to store classified information. He also worked with Thorn, designing the software they use to help law enforcement find and take down human traffickers. Chris designed some of our databases."

"That's how Brayden and Dane got their information,

that's why they took Chris and Susan." The penny dropped so hard I heard it bounce off the lining of Kurt's stomach. Kurt walked to the door and whistled. Lee appeared moments later.

"Did you want something?"

"We cracked it." They man-hugged in the doorway. "Give Josh Konstram a shout, let's get the police to pick up the suspects."

"Names?"

"Nazario Moretti. Tell Josh he needs SWAT with him for that one. Have him pick up Jenoah Moretti too, suspicion of involvement in kidnapping." Kurt looked over his shoulder at me. "I think Iverson wants to take down Dane Moretti-Willows, so we'll pick up that young man."

"I'll make the calls and meet you all in the meeting room in four minutes." Lee looked over Kurt's head at me. Not many people can look over Kurt like that. "Good job, Chicky."

If it was such a good job why did I feel like there was more to it and how did the Morettis know about the list six months ago? "A question. Is it more likely that the Moretti family accessed the database alone six months ago, or that the evidence for this is mistaken or can be interpreted in a different or more realistic way?"

Kurt faced me. "Hume's Razor. Extraordinary claims require extraordinary evidence."

"I could be wrong but I don't see a crime family like the Morettis bumbling across a secure database within the FBI system on their own, six months before snatching Chris and Susan."

"And we proceed how?" Lee said.

"As before, but with our eyes wide open. I'm certain they're involved with Chris and Susan's disappearance but something else is also happening here."

Chapter Thirty Seven
Imagination

Misha's accent swallowed everything he said and tied it in an exotic Russian bouquet. As per normal, I struggled to concentrate on the words left on my voicemail, and their meaning, through the distraction he called his *Normal'nyy golos govoryashchiy*. Normal speaking voice. What is it about the Russian accent that I love so much?

Slowly the words emerged. "Passports were used. The Iversons are on board an Emirates plane, destination Perth, Western Australia. They boarded Emirates flight Echo Kilo zero-eight-two in Lyon, France."

I scrambled to clear my head. How? He didn't say, but he had more to tell me.

"ETA Dubai, six hours. Lyon, France to Perth via Dubai, estimated time gate-to-gate nineteen hours and fifteen minutes."

I checked flight times from Dulles. I could be in Dubai in thirteen hours but they'd be there in six and gone again within eight. They'd be in Perth in nineteen hours and change. It would take me twenty-nine, almost thirty hours, including five hours twiddling my thumbs in Dubai, to get to Perth. Pretty sure five hours in Dubai would end badly, because it's me.

There was no hope of intercepting them anywhere, so I

discounted Dubai altogether and just checked for flights to Perth. Looked like Chris was right about Lyon, and about the Antipodes being a destination. Perth qualified.

Perth? Brayden Willows's stomping ground. Well, that's not suspicious.

I ran Chris's credit cards. He paid for three tickets one-way on his American Express. I needed to know who the third ticket was for. Picking up my phone I pressed two numbers and waited.

"Kirstie, is the Director back from her meeting with Our Cheeto Overlord?" I bit my lip and braced myself, expecting a less than cheerful reply after my nickname for our President slipped out.

"No." There was a small crack in her voice that let humor through. "But she left instructions to put you through immediately." Her voice dropped to an amused whisper. "Yesterday I heard him referred to as The Great Pumpkin."

Nice but I prefer Our Cheeto Overlord.

I waited for what felt like forever listening to the hold music. Then Cait's voice greeted me. "I'm on my way and will be with you in the meeting soon. Traffic is heavy." Muffled traffic sounds filtered down the line. Her driver spoke. I heard his voice but not the words. "Is this about something else?" Cait said, her voice drowning out the background noise.

"Yes and no. I need your help."

"Tell me what you need."

"There are three people flying Emirates from Lyon,

France, to Perth, Australia, and I need to confirm two identities and find out who the third is."

"Of course you do. Have you contacted the airline and asked for passenger details?"

"Not yet. Before I start an international incident, I'd like you onboard."

She laughed. "All right, what's going on?"

"My brother-in-law's credit card purchased three tickets from Lyon to Perth. Their passports were scanned so they could be on that international flight. Don't know who with."

Silence.

Silence with almost audible thoughts. Cait spoke, keeping her voice low, "Last I heard, this was a Delta B problem. How is it you were notified regarding the passports and flight?"

Snapped by the Director messing in a case that isn't mine. Dammit. "Misha Praskovya told me."

"How does Misha fit into this?"

"I asked him to check on Chris and Susan when we recovered Harley because they weren't answering their phones."

"And?"

"I might have forgotten to tell Delta B that Misha was on the ground working with our State Department in Germany." Might have slipped my memory. If they were any good at investigative work, they'd know Misha was there. They wouldn't need me to tell them anything.

The room shimmered, black lines appeared, my office

became a pencil sketch. Chance popped his head around the door and said, "Don't go down that road, Ellie, it'll end in you being slapped for withholding information and that will give Owen ammunition to further her cause."

I gave him a thumbs up and he disappeared into an inky puddle. Leaving my office as it was. No black outlines in sight. My fingers crossed. "I think Chris Iverson may have something to do with the dead formerly deceased agents."

"Elaborate."

"I think he knows something about our case. There was a drone at one of the crime scenes, it was an Iverson prototype controlled from Chris Iverson's phone. We secured the phone and the drone."

If I was right about my earlier suspicions regarding the Morettis, then Chris definitely had something to do with our case.

It went very quiet on Cait's end of the line for what felt like forever but was in fact only eight Mississippis. The silence broke with fingers tapping on a keyboard.

"This is what I'm going to do," Cait said, amidst the tapping. "I'm directing Delta B to hand the case back to Delta A in the belief that the Iverson situation is tied up with the Wayward Son Protocol."

"Thank you."

"I am instructing legal to request the passenger manifest. Give me the flight number."

"Echo kilo zero-eight-two."

"Don't make me sorry I turned this over to you."

"Understood." I hung up.

Moments later I stood in the doorway of my office and hollered for Kurt. Classy. So Classy.

"This is what we do now?" Kurt said as he emerged from the bullpen doorway. "We holler? Couldn't text or make a phone call?"

I shrugged. "Seems not."

"Problem, Iverson?" He walked toward me, closing the fifteen feet in seconds.

"Yes."

"Explain." Kurt's gaze danced across my face looking for hints.

"Do you like Australia?"

"Why?"

"A development—"

"Wayward Son?"

"That's the interesting part."

He took another step toward me. "Your office or are we talking and walking?"

"The latter." We walked, I filled Kurt in.

At the stairwell door, he stopped moving. "You're sure he's involved?"

"Yes. What I have is a handful of coincidences hinging on the use of scopolamine, his drone and phone, a hack attempt that was a code from Chris – we think ... do I need to go on?"

Kurt shook his head. "Let's say he is involved, is it an unfortunate accident or did he orchestrate his involvement?"

"I'd like to think it's accidental." I'd like to, but I can't rule out the possibility that it's not. Except that the Morettis appeared to be involved and that changed Chris's involvement to victim, rather than co-conspirator, and that made me happier.

My phone rang. Misha. "*Privet*," I said. Hello.

"*Privet*, Ellie. I am sending you CCTV photos of the travelers."

"*Spasibo*." Thank you.

"They are not traveling with their original luggage."

Now that's weird. Someone went to the trouble of uplifting their passports but not the luggage. "Why and how?" I knew he'd know what I meant.

"No time perhaps. Whoever picked up the passports knew where they were and had a room key."

Could've been another guest. That way no one would be suspicious. "Misha, who was it?"

"Same person who flew out of Lyon with them, but they were not seen together until the French airport. Photo should be with you."

My phone buzzed twice. I opened the text and found the photo. Misha had surveillance outside the Iverson's hotel room door.

Jeez. I showed Kurt.

"A look-a-like?" he said, taking the phone for a closer look.

"Kurt?" Misha said.

"Yeah, Misha, have you a clearer photograph?"

"I was able to get airport security to give me still photos as they passed through security."

Another buzz from my phone. Kurt checked the text and handed me the phone.

Holy crap balls. "Gerrard is alive."

"What the hell is he doing with Chris and Susan?" Kurt muttered.

"I do not know," Misha replied. "My sources tell me someone else of interest is on that flight."

"Who?" I said, staring at the image of Noel Gerrard on my phone. Pleased he was alive but confused as to why he was with Chris and Susan.

"Grace O'Malley."

Kurt and I looked at each other, frowns mirrored on one another's foreheads. "I take it we are not talking about a sixteenth-century Irish pirate?" I said.

"No. This O'Malley is considerably younger and more alive." Misha's voice bore a strained quality. "She's a wet-work specialist."

"And she's on an airplane with Chris and Susan and Gerrard?"

"Yes. I am not thinking this is a coincidence."

Me neither. Fuckadoodledo.

I didn't think Gerrard would make it to Dubai alive, let alone Perth.

Chapter Thirty Eight
You Got The Silver

Hushed voices in conversation filled all available space. Everyone was there including Debbie Barnes. Director O'Hare made eye contact and smiled. I moved toward her and spoke softly in her ear. "Confirmation from Praskovya that Gerrard is on board that flight with Chris and Susan. I don't know why he's with them. This could be a rescue or something else. We have another problem. Misha said a mercenary by the name of Grace O'Malley is also on the flight."

"I'll see what I can do but I think we're screwed until that plane lands."

"Me, too." I straightened up and listened to the murmur of voices in the room. Once upon a time, a room like this would've intimidated the hell out of me. My, how I've grown.

Out of respect, there was an empty chair at the table next to Lee.

"Let's get down to it, shall we?" I said, deliberately keeping my voice low. The hum ceased. All eyes turned my way. "Thank you all for coming. We have a pressing situation and it's going to take all of us to prevent more deaths." I glanced at Sandra. She dimmed the lights. The white wall at the end of the room lit up. The first page of names.

"Some of you know Delta A is investigating the deaths of former agents. Information came to light that led us to Debbie Barnes and her unique team. She confirmed the dead agents are from a list of forty-five agents." The image changed to another page of names. "Dividing the list will give us the best chance of preventing more deaths."

"Why are they dying?" Andrews asked.

"That we don't know. Until about twenty minutes ago we knew even less than we do now. And even now, we're joining the dots blind. Apart from the fact they're all on the same list, there was no obvious connection."

"Was?"

"It's starting to look like revenge on several fronts. And to a point, the perps are working together."

Lee cleared his throat. "Fairfax PD is bringing Nazario Moretti and his brother Jenoah Moretti in for questioning. We hope they'll help us with our dot-to-dot."

"As part of our investigation, an FBI team from Canberra Australia is flying to Perth as soon as possible to speak with Brayden Willows, who we believe orchestrated the kidnapping of Harley Iverson. Revenge seems the likely motive."

Kurt spoke, "What we know for sure is that Eric Simonsson is linked to the Morettis and to the Willows. And that his biological daughter was killed by a drone strike while she was in WITSEC."

I stole a glance at Cait O'Hare and tried to decipher the look on her face. For a split second, I let myself think the

Director was impressed with our work so far. It faded fast. We still had a long way to go. People were still in danger.

The image changed again. A collective intake of breath told me they'd seen Gerrard's name.

"Not just FBI?" Caine said, staring at the wall.

"No. We have CIA, NCIS, FBI, and potentially other agencies." I looked at Debbie. "Can you explain?"

"Sometimes we are called upon to create new lives for external agencies. It's rare but depending on who they're working with at the time, it's what we do."

"Seconded?"

She nodded.

Gerrard seconded to the FBI? I looked at the Director. "Gerrard is FBI?"

The smallest nod. "He retired from NCIS and took a position with the FBI. It was not publicized. He was working a particular case for my office."

Man. That didn't complicate shite much. "Did you know where he was until I told you?"

She shook her head. "My office lost contact with him several weeks ago."

And yet she never mentioned any of it. Great. "Director, Cait, can we know what he was working on?"

"No."

A frown burrowed into my forehead. "In the interest of open communication, I know where Gerrard is and as of ten minutes ago he was still alive." I felt all the eyes in the room on me. They were listening before, but now their penetrating gazes bored into my skin. "Gerrard boarded a plane in Lyon, France, with my brother-in-law and sister-in-law. They're flying to Perth via Dubai."

"You didn't see him at the cabin?" Director O'Hare said.

I was pretty sure I'd said in my report that we were at Gerrard's cabin and that we hadn't seen him. "No. He left us information, it was coded. He didn't say what he was working on and he never mentioned leaving the country."

"You didn't see him?"

Everything had turned to shit before we could find out what was going on. "No," I said. "But he seemed to want to talk to all of us together and I believe he was there or planned on being there." The way he laid out the coffee and the cups implied he presumed we'd all be there. I'd felt he would turn up. Then Miller happened.

"I appreciate how chaotic that must've been, and that certain things were pushed aside with Sam's sudden death." O'Hare glanced around the room; she met Lee's eyes briefly then she turned her attention to me. "Rowan Grange's appearance, John Miller shooting at the cabin ... I'm sure they were things Gerrard didn't envisage."

"If we can't know what Gerrard was working on, then we have to carry on without that information. What I want is everyone on the list found and brought to safety." My cursor paused over the page on the wall.

Squirrel held up his index finger. "Is everyone on the list still federal?"

"No. About ninety percent of them are either federal or

associated with a federal agency though."

"Do we have better photos available?" The look on Squirrel's face suggested he already knew the answer.

"No. I know they're not great but it's all we have."

What photos we did have were old digital photographs from employee identification cards. Thumbnail size and low resolution. About as useful as a steering wheel on a mule.

"Are we moving on their home addresses or places of work?" Moose asked.

"You've all got both addresses. Take a few minutes and check where your target could potentially be before you go knocking on doors." I stared at the list on the wall. "We don't have family information. If the target has married, had children, living with a partner or whatever since the new life began, we don't know that. Go easy."

"Good point," Lee said. "How are we proceeding?"

"Dividing the list geographically seemed the best way to move on this."

"How many teams?" Lee said.

"Four main teams and within those are four paired teams." That was everyone plus extras. "Andrews, you're North from Pennsylvania Ave. Delta A is South, Delta B, West, Delta C are taking East." I looked around the table. "Any questions?"

No one said anything. I slid pieces of paper to each team leader and kept one myself. Each paper contained a list of names.

Familiar footsteps near the closed door behind me

caught my attention. No one in the room paused or stood. I turned back to the group at the table and a quizzical glance from Kurt. I shrugged. Phantom footsteps?

Claude spoke after skimming his list. "Reporting how often?"

"After you've located each person," I said and looked over at Debbie. "Debbie Barnes will be the point of contact for everyone once the agents are located. She needs to know who you have." I smiled at the nervous woman.

She cleared her throat. "Do we have safe houses we can use? They shouldn't be brought in here."

"Yes, we do. In the interest of keeping these folks alive, each team will use their own safe houses. Operate on a need-to-know basis," Director O'Hare said.

Debbie nodded. "I can do most of what's needed without meeting with anyone. As soon as I get confirmation that the person is alive, I'll start working on their new identities." She paused. "Would you please text their current Social Security Number to me once they're safe? I will need good quality ID photos but we'll cross that bridge when we come to it."

A murmur of approval ran around the table.

"Us?" Squirrel said.

The Director spoke before I did. "You and Moose are now officially seconded to Delta A until further notice and will use their safe houses."

And forever more they'd be known as Squirrel and Moose by Delta A and Director O'Hare.

"Thank you, ma'am," Squirrel replied with a small smile.

Footsteps paced outside the door again. No one reacted. Odd. I stood, walked to the door, and swung it open. There was no one there. I glanced up and down the corridor, my eyes pausing on Sandra's desk. I blew out a long breath; this was tougher than I expected. I resumed my seat at the table.

"Problem?" Kurt asked.

"Thought I heard footsteps. Just my imagination."

And with that, the Rolling Stones filled all the crevices in my brain. All I could think about was Sandra and Sam. The music grew louder and louder. I searched for the volume control but found none. From around the table, I saw mouths move but all I could hear was the song: Mick Jagger at full volume.

I didn't think I could speak over the noise. My hand reached out and touched Kurt's arm. He turned to me, his expression changing from neutral to alarm. I angled toward him more to shield my hand movements from the rest of the table. I touched the side of my face by my mouth then next to my eyebrows. Head. Touching my ear then shaking both hands. Noise. Kurt responded with a nod.

We'd danced this dance before. A long time ago. I knew he hadn't forgotten. Making sure I could see his lips, he signed while speaking. "Deep breath." I heard nothing except Mick Jagger. Breathing in deeply through my nose, I watched Kurt sign as his lips moved. "Breathe out through your mouth."

Doing as instructed lowered the volume increment by increment. I imagined my outward breath knocking Mick on his ass on the stage. My eyes never left Kurt. He continued to offer instructions. I followed them without question. The volume slowly decreased. Each breath pushed Mick closer to the edge.

Suddenly he disappeared. My ears popped. Normal service resumed. No one seemed any the wiser.

"Iverson?" Kurt said, in a low whisper. He leaned close, his left arm now resting on the back of my chair. "You good?"

"Yeah. Thanks."

"Was it a song?"

"Yeah, Rolling Stones. 'Just my Imagination.'"

"Sam sang that for Sandra."

He sang it then proposed to her. "I remember."

It wasn't that long ago. At my wedding dance, Sam took over the dance floor and proposed in front of all of us. I'd never forget. None of us would. Especially now.

The ripples caused by Sam's untimely death were far reaching and had tidal wave potential as they gathered momentum.

"Are we done here?" Lee said. He looked so lost.

I nodded. "Let's get this show on the road." I smiled as faces turned my way. "Okay, team, alert and safe out there. I want you all back in one piece."

Chairs scraped on the coarse carpeting as everyone stood. The buzz of conversation drifted to the door.

Sandra excused herself. The Director followed the last team out. Pretty soon it was just Delta A field agents and Caine left.

Caine held out an arm. "Gather up." Moose and Squirrel hung back. "Get over here, you're Delta A," Caine growled.

Neither man looked pleased. Time for intervention. "Squirrel, Moose. Caine is our SAC. He is family. He is also the grumpiest old bastard who ever walked the earth."

I felt I was failing in my description. "He's a teddy bear … with the ability to rip off your face." Pretty sure that helped.

Caine glared at me. It felt like a warm embrace. I'm a strange woman.

"Anything you need, get in touch. Anything that feels even remotely hinky … get out and call for backup," Caine said. "We're not losing anyone else. Got it?"

"Yeah," I said, my voice lost under the affirmative replies from my team.

"Ellie, I don't want you busting down doors," Caine said.

"I won't be. We're just bringing them to safety not busting down doors." I didn't see it as a door-breaching-guns-blazing type situation. Guess the potential was always there.

His guttural growl told me he wasn't convinced. Sam was the doorman. It was pretty much always his job to breach doors. He'd loved it. I'd lost count of the number of times I'd heard him say "Knock knock, Avon calling," before blowing the hinges off a door. We all knew if it had to be done and if I was there without Sam, I'd do it without hesitation. I liked it too.

Caine turned to Lee and Kurt. "She is not to bust down doors."

"Got it," they replied with shit-eating grins.

Just what I needed. Delta with orders to mollycoddle me. Expletives grew to a crescendo in my mind. I hoped they stayed there. Hope and reality were two different beasts. Caine kept on with his special brand of caring by handing out more instructions. Cringe-worthy stuff.

Squirrel and Moose looked on. I think it was glee I detected in their expressions. Perhaps glee heavy with unasked questions?

Caine must've noticed because he rasped out a short explanation. "Ellie is pregnant."

"Seriously?" Squirrel said with a shake of his head.

"What was that?" I said, directing a frown his way.

He shrugged. "Shouldn't you be home resting. Or doing needlepoint or that thing with yarn." He paused, his eyes twinkled as he spouted more stupid. "Knitting, that's the word I was looking for."

"You ass."

The glitter is his eye told me more than his ridiculous comment. Baiting me wasn't a smart move.

He grinned then turned back to Caine. "Don't worry SAC, we've got this."

"This ... bullshit ..." I waved a hand at the group of

men, "... is why I don't want people knowing until I'm ready to go on leave."

Caine grimaced. His mouth twitched. "And this ..." he waved a hand in my direction, "this attitude is why I want this team on the same page."

"Get fucked," I muttered under my breath. "I'm not the first person to have a baby."

"Nothing wrong with my hearing, Ellie. Settle down."

A snarl threatened then dissipated. I took a breath and reminded myself that Caine spoke from a place of caring and love. He didn't want me to feel less capable. He wanted the team to be aware. The complaining in my mind continued as Caine left the room.

"We moving out?" Lee leaned on the wall and looked at me. "We're only two and a half teams."

The door opened, Caine walked back in. "You need another person."

I smiled at him. "Yes, we do. Have anyone in mind?"

He growled out a monosyllabic response, "Me."

Lee extended his hand. They shook. "Happy to partner with you, Caine."

Problem solved. "When were you last in the field?" I said.

Caine gave a guttural grumble. "It's like riding a bike."

Sure it is. If the bike has no brakes, is missing a pedal, the handlebars are crooked, and someone's shooting at you. Then it's just like riding a bike. He and Lee left.

"Kurt?"

"He's the SAC. You going to stop him?"

I shook my head. No one could stop him. "He can ride the crazy bike if he wants."

Squirrel and Moose waved as they too headed out of the door.

"Keep in touch," I called after them. Not sure if they heard me or not.

Chapter Thirty Nine

Life On Mars

Kurt drove. I thought. I talked when I stopped thinking and I don't know which was worse.

"We're bringing Dane Moretti-Willows in first, yes?"

"Yes. That's the plan." I checked his address. Checked my weapon. The thoughts I'd been thinking tumbled out. "O'Malley might kill Gerrard before we can find out how he came to be with Chris and Susan?"

"That would be painful and we'd probably never know how he found them."

"It could be a coincidence."

"O'Malley being on the plane?"

"Yeah. She could be going on vacation to Dubai or Perth." Pirates probably take vacations. There's a chance they're not all death and argh-me-hearties-pass-the-rum.

"Iverson, we can pretend that O'Malley is going on vacation if that's what will get your head back in the game we're running now."

"I think we should."

"Done."

Fifteen more minutes of trees, houses, and traffic followed. It was almost enough to put me to sleep. Almost. Reading street signs was a fun way to pass the time. Not.

"This is his street," Kurt said making a left turn.

"Should be about halfway along," I said, watching the uninspired houses as we passed them. The house we wanted was forgettable in every way. The only difference between that house and every other house in the street was the number on the letterbox. Kurt drove right the way down the street and turned around. He parked a few doors away.

We walked back playing rock, paper, scissors. Best two out of three. I won. "You go to the back," I said. "I'm all set to enjoy this."

"Don't enjoy it too much," Kurt said with a small smile. "No busting down doors, remember?"

Adulting like a champ, I stuck my tongue out as he walked down the driveway and skirted the garage.

My approach obvious to anyone in the house, I walked straight up the front path and knocked on the plain wooden door. I didn't even care that I was wearing a bulletproof vest and had my badge around my neck. Nothing stealthy about me. The little dweeb inside the house needed to know right off the bat what he was up against. That way when I drew my weapon, I wouldn't feel bad, at all.

I didn't knock so much, as smack the side of my closed fist into the door three times. Waiting was hard. My patience had flown. I smashed on the door again.

Wood vibrated. The window next to the door rattled. No one answered. I tried the door handle. It turned. The door popped open. I blew on it while giving it a tap with my foot.

Whoops. Looks like the wind blew the unlatched door open. "Hello!" I hollered into the house. "I'm looking for Dane Moretti-Willows."

No answer. Silence filled the hallway. I remained outside the door, on the porch, not breaking any illegal entry laws. I took a breath to holler again. A sweet cloying green scent hit the back of my nose.

Was that pot? Yep. Pot. No wonder he wasn't answering the door. He was smashed. "Dane Moretti-Willows, exit the house by the front door!"

I heard a noise. Listening, I heard it again. Coughing. Muffled coughing. Knocking from the back door, followed by Kurt's voice calling for Dane Moretti-Willows to exit via the front door. More coughing. He wasn't going to come out. I called Kurt's cell.

"He's not coming out. I can smell pot. Someone's coughing. He's probably smashed and hiding."

"Can you get in?"

"Um, yeah, the front door just popped right open."

"Uh-huh. Give me a second and I'll see if the back door pops right open."

I hung up and stuffed my phone in my back pocket. While I waited to hear Kurt enter the house, I listened to the muffled coughing to determine where it was coming from. The front door opened into the living room, which seemed to flow to the dining room and I guessed it extended around the corner into a kitchen. Open plan. On the wall opposite the front door was a doorway, beyond that was a hallway that led to the left. Somewhere down there was a pot-smoking cougher.

Kurt appeared in the hall doorway with a grin on his face. He beckoned to me. We trundled down the hallway. Two empty bedrooms. Actually empty. No furniture at all. A small bathroom. A separate toilet. A closed door. And a strong smell of pot.

I knocked on the door. It flew open revealing a startled young man. "You can't just walk into my house!" He backed away, tripped over a large cushion, and landed on his backside. "You pushed me!"

Oh, here we go. Another idiot. "Dane Moretti-Willows?"

"Yeah. So. Anyway, no one calls me that." He lay where he fell on the floor. Cushions were scattered all around. There was a bed, a chair, a chest of drawers. At least this room had furniture.

"Which bit don't they call you?"

"Willows. I'm Dane Moretti."

"We'd like to ask you a few questions, Mr. Moretti."

He started laughing. "That's my grandfather."

Yeah, I know.

"Come on, let's go," Kurt reached a hand down and pulled him to his feet. "You can come with us."

He hesitated for a moment then the mellow took over. "Where are we going?"

"To our office. We have this really cool room we let people use, and it has coffee, and snacks," I said with a warm smile, the guy was so smashed he was going to be fun in an actual good way.

"Can I bring my shit?"

"Probably best not. Everyone will want some," Kurt said, ushering him out of the door. "Hey, where are your house keys?"

Dane led the way to the kitchen and handed Kurt a bunch of keys. "This is the front door key," Dane said, pointing to a blue key. "And the purple one is the back door."

"Thanks. You go with Ellie, she'll make sure you're safe in the car while I lock up for you."

Dane nodded, smiled, and glazed over. I figured he'd be asleep before we got him back to work. Probably not bad. But he didn't go to sleep. Dane wanted to chat.

"So were you celebrating something big, Dane? You're looking pretty happy." I was sitting in the back with Dane while Kurt drove.

"Yeah. I got this friend, Grace. And she's so cool."

"Is she your girlfriend?"

"She's a girl and she's my friend." He chuckled. "She'd be an awesome girlfriend. Grace is smokin' hot."

"What is it that you were celebrating?"

Kurt adjusted the rearview mirror. I raised an eyebrow at him. He winked. Nothing wrong then.

"Sometimes it takes a long time to fix stuff."

"Sounds cool. What stuff?"

"It's a long story, really long, took a few years. But today Grace told me she was going to Perth."

"I hear Perth is nice."

He shrugged. "I wouldn't know. Never been."

"Why is Grace going to Perth today?"

"She's going to meet my Uncle Bray."

She's going to kill Brayden. She's going to kill all of them. That means they'll be safe on the plane, because she needs to get to Perth to complete the job. "Do you like your uncle?" I said.

Dane sank into the car seat. "I'm sleepy."

"You should sleep."

"I like my uncle. My other uncle wanted Grace to meet him. Said because she's important to me, she should meet the family, all of the family."

My eyes hit Kurt's in the mirror. Everything in my being hollered "We have to stop O'Malley."

"Did they pay for her trip?"

He nodded. "Uncle Naz, he's so cool. He said he'd pay and then Grace would come out here and be with me. So she could meet Michelle." A sadness crept over his face. "But she can't meet Mom or Dad or my little sister Em."

"Oh, why not?"

"Em died. Mom and Dad, no one knows where they are. I think maybe Naz did know, but not now."

He's a pawn. He's just a fucking pawn. He's a stoner and they used him. "Hey, Dane, how about we get your uncle Bray to come here, then you can be together and meet Grace?"

"That'd be great. But Grace is already on the plane."

Yeah. "What'd Nazario tell you about Grace? He introduced you right?"

"Mhmm, he said she was an independent contractor. I

thought it was funny. She's way too pretty to build things. He must've been kidding."

"Did he say anything else, or have you heard anything else about what Grace was doing in Perth?" I needed to know the intent was to murder Brayden, then we could arrest her at the airport.

"She was going to hit a couple of people. Friends of hers were on the plane or something … it was something to do with them."

Kurt's eyes screamed 'Are you kidding me!'

"What does 'hit' mean?" I wanted to see what the stoner really understood.

"I dunno, hope it doesn't mean sex. I really like her, you know." He rolled his head on the headrest until he faced me. "She wouldn't have sex with other people, would she? She's coming to see me. She told me she really liked me."

"She told you?"

He struggled with his pocket, finally freeing his phone, which he handed to me. "Read the texts and tell me what you think." He touched the fingerprint identification then handed me the unlocked phone.

Holy crap. I smiled at the kid and opened his messages. They'd been texting for a few months. I scrolled back and forth through them looking for anything incriminating. Nothing on his part at all. I found something from her though. "Kurt, Grace told Dane she has a job to do for Nazario in Perth and then she'll come to Virginia and join him."

"Loose ends."

I nodded. "Looks that way."

We needed to get Brayden out of Australia before the plane landed. I knew Kurt was thinking along the same lines. He made a call. I heard him speaking but not what he was saying, mostly because Dane was singing. Singing a Justin Bieber song, 'Love yourself.' Part of me hated that I recognized it at all. Damn teenager music.

Kurt made another call. Couldn't hear him that time, either. But I read his lips when he looked into the mirror and whispered what he'd done. Australian Federal Police would meet the plane, along with our FBI colleagues from the Canberra office. Grace would be arrested and held in Australia pending an investigation into contract killing. Gerrard, Chris, and Susan would be met by FBI and repatriated as fast as possible. Brayden was to be picked up by Australian Federal Police and repatriated via Adelaide Airport in South Australia.

My phone rang. O'Hare. Director O'Hare started talking as soon as I answered. "I managed to get a coded message to Gerrard via the pilot of the airplane he's on. A heads up about O'Malley. There is a security officer on that flight. The airline was most forthcoming and will notify the officer regarding the delicate situation."

"Thank you."

"I see Kurt has expedited a team to meet the plane and bring our people home."

No flies on the O'Hare, that's for sure. "Yes, ma'am."

"Alert and Safe."

The call ended. I glanced over my shoulder at Dane. Eyes shut and humming. "Dane, you should have a nap when we get into the building. The room we'll put you in has a bed."

"You're very kind," he said, yawning once then singing quietly to himself.

Chapter Forty
Leaving The Table

My phone rang telling me Josh Konstram wanted to talk. "I've got Nazario Moretti in custody. We've had a chance to talk."

"Chatty?"

"Not really. He's a smug prick."

"Anything at all?"

"Yeah, he said, 'You'll never get to them all and he can't stop it.' Then he laughed."

"Dig around in his annoying head and see if you can find out why he can't stop it and what exactly he can't stop."

"Will do. Take it easy out there."

I had our list on my knee, with red marks next to the targets who might be at home and blue marks next to the ones we guessed would be at work. I read out the first address.

"That's ten minutes away. Buckle up."

Seriously? "Just drive."

"Cranky."

Tired, not cranky.

Ten minutes later we pulled up outside the last recorded address of Brad Armstrong, formerly Duane Wilbank, before his death in 2011.

"Might be at work," I said peering out the windscreen

at the house.

"Do we know where that is?"

I shook my head. "There was no place of work for this one. He's not federal, or if he is, it's not mentioned."

"Let's go knock on the door and make his day." Kurt swung open his car door and climbed out. I followed suit. He glanced over his shoulder at me. "Dragging a bit there, Iverson."

My hand flicked up and a finger flew in his direction. He chuckled. "No sense me hitting the porch first. We both know you're going to knock," I said.

"Orders are orders." His shoulders squared off and his right hand moved to his hip.

"Since fucking when," I muttered under my breath. "Just give me the word and I'll go sit in the car and knit."

"I'd like to see that," Kurt replied. "Someone's home. That curtain just moved." He pointed to the window beside the door as he crossed the porch and knocked.

Watching from the walkway, I glimpsed movement. "Someone's there."

Kurt knocked again. The curtain twitched. I stepped sideways. Twitching curtains don't fill me with a lot of confidence. People who are happy to see you don't twitch curtains, they open the door.

"Hello!" Kurt called.

I could tell he wasn't keen on saying he was FBI. That often ended badly. A smirk wriggled around my mouth looking for my lips. As if anyone couldn't tell by looking at Kurt. He almost screamed FBI, in a tastefully expensive suit of course, not the polyester atrocities that Moose and Squirrel wore.

The door flew open. A man stood in the doorway glaring at us. My Glock was in my hand. Kurt stepped sideways adjusting his grip on his weapon.

"What?"

"Are you Brad Armstrong?" Kurt said.

"That necessary?" he man replied tipping his head toward Kurt's gun.

"You know it is. Are you Brad Armstrong?"

"What if I am?"

"Sir, I'm SSA Kurt Henderson, this is my partner SSA Ellie Iverson. We need you to come with us."

He stepped back and the door slammed.

I joined Kurt on the porch. "That went well."

"You're up. Break out that famous Iverson charm."

I knocked. Charm coming right up. I knocked again. "One more time buddy and I'm coming through the door."

"Charm, Iverson," Kurt cautioned.

I shot him a look. "Stay close, I'm about to go from charming to fucking adorable." Dane Moretti took up time, we had eight more on our list, and the clock was ticking.

There was a huge temptation to grab the shotgun from the car, unlock the door the hard way and storm in, channeling my inner Arnie. I'd be a good Terminator.

My hand poised over the door. I heard the lock tumble. I let my hand fall to my side. As soon as the door opened a crack, I shoved it. "Ready to listen?" I said to the annoyed looking man, unable to shut his door.

"What do you want?"

"To save your life. If you're interested, then we need to get out of here and go somewhere safe. If not, we've other people to help." I let the door go, turned, as if to leave. "We'll see you ... when we identify your body."

"Hold up. What's this about?" He stepped onto the porch, with a short glance behind him he pulled the door almost closed.

"Is there someone else in the house?" He nodded. Dammit. That complicated things.

Kurt cleared his throat. We both looked at him. "Who's inside?"

"My daughter."

"How old is she?" A wail penetrated the almost closed door. Young by the sound of it.

"She's ten months old. What's going on and who the hell are you?"

I flipped my ID at him. He checked it out, looked at me, nodded and handed it back.

"People are dying. Former agents who now have new lives are dying."

"And?"

"And your name is on the same list. We need to get you to a safe house." I could see the cogs and wheels turning in his head.

While they turned Kurt spoke, "Your wife?"

"She's shopping. We just got home from vacation."

That explained why he was home and it might've saved his life. And we needed to take three people not one. "Tell her to meet us …" I scrambled for a meeting place that wouldn't cause suspicion. "Is there a park where you usually take your daughter?"

A frown deepened in his brow. The baby howled louder. "Yes."

"Text her now. Pack and do it fast. Important documents. Whatever you need for the baby, your wife and yourself. In particular, medications."

Brad sighed. "This isn't supposed to happen."

"Please. Time is ticking." He hurried into the house. I called after him, "Don't forget the baby seat and her favorite toys."

Pretty sure he didn't need my prompting but we weren't going back for anything. He was right, it shouldn't be happening but it was, so we deal.

Kurt and I waited. Keeping an eye on the street and an ear on the movement inside the house.

I leaned a little closer to Kurt. "Do you think he's in danger? The other victims were still working in whatever capacity as Feds, this guy isn't."

"He's on the list. We don't get to make that call."

That was true. I'd hate to deprive a child of her father because we decided to do nothing. I watched as two cars drove past. Another came from the opposite direction. I had no way of knowing how much traffic was usual for this particular part of suburbia. Something prickled in the back of my neck. Another car went by.

Kurt nudged me when yet another car appeared. "We saw that red car a few minutes ago."

Yeah, we did, I remember the crease in the side panel. "Could you see the occupants?"

"No. We're too far away."

I rapped on the front door. "Hurry up."

Kurt watched the street. "Three times. We're going!" He had his weapon in his hand.

I yelled into the house, "Time's up. We gotta go. Now."

Kurt opened the car doors. Ready.

A voice called back, "Coming."

I ran in to help. We met in the hallway. He had the baby in her car seat, a nappy bag, and two backpacks. I grabbed the backpacks.

"Kurt, coming out ..." I said from the relative safety of the hall.

"Get them in the car." Stress cracks resounded in Kurt's voice. "... Iverson."

I stepped out of the doorway, making sure I was between our charge and the road. I pointed to the car, about eight feet away. He nodded, hoisted the car seat into his arms and hurried to the back of the car. As soon as I heard the seatbelt click around the baby seat, I pulled the front door shut and ran over, chucked the backpacks in next to her, shut the door and then slipped into the front passenger seat. Kurt climbed into the driver's seat.

As we got to the road, a red car raced toward us then passed us. I saw the crease in the side panel.

"Buckle up."

Again? Buckle up has become his favorite phrase. I glanced in the wing mirror. That car had turned and headed our way. Again. Fast. With a deep swallow, I braced myself and pulled my phone out of my pocket. Touching the home button on my phone, I said, "Call Caine." A corner loomed.

Siri's voice repeated my command and the phone rang.

"Problem?" Caine said as he answered.

"Yeah. We need a car intercepted."

A beat went by and I heard Lee. "Got your tracker. We're coming. Just stay on the road and don't engage."

"It's a red Ford, a Territory, I think."

"It is," Kurt said, adjusting his wing mirror.

I hung up. "Hear what Lee said?" I said to Kurt. He nodded. "Wish Lee'd told the guy in the red Ford not to engage."

I looked behind me. The baby was fine, her dad looked worried. Fair enough. The Ford was gaining fast.

A phone rang from behind me. It stopped abruptly when I heard Brad's voice. "Heather. Stay where you are. I'm on my way."

I reached back and took the phone. "Heather. I'm SSA Ellie Iverson. We are coming to you at the park. Please stay put."

"Where's my baby?"

"With us. We'll be there soon."

A siren wailed in the distance. Coming up behind us I saw flashing lights. Ambulance. Cars pulled over to let the paramedics through. The red Ford stayed on our bumper. At the last minute, it pulled over, allowing the ambulance to pass. Kurt stayed, turned our flashers on and kept ahead of the ambulance until he took a sharp left. I turned the flashers off.

Kurt pulled over and watched the rearview mirror. "Can't see him."

An oncoming black Suburban flashed its headlights at us. "Lee and Caine," I said, as the car leveled with ours. Windows rolled down.

"Everyone okay?" Caine asked.

"Yeah. We lost the car," I replied.

Kurt growled. "No. We hoped we did." He was still watching in the rearview mirror. "Cruising up the street now."

"We got it," Lee said. "You do what you do."

Chapter Forty One
From The Ground Up

The explanation delivered to Brad Armstrong's wife was short and dealt with on the move. We sequestered them in one of our safe houses without further incident and contacted Debbie Barnes.

We sat in the car down the street from the safe house for a few moments. I checked messages on my phone while Kurt took a call from Caine. Nothing from Perth but then no one would be in place yet.

The meager contents of my stomach writhed. I settled it with some calming breathing and the knowledge that I'd put everything I could in place to ensure a good outcome. Mitch knew something was up but not what. Harley was blissfully unaware because, despite my pinky swear, I couldn't deal with telling her right now. CPDs were doing their jobs.

Eight of the people from the main list were now safely in our protection. No one else reported any incidents. Typical. Guess I'm still attracting trouble. If Nazario Moretti talked, we might have a better chance of getting everyone to safety.

"Next?" Kurt asked.

"Manassas field office. Our next target is a working agent. Noah Bailey."

"And he's at the office?"

"Yep. Sandra verified his whereabouts and he's expecting us." She'd given him some story about a cold case we were looking into, having dug up something he was involved in a few years back.

"This one might be easier," Kurt replied with a derisive laugh.

"Caine and Lee okay?"

"Yes. That car that was following us disappeared."

"Seriously? What is it a ghost car?"

Kurt and I scanned the street ahead of us. A harried-looking mother pushing a stroller with one hand and holding tight to a small girl's hand with the other; the little girl ran to keep up. They hurried past an elderly man waiting at a bus stop before they disappeared into a nearby building. The sign above the door told me it was a daycare.

That woman was my future. "Let's get going. There's not much happening here."

Twenty minutes, a lot of traffic and a bridge later, a red car with a suspicious crease in one of the side panels was parked on the side of the road.

"See it?"

"Yes." He pulled in behind the car. "What are the chances?"

"I wouldn't have expected they were that good."

We both approached the vehicle – weapons in hand. Kurt opted for the driver's side, I approached from the passenger side.

There was no one in the car. I looked at Kurt over the

roof. One eyebrow elevated.

Kurt responded, "Abandoned." He tried the door. It sprang open. Looking quickly through the car he couldn't find anything to connect it to an owner. I called comms and had them run the plates.

"Stolen plates. The plates match a black Honda Accord stolen from Alexandria this morning."

"Not a Ford Territory ..."

"Nope."

"Think it was the same person that followed us?"

He nodded and called Caine to let him know. A few minutes later we were on the road again. The car bugged me. Whoever was driving it before was now in something else and could pop up anytime anywhere. I evaluated the likelihood of the car that had followed us being innocent.

Slipping my phone into my hand, I glanced at Kurt. "I think we should turn off the tracker on our car."

The words hit the windscreen and slid down, letter by letter, forming an inky puddle on the dash. It spilled over, dripping down the console and onto the floor. Kurt said nothing for several beats. I could see his mind whirring and knew the exact moment when he caught my wavelength and succumbed to the idea that someone was using our GPS for all the wrong reasons.

"Can you do it?"

"Yes." I accessed the app on my phone and turned off our GPS, and turned off both our phone trackers. "Sandra activated the app on my phone when Sam went missing. I'm leaving Lee and Caine online."

Kurt nodded in agreement. "No one else reported a tail or anything out of the ordinary." His grip tightened on the steering wheel.

Neither of us was willing to say the words aloud but we both knew it was either someone within the FBI tracking us or someone smart enough to hack into our GPS.

My phone rang. Sandra's image appeared on the screen. I knew that one of the screens on her desk would have our locations on maps. Sandra had three screens arranged in a semi-circle on her large desk and a laptop behind her on another desk. She could swivel in her chair and use the laptop with ease. She often had a multitude of windows open on all the screens and programs running on the laptop.

"Hey," I said touching the speaker icon. "You're on speaker."

"O Esteemed Leader ... what's going on out there?"

"We're going dark for a few hours."

I heard her fingers typing and knew she'd just discovered I'd overridden her access to our trackers. "That's dangerous. I can't see the car or your cell phone trackers." Her fingers tapped again. "You're blocking me from turning them on from here."

"I know. Keep an eye on Caine and Lee, we'll be in touch."

"Does Caine know?"

"No. This stays between us."

Her voice changed, sadness overtook the perkiness she always displayed. "Please be careful. We can't lose anyone else."

"We will."

And the perk came back. "Stay safe, O Wrangler of the Wayward."

"We'll be in touch." My fingers crossed in my lap. All going well, this next person would be a smooth pick up and we'd be back on the grid before long. A laugh slipped out of my mouth before I could stop it.

Kurt turned to look at me. His expression changed from confusion to quizzical. "Something funny?"

"I was just thinking that if no one could track us, then the next seven pick-ups might be smooth sailing."

Kurt smiled and adjusted his hands on the steering wheel. "Think you just jinxed it, Iverson."

I scanned the car interior for wood, nothing, so I tapped my head. Because we're twelve and jinxing stuff is a thing.

"I hope Noah is waiting for us," I said. My finger followed the line with his name on it to a death date and previous name. "He was David Yarbrough before his death in 2012."

"I know that name. He was FBI."

"Yes, he was out of State though."

Kurt nodded and kept his attention on the road. From where I sat, I watched small storm clouds gathering across his face. "Yarbrough was a doctor."

"Seriously?"

"Remember when we went undercover in Lexington at the hospital?"

How could I forget? Sisters killing patients. One sister was a doctor and the other a nurse. They sure made an effective team, murdering badly behaved patients who came through the emergency department at Stonewall Jackson Hospital.

"Uh-huh ..."

"Yarbrough did something similar in Texas. From memory, it was a nurse killing elderly patients."

"How'd you know?"

"The medical community isn't that big. The medical and FBI community overlap is much smaller. We all meet up eventually and there have been conference-type situations. Our roles within the agency are constantly being redefined and honed."

"Will he recognize you? And will that be a problem?"

"Not for me."

"Did you know he was dead?"

Kurt nodded. "Small community, remember."

"And you haven't heard of Noah Bailey?"

He shook his head. "No. He wouldn't have been able to remain a doctor if he required a new life. Too obvious."

"How hard would that be? Walking away from all those years and the oath you took?"

"Very."

"Could you?"

"No."

"But he did?"

"As far as I know, I haven't seen the name Noah Bailey in regard to anything medical. A new doctor on our list would stick out."

"We're almost there," I said, looking at the buildings we passed and noting the build-up of traffic.

"So far so good." Kurt slowed. "We'll park down the street and walk."

Chapter Forty Two
Get Up, Stand Up

Running footsteps came up behind me. I stepped out of the way but wasn't fast enough. The man knocked into me. "Hey, buddy. Slow down." He glanced at me. Fear flashed across his face. "You all right?" Frown lines formed on his forehead, his eyes darted across the street and back. Where'd he come from?

"There's something down there—"

"Where?" I looked around and saw nothing.

"The alleyway."

There's an alleyway?

Kurt spun on his heels and headed down the street, calling over his shoulder, "Stay there with SSA Iverson."

"SSA?" the man said, catching his breath.

I flipped my badge open and showed it to him. "FBI. And you are?"

"Robert Bolton." He seemed to deflate.

"And you're running up the street why?"

A small smile flickered and disappeared. "I usually walk. I cut through the alleyway from work, going for coffee." He pointed to a coffee sign on the pavement up the street. "I go there every day."

From the direction Kurt went, I heard a high whistle. Looking I saw his arm twirl in the air.

"Come with me," I said to Bolton. "My partner has

something to show me."

He backed away about two feet. His head shook. "Not back there."

"'Fraid so. You'll be fine." I saw Kurt using his phone. With an encouraging hand on Bolton's arm, I walked him to meet Kurt. It wasn't until I was almost there that I noticed a dark wet area on the right cuff and sleeve of Bolton's suit jacket.

Kurt stepped into our path. "CCTV cameras owned by the bank service the alleyway." He pointed to a building that shared a common wall with the alleyway. "Bank."

"What do we have?"

"A dead male beside a dumpster. He died bloody."

My heart thumped harder. What were the chances of a random person dying when we were on our way to pick someone up? My eyebrows rose.

Kurt nodded.

Dammit.

Bolton tried to pull away from my grip. My hand tightened. "Mr. Bolton, did you touch the body?" Not did you kill Noah Bailey? That would wait.

He shook his head.

"You sure about that?"

He nodded. The last remnants of color faded from his face. Tiny beads of sweat broke out on his brow.

"Let's get that bank footage," I said

Bolton tried to pull away.

Kurt nodded. "I called the field office. They're sending a couple of agents down."

"Why?" Bolton said, renewing his extraction effort.

"Because the guy in the alleyway is an FBI agent and killing a Fed is monumentally stupid—"

"And now the death penalty is on the table," said Kurt.

A warm gust of wind tugged at my jacket and twirled dust on the sidewalk. It dropped away, leaving dust swirling for a moment.

"I didn't have anything to do with his death," Bolton said, his shoulders drooping under an imaginary weight.

"Maybe you didn't," I replied. "But you have what looks like blood on your jacket cuff and sleeve and you came from the alleyway and there's a body in the alleyway."

A black Suburban pulled up alongside us. A female voice rang out. "Henderson, is that you?" The owner of the voice crossed the sidewalk and approached us.

"Dawn!" Kurt said, with a grin. "Didn't know you were in Virginia."

"Haven't been here long," she replied, shaking his hand.

Kurt turned to me. "Ellie Iverson, Dawn Alvarez."

Dawn smiled. She was pretty, my height, long dark curly hair, brown eyes, athletic looking. "The famous Ellie Iverson née Conway."

"Infamous probably more than famous," I replied with a laugh.

"This is Sal Keating, my partner," Dawn said, introducing the man on her right.

Kurt gave them a rundown on the alleyway and its

contents. Dawn disappeared into the alley. She came back and confirmed it was Noah Bailey.

"We're going to go check something at the bank. Can you two deal with that?" I said, waving a hand toward the alley.

"Yeah. He's one of us. We'll get uniforms here and secure the scene."

"Thanks," I said. Kurt headed to the bank. I pushed Bolton along behind him. "Let's go see, shall we?"

He shook his head. "This is ridiculous."

"Possibly." I held the door open for him and motioned him to follow Kurt. "Let's view the footage and remove all doubt. Easy as that."

He let loose a resigned sigh.

"If you had nothing to do with it, there is nothing to worry about," I said, mustering brightness. He could be innocent. Big Foot roams the Appalachians. Regan MacNeil needed a Ouija Board instruction manual. No one ever lied to a Fed.

Kurt spoke to a well-dressed woman. She glanced at Bolton and me, then back at Kurt. With a tight smile, she ushered us all into an office. The nameplate on the door said manager.

"I'll have our security company show you the footage, Agents." She picked up the phone on her desk and made a call. At least she didn't ask for a warrant. Nice. Cooperative. I like that in people.

I encouraged Bolton to sit in a chair by the door and stood next to him. Kurt sat by the manager's desk.

Her bland office felt almost sterile. A big, uncluttered white desk sat almost in the middle of the room and faced the door. Behind the desk was a row of white filing cabinets, flush with the wall and extending right across the room. A large floor-to-ceiling window gave an unobstructed view of the bank interior. Her office reminded me of a goldfish bowl. Green carpet. Green chairs. Everything else, including the walls, was white. No personal touches anywhere. No personality.

The manager replaced the phone. "O'Hare Security handles our CCTV, they'll have someone here in a few minutes with the capability to view the footage."

"It's kept off site?" I asked. It was a good idea if it were.

"Yes. We can't access the camera feed at all from here."

Guess that was one way of making sure the cameras weren't tampered with, or rather the footage from the cameras. "Who's coming from the security company?"

"Trent Cambrook."

I suppressed the smile that tried to wiggle free. We knew Trent. He was part of the team that monitored my private security system before he moved to Manassas and to the office O'Hare Security had out here.

There was a buzz from the desk. The manager answered then looked at Kurt. "Two agents just entered the building looking for you."

"Thanks. I'll be right back." He smiled at me on his way past and out the door. Closing it behind him.

Bolton shifted in his seat. "This will be over soon," I

said. We'll either turn him over to Manassas or turn him loose with an apology and a card to access our victim support services. We're not heartless. Or stupid.

The last thought seemed to route through the Hoover Building and pick up Owen on the way back. My phone rang and I could see her irritating name pop up on my screen. As tempted as I was to ignore the call, I knew I had to see what the Evil Queen wanted.

"AD Owen, how can I help?" I said, with much restraint. Saying "AD Owen, how can I kill you?" probably wouldn't go down well.

"Where are you?"

"Working, ma'am."

"I can't seem to get hold of anyone from Delta."

Yeah, that'll be because we're all working on this issue. "Is there something important, ma'am?"

"I would like a report. I want to know what everyone is working on. I do not appreciate you withholding information from me, Agent." She paused. Her voice sharpened. "There will be ramifications."

I just bet there will. "We're on a time-sensitive assignment sanctioned by the Director. Perhaps you should ask her for a briefing?"

She huffed air into the phone. "I am AD of the Criminal Investigation Division. I should be notified by you when an operation extends to all three Delta teams."

Die screaming. "I'm aware, ma'am. This is a unique situation."

"I am the Executive Assistant Director you report to,

Agent Iverson – I demand answers."

Maintaining a quiet yet authoritative tone wasn't easy for me. The witch pushed my buttons. I hated that she could do that. Through semi-gritted teeth, I replied, "Yes, ma'am, you are. In this case, the Director overrides you."

"I will not stand for this nonsense, SSA. I expect a full report on my desk by nightfall and a personal briefing to follow."

"Sorry, ma'am. That will have to be cleared by Director O'Hare." I could almost feel the steam pouring from her ears.

"Why isn't your car visible on the system?" she snapped into my ear.

"I don't know, ma'am. A glitch maybe?" My fingers crossed in my lap.

"SSA, this is unacceptable." She hung up.

EAD Owen: Pissing agents off since eons ago.

I breathed a sigh of relief even though I knew it wouldn't end with one phone call. She'd be on this like Batman on Robin. I shuddered. A voice in my head broke through and instructed me to leave Batman and Robin's relationship out of the equation.

The door opened. Kurt strode in with Trent and Agents Alvarez and Keating. Good thing the office was as large as it was bland. Trent had a ruggedized laptop under his arm. Pangs of jealousy raced through me. I coveted his laptop: The next item on my purchase list for Delta A was ruggedized laptops. The priority wasn't super high but the cool factor was unbelievable.

The manager, her name eluded me, spoke to Trent. "Hope you don't mind me calling you over like this."

"Of course not, Eloise, I'm happy to sit with Agents Henderson and Iverson and show them the footage from camera five," Trent replied.

Eloise. Old-fashioned name. Suited her.

"It's an unusual situation."

Trent swung around to me. "Hey, Iverson, what's the suit got to do with this?" his head inclined to Bolton.

"Not sure yet. Hoping to confirm with the video footage."

Trent nodded. "Let's get to it." He looked at Eloise. "Is there a spare office we can use?"

"Use mine. I'll be on the floor if you need me." She stood, pushing her chair back with her legs and rounded the desk. "Take all the time you need."

"Thanks," Trent said with a smile.

I watched her walk past him and try not to look in his direction. And his reaction. They were an item.

Kurt addressed Bolton, "Anything you want to share before we view the footage?"

He said nothing.

Trent sat in Eloise's chair and fired up the laptop. "It'll take a few minutes to bring up the morning's footage. Got a particular time?"

I nodded. "Let's roll back to an hour and fifteen minutes ago."

"No problem."

Bolton stopped fidgeting and just sat while Trent

typed. Within a few minutes, we were watching the alleyway camera footage.

Noah Bailey entered the alley talking on his phone. The way he looked around made me think he was waiting for someone, or expecting to see someone. He looked up and turned away from the camera. A second or so later Bolton came into view. We got a brief glimpse of Noah's face.

"He smiled," I said. "At you, Mr. Bolton."

Trent paused the video then played the section back. I saw the smile again. The video ran on. Bolton acknowledged Noah with a head nod and a smile. His right arm moved.

"Stop it right there. Can you magnify the image?" Trent rolled back to Bolton's right arm moving and magnified the image. "Zoom in on his hand. What does that look like?"

Both Kurt and Trent said, "A blade."

The video moved on. Four seconds was all it took for Bolton to ram the blade into Noah's neck, twist, pull, and stab again. I saw how the blood marked his suit cuff and sleeve. Blood covered the blade.

"I don't need to see any more." I stood. "Stand up, Mr. Bolton, and turn around." I took my cuffs from my belt and dragged his left arm behind his back, snapping a handcuff link on his wrist. I repeated the maneuver with his right arm. "You're under arrest for the murder of a Federal Agent."

His whole being changed in that instant: he showed no

remorse or sorrow. Instead, confusion and disbelief mingled with realization.

A tremor raced up my spine.

Bolton said nothing. I motioned to Alvarez and Keating. Alvarez took Bolton, Keating followed them out the door. As they left the room, I heard Alvarez reading the Miranda Warning. Always seemed redundant when we came up against cases in which someone was caught on tape doing whatever we've accused them of, but, the law says we do it. The law says innocent until proven guilty. Doesn't matter what we saw. A jury of his peers will decide his fate, not us.

"Next?" Kurt said. There was nothing we could do for Noah Bailey now. Time moved on with never-ending precision and we had to move onto the next.

I consulted the list. "There's another one out this way, let's get him now." If we can get to him before someone else does.

Trent was packing up. "I'll send the footage to Alvarez," he said, standing and moving toward the door.

"Thanks, that'd be great," I replied.

"Take care." Trent smiled and left.

Kurt and I looked at each other for a moment. I knew he was on my wavelength. "This mission has been shitified," I said.

"No argument here. Let's see if we can bring it back around."

Time to take a run at Liam Connor, previously Caleb Steele, and now working for the DEA.

Chapter Forty Three
It's Not Unusual

We were in the car and moving before I suggested a change of plan. "I'm not buying Bailey's death was a random act by a befuddled office worker who accidentally ran into us."

The temptation on my part was to skip Connor and go right for Ethan Guarino. The gnawing in my gut made me think we might not get to Connor in time. I knew it was a response to Bailey and tried to ignore it.

My comment about the befuddled office worker spun me back to Harley and the drug used to zombify her. "Could you make someone kill if they were under the influence of Devil's Breath?"

I watched scenery flash by and tried to determine where we were in relation to Connor.

"Devil's Breath removes the victim's free will. They don't seem to be able to think for themselves. It's possible that people could be told to kill while under the influence and follow the instruction."

"Bolton?"

"He was pretty confused. I don't think it was an act."

"So Nazario Moretti could be, I said 'could,' not 'is,' using innocents to kill?"

"If that's happening then we've got another problem on our hands. Moretti is in custody and his plan is in motion. He never needed to get near the target, just near someone who knew the target or came across the target during the course of a normal day."

"Anyone could be a killer."

"Of course, this is all conjecture until we know for sure." Kurt passed me his phone. "Alvarez's number is in there. Call her and suggest strongly that they have Bolton screened for drugs and in particular scopolamine."

I made the call then dropped his phone into his lap.

"We're really close to where Connor is," Kurt said, his eyes flicked sideways to mine.

"Let's do it." My wanting to jump ahead and save people I considered I could reach overridden by my desire to leave no man behind.

I let my inner voice do some talking. Okay, God, here's the thing. We need a chance to save these men and it feels like you've dropped the ball again. Little help, please.

The lack of an answer just cemented what'd felt for a long time that God doesn't give a shit. Maybe I'm better off asking Chance for help.

A pen nib appeared in the corner of my mind and slowly traced the world until everything had a thin black outline. Muted color filled the scene, bringing the flat lines to life. I touched a desk. It felt solid, three-dimensional, not like pen on paper. A door opened. Fresh air rushed in, lifting and curling the bottom of the page. I flipped the page over and found myself in another room. A living room. A fire roared in a big stone fireplace, filling the room with dancing shadows and warmth. A patch of blond hair was just visible over the back of a large leather armchair in front of the fire. Another chair sat next to it, empty. A well-known disembodied voice said, "Have a seat, El."

Unsure whether the chair would be a chair or a drawing of a chair, I felt reluctant to commit to sitting. The voice laughed at my hesitation. I sat. The chair was a chair. I saw the owner of the voice and the blond hair. Chance.

Hard not to smile when face-to-face with Christopher Chance. "Are you going to be helpful or annoying?"

"Little hurtful, El. I don't think I'm ever annoying."

"Trust me. You can be."

"With that attitude, you shouldn't be surprised." He folded his arms across his chest.

"Annoying is harsh."

Good going, Ellie, you've offended a hallucination. "Chance ... why am I here?"

"Because you opted to ask me for help. Something about God dropping the ball."

Old Butterfingers can't seem to get a grip on the ball at all these days. "Not so much dropped it, as can't pick it up." At all. Ever.

"I used to play a bit of rugby once upon a time ... give me a shot."

"Rugby? Like Kiwi's play?"

"Uh-huh. Don't let your brain explode thinking about it." His grin brought dimples with it. "Tell me how I can

419

help."

"I believe Harley's kidnapping, the disappearance of her parents, the human trafficking, the use of scopolamine, dead agents, and the list are all connected to Moretti. But I don't know what Gerrard has to do with it all. I don't know why the CIA is trying to shorten his life. I don't get why Rowan was kidnapped. I don't get the NSA reference that Chris gave me."

"What do you know for sure?"

Nothing. I know nothing. Tendrils of fear wound around my heart. Thoughts raced in every direction at once and came back with nothing. Proving once and for all, that I didn't know anything concrete. A wild thumping in my chest increased until I could hardly breathe. I pulled at the neck of my shirt, trying to loosen it.

"Hey, El, look at me. Slow your breathing."

"I don't know anything more than what I told you," I said, my words distorted as I tried to suck in enough air to speak. "I can't get those last pieces to fit."

"Slow. It. Down." Chance's calm quiet voice gave me focus. "I can help. Just slow down. Breathe."

Listening to Chance repeat his words over and over helped.

"You good?"

"Yeah. Thanks."

"No problem. Now, tell me what you know about Chris from the beginning ... don't think, just talk."

What do I know? Nothing. It won't take long. "Chris

left a code in a hack. We found an Iverson drone at a crime scene. Emma Moretti-Willows was killed by a drone."

"Okay, so Iverson Tech is being targeted. Revenge?"

"Yeah." I knew there was more to it.

"What does Chris do that makes him so valuable beyond the drone?"

"He's co-owner of Iverson Technology."

"I know that, but what is his area of expertise?"

"Design. He's a software engineer." Flashing LED ropes wound together to form an exclamation mark and all the colored lights merged.

"Do I need to continue?"

No. I shook my head. The black lines wobbled, spiked, and disappeared, taking Chance and the fireplace with them. I jumped to my feet before my chair vanished from under me. Blinking slowly cleared the last of Chance's comic-book life out of my head.

Chris Iverson is a software engineer. He designed the apps on Harley's iPad. He designed the operating software for the drones. What else did he design? Why didn't I think to investigate him before now?

Because all hell broke loose and distracted me from his disappearance. He's family. I need to do better than that. I made a mental note to look closer at my brother-in-law and what other things he was involved in.

"Wakey wakey, Iverson."

"What?" I turned my head to see Kurt glance in my direction.

"I thought you were asleep."

"No … Thinking." I looked out the window. "Where are we?"

"Connor's house. There's a car in the driveway. He might be home."

And dead already. "Let's go find out," I said with as much positive energy as I could muster, fooling no one, not even myself.

We walked together, neither speaking. I focused on the task ahead and pushed my conversation with Chance out of the way.

A door closed. Someone stood on the porch of the house. The person took a few steps to the edge of the porch and called out, "Can I help you?"

"Hope so," I called back.

"You're not Godbotherers are you?"

I detected a smirk on Kurt's face. It disappeared rapidly. "No, sir, we are not." I took my badge from my pocket and handed it to him as I got to the top of the porch steps. "SSA Iverson and SSA Henderson. There's a security breach – we'd like you to come with us to a safe house."

He handed me back my badge. "Agent Iverson, I'm no longer with the FBI."

"We know, Mr. Connor. You're in danger." I clamped my lips together before the famous words of the Terminator could break free. Enough with the Arnie crap already.

Connor looked at Kurt then at me.

"Please," Kurt said, motioning to the door. "Get what you need. Time is not on our side."

Knowing full well what that phrase would do to me, Kurt flung a grin over his shoulder at me right when the Rolling Stones blasted onto the stage in my head in full vocal force.

Connor went inside, leaving the door open. I shook Mick Jagger from the stage and watched as he tumbled into the orchestra pit taking the rest of the band with him. Charlie clung to his drum kit for dear life as it slid across the stage before another shake of my head dislodged him and the drums. An almighty crash echoed through my head. I jumped.

"Iverson?"

Dammit, Kurt must've noticed. "Yep?"

"You good?"

"Just peachy." My left hand plunged into my pocket as my fingers crossed.

Kurt sighed. He turned his attention to the house and the open door. "Mr. Connor, let's hurry it up!"

From deep inside, I heard a door quietly shut. Shit! He's running. I drew my weapon and ran inside yelling at Kurt as I went, "Stay here in case he comes this way."

I ran down the hallway, checking every room as quickly as I could on my way to the back of the house. I emerged in a large airy kitchen. From the window I glimpsed a foot going over the back fence. My mind scrambled through maps trying to recall what was behind the street we were on. Another subdivision and a golf course.

I opened the back door and whistled to Kurt. Moments later pounding feet came up the side of the house. "I think he went over the fence," I said, pointing to the high wooden fence in the backyard. "He's an idiot."

No argument from Kurt. "Leave him," Kurt said. "Let's get the next one."

"Yeah, I'll go to the back you can take the front door." I took my card and stuck it to his refrigerator door with one of the many magnets I found there. Looked like he collected them. We locked up the house and left. Just because the guy was an idiot didn't mean we wanted him to get burgled. Or dead.

We hadn't gone a mile down the road before my phone rang. "Whaddaya bet this is Connor?" I said, seeing an unfamiliar number on the screen.

"If he's come to his senses it will be." Kurt pulled over as I answered the call.

"Agent Iverson."

"What sort of breach are we talking about?" a male voice asked.

"You are?"

"Connor."

"How do I know you are Connor?" Nothing. "I'm not kidding. How do I know who you are?"

"You don't."

"Disconnect. I'll call you."

He hung up. Instead of making a voice call, I video-called the number. Call me paranoid but I'm not about to tell someone killing our guys what we know. The call was answered fast. There was Connor looking at me via his phone. "Good. You alone?"

"Yeah."

"Grab your stuff, lock up, start walking south. We'll pick you up."

"What sort of breach?"

"I'll tell you when we know you're safe." I hung up.

Kurt turned back to Connor's place. A few minutes later Kurt did a U-turn and pulled up alongside Connor.

He clambered into the back of the car and slammed the door shut. "What's going on?"

I swiveled in my seat so I could see him. "Someone has accessed a list of 'deceased' agents and their current names and whereabouts. Now we've got previously deceased agents dying all over again."

"That shouldn't be possible." He ran a hand through his hair. Disbelief crowded his features.

"We know. We're bringing everyone on the list in, you're all getting new lives."

"Again," his voice held a deep sigh of resignation. "Once was bad enough."

I waited for the questions I knew were coming.

"Do you know who?"

"We have someone in custody in relation to this matter but that hasn't stopped it."

"How are they dying?"

"In the line of duty mostly. Whoever is doing this knows an awful lot." Having the list is one thing but knowing where everyone is and how to get to everyone, now that is labor, time, and planning intensive.

"Christ." He stared out the window for a moment. "Why?"

"Don't know that either for sure. Looks like revenge but this is extreme. As far as I can figure out, the only connection you all have is the list. That list was on a secure server within the FBI. Not directly accessible from the outside."

Turns out 'not directly accessible' doesn't stop someone who knows where the information is stored and is a clever little hacker. And that wasn't the only connection they had. Someone put them on the list. I needed to talk to Debbie Barnes again. Someone also designed the software. I filed that for later. I really needed to know what else Chris Iverson was involved with design-wise.

I called Debbie's direct dial number. As soon as she answered, I said, "Debbie, it's Ellie, can you meet me?"

"It's Michael Addison speaking."

What now? Sounded like Debbie. "Is Debbie in?"

"No sorry. She's not."

"No worries I'll ring her cell." I hung up and stared at the phone screen for a moment.

"All right?" Kurt asked.

"I think so. Debbie's not there. Someone called Michael Addison answered."

"She's probably busy, she's got a lot on her plate now."

Yeah. All the new identities to create. "It's just ... he

sounded like her."

"Distortion maybe."

I nodded. Yeah, that'd be it. She wouldn't say she was someone else.

"Michael Addison gave me my new identity," Connor said.

I swiveled around to look at him. "Not Debbie Barnes?"

"No, I dealt with Michael."

"Did you ever meet Debbie?"

He shook his head.

I sat straight in my seat again. That changed things. If Debbie wasn't solely responsible for the new identities, then I needed to talk to Michael as well.

Addison. The name rolled around a bit then settled. Caine gave me two names when I asked for help. Debbie Barnes and Michael Addison. He didn't know who would be available.

I called Caine. "Real quick ... Debbie Barnes and Michael Addison, do they job share or are they both on deck at any point?"

"Job share, I believe. As far as I know, there are no set times when you'll find Addison or Barnes. Bit of a lucky dip as to who is in the office."

"Thanks." I hung up.

That could mean both of them handled the same cases, sometimes. One could start and the other could finish depending on their schedules. By the time I'd finished thinking about the possibilities of there being a crossover with some of the cases, Kurt had pulled up outside one of our safe houses. We settled Connor into the house and told him we'd be back.

Before we left, four other teams checked in. There were now twelve from the list in safe houses. And one more deceased. Just us with the dead formerly deceased agent. There are words I never envisaged would be strung together even in my world. Dead formerly deceased agent were some of them.

I looked at Kurt as he turned the ignition key.

He looked at me; guess he felt my eyes on him. "Got something on your mind, Iverson?"

"Yeah."

"Spill. Many hands or minds or something or other are good."

I laughed. "Mitch's brother, Chris, is a software engineer."

"Did Iverson Tech have something to do with the computer system that we think was hacked?"

"I don't know but Chris has designed and developed some impressive stuff and Mitch said they've done quite a bit of work for governments, not just ours."

"Let's find out if any of his design work involved programs and systems we use." His brow creased.

My mind careened along another pathway. "Why do you think Bolton killed Noah Bailey?"

"He had no reason. There was no motive to murder Noah."

"You're sure?"

"Uh-huh. I've heard from Alvarez. Nothing links Bailey and Bolton at all, apart from that alleyway and a knife blade."

And their names start with B. I was pretty sure their names starting with B wasn't relevant, unless the mastermind had some kind of OCD that required him to match up killers' names with the victim.

Stop it! Jeez, Ellie. Another tangent you don't need. "Did they find the knife?"

"Yes. And prints matched Bolton's. Also, traces of scopolamine on his clothing. It was blown into his face."

"There was no one else in the alleyway?"

"Apparently there was. And if we'd gone back a few minutes more, we would've seen a shadowy figure approach and speak with Bolton."

"Did that shadowy figure blow something into his face?"

"Potentially. Although that wasn't caught or seeable from the camera angle."

"It's not a coincidence, Kurt. Scopolamine used on Harley and then it starts showing up all over the place. Zombifying people. Could that be how the others were killed? By random strangers?"

That fitted with the crazy old God-fearing woman and Nathan Moffat. "If Nazario is behind this he's worked very hard to construct various levels of involvement to make sure no one knows too much. In case they're caught."

He stared at me. "Random strangers," Kurt said in a

hushed almost croaky voice. "Potentially. Except in the first death. He was at the house for some time prior to being killed. And so was Shaun Rowe."

"Who kept him there and who killed him could be different people."

He nodded. "Could be."

Or not. Maybe whoever kept him there wanted something. What did Simonsson know or have that was so valuable and took so long to get? If it was Nazario who held him, then he probably wanted information, a way of finding his sister, and/or to find out how much Simonsson knew about the family business ventures.

"We didn't have reason to check his clothing for drug residue ..." I snatched my phone from the floor where it'd fallen and called the ME. "Caroline, it's Ellie. The first victim from case three-zero-six-HQ-six-seven-one-eight, Eric Simonsson, do you still have his clothes?"

"Hang on, checking." Her fingers typed, there was a slight pause then she answered, "Yes."

"Can you have them tested for drug residue? In particular scopolamine."

"Sure thing, Ellie. I'll have the lab run swabs."

"Thank you."

Caroline hung up.

"Why would anyone remain in a garage and not fight back?" I said. "He was FBI, he was once a deep-cover agent. He died CIA. People like that don't just sit around waiting to be killed. Especially when they have a phone on them."

"You think both the victim and the killer were drugged?"

Apparently, I do. It explained why he didn't use the phone to call for help. "Yep. It doesn't just explain why our first victim didn't call for help, it explains why the next three didn't call either."

So did that mean the other three had information the killer wanted or was it a game? To keep someone alive and zombified, for hours, for the hell of it? Probably information gathering. My mind considered the other deaths and what I knew from the three phones we had in our possession. They weren't held for as long as McEwan. What did that mean?

I felt Kurt watching me, wanting to penetrate my thoughts. "Simonsson, or McEwan as he was before he died, might have a connection to Chris Iverson or Iverson Technologies. We know he had a connection to Shaun Rowe. Potentially Rowe had a CIA connection."

"He was CIA," Kurt stated.

"Yeah, but even CIA operatives have friends?"

"True. You think Mitch knows his brother's friends?"

I made the call. "Hey, babe. Did Chris ever mention a guy called Wayne McEwan?"

Silence filled the air between us until Mitch said, "Don't think so. I'll ask Harley."

"Good thinking, Batman."

"Call you back." He seemed distracted, not my usual, happy husband.

"Everything all right with you?"

"Someone has accessed our system."

"Shit."

"Yep. Could it be Chris again?"

Yeah. Nah. He's on a plane. "I don't think so, babe." I sensed something else. "What's up?"

"When will you be home?"

"Tonight, hopefully."

"Good."

"Three things."

"Three things."

I heard the smile bounce back into his voice and it made me smile. Maybe he was tired. I knew I was. Worry was also an issue. I didn't want to add to it by telling him Chris was on a plane with a contract killer.

Chapter Forty Four

I Will Drive You Home

"Iverson?"

Until Kurt spoke, I hadn't realized I'd been staring at my phone screen. It was black. I looked out the car window and had zero clue where we were. "Henderson?"

"We're getting steady reports. Two more deaths."

"How many people are out there killing?"

He shook his head. "No idea. Arrests were made for the two deaths. Neither person had any relationship with the deceased."

"Devil's Breath again?"

"Looks like it."

"So people are running around Northern Virginia blowing shit in random faces and telling them to go kill a specific person ... we've got Nazario and Jenoah in custody, so it's not them running around doing this."

"The Morettis are an organized crime family, they don't need to get their hands dirty ... they just need to tell people what they want to happen."

I leaned my head against the head rest. "Then how do we stop them?"

"It's not our usual kind of case. This is organized crime, we are serial crime, usually."

"What are you saying? That we're out of our depth?" He wouldn't be wrong. Definitely felt like we were drowning in the unknown.

"We need help."

Staring at my phone wasn't helping. I made a call to Marshall Joanna Brock.

"Hey, Joanna, it's Ellie Iverson. Something that might interest you and also, we need your help."

"Go."

"Josephine and Callum Willows are still in danger. Dane Moretti-Willows was used by his uncle Nazario and probably Jenoah. They twisted him and kept him stoned. He's in custody. Nazario and Jenoah are in custody. We have a developing situation on a plane headed to Dubai. We have agents dying because Nazario set up situations to play out regardless of his involvement. Even catching a killer leads us nowhere because that person doesn't have any information except for their part, or the killer is drugged and has no clue what happened or what they did."

"Shit."

"Yeah. The thing is, we're out of options and people are dying. Who would Nazario use, who does he trust, but also who is expendable?"

"I'll get back to you. Keep on doing what you're doing. I'll see what I can find out."

"Thank you."

"This is a family that needs to be put down." Joanna hung up.

Six feet isn't far enough. "I need to talk to Mitch, I need to find out why this seems to be about Chris more than about the drone that killed Emma."

"It's like both sides want Chris. Which means ..." Kurt said, his eyes on the road.

"Only part of it is about the drone, and that part was Brayden Willows's involvement. He wanted Iverson Tech to pay for Emma's death. Nazario used the damn drone, he killed the kid. Nazario wants Chris for something completely different." A horrible sense of dread blanketed me. "We think O'Malley is going to kill them all, but what if she was only supposed to kill Brayden and Susan. What if she's supposed to bring Chris back with her?"

"What does Nazario want with a software engineer?"

"What is Gerrard doing on the plane with Chris and Susan?"

"Are we handing the agents we're picking up back to the very people who want them dead by putting them back into the system controlled by Debbie Barnes and Michael Addison?"

Whoa. Holy crap. "And I thought I was the one who made quantum leaps."

"It's not a quantum leap, Iverson. It's a twisty web of lies in a house filled with smoke and mirrors."

"Okay, I'll play ... go on."

"How did Nazario Moretti know Simonsson was still alive?"

"That, Henderson, might very well be the zillion-dollar question."

"Only a zillion?"

Laughter bubbled up from nowhere. Today sucked and yet my sense of humor remained intact. Lucky, really. The potential was there for the darkness to take hold.

"We are at our next pick up," Kurt said, parking by the curb of a tree-lined street.

I went to check the list but it was gone. I discovered it half under my boot in the footwell. Smoothing the crinkled paper with my fingers, I found the next pick-up's name. Dave Smith, formerly Valentine Mendelovitz. He was FBI and now a graphic designer, working from home.

"Here we go again." I paused, my hand ready to open the door, my brain unwilling to give the command. Didn't take a genius to work out the problem. "Kurt. What are we doing?"

"Going to pick up Dave Smith and take him to a safe house."

"What if that gets him killed, maybe not today, but down the road when everyone feels safe again?" That's on us. I don't want any more deaths on us.

"We can't play the 'what if' game. If we do nothing he could die today. If we take him in, he could live another thirty years happily doing whatever, or he could get hit by a bus on a sunny Tuesday morning, or there could be another breach and he could die bloody one day."

"If Debbie Barnes or Michael Addison did something—"

"That would suck, but we don't know that. We can act on what we know. We can act on what's happening right now. We'll pick up Smith, make sure he's safe, for now. Then we'll go visit sub-basement four."

"Okay." This time my hand got the instruction and opened the door.

Kurt knocked on the front door of the tidy two-story colonial. The door swung open. We were greeted by a wiry man in his mid-fifties. He looked pretty good for someone who'd been dead seventeen years.

"Dave Smith?" Kurt asked, moving his jacket so Smith could

see his badge.

"I am. You are?"

"SSAs Henderson and Iverson."

"To what do I owe the pleasure of an FBI visit?" He leaned casually on the doorframe and didn't appear at all perturbed by our presence.

"There has been a security breach, we need to take you to a safe house. Now," Kurt said.

"Has there indeed? How inconvenient. What's the procedure here, Agents?"

"You pack, fast, get all your identification documents and anything you need medication-wise. We take you to a safe house where your life will begin again."

"And if I refuse?" He remained calm and pleasant.

I just wanted to tell him to grab his gear and get moving but I knew it was better to let Kurt handle Smith.

"It's your right to refuse. We need to warn you that there was a breach and that your identity is compromised. We are here to take you to safety."

"I appreciate that, Agents. My life is here. I don't have the energy or the desire to start over for the second time."

I understood where he was coming from. I didn't like it but I understood it. "Do you have a family?"

"Yes. I got married almost eleven years ago to a high school teacher."

I didn't want to rush him, but I really wanted to go. Preferably with him. "We can take your wife."

He smiled. "Agent, we're happy here. Our kids are in school here. Our lives are here." He straightened up. "I'm on the PTA, for God's sake."

Kids. PTA. Life and a wife. I gave him my card. "If you change your mind, we'll come back. It's not a problem."

"Thank you. After all these years, I doubt anyone will care that I used to be FBI. I'm Dave Smith, graphic designer, now."

I turned to leave and saw a car drive past. My heart ramped up to thumping. The driver didn't even look our direction. I took a breath and told myself to get a grip. Kurt said goodbye to Smith. We walked together down the driveway to our car. He pressed a button on the fob in his hand. The car beeped, and the doors unlocked.

I swung the door open, slid in and saw the same car coming back. This time a window in the back rolled down. A puff of smoke. *Pfft.* The chink of metal hitting metal followed.

"Crapadoodle," I muttered. "Where'd that go?"

Kurt shook his head. "Into the side panel, I think."

The car was coming back around. We had two choices. Run for the house or use the car as cover.

"Go, go, go," Kurt said, flinging his door open and jumping out.

I followed him. He grabbed my arm as we sprinted for the house. The front door opened. Smith stepped aside, then slammed the door after us. I found a vantage point. The car pulled up. Four men piled out, all carrying rifles.

"There's a bit of firepower out there," I said.

Smith moved up beside me. "There's a bit in here, too."

"Where is your family?"

"School."

"How long before school gets out?" I watched the men

outside. Four of them getting ready to shoot their way in. Jeez. This was not going to end well.

"An hour and a half, two hours before they're home."

I glanced at him. "Firepower?"

He left the room. Kurt was at another window and on his phone. He pocketed the phone and joined me. "THU are coming."

"How long?"

"We have to hold them off for twenty minutes."

Smith came back carrying two rifles. He was wearing a sidearm. "Who wants one?" he asked holding a rifle out.

I grinned and took a rifle. No-brainer.

"Behave, Iverson," Kurt said, his voice low and raspy. "No heroics."

"I'm not going out there, or climbing on the roof. We're defending, that's all."

He patted my shoulder. "I almost believe you."

Yeah, me too. But fuck this shit. "Ammunition?" I said, directing my question to Smith.

"Plenty." He pointed to a box on the coffee table.

Awesome. "Back door?"

He pointed down the hallway. "Through the kitchen on the right."

I shoved some spare rounds in my jacket pocket, loaded the rifle, and headed for the back door. "Gimme a heads up when those losers move."

Chapter Forty Five

Living With The Ghost

I opened the backdoor, then closed it again. I leaned the rifle in a corner, lifted my Glock from my holster, and carefully crept back through the house.

Smith was too calm. He was too damn calm. He'd been out for seventeen years living his life and when we tell him it's all over, he's obliging and calm. Yeah. Nah. Teacher. His wife was a teacher.

At the living room doorway, I paused. I couldn't see Kurt. Part of Smith's leg was in view. I needed to step in to see what was going on.

Then Kurt said, "THU are incoming. This is not how you want to end your life."

Breathe. Just breathe.

"No one was ever supposed to get this far," Smith said.

"You can't trust criminals."

I peered out the window near me. Two men were near the porch. The other two must've gone to the back.

"Your partner is smokin' hot. Always a shame when the hot ones get terminated. She looks like she's fun too."

Nice that he thinks I'm hot. I'm all kinds of fun as well. I took another breath and stepped silently into the room. Smith had his back to me, his holster empty. I looked over his shoulder and moved my left hand. Kurt never took his gaze off Smith, but I knew he'd seen my hand.

No warning. I fired. Kurt dove. Smith fired. My bullet hit Smith in the shoulder blade. Before he could turn I fired again, taking his left leg out at the knee. Kurt jumped to his feet and grabbed the handgun from Smith.

The sound of helicopter rotors thumped in the air. I saw one man make a run for it down the driveway. He wouldn't get far.

Taking my cuffs from my belt, I grabbed Smith's right hand and yanked it good and hard behind him before snapping the cuff on.

"Argh!"

I snatched his left wrist up and snapped the second cuff on. Then tugged him by the elbow to the nearest seat. With a shove he landed on the chair, covered in blood and looking pretty sorry for himself.

"You have some explaining to do," I said, giving his bloody leg a nudge with my foot.

"I have nothing to say."

Kurt tapped me on the shoulder. I looked up and saw a rope hanging from the sky. Man, THU has all the fun. Helicopter envy is real. Yelling came from outside. Someone fired from near the house. Returning volleys silenced the shooter.

A knock on the front door was followed by a loud voice. "FBI. Weapons on the ground."

I hollered back, "Scene secure. FBI inside."

A tall man wearing tactical gear came into the room from the hallway. His gait reminded me of someone.

"Iverson, Henderson. Everyone okay?" Tyler Nicholas.

Last seen taking Sam on his last ride.

"Yeah, Tyler. Except for this idiot." I pointed to Smith. "He's bleeding all over the place."

For the first time in forever, Kurt wasn't administering medical help. Kurt was sitting on the couch. Everything rushed at me at once. "Kurt!" I spun around and knelt next to him. "Kurt?"

He slowly lifted his head and looked at me. Then pulled his hand out of his jacket. Blood dripped from his fingers.

I waved a hand at Tyler in the room. "Got a medical kit on you?" He strode over, talking on his comms unit, and handed me a field dressing pack.

Dropping the pack on the couch I moved Kurt's jacket aside, there was a bloody hole in his shirt just above his waistband on the lower left of his abdomen. I ripped his shirt open revealing his bulletproof vest. "That's unlucky," I said, noting the bullet hit the quarter inch gap between his bulletproof vest and belt. "Sorry." Felt right to apologize before undoing his belt and pants. I needed a better look at the wound.

"Iverson, is that necessary ...?" Kurt said, his voice trailing off.

I moved the fabric out of my way, felt behind him, and then looked at my hand. Blood. Through and through. I covered the front wound with the gauze, took his hand, and pressed it against the pad. Then grabbed another gauze pad and some paper tape. I moved Kurt's clothes, wiped blood away with my hand, and stuck the dressing to his back, shoving some of it under the bottom of the vest to hold it in place better. "It's on your left."

"It wasn't you."

I breathed a sigh of relief. "You okay apart from the red drippy stuff leaking everywhere?"

He nodded. "Suppose it had to happen one day. Hanging around with you." He tried to laugh but failed.

"Hurts a bit, don't it?" I said, with a smile.

"Little bit. I'll live."

Tyler applied a compression dressing to Smith's leg wound and stuck a dressing on his shoulder. "We've got two ambulances on the way in."

"Good. Thank you," I said, standing up and stretching.

Tyler nodded. "Happy to be of service."

I walked over to Smith and gave another nudge to his injured leg. "We need to talk. Now."

He snorted. "Don't feel like talking."

"That's okay. You can just listen while I talk about your pal, Jenoah Moretti." He flinched but that could've been because my foot slipped and tapped his leg. "Also, I'd like to talk about how you know my brother-in-law, Chris."

He tried to move. It didn't work for him.

"What was it, Smith? What brought you all together? Because something did."

"Iverson, his wife is at Oakton High," Kurt said, showing me the school website.

Tyler was on his phone as well; by the look on his face, I'd say he was Googling up a storm. "Two years ago, see who the guest speakers were at Oakton High career day."

Smith didn't look happy. Beads of perspiration gathered on his forehead. Clammy, pale, shocky. Not a good look.

"Got it," Tyler said. "Guest speakers at senior career day ... Chris Iverson, talking about Iverson Tech and his philanthropic work designing software to help charities. Second speaker, Debbie Barnes with the FBI. Her specialty subject was undercover work within the Bureau, and the third and final speaker for the day was Dave Smith, talking about graphic design."

Kurt leaned back. He was pale but holding it together. "That's the link we couldn't work out, Iverson. That's where it all came together. Something Chris talked about during the career day triggered a spark in Moretti."

"Let's hope Chris and Susan make it out of this alive."

Smith started to laugh but pain took over fast. "If he'd just done what Nazario wanted, it would've been so much easier."

I ignored him. Because Debbie Barnes was there that day too. "Who gave you your new life?"

"Michael Addison," Smith said under a groan.

I had no idea he'd been doing that job for so long. "I'm going to have a stab in the dark here ... two years ago, three people came together at Oakton high school. Jenoah Moretti was one of the teachers present. He listened to Chris Iverson talk about his passion for drone design and knowing Chris, he probably had a demonstration model with him."

I heard sirens. Time to pick up the pace. "I bet Chris

444

talked about his charity work and how he was designing software to help locate child traffickers and bring trafficked kids home."

Smith groaned. I figured I was on the right track. "Debbie talked about the FBI and how she creates new identities for people and about her work with undercover agents. Bet that sounded super exciting to a criminal like Moretti."

Another groan. "And then there was Dave Smith, someone who knew about new identities firsthand but couldn't say anything. Who used to have a cool job but couldn't say anything. He got to talk about graphic design. Bet that didn't sound real exciting to the kids after the other speakers."

Tyler chuckled; when I looked over, he was crouched down by Kurt taking his pulse.

"Poor Dave, boring old Dave. But he was friends with Jenoah Moretti because his wife worked with him and when Jenoah had a few drinks one night and said how cool it would be to steal a drone and hack into the FBI database and find all those new identities ... bet that caused a bit of panic."

"Jenoah is a smart guy ..." Smith said, rallying. "He doesn't do things for fun."

Sirens screamed up the street. "Why did he hack the database?"

"I can't tell you that."

"Won't and can't are different."

"Jenoah wanted to find the guy who married his sister.

He was supposed to be dead but someone said they saw him at Dulles airport about five years ago. Then he heard Jeb Warner had a new identity."

"Heard from whom?"

"I don't know."

"That wasn't so hard, was it? And kidnapping Harley Iverson and Chris Iverson?"

Smith's groan became a moan. "Iverson designed software that helped put his brother in jail. If hadn't been for him, they never would've caught Angelo."

"You seem to know the family quite well," I arched an eyebrow at Kurt.

He attempted a smile in return but it wasn't quite there, his ghastly appearance told me he needed to be in hospital.

People in green flight suits hurried past the window. Paramedics. Tyler went to meet them. He pointed them to Kurt. The second crew would deal with Smith. Kurt was quiet, Smith wasn't.

"My wife is Christina Moretti. She's a cousin."

"How many times did you blow scopolamine in some innocent person's face and make them do something unspeakable?"

"Four times."

"Is the whole family involved?"

"Yes, the whole stinking lot of them."

"You're a dead man walking." I left him to his pain and walked outside beside the gurney Kurt was on. "You going to be okay, Henderson."

He lifted the oxygen mask off his face. "Yeah. Call Rachel."

"Of course. Want me to come with?"

"I'll be okay. I'll see you at Inova?"

"I'll be there."

"You did good, Iverson."

I put the mask back on his face and brushed his hair off his forehead. "We're a good team."

The second crew of paramedics passed us going in.

Chapter Forty Six
Keep On Dancing

I called Rachel, Kurt's wife, and asked her to meet us at Inova Fairfax. My next call was to Director O'Hare after switching our tracking back on.

"Kurt is en route to Inova. GSW to the abdomen. We've made an arrest, THU is handling it. Looks like the Moretti family are behind everything with the exception of whatever is up with Gerrard."

"Good job, Agent. Where are you now?"

"Following the ambulance."

"I'll meet you in the Emergency Room."

I ended the call and concentrated on the road as best I could. There was still something bugging me. How did any of the Morettis know Simonsson was still alive, how did they know Jeb Warner was Eric Simonsson? I smacked myself in the head. Idiot.

His phone.

Why did he go to New Brunswick if his family were no longer there? Because he didn't know they weren't there. He went to see his kids and they were gone. He decides after eighteen years to see his children. I just bet he'd tried before. "Hey, Siri, call Tracey Games."

"Calling Tracey Games now."

I love Siri.

He answered fast. "Hello."

"Mr. Games, it's Special Agent Iverson. I have a question about Wayne."

"Of course, please, carry on."

Behind his words I heard soft music playing, I strained to hear the artist. Adele. Then a glass clink against a bottle but not close to the phone. He wasn't alone.

"How often did Wayne travel to Canada?"

"A couple of times over the last five years, I think. He liked to fish."

"He fished?"

"Yes."

"Were you happy, Mr. Games?" His pause told me the answer was no.

"Marriage isn't always easy, Agent. We were happy more often than not."

"Mr. Games, I know you are CIA ... have you ever had cause to investigate your partner, Wayne McEwan?" The music stopped. He'd moved away from the music. Interesting.

"Why would I do that?"

"Because you believed he lied to you."

He puffed air into the phone. "That's quite an assumption, Agent Iverson."

"And that's not denial."

"I didn't investigate him, Agent."

"Then how did you find out that he wasn't Wayne McEwan?" I pulled into the gray parking area at Inova Fairfax, locked the car, and hurried over to the ambulance bay.

"Mr. Games, I'm about to go into an emergency room to be with my partner who was shot today investigating the case involving your husband. The missing piece, Mr. Games, is how the hell the Moretti family found out Wayne McEwan was Eric Simonsson and subsequently Jeb Warner."

"Will he be all right?"

"I don't know. Talk!"

"I had a photo of Wayne on my phone and when I was trailing new facial recognition software at work, I used his photo."

"Bet that was a surprise."

"Yes. I didn't expect to see my husband's face on a wall of deceased FBI agents."

"So you knew. What happened after that?"

"I dug a little further and discovered he died as Jeb Warner and was married with kids. He never told me about the kids. I was hurt. He'd lied."

"When was this?"

"Seven, maybe eight months ago."

"What did you do?"

"I went to a bar and got drunk. Not my finest idea."

I waited by the door to the emergency department, watching Kurt being unloaded from the ambulance.

"Who did you tell, Mr. Games?"

"The bartender."

"I'm going to reach down the fucking phone and rip out your tonsils if you don't start talking faster."

"Paolo Moretti, I go there a lot, he's a friend."

"Of course. Congratulations, you got your husband killed."

I hung up and grabbed Kurt's hand as the gurney stopped by me. "Tracey Games – he told the Morettis that Jeb Warner was really Eric Simonsson and that he was alive."

Kurt lifted the mask long enough to say, "Tangled web, Iverson."

I followed the gurney in then paced the waiting room. Wasn't the first time I'd paced up and down that room wearing a track in the industrial carpeting. I saw Rachel enter through the main doors with her young daughter on her hip. Olivia waved when she saw me.

"Mommy, Mommy! I see Ellie!"

Rachel stopped and peered around the child. "Where is he?" Panic rampaged in her words and face.

"Surgery. They took him straight in. He's going to be okay. It's Kurt." Shit like this doesn't happen to Kurt. I swallowed fear and a large lump in my throat. He's going to be okay. It's Kurt.

She fumbled for words. This was her first time. I pulled back when an older woman hurried through the door and called out. "Rachel."

"Mom, he's in surgery."

"I'll leave you with your mom," I said with a small smile.

It seemed a good idea to go back to wearing a track in the carpet while I decided whether I'd stay or go. I convinced myself to wait for O'Hare. She texted as I resumed my pacing saying she'd been held up. Rachel and Olivia were okay, they had family with them and didn't need me. Home felt like where I should be.

Before I could escape, I saw an overcoated-fedora-wearing man walk purposefully toward me.

"Why are you here?" With zero attempt on my part to hide my displeasure at Tierney's beady-eyed, hook-nosed presence.

He ignored my question and my tone. "I had nothing to do with Jackson's death."

"You came down here to tell me that?" I turned away from him and started walking. It was time to go home.

"Demelza."

I spun around and glared at him. "Don't, Tierney. She's dead. She died a long time ago in a land far far away."

"You'll always be my Demelza. You were good. Very good."

"Are we done?" Stone cold. "Let's keep our focus on the present."

"Gerrard is not our target. He was protecting our target. He just kept getting in the way." Tierney snorted with irritation.

"Miller wasn't after Gerrard?"

He bared his teeth in a tight-lipped rendition of a smile. His bird-like head twitched. "You know Gerrard. You know how good he is."

That makes two of us. Wonder if Miller will come after me next. That thought took over for a moment. Maybe that's how I die. I blinked and realized Tierney was still speaking.

"... every time we got close, they disappeared again."

"Miller was trying to remove him from the equation," I said, as his words sunk in. "O'Hare told me Gerrard was working for her. Some special operation."

He arched a bushy eyebrow. "Yes."

"Who is he protecting?"

The edges of his mouth pulled upward, rendering his already taut skin fit to split. "The Creator."

"God?"

"Not that creator," he replied dryly. "The Creator is responsible for the special program that in turn adds names to the list."

"I'm tired of games and cryptic shit. Just tell me, Tierney." I'm tired, period. Tired is my new barely functioning state of being.

"Levi Riggs, or as he's been known since nineteen eighty-seven, Sly Dixon."

I'd seen that name on the list. Former FBI, now retired but retired from what I didn't know. There was no occupation recorded for anyone of retirement age on the list. "Gerrard is protecting an old man—"

"Careful, Demelza." Gravel filled his voice. "Old is subjective."

"Stop calling me that." I glowered daggers at him. "Why is Riggs-slash-Dixon so important to the FBI and the CIA?" One wants to protect him and one wants to kill him.

"The program is his creation, and therefore he created the list. He put this together for the former Director, with his blessing, but the real purpose of the new identities was never disclosed to the Director."

"And that is?"

"A lot of the 'dead' in the early days were criminals or criminally stupid, they were agents who were caught up in their undercover worlds." He shrugged. "That can go either way. They can go off the reservation, or they can lurk on the fringe of the reservation. A foot in both worlds."

"Messy."

"Riggs saw a way of pulling them back in, but not all of them folded back successfully."

"You're telling me that among the agents who desperately needed to be safe and to live fresh lives there are agents who didn't deserve that, who deserved prison time?"

He nodded, his beady eyes darting over my face.

"Why kill Riggs?"

"He grew a conscience with age and was going to expose everyone in the program, not just the ones who should be made accountable for their actions while they were undercover agents. That list contains all the names."

"Some we've found were CIA and NCIS, this isn't just FBI is it?"

"No. Riggs was offering an out for his buddies."

"The former Director, did he know anything?"

"Maybe, but I doubt it. He was influenced greatly by Riggs. Trusted him."

First rule of our world: Trust no one. "Wayward Son Protocol. Tierney, what's that really for?"

One corner of his mouth twitched upward. "Clean up on aisle five."

"Our Smith and Wesson, do they know they're clean up?"

He shook his head. "That would've been a directive given face-to-face by Riggs. Earlier teams would've more than likely been given a clean-up directive."

"We're law enforcement agents, not assassins." There was no stopping the hiss on assassins. "Riggs maintained control over the list occupants after he retired?"

"Yes, he did."

"O'Hare?"

"She has no clue. She's been protecting Riggs, or Dixon, as she knows him, believing his bullshit about how he needed protection."

He'd have to be convincing. She's not stupid. Cait did not get to be appointed Director by being stupid. "How the hell did O'Hare even get involved?"

"Riggs went to her when we heard he was thinking of releasing the names on that list."

"What did Riggs say to her to get her to put Gerrard onto him?"

"I don't know. Despite popular opinion, we don't listen in to conversations inside the Director of the FBI's offices."

I rolled back to Moose and Squirrel. "Do we know for sure that Dane Wesson and Stewart Smith are clear and not running around killing the previously dead?"

Another upward twitch of the corner of his mouth. "They are not killers. You could keep them. They're like you."

So I've been told and am starting to see. Guess I'm not the only freak out there. While Tierney was feeling chatty, I asked another question, one that had irked me from the moment I saw the photo of Gerrard at the hotel in Hamburg. "Why was Gerrard in Germany?"

"He stashed Riggs offshore. They went out through Canada to Europe." He buried his hands in his coat pockets and hunched his shoulders forward. "We got Riggs in Germany. I knew about Praskovya and your brother-in-law. It wasn't easy to follow the trail, but you helped a lot by cracking the code Iverson left."

"How the fuck did you—" I held my hand up. "Don't bother, I don't want to know."

"It doesn't matter how bad you think I am or what you do, I told you once I was always watching and I always will be."

That's not creepy. "Gerrard?"

"We helped him find information about the move to Lyon and he acted alone. He didn't know Praskovya was there already. He didn't know about O'Malley. We didn't know about O'Malley."

Ha. So, they don't know everything. I felt more satisfaction that I should have. "Stop watching me. It's not right." I took two steps away then threw words over my shoulder. "Thank you, Jonathon."

Chapter Forty Seven
Every Road Leads Home To You

I sat in the car for a few minutes outside our front door and tried to rid my mind of most of the day, and the week. The security lighting flooded the car interior making life seem brighter than it was. Everything was falling into place.

Kurt would be okay, he'd be in hospital for a few days. Chris and Susan would hopefully make it to Perth alive and then we'd bring them home. I couldn't do anything but wait, and I didn't want to tell Mitch or Harley. No sense everyone being upset and feeling helpless.

The large Moretti family saga would continue for quite some months, as every agency with an interest took a shot at them. I wasn't sorry. Their empire was built on the lives of minors and on a culture of revenge disguised as family loyalty. May they all rot in hell. Every last freaking one of them. That was when the man with the partially missing finger popped back into my head. Was he a Moretti?

I called Sandra. "A real quick request, then I want you to go home, please."

"Yes, O Genie of the Underworld."

"Do you know where Jenoah Moretti is?"

"Uh-huh, right here, in one of our interview rooms."

"Take your phone, go find him, photograph his hands."

"Okay."

"Send the picture to me when you get it."

I hung up. And waited. Two long minutes ticked by before my phone buzzed. I looked at the photo of Jenoah Moretti's hands.

Holy crap. I called Squirrel, because Lee would kill the bastard. "Jenoah Moretti was the man who drugged Sam. He does not walk. Get legal now, get them to add homicide of a federal agent to his list of charges."

"Do we have autopsy results confirming manner and cause of death?"

"Not yet."

"I take it you're pretty sure the drug caused Sam's death."

"Sure enough."

"I'll make sure legal charge Jenoah Moretti with murder. You need anything else, call me."

"Thanks."

My phone rang. Sandra. "What's up?"

"I have a message from Rowan Grange. He said you asked him about Iverson Tech."

"Uh-huh."

"He called to say he spoke to his record company and asked about any software designers or tech companies they used. They use software created by CS Industries. It tracks illegal music downloads and removes the links from various search engines."

CSI. I do not believe in coincidence. I crossed my fingers and hoped for a useful outcome.

"Tell me you know who owns CS Industries?"

"O Genie of the Twisted Web, I do indeed. CSI is owned by Chris and Susan Iverson. It's a lucrative business that has nothing to do with Iverson Tech."

Isn't he the busy little developer? "Thank you, now go home!" With a smile stuck on my face, with sheer willpower I got out of the car and opened the front door. "Hey, family! I'm home." I stepped inside the house and closed the door behind me.

The strangest noise greeted me. Clattering of paws on tiles. A blur of black and tan barreled down the hallway, pulling up just before my feet. Hot on the furry beast's heels was Mitch, laughing.

"He can move," he said, sidestepping the dog and taking me into his arms.

"And he is?"

"Argo."

I looked down at the German Shepherd looking up at me. "Pleased to meet you, Argo."

The dog cocked his head to one side. And just like that my smile was real. "And Argo is here because?"

Mitch wrapped an arm around my waist and encouraged me to walk to the living room. Argo walked next to me. I readied myself for a really good explanation as to why there was a dog called Argo in our house.

We sat on the couch. Argo sat on the floor close to us.

"I found him and he needed a home, and here he is."

"Wandering the streets was he?"

I reached down and scratched the dog between the

ears. His fur was soft and warm. Matched the look in his eye.

"Not exactly."

"Lost?"

"No."

"Mitch, why do we have this beautiful dog in our home?"

"Because we need him. I need him. And he's nicer to look at than the CPD."

I'd almost forgotten about the CPD. Then I heard more noises. People noises. Murray and Diego in the kitchen. Argo listened. I watched him, his ears swiveling to hone in on the sound.

"I have a small issue."

Mitch pulled me closer and kissed me. "Small?"

"Uh-huh. You know I used to have a cat ... Aiden ended up with it because I couldn't remember its name half the time and was away a lot, and forgot to buy cat food."

"Things are different now. You've got me. You've never forgotten to feed me, and you haven't forgotten my name."

"You do most of the cooking ... your name is ingrained in my soul, makes it easy to remember. Has Harley met the furry creature?"

"Not yet."

I looked around. "Where is she?"

"Movies with her CPD and two friends."

Okay. Good. Glad she's occupied and not moping around or worse, asking questions I don't want to answer. "Argo ... do you want to live here with us?"

He sat up and rested his head in my lap. I rubbed his muscular neck and felt stress melting away. Maybe we did need him. Maybe he needed us too. "You never did say where you got him from?"

"He was supposed to be a police dog but he's too nice and failed to qualify. He's been living with a lady who couldn't take care of him anymore. That cop you know, Josh. He called up and told me about Argo."

Josh Konstram. Figures. "Looks like we have ourselves a dog." Like a real family.

Wow.

The next few days would be emotionally hard. It'd take everything I had to get through saying goodbye to Sam, not to mention the stress of trying to get Chris and Susan back and Gerrard. I'd been so worried Gerrard was into something bad and the whole time he was just doing his job.

Don't think, just be. My eyes closed and I snuggled into Mitch; my left hand stayed on Argo's head. I think we'll get along just fine.

I opened an eye and looked at Mitch. "He doesn't sleep on the beds and he doesn't sit on the furniture."

"Deal."

Chapter Forty Eight
The Sun Will Rise Again

Two days later, I held a radio in my hand as I stood next to Kurt's hospital bed.

"You're all here," Kurt said, opening his eyes and giving a half smile. "Everything okay?" His eyes moved across our faces. "I'm not dying, am I?"

I smiled. "Nope. Looks like you'll live." The corners of his mouth turned up. "Quick update. Chris and Susan arrived home this morning. Most of the Moretti family is locked up pending trials. And Mitch got us a dog."

"You got a dog, Iverson?"

"I know, right?" We fist bumped.

"If I'm not dying, why are you all here?"

"Fairfax PD wants to do a final call for Sam," I said. All humor drained from the air.

We worked quite closely with various officers from Fairfax PD over the years. They were regularly invited by us to Murphy's when we closed cases as a way of thanking them for their support.

"Help me sit up a little," Kurt said. I gave him the bed controls and rearranged his pillows as he inched his bed into a forty-five-degree angle. He looked at us all, one by one. "I want to stand."

I wanted to tell him over my dead body but I knew it was useless. He'd stand with or without my help. Someone had to hold the back of his hospital gown closed. Lee and I stood on either side of Kurt, in the space next to his bed. Close enough that we could get him back on it if necessary.

Caine, Sandra, Squirrel, Moose, and Cait O'Hare joined us. Shoulder to shoulder we stood in a circle waiting. A light knock on the hospital room door caught our attention. My breath caught in my throat hoping Owen hadn't decided to visit. All of us looked at the door, watching as it opened.

Noel Gerrard, sporting a black eye and a shoulder sling, waited in the doorway for permission to enter. "Am I welcome?"

I nodded and let a slow sigh of relief fall from my lips. Gerrard shut the door and crossed the floor to take his place. The combined sadness in the room weighed heavily upon us.

The radio crackled then a female voice said, "Calling Special Agent Sam Jackson. Calling Special Agent Sam Jackson. Calling Special Agent Sam Jackson."

Silence.

"All units stand by for the tone out. Code 33 this channel for a final call. This is the final call for Special Agent Sam Jackson five-five-six-seven. SA Jackson died while answering a call of duty. He gave himself while serving the United States with courage and valor."

I wiped tears from my eyes before they could break free.

"The men and women of the Fairfax Police Department are forever grateful and proud to have served with FBI Special Agent Sam Jackson and will never forget his ultimate sacrifice. All units break for a moment's silence."

I felt Lee move. He and Gerrard saluted. Tears ran down my face unchecked.

"Special Agent Sam Jackson, may you rest in peace knowing your strength lives on with your colleagues and your family. Your honor will continue on with all of us."

The radio crackled.

"Special Agent Sam Jackson, thank you for your service. SA-five-five-six-seven your watch has ended. Godspeed, Sir."

I swallowed hard trying to bite back sobs.

"Code 33 is lifted. Control clear."

The radio fell silent.

I felt the air rumble on a deep whisper as Lee said, "Godspeed, my friend. Your watch is over. We'll take it from here."

Kurt's hand found mine.

"Delta A out.

Acknowledgments

This was the slowest book ever to write. Seriously slow.

The End came hours before a deadly magnitude 7.8 earthquake hit the middle of New Zealand and ruined a perfectly goodnight's sleep.

But the end did come and not in a biblical way.

I'd like to thank my eldest daughter, Bex, for being such a keen beta reader and the rest of my children for their encouragement and support.

Thanks to Ian for offering up Debbie Barnes as a character and for his help in creating her.

Special thanks to Jayne Southern for her editing excellence and for still believing in me.

And to Ellie for still talking to me.

About the author:

Cat Connor is a prolific crime thriller author hailing from New Zealand. Her expertise in the genre is reflected in her engaging and suspenseful narratives, which have garnered a loyal following. Her work is known for its intricate plots, dynamic characters, and relentless pace, keeping readers on the edge of their seats until the very end. She has authored multiple books, including the popular "Byte" series, which follows the exploits of an FBI unit that investigates serial crime.

Cat's passion for crime and espionage is evident in her writing, as she strives to create a world that is both authentic and thrilling. Her meticulous attention to detail and extensive research have won her critical acclaim and accolades from readers and peers alike. In addition to writing, Cat enjoys speaking on topics related to writing and publishing. Her talks are known for their candidness, humour, and practical advice. With her unique blend of talent, expertise, and passion, Cat Connor has established herself as one of the most exciting and accomplished authors in the crime thriller genre.

Her other passions include music, reading, tequila, red wine, coffee, and chocolate. When she's not writing she can be found binge watching TV shows and spending time with her much adored animals; Diesel the mastador, Patrick the tuxedo cat, Dallas the tortie Birman, and Jimmy the thug.

You can follow and contact Cat at the following places:

Website: www.catconnor.com
Twitter: @catconnor
Facebook: @cat.connor
Instagram: @catconnorauthor
Bluesky: @catconnor.bsky.social
Threads: @catconnorauthor

Also by Cat Connor:

.

And for more from this author ...

Please turn the page for a preview of the next exciting book in the byte series, *Qubyte*

Qubyte

Walking in Light.

"Iverson, are you hearing me?" Kurt sounded irritated.

My attention swung to the phone call. "Sorry. Say again."

"I need you in Rockbridge County."

"Henderson where exactly are you?"

"Stonewall Jackson Hospital, Lexington."

"What?" I really must've missed everything he'd said.

Mitch threw off the covers and climbed out of bed and walked to the bathroom.

"We have a situation. Cait O'Hare is in Stonewall Jackson Hospital. Police are saying she had an accident while riding."

Riding accident. His words plucked at every sinew in my body. "And you're in Lexington?"

"Yes. Sean called me late last night. I drove down."

"How bad is it Kurt?"

"Bad."

"Where was this accident?"

"Mauryville."

I knew the sheriff down there. Cait and I both lived there for a time; small town life used to hold a lot of appeal. A shiver ran up my spine. Bad stuff happened in Mauryville and it didn't quite feel like another lifetime ago, yet. Some good happened there too, no sense getting all bent out of shape over one aspect of the past.

"And you want me down there?"

"She's our Director and a good friend to Delta A."

Seriously? There's nothing wrong with my mind.

"Henderson, I'm aware who Cait is. What I don't know is why you want me down there if she had an accident?" Snippy edged into my tone. "While I'm at it, how about Squirrel, Moose and Lee?"

"Long night," he said, sounding almost apologetic. "Can't hurt, assemble the gang. I'll expect you in five hours."

"Was it an accident?"

"I don't think so. It makes no sense to me. Get down here."

"We'll be there."

My phone fell silent. The black screen confirmed Kurt had gone. I lay still for a few minutes and listened to the shower running and my alarm announced the time.

I dropped my bag on the sofa in the corner of the office and planted myself behind my desk. Morning settled on me with a sense of foreboding and a general feeling that something hinky was happening. Kurt's phone call had started a chain of events in my already acrobatic mind.

Voices floated in the air outside my office.

I concentrated harder on the screen in front of me. A new case arrived during the night and I needed to make a decision. Delta A could work it without Kurt and me, or we could postpone it until the Director's situation was resolved.

A split second after the conversation landed outside my closed door a knock rang out.

"Enter!"

The door opened. I felt the barometric pressure change. The door closed. I shut my laptop lid and looked up to see Dane, Stewart, and Lee standing in front of my desk. Sam's sudden death left a big hole in Delta A. We plugged it with Dane Wesson and Stewart Smith also known as Squirrel and Moose. Fresh blood. It's gotta be good.

"Thank you for joining me. Have you all seen the new case details?" They nodded. "Pull up chairs and let's get into this."

No one moved. Curious. "Or stand," I said, opening the laptop again and re-reading the brief Sandra had sent. A water-logged body found on the sidewalk of 9th Street SW. "It's been sixteen years since the last water-logged body was found in D.C and now the Unsub is killing again?"

No reaction. No movement. Curiouser and curiouser. "Spill." I made eye contact with Lee, my eyes probing his before moving to Dane, then Stewart. "You seem to have something on your minds."

I waited. No one seemed to want to speak first. Not a good sign.

Lee shifted his weight from foot to foot.

"Say it!"

A piece of paper appeared in Dane's hand. He dropped

it on my desk. I raised an eyebrow.

Picking up the paper I skimmed the single page, taking note of the FBI letterhead used. From the office of the Executive Assistant Director.

Bold red lettering centered under the letterhead.

EFFECTIVE IMMEDIATELY
Delta teams must immediately cease all working relationships with Russian FSB officers.

I clamped my lips together to prevent a barrage of profanity.

Owen. Again. She didn't waste any time stepping into Cait's role. Jump in her grave as quick? A shudder ran from the base of my spine to my head.

No explanation but to be honest it wasn't a surprise given the current political climate. Russia wanted an enemy and we were fast becoming exactly that.

"Owen is Acting Director?" The hinky feeling from earlier intensified.

Dane shuffled his feet. Lee adjusted his expression from irritated to stony.

"What haven't I heard?"

"The rumor I heard is that Owen is angling for the top job," Stewart said.

I failed to hide my utter horror at that comment. She's not Director material. She's not even human material.

"Why would anyone consider her?" Lee grumbled, shifting again.

"Think about it, Lee. She's feminine, stupid, Republican, a total suck-up and—" Dane said.

"All the things he likes in a woman," Stewart finished. "And a freaking puppet."

"There's more to that. I heard she's a personal friend of the Overlords," Dane said. He grinned at me. "I might've done some digging."

"Good job." I knew he was right for our team.

"O'Hare has held the Director position for ten years?"

"Wow, it must be. That means only one other Director has done the job longer."

Dane nodded. "Rumor has it she'll stay at least another two years. She'll retire as Director eventually. Even POTUS doesn't want to mess with O'Hare and the job she's doing."

"Owen being a friend makes sense," Lee murmured. "Sure as hell isn't job performance."

No argument from me. Always amazed at how she managed to hold her job, I leaned back in my chair and gave consideration to the new case, weighing it against the possibility of foul play in Lexington. Nothing I'd read that morning indicated an escalation in water-logged bodies. Dead people don't mind waiting. On the other front, everything felt weird and somehow touched by Owen's manicured nails.

"We're going to hold off on this new case. There's a more pressing issue." I surveyed the men in front of me. "Road trip to Rockbridge County."

"Nothing's come through about a case down there ..."

Dane said, scanning the tablet in his hand.

"Kurt is there now. He believes there's a case. In light of the current climate here, you can choose to come with, or you can stay and carry on here."

That tweaked their interest.

"What are we investigating," Dane said.

"Cait O'Hare has had an accident."

"Is she all right?" Lee asked.

"I don't think she's great, Kurt is there with her. Sean asked him to go down. She's in Stonewall Jackson Hospital."

Half a smile scratched itself into Lee's face. "Lexington feels like full circle, Chicky."

"It's where this Delta A really started," I said, hoping to settle the seething questions I felt mounting in Dane and Stewart. And maybe where it ends.

Stewart flashed his eyes at me. He shook his head so subtly it would've been hard to miss.

"Iverson, you don't want that to become a self-fulfilling prophecy," he said, in a harsh whisper.

His mouth never moved yet I heard him clearly.

Lee spoke, "If you two are done playing mind games. Any clue how we explain the sudden absence of Delta A?"

"Caine," I replied in synchronicity with a knock on my office door.

The door swung open and Caine entered.

Lee grinned. "More spooky shit, Chicky."

"Maybe."

Caine approached, the men stepped aside, letting him

through. "Kurt's been in touch. I'm officially sending Delta A to Rockbridge," he said, his voice full of gravel, with a hint of menace.

I looked up at him. "We have a new case here."

One corner of his mouth twitched. "I suggest you get moving."

"The case?"

"I can handle things here while you're gone."

"I'll give you a hand," Lee said.

"You sure?"

"We made a good team so not long ago. I'd like to help, wouldn't hurt to have a Delta A presence around the office."

To throw Owen off the scent: Definitely a good idea.

Caine's lip twitched again. "Glad to have you holding the fort with me."

He almost sounded glad. That gave me pause. I shook it off and turned my attention to the job at hand. "Okay, the three of us will head south," I said, "You two stay safe."

I stood and pushed my chair back. Time to go.

A little yellow duck with a noose around its neck waddled across my desk quacking. I watched as the duck toppled head first over the edge. The rope caught. One sharp snap and the duck flopped lifelessly from the end of the rope.

9MM PRESS